I0606728

He'd thought logging was a dangerous occupation, but it had nothing on insurance adjusting…

Under the boat, Ernie heard the whirring noise of the air saw and turned to see a man coming at him. At first, he first thought the coast guard had arrived.

Innocenti expected there might be a deck hand, but had not expected to see someone underneath trying to fix the shaft log. Seeing the man, he moved in aggressively with the air saw, tethered by the yellow air hose to the pump in the speedboat. Swimming rapidly toward the man trying to fix the shaft log, he charged forward, without fear, attacking with his air saw whirring at five thousand rpm, followed by little bubbles of air after the pressurized air spun the saw.

Completely surprised to meet someone trying to kill him, Ernie was startled and instinctively backed up, but not fast enough. The assailant struck Ernie in his side, and the spinning blade went through the skin to his ribs. But fortunately for Ernie, his jumping back had kept the saw blade from cutting deeply into him and severing his ribs.

Ernie pedaled back a few more feet, blood coming out of his side. He then knew it definitely was not the coast guard, and this would be a fight to the death.

Ernie, an experienced logger from rural Washington State, loses his job when the logging operation he works for is shut down due to an anonymous sighting of a spotted owl. When he goes in to apply for unemployment, Ernie is persuaded to take a job out of state as a temporary insurance adjuster in Los Angeles. While he knows that Los Angeles will be a lot different than Sedro Woolley, Washington, and insurance adjusting a lot different than logging, really, how hard can it be? And there are lots of downed trees in Southern California after the recent earthquake and storms they had there. So packing up his trusty chainsaw in his saddlebags, Ernie hops on his motorcycle and heads south. But to his dismay, Ernie discovers that LA is a lot farther from Washington in more than just miles. Unprepared for the corruption and callousness rampant in the insurance industry, Ernie soon finds himself not only in trouble with his job, but on the top of an assassin's hit list. Still, although Ernie might be a hick from the sticks, he's far from stupid. Blessed with an innate intelligence, an abundance of common sense, and a redneck sense of humor, Ernie will give his enemies a hilarious run for their money…if he can just survive long enough.

KUDOS for *Ernie & The Evils of Insurance*

In *Ernie and the Evils of Insurance* by Brent Ayscough, Ernie is an unemployed logger who takes a temporary job with an insurance company as an adjuster. With few options when his logging job in Washington is canceled due to an alleged spotted owl sighting, Ernie leaves his home in rural Washington and heads for Los Angeles. When he gets there, he is shocked at how the insurance company handles claims and is unprepared for the corruption in the insurance industry. When he accidentally saves the life of a gubernatorial candidate the insurance company is trying to kill, he paints a target on his back for both the insurance company and the mob. But Ernie seems more than up to the challenge. The book is well written, fast paced, and intense, with flashes of humor at the most unexpected times. ~ *Taylor Jones, Reviewer*

Ernie and the Evils of Insurance by Brent Aycough is an interesting tale. Our hero Ernie, naturally, is a logger by trade and happy with it, until a spotted owl sighting closes down the logging operation and puts him out of work. The unemployment office convinces him to take a ninety-day job as an insurance adjuster in Los Angeles, so Ernie hops on his motorcycle and heads for California with his trusty chainsaw as he assumes he has been hired because of all the downed trees from the recent storms. But he's in for a big surprise. His smarts and common sense make him an extremely effective claims adjuster, but it isn't to be. Ernie soon screws up everyone's plans by savings a man's life, and now everyone is trying to kill him. The insurance company fires him, but he doesn't stay unemployed for long. No, the FBI wants to hire him as bait to draw out a mob assassin, and all he has to do is survive. *Ernie* is a fun and fascinating tale about a strong, smart, and clever man a little out of his element. I found it very hard to put down. ~ *Regan Murphy, Reviewer*

ERNIE AND THE EVILS OF INSURANCE

BRENT AYSCOUGH

A Black Opal Books Publication

GENRE: MYSTERY/THRILLER

This is a work of fiction. Names, places, characters and incidents are either the product of the author's imagination or are used fictitiously, and any resemblance to any actual persons, living or dead, businesses, organizations, events or locales is entirely coincidental. All trademarks, service marks, registered trademarks, and registered service marks are the property of their respective owners and are used herein for identification purposes only. The publisher does not have any control over or assume any responsibility for author or third-party websites or their contents.

ERNIE AND THE EVILS OF INSURANCE

CHAPTER 1

On Saturday afternoon in Southern California, Lisa Doty prepared a barbecue. From the doorway she called to her husband, Dave, "Honey, we need dried cranberries for the Waldorf Cole Slaw. Will you zip up to the local market?"

The guests soon to arrive were her husband's brother and wife and two other couples.

Dave was pleased, as he'd just finished waxing his most prized possession, a very low mileage, supercharged, Mustang Shelby GT500, black in color. A recent acquisition, bought second hand, it was like new, and the interior still had the odor of a new car. The prior owner had found himself in a divorce, perhaps due in part to the Mustang itself, and so Dave was lucky to get it for a distressed price. He had always wanted a Mustang, ever since he saw Steve McQueen in the quintessential chase in the 1968 Ford Mustang GT in the classic movie *Bullitt.*

Tossing the last of the polish rags in a pile, he shifted his focus from detailing to actually driving the essence of a perfect car. Conveniently, he concluded, the Mustang would be perfect for the mission to the market several blocks away. A nice day, he put the windows down, leaving the air conditioning off, which would help orchestrate the sensuous exhaust.

The supercharged V-8 bellowed and the car rocked from its torque, the sound mesmerizing. Once in gear, the perfect mix of man and machine rumbled down the street toward the grocery store.

Typical in older, upper-middle class Los Angeles neighborhoods, the houses were on small lots designed and built years ago at a time when the lots were smaller, and the homes cheaper when homeowners had less income and fewer possessions. The current owners, flush with greater income, many with both spouses working, squeezed around their homes a variety of things that they had no place to house. These included jet skis on trailers, quad off-the-road vehicles, dirt bikes, ski boats, and motor homes. Most of the larger things were kept outside next to the garage, many in canvas covers. The already-over-stuffed, two-stall garages usually housed the best two of the owner's three cars, an extra refrigerator, excess furniture, tools, gardening items, boxed decorations for Christmas, hobby items, and workout equipment that never got used after a few months from purchase.

Dave's garage was one, too, but he lacked the motor home.

A man hiding behind one of the motor homes several houses down the street, atop a Japanese crotch rocket motorcycle, fired up the four-cylinder, high-revving motor. He leaned over into the contest-position and let lose the clutch, pulling out to follow. Everything he wore was black—the pants, boots, jacket, and full-cover helmet with dark tinted face shield. His identity was completely cloaked.

Dave turned left on a side street to avoid the traffic of the major street ahead.

When the Mustang stopped at a stop sign, the motorcyclist quickly pulled up right next to the driver's side and stopped. He turned his helmeted head toward Dave as though he wanted something. David turned to him, his window open.

The motorcyclist, in a swift movement, drew from inside his jacket a .357 magnum, eight-shot Smith &Wesson revolver.

The first bullet entered his forehead, then three went into his chest over his heart, a kill certain. Dave's foot came off the manual clutch pedal causing the stick-shift Mustang to jump and stall.

The last thing Dave Doty saw at that last instant of his life was a flash of light that some would like to believe is the start of a journey to a better place.

In barely an instant, the black-leather-clothed rider returned the revolver to his inside jacket pocket and sped off.

A housewife, washing dishes in her kitchen, peered through the small garden window above her kitchen sink and would later report, as the sole witness, that she saw a motorcyclist in black leaving the intersection.

❧❧

The massive turnout at the funeral underscored Dave's popularity. The entire extended family, neighbors, school friends, as well as friends from the Los Angeles office of the FBI, all attended. Inside the small church, the pews filled to capacity and people stood tightly together in the rear and along the sides of the pews as the pastor lamented as well as celebrated Dave's life.

"A federal agent, David Doty, was more than just an honorable man and asset to the community," the pastor began. "He was an asset to life itself. He was one of two siblings, both of whom became FBI agents. His younger brother, Dan, was recently transferred to the same office here in Los Angeles. Dave is survived by his lovely wife Lisa and their two children, Brian and Brandy."

From there it got very personal, and the family began to sob, so much so that the crying became infectious. After the ceremony, most people lined up to hug and kiss the family, tears streaming down their cheeks. Even some of the FBI agents who knew him joined in the tears.

When everyone was dissipating, Dan, Dave's brother, walked over to Lisa, leaned over to speak softly in her ear, and, squeezing her hand smartly to emphasize his words, vowed, "I'll never rest until I get the guy who did this."

CHAPTER 2

"Ahhhhhhhhhhhhhhh!"

Ernie exhaled his first big breath of mountain air in the morning, as though it was the original breath of life from the freshness of the spring snowfall. A magnificent odor of forest on a damp morning permeated the air and now Ernie's lungs. The snowfall was light and blowing around from the wind.

"Mornin' Ern," Chuck, the big rig driver, said in greeting.

"Hi, Chuck, Jake, Bill," Ernie hollered to those arriving.

Some, not prone to oral salutations, just gave a nod.

Ernie had come to the job site as usual in the "crummy," the logger's term for a four-door, four-wheel-drive pickup, which he had met at the logging supply store, Woods Logging, at 5:00 a.m. along with Bob, Ted, and the driver, Sammy, to ride to the site.

Ernie's truck was broken down, and so as usual he rode his motorcycle to Woods Logging in the daily Washington rain. He parked it under an area in the back of the shop that had a roof, but no walls, at least keeping the rain off. From there he took the crummy to the logging site.

After work, the owner of the shop allowed Ernie to leave his saw inside overnight.

"Look!" Chuck said to Ernie, pointing toward a deer a short distance away in a clearing. "They go to those clear-cut areas for the forage that won't grow in the uncut area due to not enough sunlight. I saw a big elk last week just up the road."

"Hi, fella—" Ernie called out to the deer as though to a friend. It was a fairly young one.

"Morning, Ernie," Clyde interrupted, standing off to one side. He'd just arrived and not seen the deer, or he would have kept quiet.

Ernie turned to the voice and, seeing Clyde said, "Hi." When he turned back to the deer, it was gone.

"Morning, Ernie," John, the crew boss and property owner, said.

"Morning, John."

Ernie walked back to the open bed of the crummy, lifted out his orange hard hat, put it on, and picked up his chainsaw, ready for work.

"It was raining at my place, but it was forty degrees," Chuck said. "It's about thirty-four here. You think the snow will stop?"

Ernie shrugged. "It'll turn to rain as soon as it warms up."

He wore his one-piece long johns that morning, as he did whenever it snowed, and two shirts, one of which could be taken off as the day warmed. His logger jeans were oversized for ease of entry and to allow for undergarments or a second pair, held up by rugged suspenders. The bottoms were cut off half way up his boots to keep from getting caught on the trees and brush, the ends frayed in the logger fashion.

John climbed up on the metal treads and then to the cab of the yarder, a crane used to haul freshly felled trees up from down the hill. The big yarder belched a huge blast of black smoke as its monster diesel roared to life. After a minute, he brought the engine down to an idle, swung the tubular steel boom toward the cliff, and let the carriage go down the hill. Leaving the big diesel idling to continue warming up, he climbed down and walked over to Ernie.

"How's that fancy new yarder, now that you've had a chance to use it for a while?" Ernie asked, trying to show appreciation for the expensive purchase.

"Fine," John answered. "That thing cost me seven hundred fifty thousand, so it better run good! 'Course, I financed it. If everything works out well, I hope to pay it off in five or six years. If things don't, I'll be in trouble."

The yarder and the trucks were parked on a small clearing

spot on the newly cut road that was bulldozed into the dense forest for the cutting operation. Gravel had been brought in for the road, as they needed to make it stable enough for the big trucks to carry out the logs.

"Hi, Snaggle," Ernie said to his wiry, chokerdog friend as he arrived.

This was the man who placed the wire cable from the carriage, or choker, from the yarder around freshly cut logs at the bottom of the hill to be pulled up the steep mountainside to be loaded on trucks and hauled out. Ernie had started out as a chokerdog and, after two years, had become a faller. Chokerdog was by far the toughest job, and Snaggle loved it. He didn't want to fell trees, enjoying the tougher job and his reputation for it.

Snaggle wore the dirtiest jeans imaginable—so full of dirt and grease, they could easily stand up by themselves. The yarder cable was kept covered in grease to prolong its life, and since Snaggle worked with the cable all day, he had as much grease on him as the cable did. Snaggle's excuse for never washing his jeans was to keep them coated in grease to repel water from the forest and ever-present rain—or at least so he said, and very few people would argue with someone who could do such impossibly hard work on the wet, precarious cliffs. Actually, it was a bad idea to take issue with Snaggle for any reason. His missing front teeth proved that.

"Hi ya, Ern," Snaggle said, with a big smile. He put a pinch of chewing tobacco in his mouth and announced, "See ya at the bottom!"

Snaggle then did one of his amazing moves as he went over the edge of the cliff to go down to where they would begin. It was so steep, to go over the edge for the average person would be committing suicide. There were fallen trees, stumps, brush, hidden rocks, all of which were soaking wet from the rain, but to Snaggle, it was only a casual challenge to race to the bottom. He went practically straight down, touching down only here and there with his boots, like an agile mountain goat.

Ernie could not accept the challenge from the daredevil

Snaggle as he had to take with him his equipment for the day: a chainsaw with its thirty-two-inch bar and chain, a red plastic container of extra gas, a small bag with extra chain and a few tools, a sandwich for lunch, and a plastic bottle of water. Ernie hoisted his saw to rest it on the suede patch sewn on his shoulder and, holding it with one hand, the gas can and bag in the other, went over the cliff. He could not risk damaging his saw, so he went down more slowly than Snaggle, but even with his saw and supplies, Ernie descended the steep incline quickly.

Three hundred feet down the hill at the spot where they were to work that day, Snaggle was already there with his wide, gapping teeth smile, delighted that he won his challenge. Ernie was used to it, as Snaggle did it practically every morning. Ernie put his bag in a safe place, and put his chainsaw on the ground. He placed his foot through the handle of the saw so he could pull the rope hard—the method of starting it when cold—and paused, Snaggle nearby.

Ernie announced the onset of work for the day. "Let's go!"

He set the choke and, with a snap of the starter rope on the crisp morning, the saw yielded and sprang to life. Ernie revved it several times to bring the cylinder up to operating temperature and then turned the choke off and let it idle while he looked for a good place to start felling trees. To Ernie, the smell of the exhaust from his chainsaw—gas mixed with two-stroke motor oil—was a logger's perfume.

Douglas firs, the popular lumber for construction, were the trees that he would fell that day. They were an average of thirty inches in diameter at the base, fifteen years old, and about to begin their journey toward making someone a nice house.

Ernie went right to work, the chainsaw winding up and cutting through the big trees, its familiar engine noise filling the cold, damp, morning air, against the picturesque background of very light snow. The snow seemed to be clearing up, and the wind made the snowflakes dance around in circles, rather than come straight down.

After he fell and trimmed seven Douglas firs, he shut down the saw to take a short break so Snaggle would not be in harm's way with trees falling around him when he wrestled the steel cable around cut trees to hoist them up. Once he had one ready to hoist, Snaggle signaled John on the yarder above with his two-way radio he kept in his pocket. The trees were hoisted up the steep hill where Chuck was waiting by his truck, ready for the first load of the day.

As the huge trees were being hauled up, Ernie looked with affection and admiration at the majestic scenery of jutting peaks sticking through the layer of fog just below him. With the raw, tangy smell of freshly cut timber in his nostrils, the activity in the woods, and his saw working properly, Ernie was nearly overcome with satisfaction, and said aloud to the mountains, "It doesn't get much better."

CHAPTER 3

The weatherman on the Los Angeles television station stood in front of the map, blocking most of it, as was the norm, as if the viewers preferred to see him instead of the weather map. A global satellite shot showed a northern view of the Pacific Ocean and the West Coast of the United States. "There's a very strong storm in the Gulf of Alaska. The winds are reported to be gale force at seventy miles per hour, with gusts of hurricane force winds over eighty-five miles per hour."

What could be seen of the screen changed to a different satellite view. "The storm is moving down the Pacific to a point five hundred miles off the coast of Los Angeles. There is a deep, low pressure, surface condition, stationary along the California coast. There is also a deep, low pressure at high and low altitudes in the inland area of Southern California. The storm is moving south and will be off shore in an estimated three to four days. When it meets those low pressure zones to its east, it will be pulled in to the east rapidly and hit California hard.

"Because of the deep low pressure areas, the storm is expected to accelerate its wind velocities to near hurricane force winds. The winds could reach over seventy-five miles per hour, with gusts of eighty or more. This is a most unusual condition for Southern California. Coastal residents, as well as residents in the local mountains and in the passes are advised to take precautions. Very heavy rains are expected to accompany the wind and, due to the size of the air masses, the rains are predicted to last for seven or more days. We'll track the storm with the satellite and provide you with updates as they are available. This is predicted to be a record breaking storm of winds and precipitation.

"Airports have been advised to check tie-downs for small planes and to add extra tie-downs for planes left out on the tarmac, or to move them inland to other airports. The coast guard has issued an advisory to boat owners to bring in their boats, not to go out, and has posted a gale warning of two red flags. The Goodyear Blimp division manager has ordered its blimp pilots to take off from the blimp tie-down at Carson, California, only a few miles from the coast, and to head inland, far from the coast, as far as the Midwest. The big blimp, if left at its Carson tie-down, could be torn loose in such winds and end up smashing into a building or something even worse."

The warnings were so strong that people canceled planned outdoor events, except golfers, who paid absolutely no attention whatsoever to the warnings.

ϳϵϳ

"Shit! This will ruin my numbers for the year! The shareholders these days look only at the current year," said Robert Bradford, President of Majestik Insurance Company, as he watched the TV weather while dressing in the Wilshire Hotel room. He had just turned on the TV a few minutes earlier for news before he went back to work. It was a workday, at 3:30 p.m. He had been there an hour and a bit more.

"How is that, luv?" Evette Evil asked him, as she put a six-foot-long, braided leather whip, into her bag.

"Homeowners and small commercial building policies that we write are going to be hit hard. We write a big chunk of those policies up and down the coast. Most of those have five hundred or one thousand dollar deductibles. This storm will be putting down trees, lifting roof shingles, skylights, and roof sections causing water damage inside, damaging outdoor furniture, causing accidents, damaging cars and boats, and that sort of thing. We'll have quite a number of trees and limbs that break and fall onto things or get blown into cars with auto policies as well. Then we'll get rain and water damage through openings. I've seen it before."

Trying to communicate with her john, she asked, "Sweetie, do you think you will have a lot of insurance claims?"

"Fuck, yes. Fortunately, we have written in lots of limitations and bullshit language and clauses in those policies that the policyholders don't know about. But this storm is going to be a record breaker, and I'll have so many claims that I'll need to bring in outside adjustors on a temporary basis just to deal with them. In fact, I had better get on that now—if I don't, there will be thousands of unanswered calls, and complaints to the insurance commissioner for not acting promptly and for denying claims. Good thing I bought that asshole insurance commissioner off. All I had to do was to contribute ten million that was deductible to some fucking kids organization that he and his wife are directors of so that they could bleed off a chunk for themselves. That alone saved me a billion on the last earthquake, as he made rulings in our favor on coverage questions."

Bradford checked himself in the mirror, combing his hair. His hair was still wet from the shower, but he was not afraid to return to the office as it was not uncommon for some of the men in the office to return to the office after a workout, racquetball, or other activity followed by a shower. The dressing area in the hotel room had a wall-mounted hair dryer, but he did not want to waste the time just to have dry hair with the shit that was about to hit the fan with the multitude of claims over what might become the most powerful storm in Southern California recoded history.

"Here you are," he said, handing her five, crisp, one hundred dollar notes. "You got me off big time!"

"Thank you, honey," Evette said.

She did not kiss him as he did not particularly like that afterward. And he did not want to get any lipstick on his face or any telltale signs of a close encounter on his clothes. The relationship was not an affair, but only one of very intense sex and BDSM. She was not new to him, but notwithstanding the fact that she was no longer novel, she was so great at what she did, and often added variations, that it was almost as good as the first time every time he'd seen her so far.

He went to the valet pickup area and gave his ticket for the insurance company car, a plain, gray, dumb Ford Taurus. He only gave a single dollar tip to the carhop, so as not to draw attention to himself. And, of course, as an insurance company man, it gave him great pleasure to cut someone's pay down below any acceptable wage and to make them suffer. The room was always rented by use of an alias, and paid for with a credit card that he had obtained in a different company name, which he paid for through a special account, also not in his name.

As he drove back to the office, he began to go into a near panic attack about the storm that was sure to create untold claims. He realized several imperatives must be set in motion at once. He took out his hand-held, dictating machine and began dictating while driving. His trusted executive secretary, Zelzah, would be the only one to hear it. He paid her so much that her loyalty was assured—she would never get so much elsewhere. And she took good care of him in every way.

"Zelzah, contact underwriting and order them to immediately halt issuing all new homeowner and business property policies anywhere near the coast until after this fucking storm passes. We don't want to get caught insuring homes or buildings we know will become a claim in a day or two. We are not in the habit of paying any claim that we can avoid.

"Then get out our list of contacts and sources for in-state and also for out-of-state temporary adjustors. We're going to have to bring in one hundred adjustors on a temporary basis to handle the claims. Our competition will be hiring also, so we should try and get a jump on them. Try locals first, to avoid the cost of transportation and per-diem allowances, and then bring in people from out of state when the locals are used up. All hiring is on a temporary basis for ninety days. Offer the usual per month, more if you have to, and a per-diem temporary living allowance for anyone not living in the area. For airfare, require advance booking of one week to make them get the best rate. For use of their own car, offer mileage at the usual rate for actual miles on the job after they arrive, or if they rent, offer a rental here under our partial reimbursement plan. There is going to be a big rush on the need for adjustors, so tell Don not to be too choosy about credentials. If the adjustor has ten years' experience or more, put him in a list for Don. Have Don set up one hundred field draft checkbooks with special draft checks that are limited to ten thousand dollars. Tell him to set up an indoctrination class for the temporary adjustors to advise them as to how to cut claims down. He'll know what to do. Tell him to get whatever else he needs for the temporary adjustors. I want then out in the field to have a look at the damages that are reported from the storm when it hits, before the evidence is removed. I'll meet with him on the issues to be addressed for the temporary adjusters."

Don McAteer will know what to do, Bradford told himself. Don was Vice President, Operations, and was Bradford's most talented technical assistant. Bradford was amazed at how cheaply people such as Don worked, considering what he did for the company. The money he earned, plus a company car and gas card for business only, was a pittance compared to Bradford's six-million-dollar salary. With stock options, a golden parachute retirement program, and benefits, his pay was more like nine million. He paid his faithful Zelzah more than Don, but Don did not know such details, and acted the perfect part of an insurance man without greed. The guy was a complete idiot when it came to his own income—but what an expert at claims!

As for Bradford's own exorbitant pay, he was worth it. He'd saved the company hundreds of millions in claims payouts since he arrived and brought the company shares up in value dramatically. What would someone like Don McAteer know about real income? Bradford recalled the secret bribe to the insurance commissioner to make him whitewash the way Majestik cheated its policy holders on the last major earthquake when Majestik was under investigation, which saved a fortune. He prided himself for the year-end numbers for the four years he had been there.

Then he thought of the goddamned storm! *It will definitely create thousands of homeowner claims. Even with all the limitations on claims hidden in the policies, and the usual methods of reducing payouts, there will be more claims paid out than premiums taken in. The stockholders will not appreciate the notion that a bad year would be attributable to an uncontrollable act of God. When the annual stockholders' meeting comes, in the annual tally of numbers, I'll sink from the limelight of "miracle man," notwithstanding the beautiful numbers in the years before. Mother nature is going to knock on the door. I could become an also ran for the year. I need to get busy at once.*

CHAPTER 4

L adies and gentlemen," the emcee in the Century City hotel banquet hall announced at the fund raising dinner after the meal. Eleven hundred fifty people, filling the room to its capacity, came for the dinner at two hundred fifty dollars per seat, except for the round tables in the front row which were three thousand dollars per seat. Corporate supporters, hoping to get favors later if their candidate won, had bought all the front tables. It was an exclusive audience largely of successful businessmen and women, attorneys and other professionals, and a few Hollywood stars. The controversial new candidate, his wife, others from his party, and several celebrities, all sat at a long table across the stage with a podium at the center. Considerable competing odors of expensive, women's perfumes were noticeable.

As the tables were cleared there were a few short speeches, and a Hollywood comedian appeared for a short comedy skit. Then the master of ceremonies, a retired politician, announced the candidate:

"I now introduce the next Governor of California, Zachary Lewis."

Roaring applause muted all other sounds. Everyone clapped, except for one man named Bradford. His wife almost clapped, going along with the sentiment of the crowd, until she looked over at her husband and remembered who she was with.

"I thank you for your support," Lewis said. "The polls show us gaining!"

Applause rang out as the crowd was still full of energy.

"I'm here to tell you about certain specifics of my platform. Since there are a lot of lawyers and highly educated people here, I'll spend my time with you tonight on the topic of insurance reform.

"It's time for reform on how people make insurance claims and how insurance companies deal with claimants. I have a comprehensive proposal that will cure problems and fix things the way they should be."

More applause filled the room from the energetic crowd.

"It's time for a change. Let's start out with the insurance policy itself. Many people think they have insurance, and only when there's a claim do they find out that's not the case, or that they don't have enough. For example, the person might have a water damage claim with mold following, in some cases stachybotrys or other toxic mold, and have to spend a bundle to get rid of it. In such a case, they find out for the first time that mold is not covered as the companies started excluding mold when the dangers of mold became known. There are many exclusions, and it usually takes a lawyer to figure them out. And you don't learn of them until you have a claim. In my new law, all new policies will have to have the highlights of exclusions written out in bold on the front page of the policy in what is called the declarations page that shows the amounts of coverage, limitations, and exclusions. In my legislation, all the declarations pages will have to be approved by someone that I will appoint just for that purpose.

"But a readable policy that a normal person can understand is just icing on the cake. Let's get to the meat of my concept which is how claims are to be handled.

"The American rule is that claimants have to pay for their own lawyers. If you have a personal injury or property damage claim dispute, you have to hire a lawyer and pay him a third or even forty per cent of the recovery. Why? It does not make sense. It's not that way in Europe and Asia where people are not so lawsuit crazy. And it costs the insurance company, although much less, as well as your lawyer, overhead just to handle the claims, which might go on for several years and, in some cases, end in an expensive court battle.

"In my proposal, when you contact the insurance company

with a claim, it has only thirty days to settle the claim. After thirty days, the burden of why a claim is not settled shifts to the insurance company. And if not settled in thirty days, you can qualify for a lawyer fee claim if you and your lawyer can show his or her services were necessary. The amount of the legal fee will be in addition to your claim, so it will not diminish your recovery. However, your case must prevail, and the lawyer has to convince the court as to why his services were necessary, itemizing the amount of services needed on an hourly basis. If the insurance company makes the lawyer spend a lot of time, then all that time should be paid for if it was necessary to achieve the desired result. The lawyer fee application will be done with your lawyer, the insurance company lawyer, and a judge, and need not involve the parties. The behavior of the insurance company, the degree of a lawyer's skill, how the lawyer applied it, his time involved, and other relevant factors will all be considered by the judge in a written set of required guidelines.

"And the insurance company's actions, or inactions, will be closely scrutinized at any such hearing. The overriding concept is that every claim is to be resolved without delay and without bad faith insurance practices. If the insurance company cannot reach the claimant, or for other valid reasons why it is not its fault as to why it could not settle in thirty days, or whatever time it takes, the time for the insurance company to settle the claim can be extended by the court on a fee application, but the insurance company will have to advance all amounts of the uncontested portion of the claim without making the claimant wait for a total settlement. The insurance companies use, as unfair leverage on claims, holding off paying anything unless they have a total settlement. In my plan, if the claimant is asking for twelve thousand, and the insurance company says it is only worth ten, then the company must pay the ten within the thirty days and contest the balance of the two thousand.

"The present law in insurance claims is archaic. As an example, you may not mention insurance in court. This is based on the outdated concept that it might sway the jury to award damages out of sympathy against an insured party if the jury knew there was insurance. But with auto insurance, you are required by law to have it, and yet required by law not to mention it in court or be in contempt. If you're a homeowner, your mortgage lender requires you to have insurance. So when you go to court, you are required to actually to lie in court. Withholding information is deceit, which is a form of lying. Is that ridiculous, or what?

"Under my plan, insurance will be openly discussed in courts. If you have a claim against someone who runs into you, and you have to sue, you sue the insurance company itself and leave the party or parties in peace.

More applause followed.

"What about a multi-car pileup? Simple. Each insurance company must either resolve the matter among themselves within thirty days and make payment, or, if not, the insurance companies must each file a single case with a judge, who will make a preliminary decision as to which company is to pay what as an advance payment. That way, the injured parties don't have to wait years. Then the insurance companies can battle it out among themselves in court for as long as they want, but without the parties, and seek reimbursement among themselves if they paid out more than they are found liable for. The parties could be witnesses at later hearings as to what happened in the accident if the court orders them to give testimony as to how the accident happened, but they still get paid right away. The judge's preliminary ruling is only to get the injured parties paid, and the amount each insurance company has to reimburse another insurance company will be adjusted later by the court as the insurance companies sue each other as to which company has to pay what portion or reimburse the other. The payouts to the claimant should occur within thirty days after notification to the insurance company or companies of the claim. My law is designed to put a stop, as nearly as possible, to bad faith insurance practices, delays, inconvenience, and grief to the individuals.

"Now, insurance companies will run expensive ads against me in the election, and later when I'm elected and propose the legislation that provides for the claimant's attorney fee if the insurance company did not act promptly and in good faith, they'll want the insurance company's lawyers to also get legal fees reciprocally. Not so. It only works one way, and I consider it a cost of selling insurance in this state and a form of penalty for not settling promptly. The plan is to not require an attorney just to get what you should get. There is a serious safeguard, however. If the claimant and/or his lawyer are found to have presented a false claim, false facts, or an untenable claim that is not supported by good faith, the judge will be required to assess an attorney fee against that party and/or lawyer, or both, to compensate the insurance company as need be so as to prevent false claims. So, it's not just one-sided.

"This concept and new law is not just for auto claims, but for most all claims. This applies for property damage claims, boat, aircraft, general liability, and most other types of claims.

"The insurance companies, in spending millions to try to defeat my new law, will tell you that this will just create a new windfall for lawyers, but that's false. An independent study we had conducted shows that it will do just the opposite and will make less legal fees available, as the insurance companies will do anything in their power, and I mean anything, to keep from paying out money to plaintiffs' lawyers. We'll see to it that they pay legitimate claims, without any undue bad faith practices, at once. And just because you have to go to a lawyer, you will not have to agree to pay him a third or more of what should come to you. So, you see? It will work."

The crowd again broke out with loud applause.

"Now some of you may think that I believe insurance companies to be condensed evil and the residence of Satan."

The crowd broke out into laughter.

"Well, this is not so—or maybe I should say not completely so."

The crowd laughed again.

"I intend to make insurance work as it should. I am including in part of my proposed legislation a section on one of the largest problems in California, which is worker's compensation. The rates are so high for some trades that much industry has moved, in large part due to the cost of labor, which includes worker's compensation, to China, Vietnam, India, Thailand, Mexico, and Africa. Much of the cost of labor here is worker's compensation. Many companies, foreign and domestic, have set up initially in or moved to the southern states of the US where its worker's compensation and injury claims cost much less. We have documented a staggering amount of cases in California where the claimant has taken off from work and is not actually injured at all, or not so much that he or she cannot work, and gets wages for not working. I propose that all medical expenses continue for any injured person, but that the period that a worker gets paid wages be cut to a bare minimum, except, of course, for any period of hospitalization or where the person is in a cast. The largest abuse is the phony claim, which is usually a claimed sprain. In many cases, a worker is not injured at all or very little, and takes off work until all benefits are used up, while sometimes working at some other job at the same time for cash under the table. This is not the fault of the insurance companies. If an employer wants to have a wage continuation plan for employees who are injured with minor injuries, that can be offered as a benefit by the employers if they wish, not one included in required worker's compensation. We cannot stop, but we can at least slow down the exodus of industry from California to keep jobs here and keep us competitive. We have no choice."

Loud applause followed.

"Regarding Cal/OSHA, the Division of Occupational Safety and Health, that agency is known for assessing large fines against companies struggling to survive. In my plan, it cannot fine a company that commits a violation without first warning the company and only then when the company refuses to put in place the safety rules. And none of the fine money will go to support Cal/OSHA."

More loud applause followed.

"I have a change for medical malpractice claims too. I propose to take medical malpractice claims out of the court system, and to initiate a form of handling the claims like worker's compensation. Any additional medical treatment that a patient needs following poor medical treatment must be provided by the insurance company insuring the doctor or medical provider. Compensation above that will be determined by a schedule, and hearings and appeals will be to panels comprised of persons appointed by the governor, who will be me, in an expedited procedure. This will remove the uncertainties of the jury system to the medical field. And my legislation sets out a new statutory method of reclassifying HMO's that makes them responsible to the patient in California as a condition of doing business here. If you have an HMO, and you have a claim for mistreatment or lack of treatment, you bring your claim directly against the HMO—not the doctor who is connected to the HMO. Many now complain that the failure of an HMO to provide treatment as a way to save money, is the source of most malpractice of HMOs, and that must stop."

More laud applause.

"As I said at the outset, I'm focusing tonight on my insurance reform as it will be a major change in our system, and the first such major change in insurance ever. But, just so you will know where I stand on other issues, I will mention briefly a few other topics.

"One of the areas of abuse of the system is the sexual harassment lawsuit. This sort of claim has struck terror into business, and naturally insurance carriers exclude it now in coverage. Most of these cases are from a disgruntled woman who leaves the employment when not doing well and then claims sexual harassment as she has heard, right or wrong, that she can make money. She claims the perpetrator, usually a lower employee of the company, violated her virtue with unwanted advances, dirty jokes, or discussing sexual matters. She then leaves the company, and sues the company as responsible. The perpetrator has no assets and who she would never sue in the first place, and she claims the company with its deep pockets is responsible. In this claim she hopes to get money from the employer for the assault on her virtues which she only just realized she had.

"Sexual harassment claims have driven companies to send employees to classes for men to teach them how to avoid this.

The accused employer is considered to be guilty just by being accused. My plan requires that, before such a claim can be brought against the employer, the claimant must put any complaint for sexual abuse or any other actionable misconduct in writing and present it to the employer. Retaliation is strictly prohibited and gives cause to go ahead and bring the claim, including a claim for retaliation. The employer has thirty days to rectify the situation. Only then, if it is not rectified, can the claim be brought. This is in addition to and must be done before help can be sought from the Department of Fair Employment and Housing. It's a safe harbor for an initial claim. This will also apply to discrimination claims of all kinds, brought under state law. I will also put a cap on such claims.

Applause followed.

"I will cut taxes. I can work on cutting California state income and sales taxes, and put the state on a budget eliminating huge amounts of waste and unnecessary expenditures. And I will try to put together a coalition of states to cut federal income taxes as well because companies are moving out of California and the United States because they are saving billions in taxes costing us money and thousands of jobs.

"Californians have a love affair with their vehicles—whether cars, trucks, or motorcycles. To make it possible for Californians to have better cars, and to be able to afford to trade them in more often, I will cut the sales tax on vehicles to the difference between the allowance of the traded-in vehicle and the price of the new one, as opposed to the present tax which is on the full price of the new vehicle. This will give buyers from one to several thousand dollars more to put toward a new car. Part of the loss to the state in revenue will be offset by more purchases and trade-ins. I will also reduce the yearly road tax on cars. I want Californians to have the best vehicles in the world."

Loud applause followed.

"Regarding drought in California, we have eight hundred forty miles of coast line and not enough water, even though we are boarded by the largest mass of water on earth. The current brain-dead socialistic administration follows the typical route, which is fining people for not using less water and then using the revenue for other causes. I'm going to introduce emergency legislation that will issue several dozen permits for desalination plants that will be exempt from coastal commission approval, and exempt from environmental contests, due to the emergency necessity. This will also greatly enhance our state's ability to grow many more crops and hedge against future droughts. We grow very valuable crops, from almonds to strawberries, and dozens more, and those poor folks are having to try to grow these without the water they need. I'll stop that with the water they need.

"I'm not going to take away your guns, and I will see to it that the existing laws on use of guns in commission of felonies get the maximum, enhanced prison sentences. And I'm going to make it easier for certain people to get concealed weapons permits if they qualify which will require an extensive screening process to determine eligibility. People need protection from certain threats such as terrorists and armed home invasions. I am also going to repeal a number of the California laws restricting certain types of weapons to be in uniform with other states.

"Regarding security in your homes, burglaries have increased dramatically. I will seek to repeal the California law that reduced burglaries to misdemeanors for property or goods valued under nine hundred fifty dollars, and make any home burglary a felony, and subject to the three strikes law. I want to make people feel safer, and I'm going to all of you safer.

"Few people with education or assets want now to become policemen. It is difficult to get educated and substantial people as recruits, as they know they are likely to be sued. I will change that. Any claim against a policeman for misconduct must be made against the police department or the municipality, not the officer, and it will be limited in amount for any non-monetary damages such as emotional distress as the state did long ago with medical malpractice cases, limiting any non-economic award to two hundred fifty thousand dollars. Police need to know that the people are behind them in law enforcement.

"Regarding fines for tickets, currently the penalty assessment and other charges can make a simple ticket cost six or seven hundred dollars, and then the insurance company, uses that to substantially raise your premiums. I will cut the fines to a reasonable amount. The high fines also turn good people against police. Police must be our friends.

"These are the nuts and bolts of my plan. I assure you it will result in a major difference in how the insurance industry operates, as well much needed changes in our laws. With that, ladies and gentlemen, I conclude my speech and thank you for coming."

The crowd stood and the applause was long and deafening.

Some stayed to shake hands and hopefully be photographed with the candidate, but the Bradfords hurried out to beat the crowd. They came to see how the audience received Lewis and to evaluate what his chances of winning the election would be. Once inside the hired limo, his wife Barbara gave her opinion. "This man has charisma. I think he's not only going to win the governorship, but has presidential potential."

Bradford's knew his wife had insight in such matters, but that did not stop his blood pressure from spiking. Attending the event had helped him gain an impression of the candidate and to better see the danger to his insurance company first hand. Bradford wasn't top dog for nothing. He looked at her and revealed, "I'm considering funding the opposition candidate. I've got to do something—whatever I can—to keep that fucking crusader out of office at any price. He'll destroy our entire way of doing business. Every time we employ our methods to reduce claims, the methods themselves and, eventually, our company, will be put on trial. I have to stop him somehow, no matter what the cost."

"But what about his announced plan to cut worker's compensation, HMO reform for medical claims, medical malpractice, and sexual harassment claims?" she asked. "Won't that save you money?"

"Fuck, no! We don't write worker's compensation or medical malpractice. And when people started learning about sexual harassment claims, we excluded those claims in our policies to avoid the risk. And we're not an HMO. So those proposals will make no difference to us. But that idea about insurance having to pay legal fees after thirty days and putting our methods of handling a claim on display will be the demise of how we do business."

CHAPTER 5

Two FBI agents sat across a desk from each other. "Listen, Dan," Frank Maxwell, the regional director of the FBI, told Special Agent Dan Doty. "There is no way the agency can allow you to spearhead this case, as you know well. Assuming you find out that your brother's murder does come under our jurisdiction, can you imagine how it would look in court if we prosecute with you coming in to testify, trying to act impersonal and detached in presenting your evidence when the victim is your own brother? It'll look like a personal vendetta when we're trying to have someone convicted of murder and we ask for the death penalty."

He was cogent and on point. But while his logical and legal arguments went against Dan's wishes, Frank's sympathies were with him in full.

"I know," Dan said, fully aware of the unorthodox situation. "But I still want to be involved. I have set it up with agent Bill Kanno so all evidence collecting is done in his name. He'll take over completely if anything turns up. Should we get a lead, I'll be sure to notify you at once and then you can turn over the formal investigation to Kanno."

"We don't yet know if, in fact, your brother's death was even a federal crime. If Dave was shot because he was working on a federal case, it would be. But if it was just a drive-by shooting, it's not federal and the FBI has no jurisdiction. All you have is the suspicion that your brother's death might have been related to something he was working on. Naturally, I would probably do just what you're doing if it was my brother who was murdered, and that's why I'm not ordering you to cease. But now, hear me out on this. You can use our resources for your investigation, but put as much of it as you can in Kanno's name and turn it over at once if you find something or need a warrant, so we don't mess up our chances of getting a conviction and have egg on our face, looking like there's a personal vendetta behind it. If you don't, your personal involvement will come out at the trial with good defense lawyers and we'll lose the case."

Dan nodded, grim but determined. "Thank you sir, and I cannot tell you how much I appreciate allowing me to look into Dave's murder. I cannot believe that this was a drive-by random shooting, or something like a test of valor for an initiation into a gang. The housewife who saw the motorcyclist leave the intersection is the only witness. It may be that the motorcyclist was the shooter, or it may be that he came on the scene afterward and just drove around the car unaware that there was a body in it. Or maybe he was a youngster with some traffic warrants out for him and he didn't want to stop. All she could say is that the person appeared to be a male, and at least average sized or larger in stature. Not much help. But whether it was the motorcyclist or not, I'm convinced that my brother was killed because of something he was about to uncover."

Maxwell made a church steeple of his fingers and planted his chin at the peak. He looked at Dan for a few long moments. "Okay, now, that warning aside, what have you got?"

Dan was ready. "The weapon was a .357 revolver. It shows expert planning as no shell casings were left that way. There was one shot to the head, and three in the heart. This shooter knew what he was doing. The bullets were from hot loads, 125 grain semi-jacketed hollow points."

Maxwell shifted in his chair as he changed topics in his head. "What have you got from his desk or computer as to what he was working on? Any leads at all? Someone who just got out of prison that he put in and wanted revenge? Someone who he was about to indict?"

"I've checked on the records comparing convictions he got and recent prison releases, and no one seems, at least not yet, to be a prime suspect. Therefore, I think it was something new he was working on, and whoever it was set out to stop it with the shooting. This means that the shooter had some information that Dave was onto something and was about to expose the activity. It must have been something big. He had nothing typed up or that he had discussed with anyone in the Bureau. In looking at active files, all I've been able to do so far is eliminate a number of them as nearly impossible or so highly improbable as not to be a good lead. But I'll keep on it."

"You really don't have much, do you?" Maxwell asked, making a point of the obvious.

"I spoke to my brother's wife and, like the pro that he was, Dave never talked to her about confidential matters or investigations. But she did know that he was feeling very good about something at work. So I think he was about to write something up. Unfortunately, only he was working on it and no one else knows anything about it."

Maxwell sighed. "I want you to inform Kanno about what you are doing—for two reasons. One we discussed, which is your personal involvement. The other is to prevent what happened with your brother so we don't lose another agent because no one else knew what he was working on." Then he smiled. "And, don't go out and start machine-gunning down suspects, if you know what I mean."

Dan was relieved at his supervisor's interest, and his humor. He smiled back. "No, sir, I certainly won't. I can't thank you enough, sir."

CHAPTER 6

The light snow turned to rain in the late morning and continued as light rain all day, but that did not stop the loggers, who continued until quitting time at four. The crew was winding up for the day. Ernie and Snaggle came up over the cliff, soaking wet from the rain, wet woods, and very sweaty from a hard day's work. Preparations were underway to shut down the equipment for the day. John was winding up the steel cable back into the yarder and positioning it for the night, by moving it back a little from the cliff's edge.

As the crew was getting ready to leave, a pickup with a state seal on the door drove up. Driving it alone was a field practices forester from the Department of Natural Resources, a person empowered by the state to sign and issue a Stop Work Notice to any logging operation. This is exactly what he had in his hand as he got out of his vehicle.

He was new in the area, and appeared to be about twenty-six or seven. He stood six feet, three inches tall and looked like he played football in school. The young official walked up to the yarder to John. He shut down the motor, stepped down on the metal treads, and jumped down.

"Are you John Billings?" the young official asked.

"Yep. Who are you?

Rudely without introducing himself, he said, "I have this for you. It's a stop work order."

As Billings looked at the paper served on him, with a single page attached mapping the prohibited area, the forester said, "A spotted owl, a territorial single, has been spotted in this area on three occasions. That makes this area a site center. Pursuant to the authority of the State Forest Practices Board,

implemented by the Department of Natural Resources, a territorial single is a Status 3 Protected Endangered Species in this
spotted owl special area, and entitled to protection. I'm
obliged to serve you with this stop work order."

John looked at it wide-eyed. "I inherited these three thousand acres from my father, and he from his. It was bought for
the timber in the first place. It has no other value. I spent all
that money and went through all that bullshit to get the goddamned permit in the first place! I had to hire some asshole
owl biologist whore and a forester just to get the impact report
to get the permit to cut my own trees. It took two years and
lots of money. Then I bought this yarder when I got the permit
to harvest the timber. Now, what the fuck are you telling me?
An owl may have flown in here, someone says, and for that I
have to go broke? After all that, I can't cut my own trees? I
own these trees. And we plant three new ones for every one
we cut. These trees don't belong to anybody else, especially
some useless piece-of-shit owl. The control of this land
doesn't belong to some asshole like you just because his
mamma and papa had enough money to send him to college
for four years."

Ernie walked up to see what John was so upset about, as
John was raising his voice.

"I didn't make the laws," the forester said. "Don't you get
rude with me. I'll have the police on you!"

"Yeah, but you signed this paper. It looks to me like you
did make this one."

"I have a degree in biology and am familiar with the spotted owl," the young man said, bristling a bit. "I'm a state official, performing my official duties."

John got steamed up and started to lose it. "You're a fucking parasite who lives off the state to the detriment of regular
working folk. You couldn't hold a job that the state didn't
provide. You probably jack off when thinking of owls! And
since you are a fucking faggot, you jack off thinking of male
owls!"

The forester's face reddened. "You don't talk to a state official like that!" He clenched and unclenched his fists, as if

thinking hard for something to say. He moved in, aggressively close and stuck his finger in John's face. "I don't take those kinds of insults from anyone. You backwoods trailer trash are going to learn to respect the law."

From Ernie's point of view, the forester had crossed the line. Ernie, who was only a few steps behind, moved in quickly to back up his boss. He grabbed the forester by the back of his pants with his left hand, put his right arm through the forester's right elbow, then grabbed the man's collar, the movement preventing the forester the use of his right arm to swing at anyone. Ernie, with twice the strength of a normal person, lifted the forester off the ground several inches with just his toes occasionally touching it. The forester tried to fight his way loose, but he was no match for Ernie's strength.

"Let me down, you son-of-a-bitch!" the man yelled as he tried to hit Ernie with his left elbow in a backward-swinging motion.

Demeaning the forester, Ernie walked him, still suspended off the ground, over to the cliff where Snaggle and he had gone down in the morning. The forester continued to yell and tried to punch Ernie with his elbow. As he refused to shut up and calm down, Ernie took a few steps forward so that the man was suspended over the cliff.

Ernie put his mouth up closely to the forester's ear and said in a normal voice, "Don't yell so loud, you might scare your fucking spotted owl."

The yelling and the struggling didn't seem to have an end, and Ernie decided that the lesson in manners to loggers was not yet learned. So he just let him go. The forester went down fifteen feet before he touched the cliff, and by then he had picked enough speed that he continued going down the hill, out of control, trying to grab onto brush and trees to slow himself down. He finally managed to stop, after sliding a hundred feet, banging into rocks and branches. He was unhurt, but very scared. He did not stand up at once, just lay there to catch his breath and to make sure that he had not broken any bones. Finally, he got up and worked his way up the hill. Climbing over the top, he went directly to his truck, saying nothing more.

All the crew watched him leave. One of team, Chuck, said as a notice to the others, "Did you all see that dumbass motherfucker slip and fall over the cliff?"

The message was loud and clear. The only witnesses were the crew, and their stories would all be the same, in case the police came around. They all nodded.

Challenging loggers, who the forester had just put out of work, in their own forest was the essence of stupidity and arrogance, and the forester would learn about that, however long it took to sink in.

"Well, guys, it looks like we're out of business," John muttered, offering to show the paper to some of the others. The light rain made the paper a bit wet, but no one wanted to see it, as reading legal documents was hardly the forte of loggers.

"What can they do if we don't stop?" Jake asked.

"They can start putting fines on me then liens on the property if I can't pay them," John said. "They could bring criminal charges."

"Where's the fucking owl?" Ted asked. "Who saw it? Probably another one of those doped-up Earth-firsters claiming another phony sighting. It was probably a UFO with a marijuana engine."

"Can they shut down the whole thing?" Snaggle asked.

"The owl gets a 2.7 mile radius," John said. "That's 5.4 miles in diameter. It's called the owl circle. That's one, fucking huge amount of trees! We only have a permit to log this area here, which is right near the middle of this area they have marked." He looked at the map attached to the order. "I have to go back and re-apply and prove to them, the bunny-huggers, that a newly revised plan will not have impact on the owl. Soon, it will be mating season, and from the beginning of March to the end of August, you can't even disturb the owls with chainsaw noise, because that they might not mate, or might push their eggs out of the nest from being startled. I doubt we can be back in business until next fall, at the earliest. Anyway, it takes a bunch of time and, therefore, money to do all this. I may take the bastards to court. I'll have to ask the lawyer. We're all screwed in the meantime."

Ernie sighed. "Unemployed again."

It was a solemn end to an otherwise good day. Everyone was quiet as they packed up their belongings, knowing that hardship had now returned to their families.

ᴄᴏᴄᴏ

Back at Woods Logging, Ernie lifted his chainsaw slowly out of the bed of the crummy and took it inside. It was a sad day, his livelihood gone through no fault of his own. He felt helpless.

His bike was just outside. He'd motor it home in the rain and pick up his chainsaw later. He was saving up to buy parts for his pickup as the front end was worn out and too loose to drive. Now that would have to wait. At least he still had his motorcycle, and he could ride it, rain or shine and even snow. Ernie lived in a doublewide trailer that was on a friend's property ten minutes from the shop, just outside Sedro Woolley.

There was a commotion in the shop as his crew and two others gathered and began to discuss the catastrophe. Ernie brought his saw up to the wooden work counter, and set it down.

The shop owner, Jay, came up behind the counter with a concerned look.

"You heard?"

"I sure have," Jay said. "Bad news like that travels fast. I'm real sorry to hear it. I think that the only truly endangered species is the logger who wants to work for his family and provide lumber for homes."

Ernie drained the remaining gas out of his saw into a can in the shop and then fired it up and ran it dry to prevent the two-stroke gasoline left in the engine from turning bad and shellacking the internal parts, as it was bound to sit idle for a long time with the shutdown. He took off the spark plug wire and took out the plug with his wrench. "Could I have a shot of oil?" he asked Greg, the maintenance man. "I'm going to have to set this up for a while. I'll swing by and get it soon."

Ernie squirted oil into the spark plug hole. He pulled the

rope to turn over the engine slowly to spread the oil around the cylinder to coat it, the piston, rings, and bearings, to keep rust from forming while it sat unused. The used gas from the cylinder coughed out of the spark plug hole. He then put the plug back in finger tight without putting the plug wire on. It might have to rest until the spotted owl left. And who knew when that would be?

CHAPTER 7

The pilot of the Cessna Citation X pulled the throttles back, and the engine pitch changed as the aircraft began descending and lining up on the small airfield ten miles ahead. The airport had no control tower, no instrument landing service, no fuel, and in fact nothing at all except for a single runway. It had been constructed by the government during the war as a training airstrip, and then abandoned. It was a desolate area with only an Indian reservation as a neighbor. It was possibly the most unlikely place to expect an expensive private jet to land.

As the jet descended the pilot winced a bit at the pitted runway. When the plane touched down, he braked hard and the Cessna came to a stop near the end of the runway, and then turned around and taxied back to the parking ramp.

Waiting at the parking ramp in an old, faded, maroon sedan was Chief No Cloud, Chief of the Chockpaw Indian Nation. There was another sedan, a faded green Chevy. The chief himself drove an old pickup, but he had borrowed two sedans to pick up the important guests. An Indian with a face like bronze pottery stood by the Chevy, which was in no better shape than the other car.

The shiny Cessna taxied up to the two waiting cars, the jet wash blowing up dust from the ancient runway. Next to the two battered sedans, the aircraft looked like a button-down preppy in a hobo camp. The whine of the jet engines subsided as the turbines shut down. The door just ahead of the wing came down and a beautiful stewardess came down ahead to assist each man coming down the steps so he did not trip.

Chief No Cloud approached the four men hand outstretched. He wore a long, braided ponytail and had a broad, Jack-O-Lantern smile, with rotted teeth and a few gone.

"Hello, Mr. Manelli," the chief said. Of the four, he had only previously met Manelli, who had visited to check out the place.

"Good morning, Chief," Salvatore Manelli said. "I've brought my business partners along as I told you I would." There was a profusion of fancy suits, and expensive, high-styled Italian shoes getting off the plane. They all looked utterly out of place at the desolate airstrip.

"Gaspare Indelicato," the nearest man said, hand outstretched,

"Fabrizio Bastini," the next man said as he shook hands with the chief.

"Fiorello Innocenti," the remaining one said, holding out his hand.

The warm smile diminished a bit when he looked into Innocenti's eyes. There was something about his coal-pit eyes, their depth and coldness—something disconcerting, as if he was gazing into the Chockpaw's face of death. He quickly gave his practiced line. "It's an honor to have you come visit our reservation. Let me take you there and show you the area where we want to build."

The group divided and got into the two sedans for the half hour trip to the Chockpaw Indian Reservation.

Once inside the reservation, they drove through the ramshackle village, which consisted of concrete block buildings with garden patches beside them and unpaved dusty streets where children played. A number of Chockpaws cast curious glances as white men on their Reservation were uncommon. Finally, at the edge of the village, at the crest of a hill, the old sedans braked to a squeaky stop followed by a rooster tail of dust.

"This is the spot," the chief announced.

Bastini's eyes narrowed. "It occurs to me that high spot might have been a sort of burial ground or something special for the tribe. Was it?"

The chief didn't want to lose the opportunity for a hotel/casino, and he was willing to make great sacrifices for that goal. He became flushed with embarrassment and stated what he had practiced, having anticipated that question. "Yep, true. But the burials were conducted by fire, and they ain't no graves here, only spirits. And our elders have spoken to the spirits and convinced them that the tribe is better off with money."

That was not totally true, as there were a few dissenters, but the majority of the elders said that they wanted the money and would allow the building even over the sacred grave area.

Bastini thought about how hard it was to get involved in building anything in places like California that were not Indian land. "Man, you couldn't touch this place with a new development project outside of an Indian reservation."

The chief turned his withered face to Bastini. "Well, all that is up to us. That's the beauty of it. And our elders have approved it."

The group of men walked around and looked over the land. Off to one side was a river, meandering in between green pastures. A freshness from the river and the green plants filled the air, so unlike the desert around Las Vegas.

Manelli, who had been there before and looked it over, nodded to the others. "This is the spot. I think this is an excellent location for the casino and a hotel. This is just far enough from the highway such that people that come here will want to stay a couple of days or more. It'll also be great for conventions which are usually for a short week of five days. We'd need a new road in so the guests that are driving don't have to come in through the Indian village—it will have to go around. And once up here, this out-of-the-way area gives a country feeling, away from the city. There can be rafting down the river for the summer guests, and there are rapids downstream for the daring. There is plenty of room for horseback riding. There are two lakes nearby for good fishing, and there is lots of property to devote to a big golf course—even two. One could be for tournaments and the other for regular golfers. There could be an indoor pool for winter and bad weather, and a huge outdoor pool for the hot summer. We should have tennis courts, and I was thinking of grass courts, like the ones I saw on TV in England in…Wimbledon, I think is the name. Wouldn't grass courts be something nice and unusual? Nobody's got them. They would be much more fun to play on.

"We could have skeet and trap ranges. We could set up a sporting clays range, where the shooters walk through trees to different stations to shoot the clay pigeons coming from all different directions, two at each station, which would be a big hit.

"As the river water is free to be taken with riparian rights, irrigation of the golf courses, grass tennis courts, and large lawns would be next to free—the only cost is for the pumps and their maintenance. We could put in a private airport on our land just far enough away that it doesn't disturb the hotel guests, big enough for private jets and smaller commercial jets. We could have a free shuttle service bus from the airport with fancy cars. I think we'd need fuel storage tanks and a maintenance hangar. If we make the runway big enough and add a traffic control tower, we could have airlines flying in junkets and tour groups. We should leave enough additional runway length, in case later things go good enough that we want to bring in bigger jets for larger convention business."

"Does the river ever overflow its banks?" Indelicato asked, looking at the river, something they should know well before starting a project.

"Not that we know of," No Cloud answered.

"How long is that?" Bastini asked.

"Maybe two hundred fifty years."

Everyone laughed.

"How big of a hotel and casino do we need here?" Indelicato asked.

Manelli cleared his throat. "It has to be fairly large, as it will be the only one for an hour and a half drive from the highway. We need to study that and come to a conclusion.

"To be successful and bring in conventions and groups, I think it should have six hundred rooms, but it might make more sense to build three hundred first and layout, in advance, the remainder as the hotel begins to need the rooms. For the three hundred rooms, the casino, and the main features to bring in guests, such as the golf course, pools, tennis courts, the new airport, the power lines, and the like, I think we need one hundred fifty million dollars."

Bastini jumped in. "If it's done in a big way, it can be a hit. It would be a mistake to do it too modestly. Otherwise, it will appear disappointing to the guests, and it won't bring in the big crowds and high rollers. It would gain a reputation for a lower-class place and always be left with that stigma. It needs to be done to a high standard, with advertising, with big name entertainers, so it will be perceived as a fashionable place to go from the beginning. I think Manelli is right about the estimate."

"We don't know how to set such things up," No Cloud said.

"That's why we're here," said Manelli. "You were smart to call on us. We'll run it for you, and we'll work out an agreeable percentage with you. How much money can you raise?"

"Chockpaws don't got nuttin' 'cept land. That's why we want the casino like the others," No Cloud replied, referring to the numerous other Indian tribes that had casinos. "But we think we can borrow. We put out the word with some politicians who have helped us, to see if there's a big company that might wanna lend to us. We gave out copies of the prospectus that Mr. Manelli got for us. One insurance company in Los Angeles is interested, and I'm gonna go there the day after tomorrow in my truck."

All four seemed to initially agree on the concept, the size, and the amount of money. They then walked around for views from different vantage points. All were impressed with the location and the excitement of being out of United States jurisdiction and control. On a hillside, when the chief was not within earshot, Manelli turned to the group. "This is like what my father said how Havana used to be before Castro, and yet it's right in the middle of the United States with its military protection and drinkable water. This is as good as it gets!"

❧❧❧

In the jet on the return trip, Manelli told the others, "The benefits are beyond belief. We must have it. We can have unimaginable success here. This land is treated by the US as a foreign country, only better! The Indians are not taxed or controlled. There's no income tax, and that alone is enough to make it a winner. There's no property tax. There's no control over crooked machines—we can bring in slot and other machines that the State of California does not allow off the reservations. On busy nights, we can easily do things like stack the decks, rig the games, and electronically modify the slot machines to increase the house odds, just enough so as not to piss people off. We can run all sorts of scams. The police will be from the tribe. On hookers, we just need to keep it quiet enough to keep it out of the news, so businessmen's wives don't blacklist it to their husbands. Businessmen will love it for conventions, getting pussy with no hassles. The men can put pussy on credit cards as something else. The concierge can book a hooker, but it'll show up on his credit card as Turkish bath or room service. We might get creative and have a charge for convention guests that show a meeting related to their convention so the pussy is totally deductible. How fucking cool is that? Pussy paid for by Uncle Sam. Yuppies with marijuana and coke won't get hassled if they keep it in their rooms."

He began to get excited and animated over the prospects as he waved his hands about as Italians do. "Our police. No tax. Legal hookers. Stacked card decks. Machines we can alter as we choose. Scams. Money laundering. This is the future for us if we are smart enough to cash in on it!"

Everyone grinned at Manelli's excitement.

The others nodded, rather than speak, as their extraordinarily attractive stewardess they had recently hired for their private jet, brought them their usual drinks. They didn't want her to hear any comments on the subject.

CHAPTER 8

S o, what do you think, Mr. Stevens?" John Billings asked the respected, middle-aged, Sedro Woolley lawyer he had hired before and knew well. "Do you think we have a chance at an immediate injunction?"

"John, my friend, we've known each other for years. I try not to exaggerate the possibilities to give false hopes. The truth is that, if we ask for an immediate injunction, we will have to show that there is something likely wrong with the decision for the new owl circle, and that the court should enjoin the Stop Work Order until there is time to evaluate it."

"Isn't putting a crew of people out of work and creating hardships for their families enough?" John pleaded.

"I wish it were. But I fear not." Mr. Stevens picked up a list from his desk and continued. "The spotted owl has been placed on the Federal Endangered Species List, and in turn on the state list, called the Critical Wildlife Habitat. Here is the list, from Washington Administrative Code, or WAC, Statute 222-16-080." He read from a book. "Bald eagle, gray wolf, marbled grizzly bear, mountain caribou, Oregon silver spot butterfly, peregrine falcon, sand hill crane, northern spotted owl, western pond turtle, and the marbled murrelete.

"The Forest Practices Board makes the rules, and it is headed by an elected official, called the chair. That official is also the commissioner of the Department of Natural Resources, and of course, that person doesn't give a damn about landowners, loggers, and the hardships of their families. It's a flaming liberal woman."

John's anger rose. "Yeah, an official elected by the three counties with that bunch of computer kids from other states, who moved up here and know nothing about the forests. The commissioner carried no other county in the whole state."

"John, it is still the majority vote, and this is a democracy. We cannot help it that a bunch of bunny-huggers moved into the state and now control it. The Department of Natural Resources implements the rules of the board, and now we have this sighting. There are five statuses. Status one is the mating pair, which they call any pair observed close together. Status two is two birds, status unknown. Status three is a territorial single, an owl seen three times in the same general area. Status four is a single, with no information other than a sighting. The fifth is an abandoned site. Statuses one to three get regulation. Four and five do not."

John threw up his hands in frustration. "But someone reported a single, and who is he to say this is not a four instead of a three? As a status four, it gets no protection. And how do we know that the mutherfucking Earthfirster didn't just make up the sighting, as they act on anonymous calls?"

"John, you know your only hope is for an injunction. But now here's the kicker. In order to go to court, you are supposed to *exhaust your administrative remedies*. You are supposed to re-apply to the Department of Natural Resources, with a new plan and then, if turned down, go to the Forest Practices Appeals Board, with three administrative judges. Then, and only then, are you supposed to be able to go to court. These environmentalists wrote the law and the procedure. They wrote it in their favor, to understate it. It was designed to bog down any process of challenge. That way they win by attrition."

"How long before you go through all that?" John asked, tight lipped.

"Maybe a year and a half. Maybe more. There is no point in my sugar-coating it and promising something sooner than I can deliver."

"What do our families do in the meantime? How do I make my payments?"

"There's some authority for court relief without exhausting administrative remedies in extraordinary circumstances. We could try it, but I would say the odds are not even fifty-fifty. I'd need to ask for the information on the sightings from the Department of Fish & Wildlife, so as to try to show that the action was arbitrary or capricious, or without substantial justification."

"So do it. If we don't, I'm definitely fucked. I realize it's a long shot, but at least I should make one stab at it before filing bankruptcy. Can you do it in a day or two?"

"I can do it, but it will take longer than a day or two. I can go in and ask for a temporary restraining order to enjoin the stop work order. I wouldn't bank on winning, but I'll try."

John lifted up his leg and farted loudly, punctuating what he was about to say. "How's that for an exhaust of administrative remedy? I inherited that land from my father, and he from his. It was bought for logging in the first place. If the fucking government wants to make me hold it for owls, why don't they just buy it?"

Mr. Stevens acknowledged John's fart by picking up a legal pad and waving it at him, as though to recognize the power of his fart by fanning any smell away. He then raised his hand in a calming manner. "John, I knew your father well, as you know. If I had my way, idiotic people, who come from cities and think they know nature, would never have their way here. But I didn't make these laws. Out of all the counties in Washington State, only three voted for the idiot, commie commissioner. But they have the population since that Gates put his big company up here, and he hired kids just out of school with degrees for high wages who couldn't hit a tree pissing toward one in the forest. This is all I have to work with, but I'll give it my best."

CHAPTER 9

A ll rise," the bailiff said loudly as the judge walked out of his chambers toward the bench in the courtroom, looking regal in his black robe. He sat on the bench, and the bailiff announced, "Skagit County Superior Court is now in session, the Honorable Walter Snyder presiding. Come to order. Turn off all cell phones. No talking is allowed while court is in session."

Judge Snyder nodded. "Good morning, and please be seated. The first matter is an *ex-parte* petition by John Billings, landowner, for a temporary restraining order to temporarily enjoin the Department of Natural Resources from enforcing its Stop Work Order, halting the harvesting permit obtained by the petitioner for the harvesting of timber on the petitioner's own private land." The two attorneys came forward and put their briefs and notes on the counsel table. Billings followed Stevens and stood next to him. The judge acknowledged the local attorney he knew well. "Mr. Stevens, good morning."

"Good morning, your honor," Mr. Stevens said. "My client, Mr. John Billings, is also here."

"Brendan Williams, appearing on behalf of the Department of Natural Resources," said the young attorney for the other side.

"Welcome to Skagit County, Mr. Williams." The judge did not know the young Seattle attorney. He did, however, recognize the large Seattle firm that he worked for, and which firm represented the Department of Natural Resources. Williams was new to the practice and had not been to the Northern Skagit County Superior Court before. "Please be seated."

"Thank you, your honor," Mr. Williams said. He appeared

a bit nervous, like the new kid at school. The two attorneys and Billings sat.

"Mr. Stevens, I have gone over your papers submitted by you on behalf of your client, the landowner, Mr. Billings. Mr. Williams, have you had a chance to read Mr. Stevens's papers?"

Williams stood. "Yes, your honor. Mr. Stevens delivered them to me early this morning here by pre-arrangement on the phone yesterday. In this short time, I was unable to provide any written response, of course. I would like a chance to file a brief for any hearing on a preliminary injunction, which I assume would be in about fifteen days."

Judge Snyder looked at Williams. "Yes, of course. But this is an *ex-parte* application for a temporary restraining order. You would be provided with an opportunity to respond in written form if a hearing is set. Mr. Williams, are you able to respond to these papers, which demonstrate that the logging will have to stop, and the logging crew will be out of their jobs if not granted?"

"Yes, your honor." Williams started in with his prepared presentation. "The fact that the logging on Mr. Billings's property is temporarily halted until he can resubmit a revised plan to show no impact on the owl that has been sighted, and the fact that there may be some good logger folks out of work is most unfortunate. But this is not a situation where the court has jurisdiction to entertain the injunction. The legal procedure has been precisely followed by the Department. The rules come from the Forest Practices Board. The Department of Natural Resources merely implements the rules. An owl was sighted three times and reported to the Department of Fish & Wildlife. The Department of Fish & Wildlife confirmed the sighting, and reported that to the Department of Natural Resources. The Department of Natural Resources relies on Fish & Wildlife. These required procedures have all been tried, tested, and approved in the court system and the court of appeals.

"The action taken is consistent with the regular conduct of the Department. There has been a territorial single spotted owl

sighted on three occasions in the area, and that makes the owl
a status three protected one, a territorial single. The nest has
not been located, but it has been given a site center. That site
center is very near the logging in question, and the 2.7 miles
radius for the owl circle that has been set by the Fish & Wildlife Department must be observed. There can be no cutting in
that area unless and until the petitioner can show it will not
adversely affect the owl. And that burden now shifts to the
petitioner."

Williams looked at his papers where he had written down
the applicable statutes. "Now, on the request of the petitioner
for a temporary stay, it is not within this court's jurisdiction to
grant it. Petitioner must resubmit a plan to the Department,
called a Landowner's Plan, under WAC 222-16-100. The plan
must minimize the impact on the owl. It has to achieve an appropriate contribution to the goals. It must describe the area,
and the features. The habitat must be mapped. The species
must be identified. There must be management proposals and
a suitable habitat environment developed. There must be training. There must be monitoring and reporting standards. And
then the plan must be circulated to Fish & Wildlife, affected
Indian tribes, local governments, other landowners, and the
public. The Department of Natural Resources then has ninety
days, which may be extended, to review the plan. The plan can
then, and only then, be approved, disapproved, or recommended to be modified. When the Department makes its final
ruling, if the petitioner is dissatisfied, he may appeal to the
Forest Practices Appeals Board. Only after that board takes
action, can the case be brought to this, or any, court of law.

"And finally," Williams continued, "the injunction sought
would eliminate protection for the owl through the mating season, which is right around the corner. The rules are clear that
the owl cannot be disturbed during the mating season, as logging can prevent these owls from mating. That includes chainsaw noise, as well as other logging activity. If this injunction
is granted, it will be immediately reversed by the court of appeals. It would be reversed on grounds of no jurisdiction and,
although we need not reach the substance of the petition since

there is no jurisdiction, I wish to add that the state's system has been meticulously implemented."

Williams put down his papers, concluding, "Thank you, your honor."

The judge leaned forward, glancing over at Billings with a sympathetic look. He then turned to attorney Stevens. "Well, Mr. Stevens, what about this problem with jurisdiction? How am I to proceed when you have not exhausted your administrative remedies by reapplying to the Department, and then the Appeals Board as Mr. Williams points out?"

Mr. Stevens stood and straightened his shoulders. "Your honor, I'm here on this ex-parte application because the plain and simple fact is that by the time that my client does all that, at least a year and a half will have passed. My client has to hire a biologist and a forester to do studies and make reports. By the time all that happens, it will be too late. My client will be bankrupt. Delayed justice is denied justice.

"Filed separately are copies of my client's existing studies and details of the law, state and federal, on the issue of preservation of the northern spotted owl. My client was given the legal rights to log the area in controversy after submitting the required expensive reports and studies that the logging of the area now put in controversy by the state will not endanger that owl. Logging is stopped just because it might *disturb* mating owls. My client's logging has been shut down based on a mystery, anonymous sighting by someone of a northern spotted owl. The sighting is most likely a fraud perpetrated by someone trying to stop the logging. We should be able to bring the person making the sighting to court to cross examine him or her."

His comments were heard by all in the courtroom, and silence followed it as it had meaning and moved everyone except Williams. Obviously well-seasoned in court compared to the younger Williams, Stevens gave a very moving address. "Let me please attempt to illustrate how capricious and unreasonable the action of the Department is. There are over one thousand three hundred site centers already. For every one of these, the spotted owl gets an owl circle of 2.7 miles radius, or

5.4 miles in diameter, just to breed. Now they want to add another site center, since someone has *claimed* to have seen an owl flying over my client's land. There is no positive proof that the owl has chosen my client's land as his territory. If it is not a territorial single, it is not entitled to status three protection and becomes a status four, just an owl sighted, and entitled to no protection. How can anyone just come into an area and state that because an owl was seen there, that twenty square miles must be set aside as undisturbed, so as not to harass the owl? The rules also prohibit chainsaw noise and helicopter noise if the owner wants to use a helicopter instead of a yarder during the mating and egg hatching season of the owl, from March first to August thirty-first.

"The Department of Natural Resources is running amok. Its actions have no reasonable relationship to reality, and especially not to landowners and loggers. The Department protects the northern spotted owl, the marbled murrelete, and some other creatures. The extended protection of the marbled murrelete is just as capricious. This bird lives primarily in rocks, and only some live in old growth trees. It appears to have, when related to human behavior, a neurotic personality, and is excited by most anything. Thus, it was easy for the Department to find some degree-holding scientist to provide a psychoanalysis of the bird that it should get up and go to bed without the sound of chainsaws, anthropomorphizing that, because environmentalist scientists don't like the sound of chainsaws, the bird doesn't either. Logging has been stopped in any range where this bird can hear the noise at sunrise and sunset, and an hour before and after on both. This little neurotic-acting bird cannot be disturbed by the sound of chainsaws in the mating season, which is April first to August thirty-first of each year, and their nesting areas must be left undisturbed."

The judge smiled at the comments on the bird. It was obvious he was sympathetic to Stevens and his cause.

"Now the Department has capriciously decided on an emergency basis that there can be no logging within two hundred feet of any creek or stream that is or might serve as a spawning ground for salmon," Stevens continued. "This is for the ostensible purpose of providing more shade for the stream banks to stabilize the water temperature. But the truth is that it is merely another attack on the landowners and loggers. Many streams are also on my client's land. The Department took this action as the Emergency Salmonid Rule, to protect salmon, as though there will be no more spawning of salmon. Of course, anyone with common sense knows that the current problems with salmon are from the fishery-hatched salmon, which mature in two years. They mix with the wild salmon, thereby coming back in just two years instead of four or five, and so when they come back early they are much smaller. The Indians are allowed to net fish them without restriction, diminishing their numbers by over-fishing. There is also widespread belief that the unusual higher water temperatures of late in the ocean may have some effect. But increased shade on stream banks? No one with any credibility believes that to be helpful to their size or numbers.

"Washington State has so many creeks and streams that this constitutes an incredible amount of forest that cannot be cut. If you look in the publication of the Department, *Our Changing Nature*, the Department psychoanalyzes the salmon as *depressed*! This is an incredible assumption to make for a mindless fish that returns to spawn at an earlier age than it did eighty years ago. This is yet another example of people, who know nothing of the real forest, making laws to back up their ill-advised notions.

"Getting back to the alleged owl nest, no one has seen it. The action by the state is only based on an anonymous call of seeing a northern spotted owl in flight which no one else has seen, let alone someone reputable, and we contend is a fraud. If the court does not intervene, my landowner client will be shut down and faced with hardships, and a hard-working bunch of loggers in a noble and wanted trade will be similarly caused hardship. This court should consider the rights of these people to earn a living and care for their families sufficiently important so as to interfere with the catering to the hypothetical decrease of a rare species of a critter that provides no benefit to ecology, any other animal, or mankind, and which animal is not in great numbers for whatever reason in this day and age.

"Millions of species have come and gone, and many will in the future. Is it not a *perversion* to try to arrest nature? What arrogance of man to deem that the will and design of God and nature is *stasis* as to preserving one of nature's critters, and that man is not part of nature, rather than apart from it? And similarly, who is man, and the Department, to conclude that bringing back a nearly extinct species to a large number is what nature intended? Nature has gotten rid of millions of species. Does the Department supersede nature? That's what it wants to do with its arrogance, and to do so, selectively. It doesn't care about coyotes and rattlesnakes, since they can attack children—but it loves fuzzy little owls since they seem harmless.

"But this is not an issue of allowing a species to go extinct. It's a question of just how much proliferation, and at what cost and hardship to men, should there be just to expand a very rare species that nature does not want anymore. This refers to both the northern spotted owl and the murrelete. They're in zoos, and they are protected with an unimaginable cost of forests and money. There are three subspecies of the spotted owl, the northern spotted owl, the California spotted Owl, and the Mexican spotted owl. The Pacific states are estimated as the home of six thousand northern spotted owls.

"The combined preserved lands for owls, birds, turtles, and now salmon, in Washington would cover a strip of land, if laid out in a line, five miles wide and three thousand five hundred miles in length. Yet, the Department says it wants to virtually seize another chunk of land to put more people in hardship. Shouldn't the children of the families of the loggers and the landowner have the money to buy new tennis shoes and get a computer one day? The families of the loggers do not have many of the luxuries of the city dwellers. Isn't their protection, and that of their children, more in need and entitled to more equitable relief than trying to save another breeding ground for a pair of owls?

"The Department bases its reasoning, in part, because, it

says, that there are three hundred percent more visits to the Washington state parks in the last thirty years. But the Department does not take action to condemn or ask for property by donation for more parks. It simply states that since the parks are getting a lot of use, that somehow everyone should equate that to a reason for not cutting down trees in the dense forests that are on such steep hills and mountains that no one but a logger can even walk up and down them, nor would they care to try.

"All concede that the clear-cut areas bring in and enhance the proliferation of deer, elk, and a number of other animals that can only find food in the clear-cut areas as there is plant growth there that they can reach to eat, whereas it is not so in dense areas where the sunlight cannot get below the entangled limbs of the canopy of uncut trees. There are three to four new trees planted for everyone cut, and they are a better variety, less vulnerable to diseases, and grow faster and healthier. These are all on private land, and not coming from some public park.

"The Department is always free to petition the court to modify or change its injunction if it issues one, and some new evidence that has any credibility comes up. Please grant the injunction and save my client's property, his family, and the livelihoods of the loggers that are working there! Thank you, your honor."

Attorney Stevens paused after his emotional and moving address and sat down. The courtroom staff and all of the few people in the gallery were absolutely quiet, having listened with great interest to the talented pleader. The court clerk behind her desk to the side of the bench forgot herself and started to applaud, clapping her hands excitedly, but then realized her position as everyone, including the judge, looked at her.

The Honorable Walter Snyder sighed. "Mr. Stevens, you are, as usual, in excellent form. You are eloquent, moving, convincing and a delight to hear. No doubt justice is on your side. But I was just reversed six months ago on something very similar for intervening when the administrative remedies were not exhausted. I'm convinced that the rights of loggers and landowners are indeed of the utmost importance, and I do not overlook them in the slightest. But the immediate problem I have is that if I intervene I'll be reversed by the Court of Appeals, and whatever I do made invalid. I cannot intervene and weigh the actions of the Department until you go to the Department and get turned down, lose, and then go to the appeals board and again lose. Only then am I empowered to review the evidence and weigh the rights of the landowners, such as your client, and the loggers, if that is the state of the case at the time.

"But there is one thing I can do, and I'm going to do it. I must rule that the petition is premature, but rather than deny the petition, I'll stay the action you have filed until you have exhausted your administrative remedies. And to prevent the Department from unduly delaying the matter, in the light of your client's contention that the delay itself is the problem, you may come back at any time if the Department takes an unreasonable time to act. If I find the Department is not acting as quickly as is reasonably practicable, I will entertain an injunction. I believe that I'll have jurisdiction to intervene if the Department is taking an unreasonable time to act. I believe that the appellate court will uphold me in that case. Mr. Williams, I want you to tell the Department that I want it to act with expediency."

Williams, relieved that he won, was nevertheless concerned that he was going to have to report back that his clients would have to move this case along, as it was to be under scrutiny of the court for timeliness. "I'll inform them, your honor."

Causing delay was his department's main stock in trade and he was unhappy about the judge's ruling as he had been anticipating a complete victory.

The judge turned to Mr. Stevens. "And if you wish to return with facts that the Department is delaying matters, Mr. Stevens, you may return on this same case, at which time I will undertake to rule on the matter, depending on what the status is at that time. At least this way you have a case pending and will not have to pay another filing fee and file new papers.

There is no need to set a hearing on a preliminary injunction at this time, as I find I have no jurisdiction to proceed. Mr. Stevens, I'm extremely sympathetic to your cause. However here, I must follow the law. If I don't, I'll be reversed, for sure.

"So my ruling is as follows. I find that the petition of Mr. Billings is sufficient in facts and persuasive enough to warrant temporary relief and to set a hearing for an injunction. However, it's premature, and the plaintiff must exhaust his administrative remedies with the Department of Natural Resources and, if necessary, with the Forest Practices Appeals Board before he can obtain relief here in the Superior Court. However, I note that the court may and will intervene if the Department takes any undue time to rule on the landowner's new plan, especially in the light of the fact that Mr. Billings already has an approved plan. I expect the Department to handle this on an expedited basis, and I want you to make that clear to your client, Mr. Williams. I stay the action, to hold it for further hearing, depending on what happens in the administrative process at the Department of Natural Resources and the Forest Practices Appeals Board. I reserve the right to reexamine matters on a showing of good cause at any time. I want a report from both sides in ninety days on the progress.

"Thank you, Mr. Williams and Mr. Stevens."

Downtrodden, Mr. Stevens, picked up his briefcase and walked through the swinging doors to join Billings, who had gone out first, disgusted with the situation. It was probable bankruptcy for him.

Outside, Billings spoke first. "We're screwed. Even with the judge's admonition and ruling to hurry things along, those sons-a-bitches will make it take over a year. Even if they do it in a year, I still lose. The probable outcome will be that the Department will pretend to compromise by allowing some limited harvesting near, but not too close, to the site center, and then only in the fall when the mating season is through. I depended on the permit I was given to get the new equipment to log that area. Even if I could go in now and log only a little of it, I would end up losing, due to the expense of the roads and the equipment. I will have to raise money for another study by an owl biologist and submit the damn thing again. In the meantime, I have to make payments on the bank loan I took out on the property to cut the roads in for the logging, and on the seven hundred fifty thousand dollar yarder and other equipment I financed after I got the permit. I have no way to make the payments. So, I lose even if I win another permit to continue logging my own land. I might as well turn back the yarder to the bank, and just face the fact that I will have no credit again, and probably end up in bankruptcy court."

"Well, at least he left the case open and warned them that if they drag it out unnecessarily, he will intervene," Stevens said. "And I think he made his sentiment clear on which side he leans, yours. Think it over for a while. Maybe you can get the permit in a year or less, and put off the idea of bankruptcy."

"What about the families of my loggers?" Billings demanded. "Now they're out of work once again over that ridiculous owl. Imagine what my grandfather would have said if, when he worked and saved and bought that fairly small piece of land, the government came in and told him that he, and his descendants, would still own the land, still have to pay taxes, maintain it, but have to hold it without logging for the benefit of a rare owl that might have its screwing upset without a 5.4 mile diameter of peace and quiet!"

CHAPTER 10

We interrupt our regular programming to bring you this special report," the newscaster said to the TV audience. "The storm that struck the Los Angeles coast this morning at eight a.m. has brought record rain and winds. Wind gusts this morning were recorded at eighty miles per hour, which is hurricane force, although the National Weather Bureau has not classified it as a hurricane, since the winds have reduced their velocity somewhat after the first half hour of pounding the coast. Presently, wind gusts are as high as fifty to sixty miles per hour and are causing considerable damage. Power outages are reported in many places. There are numerous reports of trees uprooted, broken, and down in residential areas, blocking streets. Intersections are flooded, in many places, with two or more feet of water, stalling cars. On the screen now is a live shot from our location camera van in the valley, showing you a flooded intersection."

A traffic intersection with water higher than the curb at one corner appeared on the TV. One small car was stalled, with its occupants already gone, and a higher SUV was going through it, spraying water up from the big wheels.

"Heavy rains are reported from Santa Barbara down to Orange County, moving into San Diego, and are expected not to let up for seven or more days. The rains are moving inland and there are warnings in place to the entire inland empire. In just two hours, Los Angeles has had a record three inches of rainfall. Pacific Coast Highway is closed at Malibu with mudslides and flooding. Flying debris caused an accident on the 405 freeway near the Los Angeles International airport, and an eighteen-wheeler jack-knifed and has backed up traffic in the northbound lanes. A large billboard has blown down from the wind on the Pasadena Freeway in the southbound lanes. There is local flooding in many areas as the drain systems are overloaded. We will interrupt our regular broadcasting to bring you updates, and have a full, up-to-date report at the top of the hour."

CHAPTER 11

The unemployment office was noisy. Over the screams of an infant in its mother's arms, Ernie was handed a set of forms at a window and took a number, waiting for his turn to be called.

When it was his turn, he went inside to the desk of a lady and handed her the forms he had filled out. He sat, and the lady looked at the forms, making a notation on one of them. "You can only qualify for unemployment after three weeks. However, there is a new program whereby several states are cooperating with each other to get people off the unemployment rolls. There are some actual shortages of labor in certain areas in some states. Much of it is only temporary work, however. If you would be willing to take temporary or permanent employment out of state, you can receive benefits at once, provided you begin the out of state employment within thirty days. Would you be willing to accept out-of-state temporary or permanent employment?"

"Temporary, but not permanent. I like what I do. I want to return to logging here as soon as something opens up."

"Good. There really aren't that many people who have been willing to leave the area. If you qualify, you can get the benefits without delay and retroactive from today, and the benefits will continue for a period of a month from now, or until you begin working at the new job. Please fill out this form for temporary work out of the state." She handed over another form. "You can do it here, as it requires only that you fill in the boxes in block letters with your name, address, phone, social security number, date of birth, and experience."

Ernie figured she must get some sort of recognition for getting people to agree to out of state employment, as she let him fill in the form right there at her desk instead of making him go back to stand in line again. He took the form and began to print his name and address in block letters in the boxes at the top of the form. The form was apparently computer reviewed, as there was no place on it for any handwriting.

After the personal information there were a series of boxes next to job descriptions and the name of the state where the job was offered. If you had experience in a particular type of job, you checked a box next to that and then in the next box the number of years of experience that you had in that field.

He looked up and down the form, and there was nothing on it for loggers. The jobs listed were for part time shortages of labor, or were otherwise undesirable. The first job on the list was: Sheep Herding, Idaho.

Sheep herding? Sounds nasty! Herding sheep around on snowy, rocky mountains, stepping in sheep droppings, and smelling sheep. There must be something better than that.

The next was: Fruit Picking, California.

Fruit picking? Ernie saw himself walking up and down steep hills with a group of Spanish speaking Mexicans picking avocados, oranges, and nectarines off trees with ladders. *No way, Jose!*

The next was: Nurse's Aide, Wisconsin.

Good Lord! Imagine changing bedpans for the aged in some rest home in some snow-ridden state! Out of the question!

The next was: Insurance Company Field Representative, California.

What's a field representative? Someone who works out in the field? What could that be? There's no clue. Time to ask.

He looked up at the lady who was working on some forms and got her attention. "Is a logger who works out in the field all the time a field representative?"

The woman was looking at something, not paying much attention, and carelessly said, "Yes."

Why not? Ernie checked the box for *Insurance Company Field Representative, California*. The box following asked for number of years of experience. Ernie put twelve, representing the years of experiences he had as an adult logger, and turned in the form.

She looked it over perfunctorily, and stamped the bottom with an official stamp. "You should be notified within a week to ten days if you will be accepted for the out-of-state employment. The employer will notify you, and you, in turn, notify us that you have the job. Accepting the out-of-state employment qualifies you for unemployment benefits retroactively from today up until the time you start the next job, not to exceed one month. This is offered as an incentive. Can you be reached at this phone number and address on here?"

"Yes." Ernie left the office with a hollow feeling, wondering if he was making a mistake about leaving his familiar home in Sedro Woolley, and the forests he loved, for the big city. But then, on the brighter side, any work was better than none, and it was only temporary. Maybe Billings could get his operation back up and running, or some other logging operation would open and need him soon.

CHAPTER 12

The freshly poured cup of coffee in Don McAteer's cup, sitting in front of him on his boss's desk, spilled over the top without anyone touching it. Majestik Insurance's high rise building began to move slowly several feet one way and then back the other direction, accompanied by a very deep growling sound like a groan from the bowels of the earth.

"Jesus!" McAteer exclaimed across the desk from the company president, "An earthquake!"

Rain pounded against the windows of the luxurious office, the predicted storm having struck. Bradford went to the wall across from his desk, opened two doors to expose a flat screen TV, and tuned in the news.

"…interrupt our regular broadcast to bring you an update," the newswoman said. "Just a few minutes ago we had an earthquake of 6.1 on the Richter Scale. Its epicenter was at Northridge. However, the shock was felt throughout the Los Angeles basin and as far away one hundred miles. We will bring you reports as they come in, and more on the hour."

"It doesn't sound too bad," McAteer said. "Only 6.1. I don't think we will have much loss on this, do you? Most of our insureds don't purchase the earthquake coverage, and those that have it only get coverage on losses over ten per cent of the structure."

"Yeah," Bradford responded. "Remember how we and the other big companies spent a bunch of money for lobbyists and stopped writing new homeowner's policies until we got what we wanted, the legislation whereby earthquake insurance only attaches when the value of the structure is damaged by ten per cent or more? This quake was too weak to do any real damage. I bet there are nearly zero homes that have cracks creating anywhere near ten per cent loss of their value. I bet you lunch we don't pay out on a single claim. Hah!"

McAteer mopped up the spilled coffee on the fancy desk with a tissue. "Well, most people don't even know about that. They think that because they paid for earthquake insurance that they're covered for any damage. So there will be lots of claims. We'll be able to deny most of them due to the ten per cent floor, which only comes into play where the structure is over ten percent destroyed before we pay the first dollar. But we better set up some diplomatic people on phones and writing letters back to policy holders that can reduce their anger when they find out we screwed them."

Suddenly Bradford slapped his forehead with his palm, as if to acknowledge that his brain had just awoken. "Do you know what? This could be a stroke of luck!"

"How so?"

"Isn't it obvious? The storm now underway is an insured event. Rain damage is covered. So, you can blame storm damage on the quake, which is not covered with most policy holders. Perfect!"

McAteer's face lit up. "Got it. I'll incorporate the quake damage into the storm claims. Where there is a leak in a roof that was lifted up by the high winds, we will deny the claim based on the contention that the earthquake caused the crack. I see what you mean. The simultaneous events are a true stroke of luck."

"Do it!" Bradford commanded. "Now, how's the program going to hire the temporary adjusters?"

"I've set in motion everything you asked for. I put out the word for one hundred additional adjusters for ninety days' temporary assignment. My office is already hiring them. With all the other companies also hiring, the locals are going fast. Looking out of state, we've found some already." McAteer raked a hand through his unkempt, already thinning, gray hair. "I'll personally conduct an indoctrination room for the adjusters, so as to involve no one else on those sensitive matters.

And, most importantly, as I know you'll appreciate, I have put none of the sensitive matters into writing, in case we get a disgruntled employee who quits or gets fired and tries to blackmail us by threatening to tell the public how we do business unless we pay unemployment or severance pay. We can defend ourselves by denying everything, as usual."

"As usual, Don, you do a fine job." Don smiled, appreciating the compliment from the company's chief executive officer.

Bradford continued, "I have updated our unpublished procedures and you should have a look. However, as you know, this is really sensitive stuff. So, I want no copies of it anywhere. The only place it exists is on my personal computer and Zelzah's. Just look at it on the secure screen at the private side office next to Zelzah. The file name is *MM*. She'll open it for you. *MM* is my little joke for *Moneymaker*."

Except for what would be shown to Don McAteer, Zelzah, Mr. Bradford's executive secretary, was the only one in the huge company who had access to such sensitive company information—that was in writing—and only because she typed it and updated it for Bradford. Possible leaks were a major problem, and a great deal of money was spent on security. All such secured material was only kept on two computers, Bradford's and Zelzah's, and required a special security code word to get in. Either could access it, and sometimes Zelzah would access it at her home to update the programs. If someone got hold of the information, the company could be sued for hundreds of millions in a class action lawsuit. A jury would award it, too.

"Zelzah," Bradford called on the intercom.

Zelzah was the epitome of loyal. Bradford paid her more than anyone in the company, and double what a comparable position would pay. Her benefits included a retirement plan, unheard of for a secretary, a medical plan, and a company car—but since she did not want to drive a Ford Taurus that the company would buy, she took the equivalent in money and upgraded herself to a Lexus. Bradford could not buy her a Lexus because the management of the insurance company had to keep a very conservative image—even Bradford's company car was a Ford Taurus. The high salary would be hard to replace elsewhere, and this ensured, Bradford figured correctly, her loyalty.

Working for the top man in the company, she was in a position of power. She had been working for him for twelve years, following him from his two last jobs to this one, the third company change for her. Never having married or having children, she was now forty-three, and it was fairly clear to her that she did not need a marital companion. Tall, dark hair, and slender, she gave a very nice appearance, al-though she was not very pretty in the face and her nose was a bit long. Her clothes were elegant and corporate, and she looked like the powerful person she was in the company as she was so close to the top—as close as anyone could get. Being next to the top had its own form of power, as all she had to do was ask Bradford for something and it would happen.

She would not trust the typing pool or anyone else to type anything for her boss, and did it all herself. She seldom went out, except for shopping in Beverly Hills and for an occasional sale somewhere. A big fan of old movies and classics, she mostly stayed home and watched movies on internet programs like Netflix.

Once a year she would take a trip, and only gone from the office for two weeks. She liked to go to someplace different each time, and had been to many countries in Europe. She had also been to China, Egypt, and Israel. She had taken a cruise to Alaska on a one week part of her two weeks entitlement to holiday last year, and had become very enchanted with the Pacific Northwest.

With few exceptions, her favorite movie stars were not the city type, but the outdoors sort. In addition to Humphrey Bogart and Clark Gable, she loved to watch Burt Lancaster acting the swashbuckler pirate, and Errol Flynn in anything. She loved Sean Connery in all his movies, and laughed at his replacements trying to act James Bond. She did not care for the smaller, more modern stars who she thought were wimps and ineffectual as heroes.

Her fantasies were always with a big, strong, outdoors sort

of person. The idea of being taken by a strong man was a recurrent dream she had while masturbating.

When Bradford called, in she came at once, her notepad
and pen in hand in her usual always-prepared mode, her effi-
ciency unexcelled.

"Zelzah, I have some new materials dictated for you to put
in my *MM* file. Don is to have access to it. Let him use the
side office next to you when he wants to view the file. But no
hard copies are to be made."

"Yes sir," Zelzah said.

CHAPTER 13

As Ernie pulled up on his motorcycle to the row of four mailboxes at the end of the drive where he lived just outside of town, to his surprise, he saw a special delivery letter was in his mailbox. He put it the inside the breast pocket of his leather motorcycle jacket, and drove up the gravel road, which wound around for a country mile to his doublewide trailer house. His broken down truck sat behind the trailer. He had made a makeshift garage to keep his motorcycle and tools. It was a rare day in the area—it had not yet rained. Soon it would, however. It was only 11:00 a.m.

He pulled up in front of the doublewide. Quiet consumed the area after the engine rumble quit.

Once inside, he opened a can of beer and sat at the table and looked at the envelope that had Majestik Insurance Company written on it with a colored logo.

Due to the storm that struck Southern California recently, Majestik is hiring outside field representatives on a ninety (90) day temporary basis. Your name has been provided by the Washington State Employment Office as having twelve years of experience as a field representative.

You qualify for the position if you have ten or more years of experience. We are offering those who qualify a ninety (90) day job at five thousand dollars ($5000) per month to work out of the Los Angeles office if you can come to work at this time. We offer, in addition, mileage reimbursement for actual miles used in work, and thirty-five ($35) per diem extra toward housing and

*meals for those who come from out of state. We can on-
ly hire those who can start in two weeks or less. Please
call the office at the number shown to confirm that you
have the requisite experience and can start in two weeks
or less if you are interested in this temporary employment.*

    Don McAteer
    Vice President Operations
    Majestik Insurance Company
    Los Angeles, California, Home Office

Wow! The offer reverberated in Ernie's mind. *That's more
than I make logging. And no owls to get me laid off. It's a
Godsend!*

Anxiously, Ernie picked up his phone and called the number. A switchboard operator answered. "Majestik."

"Can I speak with Mr. Don McAteer about the temporary
employment, please?"

"Mr. McAteer is presently unavailable, but I'm his secretary, Judy Canton. Did you receive a letter from Mr. McAteer,
offering you a temporary assignment?"

"Yes."

"I sent all of those myself on his behalf. I can take the matter up with you, unless you need to speak to Mr. McAteer personally."

"No, no. I don't really need to speak to him personally."
Ernie said, sheepishly avoiding demanding an audience with
McAteer, relieved he did not have to give a phone interview to
such an important person. "I'm out of work now and need a
job."

"I'm told that, if you have the requisite ten years' experience, I can confirm the temporary job offer for you at this
time."

"I've got twelve years' experience with falling trees," Ernie said. "I assume that's why I was selected, because there
are so many trees down from the big storm I saw on TV."

He used the words *falling trees* as a verb phrase to mean
that which a tree faller does. But it was interpreted by Judy as

an adjective describing downed trees. Ernie did not understand the grammatical distinction. He *felled* trees. The terms *faller* and *fell* in relation to trees were not used in Los Angeles, and Judy heard *falling* as *fallen,* understanding it to mean that he was familiar with the handling of insurance claims on fallen trees, of which there were many, due to the storm.

"You've got the experience. Good." She determined he qualified, trying her best to handle the matter herself as a valuable assistant to her important boss Mr. McAteer and to insulate him from unnecessary disturbances over petty matters. "I'm sure that Mr. McAteer will be very pleased to have someone with your experience. I'll put you down as accepting and can confirm that you have the job, if you can come to work within two weeks."

"I can be there in a few days!" Ernie proclaimed, ready to roll for the opportunity.

"Good. Please come to the Los Angeles office at the address in the letter. You will be reimbursed for your airfare or mileage upon your arrival as the letter states. Mr. McAteer will be giving an indoctrination class."

"I'll be there," he replied exuberantly. *Wow! Finally, luck comes my way.*

CHAPTER 14

Chief No Cloud got off the elevator at the top floor of the Majestik Insurance Building. Wood paneling and granite floors distinguished the top floor from the rest of the building. There was a reception area with several women at it and some very luxurious chairs. The back, not visible from the reception area, was just for the president—his waiting room and secretary. There was also a huge, long room with a long table in it for board of directors meetings. There was a kitchen off to the side of the board room, but it was only staffed when there was a board meeting.

The storm was pounding rain when Chief No Cloud arrived in his old truck. The driver's side door had fallen off some time ago, so he fixed that before the journey—however, with the way he fixed it, the door would not open and he had to get in and out on the passenger side. He wore his Stetson, wet from the rain, which he took off as he exited the elevator, his long hair tied into a braid down to his waist. He wore jeans, cowboy boots, and a western shirt. Around his neck was a woven leather necklace passing through a large, real, eagle talon.

Once off the elevator, he approached a brace of secretaries typing away. His discomfort with the lavish surroundings showed. The nearest one looked at him, as though to beckon. No Cloud held his Stetson in hand and shuffled toward her, worried that he might be disturbing someone. "Hi."

A secretary looked curiously at his attire and long hair and impatiently asked, "Name please?"

"Chief No Cloud. I'm here to see Mr. Bradford."

"Very well, Chief No Cloud, if you would care to have a seat, I'll contact his office." She picked up a phone and spoke to Zelzah. She then pointed. "Go right on down the hallway, just through there."

He walked slowly down the hallway and turned into the private office area of the president. He was yet more intimidated at the overwhelming opulence of the seating area.

Zelzah's desk was just off to the side of the president's door, where she sat like a sentry. She stood to receive him. "Chief No Cloud?" She requested confirmation of his name, as though trained as an ambassador's staff assistant. She was far too professional to smile, as many of the callers did not come on friendly business. Her expression was stoic and painfully professional, a robotic greeting without a discernible trace of opinion.

"Yes."

She picked up a phone. "Sir, Chief No Cloud is here." After a pause, she said, "Go right on in, sir. Mr. Bradford is expecting you."

The walked up to and entered the big door, frightened, his knees were weak. His awe showed as he entered the office which was more spectacular than any he had ever seen, including on TV shows. The ceiling was done in raised three-foot-square cherry-wood frames with burled elm panels in between. Opulence abounded. Large windows promised a look at the world, but they were covered by loosely woven blinds that allowed light in but which no one could see through from the outside—Bradford did not like the idea of someone being able to see him, in spite of the city view he lost. The walls were of paneling of the same burled elm that were in the inserts of the ceiling, divided by cherry wood wainscoting matching the ceiling. The floor was multi-toned brown granite, with a huge, authentic, Iranian hand-woven carpet in the middle.

"Chief No Cloud." Bradford greeted him by standing up and offering his hand. "I've heard a lot of good things about you." He often said that at introductions and made it sound true.

The chief had rehearsed his salutation for his meeting with the important executive and performed it. "Mr. Bradford, it is an honor to meet you. I thank you for taking an interest in my humble tribe and our reservation. My tribe hopes you will loan us the money for the project."

Motioning for the chief to sit down at one of the chairs before his desk, Bradford put on his most sincere face. "Well, we here at Majestik have a charitable heart. I heard through some politicians who support the insurance industry that your tribe was in need of a loan for a hotel and casino, and so that's how I got the lead. I've considered whether or not this is the sort of thing that is appropriate for Majestik to get involved in. On the financial side, I have been provided with a prospectus from an investment-procuring firm from Los Angeles and a CPA firm out of Las Vegas on expected building and operation costs." Bradford leafed through a file he had been provided on the proposal that Zelzah had put on his desk earlier for the appointment. Experienced at evaluating a prospectus, he wanted to know the source, as that could skew the bottom lines. "Did you have these done yourself?"

"Not me personally. Nobody on the reservation knows nuttin' 'bout these things. I found some experienced hotel and casino operators in Las Vegas and they got those things. If we get the loan and build it, this group will provide management and also to put up ten million dollars for operating capital. All we got is lots of land. We need a loan to build it, and that's why I'm here. We believe we can make it a success and repay the loan on time."

"Very wise to bring in experienced management. It makes the endeavor much more likely to succeed. I see you have no other loans or indebtedness. You will need, according to this, one hundred fifty million dollars in total, with an advance of one million dollars for soils testing, architectural plans, engineering for plans to bring in power, road engineering, sewage, design of an airport and other initial expenses. This I understand well. Apparently you are going to build three hundred rooms initially, and put in all the amenities to create a draw to the hotel, which is some distance from other attractions."

"Yep."

"This is an unusual type of loan," Bradford continued. "We may not be able to put a usual type of enforceable encumbrance on the land, since we really would have no way to foreclose, as it is considered another nation. If you default on the loan, we cannot foreclose with our courts because they have no jurisdiction over Indian Territory, which is treated as foreign soil. However, you do have quite a lot of land to be sure. And you have several contracts with the state and federal governments. I think that if your tribe is willing to sign a comprehensive pledge of its assets, which would include an assignment of benefits under existing contracts in the case of default, and stipulate to jurisdiction in our state court in the event of dispute, Majestik would consider that adequate security. There is a certain amount of goodwill that we can advertise in helping out a group in need. And the venture looks promising. We have to look at passive investment with our reserves, and this could be a good one, if everything works out. You would like to borrow one hundred fifty million dollars then, with a one million dollar advance, is that right?"

"Yep." The chief then went into his practiced selling pitch, much of which he had learned from his new Las Vegas management group. "The other reservations make good money off their casinos, but almost none got a hotel. We ain't close to no major city, and too far from the highway to get people in just for the day or evening like other reservations do. So we need a hotel to make it work. We got a beautiful spot for it, overlooking the river from a hill. We got plans for a big golf course for regular golfing. We got room for another golf course if we can get major tournaments, so we can have golf for pros and guests at the same time. We got no taxes and free water from the river. We ain't worried about no drought.

"The California droughts don't affect us as we got all the water we can use from the river for free. We just need to buy the pumps. We can have river rafting, horseback riding, skeet, trap, and sporting ranges, real grass tennis courts, and fishing in the river and lakes. The lakes got fish. We can have swimming pools, outdoor for the good months, and indoor for the bad weather. But we need a good road in, and a small airport with fuel for the planes. If the hotel is run good and priced right, we can bring in lots of folks. We want those conventions and some of those entertainers like Las Vegas and Reno got."

"Very ambitious," Bradford said, as he leaned back in his chair and pondered the concept.

The chief could see Bradford was interested, and so he moved on to the big selling point. "The reservation is not subject to the laws of the United States and so the convention people and guests can only be policed by our own people. We'll have some of our young men who want to become policemen make up the police. They will answer only to us tribal elders. The customers will find that they can have a very good time, like going to a foreign country, except safer."

Bradford had not previously thought out the implications of what the chief was revealing. It was almost too fantastic to be real. He listened intently, thinking of how prostitutes could be legal. He thought about Evette and his leg twitched.

"We don't pay no taxes and can have slot machines that the casinos off the reservation cannot have. Unions can't come in and take over and can't get no court relief 'cause any dispute with the reservation must go to our own court of tribal elders. So we got a big advantage over a regular casino in Las Vegas or Reno. The only thing that they got is the huge money that put them there, and the attraction of other casinos nearby. Ours won't have no other casinos nearby, but we will have gardens, horseback riding, lots of grass, and good country life just outside the hotel doors. As it ain't as hot as Las Vegas in the summer, the outdoor activities can be enjoyed more. So, if we get the money to build a big one, we think we can be a big success and repay you in ten years."

Bradford was impressed with the lack of any governmental control. "I see what you mean. I wish we had some of those privileges." He let his mind drift for a moment, wondering what it would be like to do business under such total freedom. Then he brought himself back to reality. "Chief, if Majestik gets interested in this venture, there may be some political contributions needed. Do you have any reasons why you would not want to make certain political contributions? It is all perfectly legal, of course." That was not true, but was a test to check the chief's willingness to bend the law.

"Nope. Some big contributors to lobbyists in California are from some reservations. Some gave fifteen million dollars and even more last year alone. They must have got some big favors for that!"

"Are you or the tribe supporting Zachary Lewis for Governor?" Bradford asked bluntly. If the chief said yes, the meeting would end then and there, along with the loan.

"Nope. Ain't he the insurance reform guy? We ain't supporting nobody."

"Good!" Bradford did not answer his question but concluded that he passed the test. "Let me be candid with you. Zachary Lewis will virtually destroy our methods of doing business with his proposed legislation if he gets into office. If he wins, I will not be in a position to lend you the money. So, he must be kept out of office. I want to put up money for TV ads to discredit him and to help his opponent. The Fair Political Practices Law puts no limit on the corporate donations that can be made to gubernatorial elections. There is no limit on how much the Chockpaws can donate as well. However, if it comes out that Majestik or a conglomerate of insurance companies have donated millions to defeat a candidate, or to defeat his proposed legislation aimed at insurance, it would backfire, and have the opposite effect. At the end of an ad on TV, the sponsor has to be announced. If the voters see it is an insurance company, it will ruin the effect of the ad. Do you understand me on this?"

"Yeah, I see." the chief answered as though he understood, but it was all coming at him much too fast.

"If Lewis gets elected, I won't be able to make the loan. But I have a proposal for you that I think you'll be interested in. I'll make you an initial loan to get your soils testing, engineering, and to get underway in the projected amount of one million dollars. But to this I want to add another twenty million dollars to contribute to a committee to oppose Zachary Lewis and to assist his opposing candidate as we direct. The one million will be written up as a loan, and the twenty million as a donation to the tribe. Of course, I will forgive the one million if I do not loan the one hundred fifty million that you need for the project, and you may keep the benefit of the million for the initial expenses. You could use all of the engineering that the one million dollars will buy to show some other lender that you are well under way in the project, and it will be easier for you to get the money from someone else. I'll have a man that will have control of the twenty million and take care of donating it on behalf of your tribe to defeat Lewis. No one may find out that the twenty million came from Majestik."

The chief nodded, but his face was as blank as a cigar store wooden Indian.

"If Lewis loses, I'll then lend you the one hundred fifty million at competitive interest rates," Bradford assured him. "I can deduct a good deal of the twenty million dollars as a charitable donation if I don't loan the balance and, of course, your tribe pays no income taxes, anyway, so it is not taxable as imputed interest or otherwise."

"We don't pay no taxes," the chief said, ignoring the imputed interest comment—whatever that might mean.

Bradford chose not to address the chief's obvious lack of knowledge on the matter. "So, if Lewis loses, we will then loan you the one hundred fifty million—but, if it gets out that the political contribution came from here, I won't make the loan to build the casino. Is that clear?"

"No sweat," said the chief with dreams of avarice, hoping his flexibility would propel his tribe into wealth never before imagined. A picture of a new, red pickup truck formed in his mind. Maybe even with air conditioning.

Bradford leaned forward and placed his elbows on the desk. "Also, if I make the building loan, I'll be funding it pursuant to a builder's control over the construction, which will take a year and a half, and I'll put a secondary paymaster, in addition to whoever you chose from your tribe, in control of all pay-outs. This is also to protect you from contractors who don't finish or pay their subs, internal embezzlement, liens, and other problems. We, at the insurance company, are used to the needed security measures in handling money, as that is basically all an insurance company exists for and does. It takes in premiums and spreads losses when paying out claims. So I would like this conversation to go no further about the political contributions. I don't want anything written about it, other than what we will prepare, which will show the twenty million dollars as a donation, the one million as a loan, and the remaining one hundred fifty million dollars to be lent if Lewis's party does not win the election. I want you to include no one else in what we are doing about the candidate. If you have to include a trusted one at the reservation, that should be all. I want the Chockpaws to come out formally against Zachary Lewis and give money to his opposition. You may, of course, disclose to your business partners in Las Vegas the fact that I am giving you the one million dollar advance and the fact that the outcome of the up-coming elections may influence whether or not the company will make the building loan. Would that be agreeable to you and the rest of your tribe?"

"I speak for the tribe. The answer is yes. We really want that casino and hotel. All we got is property. We are property poor. How soon before we get the million?"

"I'll have your one million dollars together with the political contribution of twenty million in a week. You will need to set up an office at the site, which is usually a house trailer with a generator and phone lines if there is no cellular service there yet. Do cell phones work there?"

"They do," the chief said proudly, as though announcing that his Indian nation was not completely backward.

Bradford nodded. "We can use cell phones initially until you bring in lines. A man from here will be sent over to show how the money is to be paid out to the engineers and others by first obtaining lien releases, and so on. And, of course, he will handle the pay out of the twenty million for the political purposes. The papers on the deal will be drawn up by my staff, and ready in a week. I'll show the twenty million as a form of charitable donation to an underprivileged tribe, which I can justify to the stockholders as being in the best interests of the company. If Lewis wins the election, I'll also write off the one million as a charitable donation, and you can keep the benefits of the engineering that it buys and no doubt find some other lender that can loan you what you need—in that case you will have a much more organized plan to present to a prospective lender."

Bradford suddenly got an idea. "Of course, if we fund the loan, we'll expect you to insure the hotel with us, as well as all vehicles, equipment, fire, and liability insurance as well."

As he thought about it, there would be considerable premiums in insuring such huge buildings and related property, making the matter profitable over a short time even with the political contribution. And if there was a claim from some individual at the hotel, he could fix it so that the claimant had to go to the chief's court, instead of the California state court system, and they could literally just tell the person what he was going to get, and he would have no other recourse.

"You'll have your own private suite on the top floor if you do this for us," Chief No Cloud offered as a fringe benefit.

Mr. Bradford was silent for a moment as lascivious thoughts swirled in his head. *Rendezvous with women. Hookers with no possibility of police intervention. All the police will be Indians working for No Cloud. And I can justify going over often to check on the investment. Barbara will never know what I'm really doing up there.*

Concealing his excitement, Bradford nodded. "Well, we'll see. Are we in agreement?"

"You bet!"

"I'll be in touch with you when the papers are ready," Bradford said, as he stood, came around the desk, and offered his hand to the chief.

Chief No Cloud stood, took Bradford's hand, and shook it excessively.

CHAPTER 15

I bought you some things to wear in the city," Lilly said proudly, putting a shopping bag on her bed. She brought out a pair of new tweed wool pants and Ernie's jaw went agape.

"They are very good wool, and medium-light weight for the warmer climate down south." She held up the pants to show the expensive present. "I had suspender buttons put on for you. See?" She turned them around so he could see the buttons on the inside of the waistband. "And look! New suspenders, the big city kind," she said as she held up a pair of brand new blue, leather-trimmed suspenders. They were not the wide, heavy duty kind that Ernie normally wore, but still much larger than the sort he had seen on TV on the yuppie men in suits in their big city offices.

"And," she continued, "I got you this jacket as well." She held up a matching, tweed wool sports jacket, a waist length, Eisenhower jacket that zipped up the front, such that it could be used on a motorcycle but gave nearly a suit look when accompanying the pants. "Try them on. I even got you two shirts and a tie." She held up a cream colored shirt with long sleeves, and another one, olive colored but with short sleeves. She then held up a plain brown tie to the shirts to show the color match. "I think this will make you look very nice in the city offices. Do you like them?"

Ernie blushed at the attention. "I don't know what to say."

"I hope you like 'em." She then started pulling the pins out of the olive shirt for him to try it on for size. Ernie took off his clothes and put on the tweed pants. The shirt was ready, and he put it on. He then tried the wool jacket. She'd had to find big sizes for Ernie for the shirts and jacket and, after going to two stores that carried double-extra-large jackets, she found what she wanted.

The fancy dress clothes made him feel out of place, and the odor of newness heightened that sense. He went to the mirror over the dresser in her bedroom to look at himself with Lilly following behind, admiring. The clothes looked very smart, giving him a sort of a country gentlemen appearance.

"Why did you do all this?"

"Because you may need these in the big city, if you have to go to fancy offices. I understand they all dress up quite a bit down there," Lilly surmised, but neither of them had ever been to Los Angeles. "You must look nice."

"I suppose so. Although I'm hired to fell trees, they might call me into some office now and then. I'm supposed to go first to the main office, and these clothes will probably be just right for that. After that, I'll need a pair of jeans." He then looked at her. She had spent her modest income on him just to make him look better for his new job. "What a gal! I sure wish you could come with me," he said, looking at her with affection.

"Well, they need me at the meat market, and anyway, what would I do? You will be back in three months, and you can call me once or twice if you want—I'd like to hear from you, but don't waste too much money on phone calls."

Lilly was the butcher at the local market. Hunters often brought in their kill, through the back door for bringing in large game to a huge table for dressing deer, bear, elk, and most anything. She had two children from her marriage to a tree faller who had gone off to Alaska to make money when the work had dried up in Washington due to owl protection. Bad luck came not long ago in the Alaska wilderness when an enormous tree he cut fell on him. Details as to how it happened were not exactly known, as he was alone at the time. It was said to be on steep terrain, and most likely the tree fell in some unusual manner, and caught him.

Although always praised by his peers as one of the best, accidents happened to fallers. Logging in Alaska was tougher than elsewhere with the extreme weather and distances. It was no place for a motorcycle, or Ernie might have gone himself several years earlier as the money was better.

Endowed with an abundance of feminine charms, Lilly was of the best looking girls in Sedro Woolley, and definitely the most fun. Lilly was always still going strong when the bar was closing down for the night, and could out-drink most of the best men. She was still in mourning over her husband, and now considering getting to know Ernie. Hearing all about his new offer from him at the bar, she decided to go down to Seattle and buy him the presents as a sort of initial offering toward a relationship.

As he took off the fancy duds and folded them with her assistance, he realized that Sedro Woolley did not have any such clothes for sale, and that she must have gone down to Seattle on the I-5 to get them.

"Come here, you!" He easily picked her up and gave her a big kiss.

She grinned mischievously. "Well, maybe you'll meet one of those big city girls with a fancy car and forget all about me." Although said as a joke, it was based on actual fear that she might be losing her chance with him to the big city and all it had to offer.

"That won't happen," he assured her.

CHAPTER 16

anelli sat across the table at the meeting room in the Equator Las Vegas hotel casino, moving his hands around in the Italian way of expression. "So, Majestik has agreed to put up one million dollars for you for the plans, soils testing, engineering, and preliminary work, but the balance of one hundred fifty million will come only if candidate Zachary Lewis loses the election. Very good! Who did you deal with?"

"The president himself, Mr. Robert Bradford," Chief No Cloud answered proudly, having hobnobbed with the top man. He said nothing about the political donation of twenty million dollars. After all, he had promised he would not, and it did not seem to affect the deal with these people, as far as he could figure. Keeping his word was important to him as a proud Indian.

"How about this guy," Indelicato said, looking around the table at his partners, also waving his hands about in the Italian fashion, finally laying out one hand, palm up, toward the chief to give him recognition. "He goes right to the top."

The chief was not used to such praise from big city people, and felt a surge of importance. He repeated what he had learned so far about the project. "We got to get plans for bringing in power, road access, an airstrip, soils checking, engineering, architecture, sewage disposal, and so many things. I'd like to go ahead and get started. There's a lot to do before we can start putting up walls."

"That's nothing compared to what you have to do off the reservation," Bastini said from experience. "You can't believe how much cheaper this will be as opposed to doing it under government regulations. If we had to run the power lines across undeveloped land outside the reservation, it would take years just to fight a bunch of long-haired graduate students and their professors from universities using grant money to find rare lizards with psychological problems, aided by some group filing a federal lawsuit claiming damage to the lizard's hearing. The cost multiplies when you have to do that. This Indian nation concept is perfect."

"We have already had some initial renderings drawn up in color for you, Chief. Here they are," Manelli said, rolling them out on the table.

He unfolded beautiful colored drawings of a magnificent hotel surrounded by two green golf courses, lawns, grass tennis courts, an Olympic-sized pool, horse trails, and a trellis walkway.

"Wow!" the chief said, gazing at the renderings like a child with a new Christmas toy.

"I wonder what the odds are of Zachary Lewis winning?" Innocenti asked the group collectively. As most Italians do, he waived his hands around in the air as he talked.

"I've heard that Californians like him," Indelicato said. "I guess we'll have to wait and see on the loan. In the meantime, we'll set up the engineering and architecture."

The chief smiled. "Wonderful."

"Contact us as soon as you have the million," Manelli instructed.

"I sure will. Can I borrow these pretty pictures back to the Reservation and show the others?"

"They're for you. They're called renderings. Take them," Manelli said, pushing them toward the chief. "Once the million comes in, we'll have a complete three-dimensional model made up as well which we'll bring up there to you on one of our trips."

"Much thanks." The chief took the renderings carefully, rolled them up as if they were original Van Gogh's, and put them in their carrying tube.

"Would you like a suite tonight at our hotel?" Bastini asked. "Everything complimentary for you of course."

"Oh, no thanks. Maybe another time. I drove down in my truck, and I want to get back. I can be home tomorrow, and I'll show these to the others, and get to work on things. I know where there is a trailer I can get for nothing that I'm going to tow over for the construction office. I'll go for that the day after tomorrow. I'm really excited!"

Once the chief left, Innocenti turned to the group and leaned forward aggressively. "We have to see what we can get on Majestik President Robert Bradford. I'll contact my LA investigator and see what he can find out. We can afford to pay whatever he charges to find out something on this guy. It would be nice to have control over the bigger purse strings. The California election is not for several months. I wonder if we should consider helping Lewis drop out of the race before the election?"

"For one hundred fifty million dollars to put us in a casino with no government regulation?" Manelli asked as a rhetorical question while he waved his hands around.

Indelicato looked very seriously at his partners. "Do you think we should? Or do you think that hitting a political figure is too risky?"

They looked at each other without saying anything.

Bastini finally provided an answer. He shrugged. "Why don't we see how the polls are going first—maybe we don't need to think about it."

Manelli chewed on his lower lip, a habit he had when doing any deep thinking. "Okay, but I gotta' say, that Indian reservation would not only be good for gambling odds and other things we can't do in Nevada, but it would also be a much better place to launder money than we have now. We had to kill that fucking fed because he was on to us. I say that we consider it unless the polls show that he is far behind in the election."

CHAPTER 17

We take you now for an update on possibly the worst storm in Los Angeles recorded history," Phillip Hartley, the newscaster anchorman said on a Los Angeles television station. "Let's take you right to our top story, the storm." The screen changed to a man in a suit standing in front of a map. "Here is Tim Atkins in the weather department."

Tim Atkins, the weatherman, took over. "Phillip, this is truly the worst storm in recorded Los Angeles history. We had a bad one in 1938, but this is worse. We have never had as much recorded rain in a four-day period—over twelve inches! The gusts and high winds that initially hit the coast were as high as eighty miles per hour, which is hurricane force, and thousands of trees have been blown down. There was considerable damage to many homes and buildings from as far north as Santa Barbara County and south to San Diego County. The inland cities have now been hit hard, as well as the coastal regions. Fifteen deaths have been attributed to the storm, and injury reports are many. The wind velocity has lowered to its present fifteen to twenty miles per hour, with gusts of thirty, but the rain continues and it looks like there will be rain for another three to four days."

The screen switched back to Phillip. "Any relief in sight, Tim?"

Then Atkins's face showed up, filling the screen. "Not for three to four days."

"Thank you for that report, Tim," Phillip said as the camera switched back to him in the news studio. "There are hundreds of reports of trees down all over the southland, and power lines are down, causing power outages. The winds have caused considerable damage to buildings and residences. There's local flooding in a number of residential areas. Our helicopter has been unable to bring you our skycam report due to the high winds, but we do have a mobile unit report to show what the flooding is like."

The screen switched from inside the TV studio to a street location showing two feet of water in an intersection, and then to a huge tree that had been blown down onto the roof of a house damaging the roof. Another view showed a huge tree blown down into the street, blocking traffic. Under the big tree was a squashed Prius.

A woman reporter appeared on the sidewalk in the rain, with the flooded intersection behind her. "Here in Reseda, you can see the water has filled the intersection. There are many more like this one. Cars are stalled in the streets from the high-water level. The runoffs are simply not sufficient to take the water away, and the water has gone up over the curbs and past the streets as it has here. The power is out in this area, and the traffic signals don't work. The residents say that this is the worst flooding they have ever seen in this area. Janey Hargrove, reporting."

The screen switched back to the studio. "Thank you for that report, Janey. We now have a special report. Just in from the earthquake center is a report of several aftershocks from the earthquake, but no damage reports as yet. We are still receiving reports from damaged caused by the main quake, but building damage appears to be relatively minor. We'll bring you updates as we receive them."

CHAPTER 18

As dawn was yawning, the quiet emphasized the sound of the American two-cylinder motorcycle engine. It was music to Ernie's ears as he rode adventurously away from his Sedro Woolley. He and his machine headed south through the rain at seventy-five miles per hour. Ernie and engines had a special relationship, nurtured over time by his constant work on chainsaws and motorcycles. The engine responded kindly to the rain with a deeper note, liking the moist air. The incoming moisture enriched the intake air with oxygen from the water, and also cooled the incoming charge which added to performance. He recalled the year before when a young man who had stopped at the local Evelyn's Bar, having ridden up on a Jap bike. He made a statement that American motorcycle engines had the same technology as Vietnamese bilge pumps. Ernie approached him asked him to repeat what he said and his opinion changed dramatically, although it was unclear exactly what he said as Ernie was holding him up off the ground by his neck with just one arm.

But even if not modern, the crisp firing of Ernie's old fashioned, two-cylinder engine provided a lovely cadence.

The rain rolled off his leathers, which he had soaked in a fresh coat of water repellent oil just before leaving. He wore a traditional leather motorcycle jacket, and leather chaps over his jeans, his usual dress for riding in rain. Ernie was no stranger to the wet, as it rained nearly every day at work, except for some dry spells in the summer.

As he motored along, he concluded he preferred the rain to those periods in the forest when it was dry. In the dry season in the woods, he carried a thermo-hygrometer, a device the size of a cigar that measured the humidity and temperature. If it got below thirty per cent moisture, the law required him to leave the forest. It wasn't really a bad rule, and he usually followed it. A forest fire could start, and usually did somewhere in the region in the dry spells. Given that the forests that were logged were not on flat land, but usually on steep hillsides with very rough terrain, the speed of an oncoming forest fire could be twice or more as fast as one could run away from it. He knew of several loggers who had bought the farm that way.

He wondered what it would be like in Los Angeles where he heard that it seldom rained. He inventoried in his mind what he had brought and wondered if he had remembered everything. In his leather saddlebags he had packed what he thought he could use, and nothing more—anyway, there wasn't any more space. In one of the saddlebags he had put his favorite chainsaw, a mid-sized saw with a thirty-two inch bar which stuck out of the top in the back of the saddlebag. He had a bigger saw, but figured he would not need it as he doubted the fallen trees from the storm in the city were so big as to need a bigger saw. And if he ran into a big one, he could handle it with the mid-sized by cutting from more than one side. He assumed the insurance company would not provide him with a saw, as loggers have to buy their own. The secretary, Judy Canton, had not said that a saw would be provided. Another consideration was that his own saw was slightly modified just as he liked it, and he would be much more comfortable and efficient with a proper saw rather than a loaner or rental. His was balanced just right, and he could do a lot with it in a day.

In the same saddlebag with the saw he also put two extra chainsaw chains, a chain link pin remover, several master links, two extra spark plugs, a sharpening file, and a few tools. He only had room for a small plastic container of gas, and small plastic bottles of his favorite two-stroke oil and chain bar oil. That would be enough to get going, and he would get more locally.

In the other saddlebag he put the new outfit from Lilly. There was no room and no need for extra footwear, and anyway he did not have any dress shoes. The logger boots he wore would have to do, although he wondered how they would look in the big city. They were rubber soled with cleated bottoms, laced up the ankle for support, and coated with water repellent oil. A small bag with his shaving things curled up neatly inside an extra half-cover helmet for a passenger in case he had to give someone a ride.

At the end of a long day of riding, Ernie had passed through Washington, Oregon, and finally across the border into California. Having accomplished a sufficient distance, he pulled over at an inexpensive motel. He would make it to Los Angeles on the second day if all went well.

CHAPTER 19

Special Agent Bill Kanno joined Dan Doty, working intently at a computer terminal at the Los Angeles FBI office, and looked over his shoulder. It was 7:30 p.m.

"Hey, Dan! Whatcha working on so late? Got anything on what Dave was working on yet?"

"One possible lead. I found some notes with the name and number of an IRS auditor in Dave's things. I called the man, and finally got a call back. He's a Russian immigrant, and new at the IRS. He did accounting in Russia. He was doing a limited IRS audit at a major hotel casino in Las Vegas called the Equator, and believes he discovered something suspicious, which got him scared, as he was used to violence in Russia with the Mafia. He turned over the information to the FBI, and the call got routed to Dave."

Kanno sat down beside him and showed great interest. "Tell me more."

"The Russian was at the Equator conducting an audit. New at the game, he was trying to find expenses that should not be allowed. He did not do well at that but it seems that for period he was at the location, he happened to see the daily receipts come in for one day from the crap tables as they came into the count room. He was fascinated at all the cash, coming from Russia, and apparently the casino did not worry too much about him as he was only auditing expenses which don't show up in the count room. He saw the summaries visually, and recalled the amount. But before he left, the next day, in looking at the summary of income for the day before, the income for that day for cash from the crap tables was much *larger* than what he saw in the tally room."

"So what's wrong with that?" Kanno asked. "Instead of stealing cash by not reporting, they were reporting more than the receipts showed. That means eventually more income tax. It's only a federal crime *not* to report income. So there's no income tax evasion to go after. Remember how they got Al Capon—income tax evasion. Maybe it was just an internal mistake."

"Three million extra in cash on one day? That is a pretty big mistake, don't you think?"

Kanno shrugged, not really too concerned about over re-porting income. "Maybe there were receipts that came in late? Maybe they adjusted the final tally to account for a different time period, as they are open twenty four hours?"

"It would be an awfully big gambler who stuck around a table and lost three million bucks. It seems unlikely that someone came in with that much money in cash and lost it at the tables. He would have to have brought in a suitcase of cash."

"Hmmm. I see what you mean," Kanno said, pondering the magnitude of difference.

Doty leaned forward and advanced his idea. "The cash from the day is brought into the secure money count room. It's always carefully added. But someone in trust adds a suitcase of cash at some point so that no one else can see it. The tally just goes up, and there are always large fluctuations."

Kanno scratched his head. "Money laundering?"

"Bingo!" Doty said with a smile.

"Who owns the Equator?" Kanno asked.

"The Nevada Gaming Commission says it's a widow of three years named Gunther. Her husband was on the licensee until he died, and the Gaming Commission allowed the license to be transferred to her. She must be worth a bundle."

"Why would a super-rich widow get involved in money laundering?" Kanno wondered aloud.

"I don't think she would."

"Then who?"

"Well, it may be that some person or persons in manage-ment at the hotel are involved and she is unaware of it."

"Well," Kanno said, "my wife is waiting at home for me. I'll see you tomorrow. I'll help you then if I get a chance."

"Thanks, Bill. If it comes time for any warrants, I'll turn it over to you. Maxwell warned me."

CHAPTER 20

Hello, Mr. Innocenti," private investigator, Jim McKinsey, said at the Yellowfingers Café in Van Nuys, California.

"Will you join me in a bowl of French onion soup?" Innocenti asked. "This place makes a great one."

"Sure."

"It's nice with a dry white wine, but not one of those sweet chardonnays that I call sheepherders' piss. Want to try?"

"Why not?"

Innocenti ordered the soup for them both, a specialty of the café. However, it was made with Swiss gruyère cheese, and Innocenti could not resist telling the waiter to have the chef add fontina cheese to the guyère to bring a bit of Italy to the flavor. He also asked for two glasses of a dry, light wine.

While waiting, McKinsey handed him a large, manila envelope. "This is what you want."

Innocenti looked around to make sure no one was listening and took out the contents. There were a number of papers, including Bradford's credit profile, properties owned, autos, and criminal record, which was clean. There was also a DVD.

"I see you have Bradford's credit profile. That's good. But is there anything I can use?"

"Yes, there is." McKinsey was a very effective investigator with very special resources for very special clients. He got things that were illegal to get, and that no one else could. "Allow me." He took back the package and leafed through it to find a typewritten report of several pages of exhibits. "Check this out."

The report was all about a girl named Julie Bailey. Attached was her rap sheet, which showed no major crimes, but did report two misdemeanor arrests for prostitution, one for possession, several warrants for not appearing, and traffic offenses. She was obviously a hooker. A copy of her driver's license showed her picture. There were details about her purchase of a secondhand Mercedes sports model and the financing from the dealer less than a year ago, her apartment, and the last three month's purchases on a credit card, which were mostly gas.

There was one charge for a car service for the Mercedes. It was obvious that she paid cash, like most prostitutes, for most purchases. The report gave details about where she came from, including her parents. That was Salt Lake City, Utah—obviously a Mormon girl who had chosen a direction not recommended by the Church.

"Why do you give me this?" Innocenti looking at the investigator and holding his hands out with his palms up, using them in the Italian fashion.

"She's Robert Bradford's regular hooker," McKinsey said. "Read on. She's known to him as Evette Evil. She's a twenty-five-year-old girl from Salt Lake City. She does well, and lives high on the hog. She no longer does any street work, as she has a referral base rich enough to keep her in style. She does an occasional referral through a special escort service in Beverly Hills, which is high price work. She lives in Marina Del Rey—her address is there, and her cell phone. She is known for guys who want the whip or other torture, and she is supposed to be good. The DVD is a short movie she made called *Mistress Discipline,* starring Evette Evil. I was able to find the producer and was told that she got two thousand, five hundred dollars for performing in it. That was before she developed a good clientele."

Innocenti's eyes lit up. "Where in the hell do you get this stuff?"

"Never ask such things, and, of course, I rarely tell. But for you, Mr. Innocenti, as my most valued client, I'll give you one of the sources on the girl. I have a source at the hotel. It's the Wilshire Hotel, and that's where they meet once a week. My source discovered that Bradford has been coming there under an alias. The man's into bondage and whips."

"Damn, you come up with the best stuff!"

"There is something else. Julie Bailey has a sister, Iris. Guess who she works for?"

"I give up."

"You!"

Innocenti's mouth gaped. "You're shitting me!"

"Nope. Up at the other casino your group manages, the Jackpot, in Reno. She's a cocktail waitress."

Not much amazed this mafioso, but this did "You are too much! How much do I owe you?"

"Is this cash, as before?"

"Yes. We sure as hell don't need a paper trail."

"Fifteen thousand, and that includes what I have to pay out for the information to my sources."

"Okay." Innocenti brought out a folded pack of hundreds from his right front pocket. "This is ten." He passed it under the tablecloth that was hanging down. He then got another batch from his other front pocket, and counted out five thousand, just below the tabletop to one side, and passed the additional bills to him, this time across the table, but out of view.

McKinsey gave the wad a cursory counting in his lap so it would be below the table and, when it became apparent that it was all there, he stopped. He was not just a little afraid of offending the cold-eyed mafioso. "Thank you sir. Will there be anything else?"

"Yeah. I want your contact at the hotel to do us a favor. Is that possible?"

"I suppose. It depends on what you need. Can you let me know first before I attempt to commit my source?"

"Sure," Innocenti said. "I have to make some plans. But now, let's try the soup since I see it coming."

The waitress arrived with two steaming bowls of French onion soup, specially made with a mix of both Swiss Gruyère and fontina cheeses over a thin slice of toast. The fragrance was all too compelling, and the white wine selected consummated the experience.

CHAPTER 21

Through the split in the cheap curtains, rays of the morning sun darted into the room like yellow laser beams, piercing the still air of the small, inexpensive hotel room. Dust floated about in the beams of light. The air was a little stale, as no window was open. The rainstorm, unusual for Los Angeles, had let up.

Ernie awoke and remembered where he was. He had arrived in Los Angeles County, after two long days on the road. He stretched after the long ride, opened the only window wide, and let fresh air in. He took in a deep breath, but found the air not like back home. He gave up that idea after the first sample.

After his shower, it was time to don Lilly's present for his appearance at the home office of the new employer, Majestik Insurance. He buttoned his dressy new suspenders to the wool pants and put them on. The new shirt was then adorned with a tie, which he managed to tie in the right place after three attempts.

He looked down at his black, oil tanned logger boots sticking out of his new wool pants, and realized that they sort of gave away the fact that he was not from the city.

He wondered if the boots were the right shoes to wear, but it really didn't matter. That was all he had. He did not bring, or even own, a pair of those sissy loafer shoes with thin soles and kiltie tassels that the big city office men wore in the movies.

He stood back and looked in the mirror at the new duds. Feeling totally uncomfortable, he thought he looked like a salesman selling vacuum cleaners.

༄

The guard at the parking lot entrance of the big Wilshire Boulevard building stared curiously at Ernie and did not show any signs of friendliness.

Still astride his motorcycle at the guard gate, Ernie asked, "Is this Majestik Insurance Company?"

"Yes sir, it is. Have you business here?" the guard asked, assessing the motorcyclist with a dubious expression.

"Yes. I'm here to report to Mr. Don McAteer for work. I'm hired as a field representative."

"I see," the guard said. He decided the stated reason sounded valid since the motorcyclist knew the name of an executive that the guard recognized. Motorcycles simply never came to insurance offices.

Ernie rode his motorcycle in until he found a spot near a pole that was too small for a car. Strangely, to Ernie, there were no other motorcycles anywhere. He parked and left his helmet on the bike, preferring not to carry it inside, as no one else seemed to have arrived on a motorcycle and he didn't want to draw attention to the fact that he had.

Inside, people were bustling about everywhere. Ernie saw a man in a gray suit pausing momentarily and he stepped up to him. "Do you know where the office of Mr. McAteer is?"

"He's one of those big shots on one of the floors near the top, eleven I think."

A capacity crowd filled the lift, forcing him toward the back. He felt claustrophobic in the tiny elevator and feared what would happen if the power went out and he and all those others were crammed in there for who knows how long. It seemed to stop at every floor, finally halting at the next to last floor, number eleven.

The elevator door opened to a plush reception area, where a young lady sat to greet anyone coming in. "Good morning, sir, how may I help?"

"I'm Ernie, here to see Mr. McAteer. I'm a temporary field representative."

"Ah, yes. I have a list with your name on it. Just a moment." She picked up the phone and spoke into the intercom. When she hung up, she said, "Just a moment sir. He's on the phone, and will call on you directly."

Out of a corridor to one side came another secretary. When she saw Ernie, she smiled. "Hello. I'm Judy Canton, who talked to you on the phone. Won't you please come this way?" She led him back to another reception area, where there was comfortable seating. "Please have a seat. I have some forms for you to fill out. We need your social security number, address, a copy of your driver's license, and, if you are going to use your own car, proof of insurance. You will be provided with medical insurance for the duration of your work."

"I don't have an address here in town yet, as I just came in last night."

Judy only nodded. "You can just call in your address when you get settled. Then all we need is your social security number for tax reporting."

Ernie handed her his driver's license and insurance card which she took to copy nearby. She returned his documents. "Please just wait for Mr. McAteer. He will be with you shortly."

While he waited, Ernie looked at the walls on the two sides of the area. They had large oil paintings of men, who he determined to be founders of the company or otherwise important people. One was a painting of a couple, instead of just a man. On the bottom was a small gold plaque that had a name on it. He looked up closely at the inscription:

Matthew and Lilly Bradford 1920

It must be someone's grandparents, he figured, given their age. As Ernie sat waiting for his interview with Mr. McAteer, down the hallway came Zelzah, dressed smartly in a black business suit. She had come down to the eleventh floor from the twelfth to give an assignment to someone. She looked at Ernie and took an immediate interest.

He didn't seem like an insurance man. His tweed outfit was completely foreign, and he wore his huge, black, oil-tanned logger boots that were completely out of place. To Zelzah, Ernie's outdoor, extra-healthy complexion made him appear clearly unique in the palatial icon of commerce that was Majestik Insurance.

His breathing was bigger and deeper than office people, as though he needed twice the breath of a normal person, and that was because he did. He did not have the pasty, pot-bellied, uptight look of the men she saw all day long. The tweed wool outfit, the cleated boots, and the look, made it clear he was out of his element in the insurance environment. For her it was like meeting Errol Flynn right out of one of her favorite old movies. Ernie was definitely, and especially in an insurance office, bigger than life. To Zelzah, this was too much to miss. Ostensibly a paradox, she had recurrent dreams and vibrator sessions of being taken by her super masculine heroes. But in business, she was aggressive, vocal, and did not waste time. She took advantage of the situation and walked over to Ernie to find a way to meet him.

"Hello, I'm Zelzah."

"Hi, I'm Ernie."

"May I ask you about your boots? Are those a new logger fashion?"

"Did you notice I was a logger?" He wondered if he Lilly's clothes didn't work for fitting in.

She laughed, assuming he had paid Rodeo Street prices of a few thousand for the boots and clothes, as though to try to look like a real logger. "You are really quite voguish. Where are you from?"

"Sedro Woolley, Washington."

"Is that near Seattle?"

"It's farther north, nearer the Canadian border."

"Fantastic! The Pacific Northwest! That's a place on my list to go! The closest I have been is going by there for an Alaska cruise ship tour. When did you arrive?" She felt a surge of emotion at the prospect of getting to know him.

"Last night."

Zelzah was taken by his voice and was silent for a moment. He had a voice to go along with the look. She regained her composure, but lost track of the question. "So you are one of the new temporaries that Mr. McAteer is bringing on?"

"Yep, that's me."

"Are you familiar with Los Angeles?"

"No. This is my first time here."

Going against her normal policy of not having anything to do with the company men, she decided to take a chance and get bold. He would only be working for ninety days as one of the new temporaries, and then he'd be gone. "I'd be happy to take you somewhere, if you like."

"Gee, that would be great. But I doubt that I'll have a lot of time to go sightseeing."

He was so different from the usual men that who were always trying to hustle her, she concluded. "How about coming over to my place for dinner?"

"That'd be nice."

"Here," she said, writing her number and address on her notepad. "Would tomorrow night at eight work for you?"

"Sure."

A little old for him, he surmised, with all her fancy clothes and all. But what a nice thing to be invited to dinner, as opposed to some early bird special at a diner.

Just then, Judy was told to bring in Ernie to Don McAteer's office. "Mr. McAteer will see you now."

To Zelzah, he was even more impressive standing. He was tall, very well built, tanned, and had the outdoors feeling she sought in her fantasy lovers, so different from the pasty complexion of insurance types.

"See you tomorrow?"

"I'll be there."

As Zelzah went back to her section on the upper floor, she had a tingling sensation in her loins and imagined that she was going to have a date with a swashbuckler from one of her classic movies.

Judy led Ernie to McAteer's office. "This is Ernie, one of the new temporary field reps that you hired."

"How do you do, Ernie?" McAteer stood, and smiled, putting out his hand. He was down to earth about meeting people.

"Very good, sir, and I appreciate the opportunity you've given me. I'm happy to be chosen to work for Majestik. I'll do my best," Ernie said, clumsily, not practiced at meeting important strangers. He held out his powerful hand to shake McAteer's.

McAteer winced slightly at the squeeze on his hand. "I'm sure you will. Have you got a place to stay yet?"

"Not yet."

"We have a list of recommended places selected for the temporary people we are bringing in. I have it here," he said, finding it and handing it to Ernie.

Ernie looked at it, not recognizing any of the cities or areas. "Do you have a recommendation?"

"Are you here with your family?"

"No, I'm not married."

He looked up, as though looking to the heavens in a dream. "Ah, a single man. Oh, to be young and single once again." Then he came back to earth. "Well, in that case, I think you might like the Polynesian. It's near the ocean, and they have furnished rooms available with everything including flatware. Linens and maid service are also available, just like a hotel. It has three pools, each with a different temperature, a clubhouse, and houses lots of temporary working people like you, but mostly airline staff on overnights between their flights. I hear it's a lot of fun there. We have set up a program with that place, whereby we pick up the room as an alternative to the per-diem reimbursement for lodging program. The one-room place will have furniture, flatware, coffee maker, linens, towels—and maid service if you want it but that is optional and not paid for by Majestik. That will be a better deal for you than the thirty five dollar per diem allowance. Does that sound good?"

"Sure, if you recommend it."

"Good. Now, there is an indoctrination class I'm giving to several of the new people in an hour. It's in a meeting room on the third floor. I'll have things that you will need. You can stay for that?"

"Of course, sir."

"See you there," McAteer said.

In the third floor meeting room, eleven others came in as well as Ernie. An ordinary coffee pot had been set up with Styrofoam cups, but, that looked like something to avoid so Ernie opted not to take one. In north Washington coffee was very good.

Seven other people beside Ernie showed up, and Mr. McAteer came in with a young male assistant bringing a box of things to pass out. Each new adjustor was given a checkbook, Majestic sample policies, release forms, a GPS receiver, and a cellular phone with a built-in camera. The assistant made sure each person signed for the items.

When the assistant finished passing the things out, and the signature cards were returned, McAteer went to the front of the room. "Welcome to Majestik. I'm Don McAteer, Vice President, Operations. Well, they say it never rains in Southern California, but we have had a doozy this time! This storm and its winds were the biggest in Los Angeles recorded history, and then combined with that, we had the earthquake. There are a lot of good, premium-paying homeowners out there who have damage to their homes and haven't the slightest idea as to what to do, who to call to have the damages fixed, and how to go about it.

"Many will rely on us as to how to get the damage fixed. That is why our president had the foresight to bring in outside, temporary help to go out and deal with the claims. With this group, we now have over seventy of the one hundred Mr. Bradford has requested we hire just to deal with the calls and claims. More are due tomorrow.

"The types of claims that you will be assigned, for the most part, will be homeowners, small commercial buildings, small business general liability, auto, and marine. Sometimes the residential or business policies cover a situation of general liability giving rise to an unusual claim. You are all familiar with these types of claims, as you were chosen because of your experience."

Ernie was not sure what all he was talking about, but he did not speak up as he did not want to look dumb. He wondered when the part about falling trees would be brought up as he was sure from the TV news that there were many trees that were split in two, uprooted, or otherwise needing to be cut down or cut into manageable logs.

"Now, I'm aware that you are not familiar with exactly how Majestik works, but I'm sure you'll find it similar to your previous experience. We'll have business cards printed for you in an hour, as we have a machine that does that. Familiarize yourselves with the new phones. You can record conversations with them, as well as taking pictures. Record all witness statements, and also statements from anyone making a claim, which you will want to get if you can before the claimant gets to a lawyer. Remember when you record a call, tell the person at the outset that you are recording it and get their okay on the tape. Very few people will refuse to talk about some accident or storm damage that has occurred. You can usually get them to make admissions, compromising their claim if you are clever at interviews. I also have a new GPS receiver for you to help you find the location of a claim."

The people looked at the things that were provided them as he spoke.

"Now, cell phones have been provided, but these are only for company use. We want you to call in to our new hot line room, which I'll show you when we finish. I'll have someone experienced there to help you new folks, and if you can't get through because the person is busy, just ask for me. My office and phone are open to you at all times.

"You have also been provided with a company draft check book. It's like a check, but before anything gets paid out there must be a counter signature before it clears. Each draft goes through our special auditor first for cross-checking before it's paid. But the person you give the check to thinks it is as good as cash, so don't be giving those out unless you are sure that the company will back you.

"You have ten thousand dollars' worth of settlement authority on any single claim. This can be very helpful to you to be able to settle a claim on the spot and can save us money. If a claim is worth five thousand, but you offer three on the spot that the claimant can have right then, he might take it if you raise the defenses and offsets. Or, if the damage is more than ten thousand, the claimant may take the ten thousand to get the money in a hurry, and we save. More than ten thousand means you must submit the proposed settlement to the next level with your recommendation. This can only be circumvented by my office. I'm authorized to increase that amount by phone, but it still must be documented later. Remember that being given this authority to settle cases and provide company money to claimants places a fiduciary responsibility on you, and we put our trust in you.

"Now, you have also been provided with samples of our policies. We want you to be familiar with them, so you can understand the limitations and exclusions."

McAteer then turned to the forces of nature that affected the claims. "This storm has been one of the worst ever, causing all kinds of damage. Many trees are down, roofs lifted, water coming in houses, and all sorts of things that follow such high winds and rainfall. We also have the benefit of the earthquake, which, I will explain, is a godsend to reduce the payouts on many claims."

Ernie heard the part about the trees, and that was what he figured he could do. But the others in the group clearly were not capable of falling uprooted or partially downed trees. Maybe they had other special qualifications?

His question about trees was answered without him having to ask.

"Now, regarding trees," McAteer said, "note on page eight of the sample homeowner's policy and commercial business property policy that, while we do insure for trees, we usually have a five hundred dollar limit on the total tree losses for any insured. This means that no matter how many trees are blown down, we only pay five hundred dollars. The homeowner thinks his trees are covered, but we are only in for five hundred dollars, although sometimes, the limit may be one thousand. If the policyholder gets angry, you can tell him that he could have increased the limits if he wanted to but did not.

"There will also be other claims, so remember that the policies usually have a deductible that apples to the total claim. You deduct the deductible before you pay anything. Clever, eh?

"Now, don't forget the exclusion for surface waters. This is a real beauty! This is the clause we got past the lawmakers, whereby we don't insure for floods. Instead of excluding *floods,* we have successfully renamed *floods* as *surface waters*. This is a brilliant way to deny a claim. Under this, you can deny coverage for any water that enters a house over the ground. If water comes in over the ground, even if there is no flood, deny the claim under that provision, such as a broken water main, backed up drain in the street, or hurricane wind blowing water up from the yard into the house. There are a lot of water damage claims out there after this big storm, and we can get out of paying on most of them because of this clause. If the water did not come in the roof or a blown out window, deny the claim as surface water, which is excluded. If it came in from both places, deny it anyway and claim it was surface waters.

"The next topic is deferred maintenance. In many cases, you can cut most claims down to near nothing, based on the fact that the damage is a result of lack of lack of useful life, or deferred maintenance, rather than from the storm. This could apply to the quake as well. As an example of deferred maintenance, if the wind blows off roof tiles, or a gutter that was rusted and hanging loose, you can claim that it was ready to be repaired anyway, and deny or drastically reduce the claim that way as deferred maintenance. If a roof is damaged, and needed work, you can apply the same concept.

"On useful life, for example, we usually put a ten year useful life on roofs. So, if the roof is nine years old, and has to be replaced, we would pay a maximum of ten per cent of the cost of the repair, not the entire roof. And then you apply the deductible to cut the claim. If the area requires a newer form of roof that has a newer insulating ability, that is another cut, which comes under betterment that also has a limit in the policy. I'll explain that in a bit. You're probably wondering what to do if you have a roof claim on a twenty-year-old roof? You tell them that the average roof life is only ten years and, therefore, we cannot replace or repair any of the roof.

"Now, one of the best things we have going at the moment is the earthquake that just occurred. In the sample policy, there is a copy of the earthquake endorsement. Don't forget that earthquake coverage is not bought by most and is a special endorsement. Even if the homeowner bought this extra coverage, note that it only takes effect after ten per cent damage to the structure. As an example, there has to be twenty thousand dollars damage to a two hundred thousand dollar house, excluding the land value, before we pay out the first dollar. And, we do not pay the initial ten per cent. You normally don't pay out on these claims in the field on first inspection, as we require appraisals and several damage estimates before we pay. We seldom pay on any of them. And we have the best when it comes to getting the low appraisals that we want. We have appraisers who do nothing else but work for us and other insurance companies. They claim they also do repairs but, in reality, they were unsuccessful as contractors, and they are happy to get about two hundred dollars from us for a repair estimate that no one will repair the damage for.

"So if there is damage that can be attributed to the quake rather than the storm, you can deny the claim, saying the damage came from the quake and the damage does not exceed ten per cent of the value of the structure. An example might be a crack in the roof. You can contend it was from the quake as that is what causes cracks. And even if the insured later proves that there is over ten per cent damage to his structure, we can still discount the claim on deferred maintenance, useful life remaining, and depreciation. And don't forget things like lead paint, asbestos, and other things that we exclude or limit as their removal is a required code update. Remember, we are not here to pay out on claims, but to reject them, delay them, and cut them to the bare minimum if we have to pay anything.

"We here in insurance in California have another really good thing going. In our policy, and other states have this too, there's a provision addressing a dispute in the repair of something. This is usually for a larger claim, like damage to a house. Here's how it may come up. The insured says he has a one hundred thousand dollar claim for damage to his house, and has a contractor that gives that estimate. We say half that. We have lists of experts who will give any estimate we want for a couple of hundred dollars.

"We sit on it and pay nothing. The contract provision in our policy says that when the two sides do not agree, each side's expert will pick a third, neutral party expert that will then determine the final amount. Naturally, this never happens as they cannot agree, as our experts will not agree to a legitimate contractor. The insured has to then go hire a lawyer, pay him hourly or give him a third. He also has to pay a lawsuit filing fee of about five hundred dollars if he files a case in court.

"Some years ago, retired judges set up a golden parachute for themselves. It is called JAMS, or Judicial Arbitration and Mediation Services. Judges go there and get their names on a list to act as arbitrators in disputes. They typically get six or seven hundred dollars an hour for every second of their time and they have no overhead whatsoever. They do not have to have malpractice insurance, an office, or even a secretary. JAMS does all typing for them if asked, but then JAMS charges the litigants for that. This means that someone suing us has to pay half, and we half. We can afford it, but most of the claimants cannot. And JAMS charges fees for itself as well as well as for the parasitic judges.

"The claimant files a case in court to make the judge fix the damages as the neutral arbitrator. Instead of doing it himself, he cuts his work load, and sends the case to JAMS where some of his retired friends work and where he hopes to go for part time huge income later. Each side has to pay half of the retired judge's pay, which they determine themselves. The claimant has to pay or lose the case. It could be ten thousand dollars total for a small case, but it is usually much higher and could be several times that, as the judges will charge as much as they think that they can get away with. As Majestik is always has a several cases there at any one time, and the claimant will have one case at most in his life, we get better treatment as we and other insurance companies are their regular support. The JAMS judges always favor the insurance industry, as that is where their bread is buttered. And the fees must be paid by both sides, half-half. We can afford that, but many policy holders cannot. So, if there is a contest over the value of a loss, and it's perhaps twenty or more thousand, go this route. This really screws over the insured. It is our best long-term asset. When the insured is faced with a bill from JAMS of ten thousand dollars or more, they will easily settle. This turns the case from one of accessible justice of the courts to something that will cost an insured many thousands.

"Regarding releases. You have also been provided with our field release forms. Under no circumstances settle anything without getting signatures on these. If you think it advisable, get both spouses before issuing a draft. If the claim is small, like a thousand dollars, you may wish to go ahead with one spouse if the other is not present. As an example, if the wife is home, and the husband is not there, and the claim is small, you could go ahead and settle with her and let her take the blame from her husband for settling cheap. Normally put in both spouses if you can, as this binds them both in to the settlement. You just have to use your own judgment on this. We have the settlement forms for auto, renters, property owners, commercial, marine, and a general one if none of the specialized ones seem to fit. We give you discretion in the field to use your best judgment.

"The next topic is used parts and aftermarket parts for auto claims. With all this water and wind, the accidents have gone way up. There could also be something like a tree falling on a car. We have been successfully getting away with the use of used parts in auto claims. For example, if you have to replace a hood on a five-year-old car, when the body shop wants to get approval from us to fix the car, you tell the shop to find a used hood from a junkyard. We have lists of the sources, and know the prices. There is an entire network of junkyards that have or will find used parts like hoods for a fraction of the price. There are also aftermarket parts. As an example, a Honda radiator from the dealer will be three time the price of an aftermarket new one. On windshields, most accidents have a broken windshield. The Chinese are now making them for most models, and they are only a third of the price. There is no need to tell the owner, but if he finds out, you just say that he is entitled to a repair, not a betterment of a new part or a factory part. If the insured wants to know where to go to get his car fixed, our list of body shops already know all these things the insured will never know. But if the insured takes his car to his body shop, or the dealer, you will have to tell the estimator what we will pay, and he may tell the insured that we should not do that. Then you just have to negotiate. There is nothing in the policy that requires new replacement parts, or factory original equipment parts.

"Now, on depreciation. If a couch gets ruined where water came into a house through the roof or a window, keeping in mind we don't pay for surface waters, depreciate it based on age. I already explained the roof example. Just like discounting a repair to a nine-year-old roof by ninety per cent because we give it a ten year life, the same is true with a couch that got soaked inside when the roof came off, except that we usually use five years for a couch. And don't forget the deductible.

"On timing, time is on our side. But, if the insured will compromise with you on other aspects of his claim, you might get a smaller settlement by a quick one such as by offering the money right away. But if it goes into a contest, then time is on our side. And don't forget mold, which I'll get to."

"Now, on documentation, most of the time, the person usually won't have the receipt that he got when he bought the item, such as a couch. You can say you will wait to get it, and many times they never get around to it or can't find it and we don't pay.

"The multiple deductible trick works well. When you are getting a statement from the person on your tape recorder, the person might say that one couch got wet on Saturday, and the big screen TV got wet on the next wave of rain two days later. If they say that, get it on tape if you can, and you can say it was two storms on different days, which gives us two claims and we then apply two deductibles. Wonderful, eh?

"Another beauty is the policy limitations on lead based paint and asbestos. We either do not pay at all for these, or have a limit. Here is how it works. Older paints had lead in them which is now illegal. If the damaged house needs to be repainted in whole or in part, such as existing paint of twenty or so years old, send out someone from our list of experts to check for lead in the paint. If you have to repaint, you can cut the claim down because we do not pay for removal of lead paint. So the owner has to pay for removal, which makes putting on a fresh coat or two of non-lead paint cheap.

"The same is true for asbestos. You will likely find asbestos in any older small commercial building around the heating ducts or in insulation. The law says that the owner has to bring out a special, certified contractor to remove the asbestos, but we don't care as we exclude coverage for asbestos. Then, the building department of the city will require new insulation as an energy saving law, which the insured has to pay for himself.

"Regarding mold. This is a real beauty. Our policies now exclude all mold damage. If water comes in a roof that was opened by the storm, or otherwise, the furniture and carpet can usually be saved if dried right away. You can call a service from our list that that comes out even at night that will lift up the carpet, and place blowers under it which will prevent mold. This has to be done right away, like within a day or two at most. But in many cases, the homeowner does not know to do this, or for whatever reason it is not done soon enough, or not at all. Or there will be moisture in places where fans are not put or cannot reach, including things like furniture, drawers, drywall, and other places. If mold sets in, and it often does, the item is useless as the mold ruins the fabric, drywall, drapes, cushions, and even things like wooden drawers. We deny the claim of course.

"Now, here is an advanced trick. I call it *Panic in the neurotic claimant.* I came up with this one myself, in a case we had two years ago." The pride showed in his expression. "I'll tell you what happened in this case and you can see if you can use it yourself.

"Sometimes the insured is neurotic. In the case that we had, one of our adjustors went to a home where there had been a rupture in a water pipe in a wall.

"By the time the couple noticed it, there was black mold all over the area. It was not all that obvious at first glance. It was in the drawers, and in the back of the closets, and in the clothes. Don't forget, if it was a slow leak we don't cover those as a maintenance item. But this was a rupture.

"The adjustor contacted me about the mold. We pay for water damage, but not mold. I told him to warn the housewife that the dark, greenish/black mold is suspect of being Stachybotrys, Aspergillus, or Penicillium. He told her that she might want to have it tested for her own health and that of her family.

"We have had mold since the beginning of life on our planet, but all of a sudden it's dangerous if you check with companies that advertise online as to just how harmful mold can be. The mold remediation company will come out free and takes swabs and send them to a lab. There could be a tiny trace of the most dangerous molds, and the service will provide the insured with a plethora of materials with color pictures that show how such molds cause neurological damage, multiple sclerosis, lupus, and cancer. She can also get these exaggerated opinions online from the companies that do mold remediation and want to scare the insured into hiring them.

"In my case, the neurotic insured panicked, and hired one of these companies. The company came out and sold her their goods, hook, line, and sinker. The company sent out a big truck, and installed a special HEPA air filtering machine, which is a short for high-efficiency-particulate-arrestance filter. The company laid plastic, walk-in tunnels from outside the house to the inside, sent in men in hazmat suits with breathers to cut out the materials that had any sign of mold. She was convinced she and her family were about to die. She moved out for two weeks, and only moved back in when nearly all of her nice things were replaced.

"Naturally the mold company had subcontractors that do the replacement of ordinary things at high prices.

"Her bill was over one hundred thousand dollars for mold damage and mold remediation which she had to pay for and we paid nothing.

"You can expect the same to happen to you if you can determine that you have such a person. The woman will insist that everything in her house that had mold on it be destroyed. If an item is subject to having air born mold spores get into it, like clothing, she will have it all cleaned or thrown out. She freaks out.

"She will be so traumatized, having left her home, having thrown away many of her nice things, and so on, that the last thing she will try to do is to make a claim for water damage unrelated to mold and relive it all again. I paid nothing on that claim, but there was a bunch of water damage that we were liable for if put to the test, except for the mold.

"Now, who here knows of what sort of clues to look for in trying to determine if such a person is subject to such suggestions?" He looked about the room for anyone that might know.

One of the new temporary adjustors, a woman, raised her hand. McAteer acknowledged her. "Neurotic behavior?"

"Exactly!" McAteer said. "Now, who can give me a clue as to what you might look for?"

She did not reply, and no one else spoke.

"I know one. Tide," McAteer said.

Everyone looked at each other, waiting to hear what he was talking about.

"Sound like voodoo to me, the pull of the moon raising the level of the sea," one adjustor said.

McAteer laughed. "Not, not that kind of tide. I'm talking about the laundry detergent."

All mumbled in the shadow of this master at cutting claims and looked at one another to determine if he was making a joke.

He continued. "If you are at the home, and you happen to see into the insured's laundry room, and you see Tide detergent there, then you can suspect you have such a candidate. Tide is three and more times the price of discount store detergent, and it is all the same stuff. But here's a woman that pays three times what she can get cheap detergent for that is every bit as good, if not the very same, as Tide. So, she thinks that she has to have the very best detergent to get rid of germs that might harm her family, no matter the cost."

There was a collective groan in the crowd.

The woman who spoke before said, "Brilliant!"

"Thank you," he complemented the woman. "As for the rest of you, I see we have skeptics. I'm just telling you what I think is a sign to look for. Perhaps you have better instincts than me, but keep in mind that I did not rise to the head of claims here with bad judgment."

Then they looked at each other, wondering if he could be right and they were the dumb ones.

"Let's move on to code upgrades. Let's start with plumbing. Older homes have galvanized pipes. This is no longer used, and copper is now the standard and in many areas required. But use of copper is an upgrade, and the insured has to pay for that. We don't pay for upgrades. Usually the upgrade to copper is the same as new copper pipes, and so we get off paying nothing.

"On insulation. If you have to replace a wall, or under a roof, the house may have either no insulation or an older insulation with a rating of R 11. If the house is sixty years old, it may have no insulation at all. If it is thirty, it may have R 11 in the wood framed walls. But you will be asked to give a settlement value in most cases before the work is done. So, you should know or try to find out what the structure needs in advance. The best way, for homes, is just by the age of the home. The owners may know, or you can check with the building department of the city hall. The building department will require better insulation than R 11 in most cases and certainly more than none whatsoever. It could be R 13, or even R 30. In our policy, this is a code upgrade requirement. We have a limit on all code upgrades. It can be a little daunting trying to know all of those things, but we have them here. Just call in. They are in California Title 24 which we have here and will interpret for you.

"Code upgrades include any and everything that is put in

the house that is better than before. The policy limit on code upgrades may be three thousand dollars for example. So, after that, we don't pay anything further. That three thousand dollars includes things like insulation, lead paint removal, asbestos removal, plumbing upgrades, and other things as well like windows. On windows. If you have to replace a window, the damaged one may not be dual glazed, that is, it may only have one piece of glass instead of a double pane or not be up to the latest energy code requirements. Energy saving codes now require the dual pane and a certain rating, so there is an upgrade that the insured has to pay for. So, we have the depreciation of the old window, which is depreciated due to age, but a similar window is probably not be legal to install now since it does not meet the current energy saving requirements. For example, the amount of the cost of materials like windows that are energy efficient and other code upgrades and their installation might be thirty thousand dollars, but we only have to pay three thousand because the owner had to put in the approved items with the upgrades, but we are capped at three thousand dollars. The three thousand cap is on the total claim, not just one item like windows.

"Now, use these digital phone cameras we are providing you in the field. McAteer held up one of them. Get lots of pictures while you are there to document the damage. In many cases the pictures can be used to reduce a claim, and sometimes to prove that the loss was from an uninsured cause, like surface waters, for example. If we get pictures that the claimant does not have which prove that the claim is larger than we say it should be, and the claimant demands copies of the pictures through his lawyer, our internal legal staff here will lose those pictures as the claimant has no way of knowing what pictures we have until we turn over whatever we say we have to him.

"If you need guidance, call in. That is what the phones are for. As some of you are not from the area, and LA is so big and full of traffic that it takes a lot of working hours to go to a claim, if you can get the job done while there, do it, rather than having to go back. Don't be embarrassed. We may have some ideas for you to reduce the claim, and we may not. We also have some in-house attorneys on the fifth floor for legal questions. They might be able to give you help on legal interpretations as to why the policy does not cover a claim. But, by and large, our in-house staff of lawyers are a bunch of kids just out of law school that we don't pay much and are just told to defend any lawsuits—settlement authority comes from me or someone in my office. They don't get any big cases. So you are probably better off contacting my office on questions in the long run. And, a second opinion never hurts.

"Oh yes, I almost forgot. If an auto has been in a wreck, and totaled, the blue book for the auto is your guide. But if the car is newer, the annual license fee in California is high, based on value. If the claimant is sharp, he will know about this. Let's say the license fee is one thousand five hundred for a second year of an expensive car. The year is half over when the car is totaled, based on the month his license fee is due. He can get us to pay seven hundred fifty dollars for the unused portion of his license fee that he loses, if he asks. But most don't know that, so don't volunteer. Once he signs the release, and gets the check, he is screwed. That savings all adds up to us at the end of the year, you know.

"Any questions so far?"

One of the new men held up his hand.

"Yes?"

"The company I used to work for believes that if you have a homeowner who has been with the company a long time it is a bad business not to honor smaller claims and lose the policy holder at the renewal. What is your policy on that?"

McAteer had an answer. "Good point. If the claim is from a policyholder that has been with the company for many years, and has never had a claim, and the claim is small, it may be good business to go ahead and pay it to keep the policyholder happy, especially if you don't have to pay very much. It's true that if they get mad about a claim they might change companies. Look at the premium. It may be one or two thousand dollars, so you have to weigh that against the amount the claim. You should use your own judgment, or you can call in here for help. That is why we are encouraging small settlements in the field on the spot, which usually result in an acceptance of an offer for much less than the claim is worth. With your checkbooks in hand, you can often settle on the spot for less. A person will usually take a check at the moment for half of what the claim is worth just to be done with it. Also, if you show the insureds the exclusions and limitations in the policy in person, they will then understand better. Most of the insureds have no idea of the numerous limitations that we have put in the policies."

The same man asked another question. "But if someone doesn't get offered what they want, won't they go to an attorney and the attorney sues to get the full amount and cost the company more in the long run?"

McAteer was ready. "We have a relatively new practice for some years now whereby we use kids out of law school as in-house attorneys that we hire dirt cheap to fight every one of the smaller claims brought by attorneys to let attorneys know that it is not profitable to sue anyone insured at Majestik. We only give them the small cases, make them do their own typing, and we work them about seventy hours a week as they are just out of school and are full of energy, and not on hourly pay. The number of claims brought by attorneys has already dropped considerably in recent years because of this strategy. So, if someone wants too much, then don't settle, and we go into the waiting game whereby we put our kid lawyers on the claim and we win a lot of by attrition. The claimants tire, sometimes miss the statute of limitations, move, forget about it, have a family crises like a divorce, a death or illness of a parent, and a variety of factors most all of which work to our favor.

"The only thing that doesn't work to our favor is when the claimant hires a very good lawyer and sues for bad faith, in which case we have outside lawyers who have talent and experience. But the concept we use is to spend a disproportionate amount of time of our in-house lawyers to set an example that we are going to make the plaintiffs' lawyers spend much more money in overhead to sue us over a small case.

"Any more questions?" McAteer asked as he looked about the room.

One of the new women asked, "Where do we get our assignments from?"

"Each of you will take files from an adjuster who is overloaded. And then new claims will be assigned to you. Now, please follow me to the computer room."

With that, he led them out the door and down the hall some distance to a work room, with computer tables on three of its walls. There were a line of computer terminals up against two of the walls, with chairs to make workstations out of each computer.

"These are for you to use. These are networked to a special company database. These are especially good for personal injury claims. Whenever we have a claim from an insured, or someone makes a claim against one of ours, we have a secretary put in the information about the claimant. Age, date of birth, social security number, driver's license number and any restrictions, residence, place of employment, and any personal information that we get about the person. If the person has medical insurance with us or one of our affiliates, we can get everything on them medically as they turn that over as part of their claim. But, you must be careful not to reveal that to them. If a person has made a claim to us for injuries, either as an insured or against one of ours, we put in a summary of the claim, and the injuries claimed. If there has been a lawsuit filed previously and we asked them written interrogatory questions about any previous injuries and claims, we put that in the computer as well. If you have a claimant with injuries, you should come by here and see if the person is in the database, or call in and we will do it for you. We have more than half of the people in the state who are of age in here somewhere. It could be that the person has made a similar claim before for the same or similar injury, and then you can deny or reduce the claim since he has already injured that portion of his body. Sometimes you can get the person to deny in writing that he or she has hurt that portion of the body, like his back, and then add the computer information to the file and we will have the claimant lying which the company can use to deny the claim or embarrass him in court as a liar.

"We also have access to all court filings online, including divorces, as sometimes the person's ex-spouse hates them so much that we can get the ex-spouse to tell us information even if it hurts the person telling it. When you check the court filings, and you can check the county in which the person lives, to see if that person has filed any lawsuits. Much of this can be done online now. If you find a filing by number that does not have the documents online, you can go to that courthouse and pull the file, and see what sort of a claim that was made and make copies there. These are all public records. Do not underestimate the value of a trip to the courthouse. If it is personal injury case, the person will probably say his injury is so bad it is permanent, and we can hold that against him in our case. In divorce cases, the spouse, for example the wife, may be so pissed off at her husband for cheating that she may file a sworn declaration that he cheated an insurance company on a claim and give details. Is that cool, or what?

"Any more questions?"

None being asked, he said, "All right then, let's get to work and get out there and beat the shit of anyone who makes a claim against us!"

Ernie was given the address of a Majestik field office to go to and told to meet a Jessica Bloom there.

McAteer and his assistants left the room, and McAteer told the new assistant of his who was following him, "God, I love this job!"

✧✧✧

Ernie went outside to the parking lot and sat down on the curb next to his motorcycle, disgusted with what he had done in coming to work for this demonic insurance company, reflecting on just where he was at this lowest stage in his life. A questionable sighting of a silly bird, that should be extinct, led him south, into the embrace of Satan.

He thought about the session. *Now I know now that the in-*

surance world is crooked. I should just go back home, forget about going to the Polynesian hotel, forget about the retroactive benefits, forget about the five thousand dollars per month, and forget this crooked job. But, damn, I don't even have enough money for gas to get home. Lilly bought me this nice outfit for the job with her hard-earned money. I feel like if I take this job I will be selling my soul to the Devil like in one of those movies. I really don't have an option at this point. Maybe, just maybe, I could work this job for a while without doing any of those crooked things that McAteer taught me. Maybe I can do something good.

He got up slowly, sat on his motorcycle, fired the motor up, and headed for the Majestik field office he had been directed to. Riding always gave him a chance to think.

As he rode, he thought, *McAteer is not an honest man, and Majestik is not an honest company. Why is it necessary to cheat people? Can't the claims be settled honestly? I could never last at such a job. But then, I accepted the job, and I must try to do my best. Surely it is possible to settle claims honestly, at least for ninety days. They might fire me for not stealing from the people like they want. I guess I'll find out. I don't have a choice, for now, as I don't have enough gas money to get home. I better save money right away for gas to get home if they fire me early for not doing what they want.*

CHAPTER 22

Ernie swung down the kickstand of his trusty motorcycle with his left boot and looked at the Majestik field office that he had been directed to. He unfolded the paper he was given to recall the name, which read, *Jessica Bloom.*

"Yessssss?" the pasty-faced young man with soft skin at the reception desk asked in a swishy voice.

"I'm here to see Jessica Bloom."

Ernie's booming voice startled the man and he jumped. "I'll see if she's available. Who may I say is calling, sir?"

"Ernie, a temporary field representative. I'm here to get work assignments from her."

"Very good, sir." He called someone and then allowed entry. "Go right on in."

Inside the door, Ernie found himself in yet another secure area, like a little jail cell eight feet square. Another buzzer went off, and the next door opened to a large room of mostly women sitting behind desks. All this security? What for? What is there for someone to break in here and take? Rape? Certainly it cannot be to protect the virtue of insurance company women. After hearing the McAteer lecture, Ernie doubted there was any virtue to protect.

Of the considerable number of women working, one was straight ahead, ten desks away, and was looking at him. *She must be the one.* Thirty-five, bleached-blonde hair with ugly dark roots, black pants suit outfit with stretch bottoms over her pregnant stomach, she did not stand but did acknowledge him.

"Hi," Ernie said in greeting as he approached.

"Hi. You must be Ernie. Would you like some coffee? There's a machine just over there."

"Sounds good. I'll go fix it myself."

"I'll put the files together for you."

Ernie poured a Styrofoam cup of coffee that tasted like a combination of used motor oil, battery acid, liver bile, and droppings of a diseased, wild animal. He tried it at the coffee station and then put the cup in the trash. He returned to her desk and sat in front of Jessica as she organized the files he would take.

"I'm so relieved that they got someone to take over my files. I really had too many."

"I was hired because of so many trees down from the big storm," Ernie said proudly. He thought that by mentioning it, the files he would be given would be limited to tree problems.

"Ah…yes, I suppose so. There are certainly a lot of tree related claims," Jessica answered. She was completely unaware that he was speaking the exact truth. She did not care about anything but her maternity problems at the moment. In the several years she had worked at the insurance company as an adjuster, she had yet to go out in the field on a single claim and was not about to start caring now. "I'm going on maternity leave, starting tomorrow. I've reassigned all my files. Some were assigned to others, but most to you. You are getting forty seven files today."

"Will there be more?"

"No doubt. The claims are really coming in with this big storm. You're mostly getting claims that arise under homeowners, small commercial building, auto, and marine policies. But there are others in there too. Many have all been already denied by me, or delayed by asking for receipts and other information. Or, in a few cases, I offered the few hundred dollars difference between the deductible and the damage, and they have not yet answered."

Ernie was puzzled. "About the ones you have denied, what am I supposed to do with them?"

Jessica did not quite understand. The actual but unwritten company practice was to deny all claims. Then she would paper the claimants to death and burn up time until they got tired and went away, let the statute of limitations pass, or took a very modest settlement. Or, let them sue and turn over the claim to those kid lawyers at the main office. If a claim was a substantial one, McAteer would assign the claim to some outside, talented lawyers. What was it that Ernie meant to ask for? Thinking he must be speaking at a higher level of insurance talk, she answered, "Oh, you know, the usual stuff."

Perplexed on how she handled a claim, let alone denying it from her desk with her big belly without going out to see the claim in person, he asked, "How can you decide what to do if you don't go out on any given file to meet the people and take a look at the damage?"

She was even more puzzled at his comment, as she never went out on a claim, even though the company would pay her mileage. After all, why leave the luxury of the air-conditioned office where you can bullshit with friends either at the office, or talk to or text them all day? She wondered if this Ernie fellow came from a rural town and smaller claims office where they actually worked the files. Finally she said, "Well, you can ask the claimant to send you pictures and estimates, and if he doesn't, you can deny the claim based on the fact that it hasn't been done or that he has not cooperated as the insurance policy requires."

Ernie found this attitude to be very unusual. But what did he know? This gal must have been doing this for some time. "Is there any reason not to go out to see the claim and meet the claimant?"

"You can do what you want," she said, giving him a curious look. She pushed the stack of files at him. "Here, these are all from the greater Los Angeles area, and no one has been out on any of these, but I have denied many of them by letter. You can have my desk here. I'm off tomorrow."

܁܁܁

The Polynesian Apartments sign did everything it could to give the essence of what someone might think of Polynesia—with a budget. The sign had a palm tree and a swordfish, all lit up at night in neon splendor.

Inside the courtyard were three, small, aqua pools, the blue water inviting fun. They were labeled Torrid, Tepid, and Frigid, all three heated to different temperatures.

Every piece of décor in the lobby furniture was in rattan bamboo. Leafy plants abound. New to Ernie were bird-of-paradise plants, and he stopped to stare, realizing that there was so much of the tropical world of plants that he knew nothing of, and that he would never know. *Is Los Angeles in the tropics?*

At the manager's office, an attractive fortyish woman came forward. "Yes?"

"I was referred here by Majestik Insurance. I'll be in town ninety days. Mr. McAteer said he had an arrangement with you for us temporaries?" He put it in a question as he was not too sure of himself in the surroundings.

"Yes. His office did call. My name is Wendy, and I'm the manager. We have a special arrangement with Majestik for those who come into town and are not set up yet. Most want the full service, the linens, plates, and all. Are you interested in that? Your cost is to be paid for by Majestik. That does not include phone calls."

"Okay."

"Welcome to the Polynesian."

᭬᭬᭬

Ernie settled in, and when evening came he had conclusively concluded that his chainsaw looked just wonderful on top of the coffee table. He waded through files given him by Jessica, reading and trying to figure out what on earth they were about.

One of the files reported that a huge pine tree had fallen on a house in Pacific Palisades, and the tree lay against the sloped Tudor roof, such that it might fall over and hurt someone or damage an atrium below. The owner stated she was unable to get anyone out to handle the problem.

Jessica had written her a letter stating that the claim could not be acted on until she got estimates for the claimed loss and telling her that there was a one thousand dollars maximum on all trees combined in her policy and a five hundred dollar deductible.

Well, now, Ernie thought, *this matter of a tree will be my first visit tomorrow. I have a GPS, so I should be able to find my way. I'll wear my jeans, instead of Lilly's new dress outfit, and take my saw. Tomorrow should be interesting. Time to earn my pay!*

CHAPTER 23

His chainsaw, sticking out of the saddlebag on one side of the motorcycle, seemed out of place for Los Angeles, but not to Ernie. He stopped at the nearest gas station and filled up his tank as well as his plastic gas can for after adding two-stroke motor oil for the chainsaw. He added chain oil to the oiler on the saw, and it was ready. Off to his first assignment he went, full of piss and vinegar.

At the address was a large, expensive looking, English Tudor house, with a high-pitched roof with a very steep angle. It was two regular stories high, but the steep Tudor roof made a slanted third story. The windows, doors and trim were in the traditional Tudor brown. That was uncommon for what he had seen in LA so far, as this roof angle was clearly designed to withstand the weight of tons of snow, obviously not originating in Los Angeles where there was no snow.

At the door, a reasonably attractive lady in her late forties, with a tired face, answered, "Yes?"

"Hi. I'm Ernie, from Majestik. I'm here about the problem you reported. My card." He handed her one of the new cards he'd gotten from McAteer.

"I'm Edna Connolly. It's wonderful that you have come! I cannot get anyone out here to remove the tree, and it is so dangerously ready to fall. Come through the house here to the back yard."

In the back yard, Ernie was faced with a huge pine tree, ninety feet tall, which had blown over from the wind, only to lie precariously against the very steep Tudor roof. It was still partially connected to the ground by its roots, but was clearly resting most of its weight against the roof. It was much taller than the Tudor roof. There was no apparent damage to the roof, as the slant of the roof was the same angle of the tree resting against it. The tree was three feet in diameter at the base. Below it on the ground to one side was a glass house for plants.

"I had a tree removal service man come by, and the fellow told me that the top of the tree has to be cut from the roof, but the roof is too steep for him or his workers to walk on to cut it," she complained, very much upset. "He told me I needed a crane to lift the tree up and out to lay it down, so it could then be cut up. I called a crane service, but the man who came said it would cost a minimum of seven thousand five hundred dollars to get one of his cranes out for a half day that would big enough to go over the roof to get to the tree on the back side of the roof of the house. He said that he would need his biggest crane as he would have to put it in the front yard and go over the roof to get to the tree, which was his one hundred fifty foot crane.

"He said use of that crane requires special permits for each city that it has to go through just to get here, and a special permit from this city, all of which is expensive, is in addition to the seven thousand five hundred dollars. Then, for an extra charge, they would cut up the tree once it is on the ground and put the pieces into a chipper to grind it up and take it off. They want a total of nine thousand five hundred dollars plus the permit fees. Worse yet, they are booked for at least six weeks because of all the trees down from the storm. I reached another crane service man but was told that he would not bring a big crane into a residential neighborhood as it created too much liability, and in any case he was too busy.

"I called Jessica Bloom at the insurance office as to what to do, and she said that I should go ahead and get estimates and that the insurance would pay up to five hundred dollars as trees are limited to one thousand dollars but that there is a five hundred dollar deductible on my homeowner's policy. I'm willing to spend the money to bring in the crane, but I can't even get the crane for six weeks due to the backlog and I think it may fall down before that.

"Can you help me? I'm so afraid it will fall and smash my greenhouse or even kill someone."

"Yep." The single word left all the details unanswered.

"What shall I do? It's supposed to rain again soon, and if there is wind, I'm in big trouble. I live alone. I'm a widow. I wish my departed husband were here. He would know what to do!"

"No sweat, lady."

"What can you do?"

"I'll cut it up. I've got my chainsaw with me."

"You're joking! No crane? Do you mean to say that you can get the tree off the roof without a crane?"

"Piece of cake."

She was silent, pessimism all over her face.

Ernie headed toward his motorcycle for his saw in the saddlebag. She was waiting for him in the rear, looking up at the huge tree when he came around the house, chainsaw in hand.

"Show me a way to the roof. I have no ladder."

She pointed up. "You could get there from the window in the sewing room in the attic."

She led him inside the back door and up three flights of stairs to the attic that served as storage and also a sewing room. A sewing machine was under a small window built out under a little gable. It was not made for roof access, the window being only two by three feet. Ernie moved the sewing machine, opened the window, took off the screen, and went out, walking fearlessly on the steep roof over to the tree, as though it was level ground. The roof was so steep only a roofer or a logger, like Ernie, would dare walk on it.

He looked down to check out where to let pieces of the big tree fall. He then yanked his chainsaw to life with the starter cord, and it fired up without protest in a salute to Ernie in the strange new climate he had brought it to, a testament to his mechanical ability to understand engines. He lived anthropomorphizing with his equipment and motorcycle, with the tiny distinction that he attributed human like traits to machines as well as animals.

Ernie cut the upper limbs from the tree and then made several cuts in the trunk, letting the pieces fall to the back yard as the woman watched in amazement, from the safety of a long distance away. The remaining tree trunk was now only as high as the bottom of the roof. Ernie went to the edge and sat back against the roof, putting his feet against the cut-off top of the big pine. He gave it a hearty shove with his legs, away from the direction of the greenhouse, and it twisted, finally tearing its few remaining roots out of the ground, began to roll against the edge of the roofline, and stopped. Ernie moved over to it, repositioning himself, and gave it another push with his strong legs. It rolled over again and began to move faster until it was clear it was going to go past the roofline and fall. The big tree fell away from the greenhouse, as planned, and into the back yard with an enormous THUD that shook the ground like an earthquake. The backyard had other large pines in it and was not visible to the neighbors, who did not know what was going on, and two called in to report another earthquake.

Ernie walked back to the little window, crawled in, sawdust and all. He replaced the screen, and went on down the steps inside leaving a trail of sawdust, and out to the back yard where she waited, spellbound.

The enormous tree safely on the ground was, for Edna, like a Zeppelin that crashed from the sky, "My God, that was amazing! I've never seen anything like it!"

"Do you have a fireplace?" Ernie asked. "I could cut this critter into fireplace-sized logs for you. I can cut the trunk into two or three foot pieces, and then each of those into four pieces if that is okay. They'll be a bit large, but they'll burn a long time. If you want them smaller, you should hire someone with a log splitter."

Still dumfounded, she hesitated. "Well, yes, there is a nice one in the family room, but I have not used it in years except for those paper-covered little logs I buy at the grocery store. I'm sure that I can use the logs in it."

"Logs from this wet pine will spit out sparks, with the sap and all. You might need a screen over the front. But it'll burn."

She was willing to go along with whatever he suggested.

"That would be marvelous. There is a place for fireplace wood just there," she said, pointing to an area up against the back of the house where he could stack them."

Ernie fired up his saw again, and began the task of cutting the trunk into fireplace-sized logs. He first cut the trunk into short lengths and set up each segment upright on a base log he used as a cutting table so as not to get his chain into the dirt, and cut each segment into four or six pieces suitable for a fireplace. The smell of fresh pine sap and freshly cut pine wood filled the air.

He stacked the logs up against the back of the house, and took the green pine branches to the front near the street and cut then into small pieces and piled them to be picked up by the trash haulers. Half a day was gone.

He put his saw back in his saddlebag, and was dusting the wood chips that completely covered him as she came back outside. Seeing her, he recalled that he had to do the paperwork. Ernie remembered that the office told him about the limitations on trees. They paid only up to one thousand dollars, but there was a five hundred dollar deductible.

"Are you making a claim for the tree? The company only pays five hundred on that."

"Oh no, I've been wanting to get that overgrown monster down for some time. I get a sore back gathering up the pine needles. And it is too close to the house, it raised the ground near the house such that water puddles between it and against the house."

Ernie shrugged, as there was nothing much to say. He had settled his first claim for nothing. It seemed to him that he was earning his pay properly.

She looked at him admiringly, wanting to do something for him. "Now, it's lunch time. I made you a turkey sandwich if you want it."

"That would be great, but I'll eat it out here, as I'm covered in sawdust."

"Oh no, come on in. I insist you sit in the kitchen with me. I'll clean it up when you're gone."

He put his saw in his saddlebag, and brought in the file on

the claim. Doing his best to dust off the wood chips, somewhat unsuccessfully, he came inside, leaving a path of wood chips.

In the kitchen she laid out a very thick turkey sandwich, a salad, and a glass of water. Ernie, thirsty, downed the water. She got a bottle of white wine from the refrigerator, and set it on the table with two glasses.

"While you eat, I'll change."

"Thanks. This looks great."

She returned quickly, before Ernie finished. She wore an expensive looking brown and ivory silk robe, her feet bare. The way that the sheer silk hung on her revealed that she was naked underneath.

He had not touched the wine. She held up the wine bottle. "Won't you join me?"

"Better not. This is my first day on the job, and I don't know what I'll run into yet. I still have the whole afternoon to go do another claim." Ernie continued eating.

"How about just a smidgen?"

Ernie gave in to be polite. "Okay, a small glass."

She poured the glasses and sat down at the table on the adjacent side, close to him. "I love the way you handled my claim. I'll be sure and write the insurance company about you. Are you from out of the area?"

"North Washington, near the Canadian border. I'm only here temporarily for ninety days to help with trees down due to the big storm."

"Fascinating!" She sipped on her glass of wine, looking at him invitingly.

He joined her, drinking some as well. Getting on to business, he produced the release form. "I have a form here for you to sign." He began to fill it in.

She looked at him, rather than the release form. "You know, I get rather lonely here all alone."

Her leg slid through the slit in the robe and she stretched it under the table to his, touching it with her toes.

He polished off the last bite of the sandwich. To direct attention away from her behavior, Ernie looked around at the big kitchen. "You have a beautiful home here. You must have a lot of things to do in this big city." He pointed to a line on the release form. "I need to get your signature to show that you are satisfied."

She took the form, without looking at it, and set it aside. "*Sugah*, in order for me to be satisfied, I need something more from you."

She suddenly stood up and, to Ernie's surprise, opened her silk robe and dropped it to the floor. "Would you please tell me if I'm still good looking at forty-nine?"

She stood and turned about, modeling and pirouetting. He realized he was supposed to admire her body, and so he did his best to comply, by looking her up and down, as though she was a heifer at an auction. She had nice big breasts, without much sag. Her waist still had suppression, rendering shape to her figure, and she was just a bit overweight, with thighs the fullness of Virginia hams.

"Yes, very nice. You certainly are still very good looking and shapely."

"Would you do a widow a favor?"

"What would that be?" he asked innocently, trying to avoid the obvious.

"You want me to sign that I'm satisfied. In order to be completely satisfied, I need something else."

Ernie lapsed into silence, his face flushed. He finally decided that satisfying the insured might be the proper thing to do. "Okay, but I have to go to another assignment, so I can't stay too long."

"This won't take long."

Leaving the silk robe on the floor and remaining completely naked, she took his hand in hers and led him into her bedroom. Centered against the back wall in the large bedroom with its high, vaulted ceiling, was a huge, old fashioned, four-poster, wooden bed with a massive headboard seven feet high. She led him to the side of the big bed, putting her arms around his strong neck and then kissed him squarely on the mouth. She then opened his belt and pants and helped him out of his clothes, sawdust falling everywhere as the strong odor of pine from the chips on Ernie's clothes filled the room. Once he was naked, she stepped back, gazing at his sex, as though to admire a prize she had just acquired.

Later, in the kitchen, she kissed him. "Now, I'll sign that I'm completely satisfied."

Not long afterward, Ernie climbed on his motorcycle, fired it up, and drove down the street, thinking of that big ninety-footer. "Since McAteer didn't have any saws to pass out," he said aloud, "it's a good thing I brought my chainsaw."

∽∾∽

The next claim was from a homeowner living not far from the lady with the tree on the Tudor house. The letter in the file was from a Ms. Nancy Scott, claiming the loss of one thousand dollars for a yellow-naped Amazon parrot.

Ernie walked up to the door of a fairly large house with a Spanish-tiled roof, white stucco sides, and with a rainbow of birds of paradise, bougainvilleas, and hibiscus plants in the front. A woman in her early forties, looking dreary, answered the door, "Yes?"

"I'm Ernie from Majestik Insurance about the parrot claim. My card."

"Oh, this is unexpected! I phoned in about the claim, but have heard nothing."

"Well, here I am."

"Please come in," she said, opening the door wide.

"This is a nice home," Ernie said, but it was a little run down as though needing a new coat of paint.

"Thank you. I live here alone now, as I am recently separated from my husband. Won't you sit down?"

Ernie took a seat in a heavy leather chair in front of a coffee table. "So tell me, what is this claim involving a bird about?"

"In fact," she said, "the bird is the reason, or at least the last straw, as to why I kicked my husband out of the house. But, actually, we weren't getting along, anyway. He moved in with his girlfriend."

"What happened?"

"My husband and I bought a yellow-naped Amazon parrot two years ago from a pet store—a male. We both got along with him fine, initially, and the bird was talking up a storm. We named him Wie Gehts. That's German for What's Happening. It was a line in a Peter Sellers movie. But after a year, Wie Gehts took to attacking any and all men, while taking a liking to most all women. He became gender conscious. We had no idea it would get that way. Wie Gehts attacked my husband and other men several times here in the house. He took a very special liking to me, and the little fellow was always on my shoulder when I was at home. If I lay down to watch TV, he would perch on me. Of course, my husband could not lie down next to me if the bird was there or he would attack him. That really irritated my husband. I thought that Wie Gehts would get over it, as a passing development."

She took a few breaths, obviously emotionally upset about the bird. "Then one day, my husband was watching TV, lying on the couch. Wie Gehts came down from his perch on the top of his cage, snuck over to the couch, crawled up on my husband's shoulder, and jumped down on top of him, going for his eyes. He almost got one, and left my husband with a small beak mark, bleeding a bit in the face just below his eye. It really scared my husband, and it was quite a shock to me as well. There really was no justifiable reason for the attack."

"Sounds like a pretty nasty bird."

"Well, he was never that way to me. After that, I agreed that he could go if we could find a good home for him. But my husband said that he would just attack someone else, and someone would end up losing an eye. So wait until you hear what he did."

"Okay, tell me."

"Come, I'll show you."

She got up and Ernie followed her to a back room that had a desk with odds and ends stored on it. On the desk, Ernie saw a contraption made out of wood from a woodworkers shop painted gray. It was three feet in diameter, square, except for the front, which was done in five plastic panels made to look like glass, put together on angles so as to provide a view, like a bay window of a home. As he looked more carefully, inside he saw a little chair with a tiny leather strap for the bird's neck, and another strap below that would go around the bird's midsection. On the outside on one side was a spring-hinged opening that could be used to drop things inside. He then realized what it was. It was a model of a real cyanide gas chamber!

"Is that what I think it is?"

"Yes! He and his friends made it. It's a gas chamber. It uses real cyanide gas!"

"So what happened?"

"After being attacked, my husband decided that our bird had to die. So he went out and bought all the materials to make this miniature model of the California gas chamber. Two of his friends helped build it. Then he arranged a party of all his friends to come and watch. He had this thing set up in the family room one night."

"If you didn't like it, was there some reason why you didn't stop it?"

"I really had no say in the matter. He is too headstrong for me to tell him what to do. And his method was barbaric."

"How was that?"

"He invited his crude friends over for a party. There were seven men, plus my husband, and six women, most of whom I don't approve of. After stupefying themselves in booze, they picked twelve for a jury trial, my husband the prosecutor, and one the defense attorney. They had the quorum, twelve men, tried and true, as they put it. They put on a trial, and voted on his guilt like a jury. They found Wie Gehts guilty and sentenced him to die in the gas chamber. One of them read him his last rights.

"They all thought it was such fun. Then they marched him to the chamber with a string like a rope around his little neck, and put him in the seat they had made. Then they all gathered around and continued embalming themselves in booze, watching the event. Poor little Wie Gehts was strapped in the chair, and I could see his fear."

After several deep breaths, she continued with the story.

"At one point one of them actually called the governor's office in Sacramento to ask him if they could get a temporary reprieve!"

"This is some story," Ernie exclaimed.

"They got through to the governor's office, saying that they were trying to stop an execution scheduled for dawn, and, worried that there might be an execution he was unaware of, the governor got up and took the phone call. He said he was unaware of any scheduled execution. But when they finally explained that it was a parrot, the whole bunch of them broke up in laughter and the governor went back to bed. Then they gassed my little Wie Gehts!"

"Where did they get the gas?"

"Oh shit, that was easy! Three of them are doctors. It was no problem for them to come up with a lethal gas. I think it was fentanyl. It was so sad, watching my little Wei Gehts die."

"Well," Ernie asked, wondering what Majestik might do, "What is it that you are claiming against the insurance company?"

"Well, since he killed our pet deliberately, my sister said that the insurance company should get me another, especially since my husband and I have parted. I really cannot afford to buy another now that he's gone. I'll have to find work soon."

"Well, this is not something I'm familiar with," Ernie said, thumbing through the various exclusions of the sample policy he had been given. "Was your husband living with you at the time?"

"Well, yes, but he had his girlfriend and occasionally did not come home."

Ernie found a section on pets in the sample policy he carried. "Pets are excluded, it says here in 'exclusions.'"

She frowned and sadness overcame her. "Darn. I might have known that insurance wouldn't pay for my Wie Gehts," she said quietly, looking down. "Anyway, I doubt that a replacement would be the same. Apart from his attacking men, he was quite a character. I miss my little friend. He was loyal, unlike my husband." Tears formed in her eyes, and then she began to cry.

Wanting to take her mind off her sadness, Ernie asked, "Do you have any other pets to keep you company?"

"No."

That just exaggerated her loneliness and she began to cry even harder. Looking through the policy, as though a solution was in it and trying to come up with something to help, he finally he realized it was up to him to do something, and it was not going to be in the policy.

"Say, I have an idea. Were you very emotionally upset at your husband for killing the bird?"

"Of course! Losing Wie Gehts meant more to me than losing my husband since he started carrying on with that slut of his. He spent a lot of money on her. He even took her on trips, the puta-sharmoota-cunt-slut-bitch-whore!"

Ernie thought for a while as she cried. "I have a suggestion."

"What?"

"Have you ever ridden on a motorcycle?"

"When I was in the university, this guy took me out on one. That was wild. He took me out in the woods and fucked me on the seat!"

Ernie was a bit shocked at the unexpected frankness of the story. "Do you have a phone book?"

"No, everyone uses the computer. Come over here." She led him to her computer table in the same room.

"I don't have a computer," Ernie admitted.

"What are you looking for?" She sat in front of it and readied for a search.

"Pet stores."

"That's easy. I know of one not too far." She found it in a jiffy and wrote down the address.

"Put on some boots and get a coat. Let's go for a ride."

Nancy's expression changed from crying to gleefully accepting the excitement of a motorcycle ride. She returned from her room wearing blue jeans, a tight bright-red sweater, and boots, looking very sporting.

⁂

As they entered the pet store, they were greeted by a cacophony of sounds, squawking bird noises, barking dogs, chirps, and other animal noises. There was an overpowering odor of animals and a sort of electricity in the air that Ernie always noticed whenever he went to the home of someone who had more than one cat. He approached the man behind the counter. "Do you have any puppies?"

"We sure do! Just go right through there," the man said, pointing down a hallway to another section of the shop.

Ernie and Nancy walked through it and into a section where there were wire cages on the floor with new litters of puppies. One had a mother German Shepherd with five puppies.

Nancy leaned over the cage. "Awwwwwww."

Responding as though it was predestined, a very cute little blonde and black female puppy pranced over to get closer to Nancy and looked up with warm eyes and a wagging tail.

"Oh, look at this one!" She reached into the cage and picked the little doggie up. "I think it's a female."

The puppy was very excited and licked her, snuggling up to her face. Nancy became ecstatic, as a complete mood change came over her. Hugging and petting the little puppy, she had found a new love, something she needed in her life.

Ernie went back up to the desk. "How much for the German Shepherd puppy?"

"Seven hundred. This dog has papers and is guaranteed against hip dysphasia."

But Ernie knew animals. "My friend, there is no such thing as no hip problems in German Shepherds, but they still make the best pets for about twelve years, so don't bullshit me. I'll give you five hundred and you throw in an adjustable choker collar, a leash, and a bag of dog food. I work for an insurance company and am required to get the best deal. I can give you a check now. As there is no credit card, there will be no commission."

The man looked up at the ceiling and thought and then looked at Ernie. "Okay, especially since it is not on a credit card. That'll save me three per cent."

"I appreciate it." Ernie joined Nancy, who was treating the puppy as though she gave birth to it, and revealed his settlement proposal. "Nancy, you are entitled to make claims under this policy against your own spouse. If you would like to make a claim against your husband for the emotional distress of seeing him murder your bird, I could consider that as a valid claim, especially since you are a long-term policy holder. I can offer you a check for five hundred dollars, which you could then use to buy the puppy. The neat thing about an emotional distress claim is that, unlike a property damage claim, there is no deductible—you get the full amount. How does that sound?"

"Oh, Ernie," she shrieked. She leaped up to him, puppy in hand, hugging him with the puppy in between them. The puppy squealed from the pressure of the hug.

"Be careful! You'll squeeze that puppy to death. And now, listen. I got you a choker collar. When she is a bit older, in about four months, use that, as that's the only way to train her. You let her know who is boss at all times, and she will make you a fine protective dog. But make sure you train her on the leash. Later, she will do the same off leash. I know these dogs."

She began dancing about the pet store with the puppy, humming a tune, as though she and the new doggie were Ginger Rodgers and Fred Astaire.

"And," Ernie said, to no one in particular, as he went out to his motorcycle to get ready to leave, "this special doggy gets to ride on a motorcycle."

Back at the house, they went inside to sign his release form, and she fixed the puppy a bowl of water. "Before you go, I want you to do something for me. Follow me." She led him to the garage and hit the electric opener button, opening the double door. There was only one car in it now that her husband had left, the other stall open and empty. "Could you please push your motorcycle in here? That way no one from the street can see us. I want to do it on the seat like I did in college."

⌘

As Ernie dressed for dinner in his new, smart, wool outfit, he turned on the flat screen TV in the furnished room. A talk show was on. He wasn't much interested, but left it on as he dressed.

In the background, as he got ready, he could hear, "Tonight on our show is Zachary Lewis, the popular candidate for governor," the talk show host said, introducing his guest to the listeners.

"Mr. Lewis, as you may have read, has proposed changes in several areas of the law that are innovative and original, and these changes would make the biggest change in our system ever. Here in our studio is the candidate himself, Zachary Lewis." He turned to Lewis. "Mr. Lewis, the polls show that you have come up in the last several weeks from behind several points to nearly neck and neck with your opponent. To what do you attribute your gain and success?"

"Well, I believe the people are aware that my proposed reforms are not just some dream, but represent genuine, needed reform. I'm extremely pleased to learn of the gain in the polls, and as more people find out about my plans, more will come to our side."

"Mr. Lewis, I would like to ask you a few questions about your proposed legislation. The hottest issue is definitely the major change you have proposed in the manner that insurance companies must deal with claims. Our sources tell us that insurance companies are spending a lot of money to try to prevent that from happening."

"You bet they are! Already in this state election, insurance companies have spent more to try to defeat me than the last two presidential candidates spent combined in the national race. Imagine that! They are bigger financially than entire nations. Insurance companies are doing anything they can to hang on to their well-established ways of systematically cheating people. My proposal will be the downfall of insurance company bad faith practices, and force settlement of claims in weeks instead of years."

"How can the audience find out how your proposals will work?"

"The best way is to go to our website. We have videos there on several different aspects of the plan, and your audience can see it there. We also have a phone number they can call, free of charge, if they have questions."

Elsewhere, in a very posh living room, the Bradfords watched the same interview. When the commercial came on, Bradford clicked off the sound and said to his wife, "You see how they talk down about the insurance contributions? That's why I gave twenty million in contribution through the Chockpaws. So far no one has found out. If they did, it would backfire, sure as hell."

CHAPTER 24

That evening, Ernie motored up to the security gate of Zelzah's Beverly Hills condominium and called her on the intercom.

"Yes?"

"Hi. It's Ernie."

"Ernie! I'll open the gate. Park behind the Lexus at number eight."

In the parking stalls were BMWs, Porsches, Mercedes, Land Rovers, Lexuses, Audis, and Volvos. He saw no American brands, and no motorcycles. He parked his at number eight, behind her Lexus.

Zelzah answered the door in a colorful, silk, embroidered kaftan. Ernie detected the fragrance of an exotic perfume.

"Come in. Then she noticed his helmet in his hand. "Oh my, are you on a motorcycle?"

"Yeah."

"How exciting! I've never done that. Will you take me for a ride sometime?"

"Why sure." Ernie could see a dining table set for two, and candles set out but not yet lit. Wine glasses were on the table, as was expensive china with a hand-painted floral pattern. "Nice of you to have me over."

"Please, have a seat, and I'll fix you a drink. Would you like wine?"

"Fine."

"You must tell me about yourself. What were you doing before you took the temporary job at Majestik?"

"I was working up near the border when the site was shut down."

"What insurance company?"

"No insurance company, I felled trees."

"You're so funny. But seriously, I don't mean to pry, but I just wanted to know a little about you. What insurance company did you work for, and where did you buy those marvelous fashions? Not on Rodeo, as far as I know," she asked, referring to Rodeo Drive in Beverly Hills, the most fashionable and expensive street in Los Angeles.

"I worked right up near the border for a man named Billings who has a logging business. The wool clothes were a gift, but the boots came from Woods Logging where I get most of my stuff."

Perplexed, she stared at him. "What were you doing up at the border?"

"Felling trees. I'm a logger."

She was dumbfounded. "Then what on earth are you doing here?"

"A spotted owl gave the Washington Department of Natural Resources power to close down the job, and everybody working for Billings was out of work. Unemployment found this job for me."

"Surely, you must have worked in insurance industry at some time?"

"Nope."

"You never worked in insurance? I typed the memo to my boss. Only insurance agents with experience were hired."

"I was brought in to take care of trees down due to the storm."

She then began to finally realize that he might indeed be a logger. It was a problem for her. There was no way she could report him as hired by mistake now that she was socializing with him unless she sent him away at once. Then she realized that it was even better that he was not in the industry as she was now going to socialize with him, and the idea of being with a real logger was infinitely more exciting than just an insurance man. A dilemma.

Her libido controlling, she decided to continue. "Well, I normally never get familiar with anyone in the company, but since you are only a temporary, we might get to know each other. After all, my boss has his own vices, I can assure you. The fact that you are not in the industry is even better. Please, take off your coat."

With that, she stood to help him with his Eisenhower wool jacket and took it to the cloakroom closet. Ernie's blue leather trimmed suspenders then dominated his outfit, and the size of his chest and shoulders differentiated him from insurance types. The novelty of this man was exciting.

"Let's have dinner. It's just ready."

"Sounds great. I'm hungry."

She led him to the table. "I hope you like this. It's called Singaporean Spicy Short Ribs."

Ernie wondered about the strange name. "Where did you learn this?"

"I got the recipe from a magazine. An inquirer wrote the magazine and said he had this in Singapore and that it was fabulous. The editor wrote the restaurant, got the recipe, and published it. It's made from beef stock, Thai chilies, soy sauce, ginger, crushed tomatoes, shallots, Worcestershire sauce, garlic, and cilantro added at the end."

"Sounds great. And coleslaw. I love coleslaw." Ernie identified with the coleslaw as he had no idea what Singaporean Spicy Short Ribs would taste like. He then sampled her efforts. "This is wonderful!"

"So, tell me a little more about yourself. What exactly does a logger do?"

"I'm a faller."

"What is a faller?"

"I cut down trees."

"You actually cut trees? How?"

"Chainsaw. How else?"

"You use a chainsaw? Wow, this is too fantastic!" She put her hand over her mouth, trying to hide her expression of surprise and excitement, almost as though she was Japanese. It was the most excitement she'd had in a long time, and she felt a stirring in her loins.

"In fact, I used mine this morning. I took down a ninety-footer off a roof for lady who made a claim. It was soft pine and cut easily. But those suckers have a lot of sap."

Zelzah wasn't sure if she was supposed to laugh at what must have been a joke. "You can't be serious."

"Yep. It wasn't much of a job. I cut it into firewood for her. She didn't want any settlement money."

Zelzah's eyes opened wide. "This is too much! You came down here and cut down a ninety-foot tree in Los Angeles with a chainsaw? I can't believe it. Where did you get a saw? The lady had it?"

"Nope, I used my own."

In spite of her ability to keep her decorum, she practically screeched, "You brought a chainsaw with you from Washington to cut trees for Majestik? This is over the top."

"Yep. Good thing too. Mr. McAteer didn't give anyone a saw at the indoctrination."

Zelzah rolled her eyes and put her hand on her forehead. She regained her composure and made up a silly question to try to hide her chaotic emotions. "Did you think you would be cutting trees in this job?"

"Yep. The lady I talked to on the phone from Washington said I was hired because of all the trees down due to the storm."

Zelzah smiled and sat back, realizing that Ernie was truly an anomaly to the insurance business, and so much the better for her and a possible affair. "I see. Well, you certainly are a refreshing change to the usual Majestik personnel. I think I'm going to enjoy this."

Ernie was perplexed at what she was referring to. But to her, she definitely had him there for her own prurient interests, not a candidate for a suitor.

He found that the Singaporean Spicy Short Ribs, that sounded so dangerously foreign, were, in fact, wonderful. He eventually polished off the meat from the last short rib bone, and complimented her. "That was delicious. I really appreciate this—being in this big city and knowing no one."

"Would you like some dessert?"

"No, thanks. That was just right"

"Why don't you relax in the living room for a few minutes while I pick up?"

"Okay. Where's the bathroom?"

"Just down the hall there." Zelzah pointed with her long nose as she had both hands full of dishes, heading toward the kitchen.

On the way back, he noticed another door across the hall and peered in. What he saw impressed him. There was a desk with a computer, a big computer screen, a floor-standing copier/printer/scanner, and related equipment one saw in an office.

He wandered back into the kitchen. "That room looks like the bridge of a starship!"

"That's my workroom. I've got complete access to the company's entire files electronically here. I'm the only one who has unrestricted access, other than Mr. Bradford himself."

"Why do you have all this here instead of at the office?"

"I don't go out much. And I like working in the evenings or on weekends. Wilshire Boulevard is not very safe at night, and this way I can work at home at nights and on weekends safely. I've been with Mr. Bradford for twelve years now, in this, the third of three different companies. He's the top man," she boasted. She switched the conversation away from her. "Are you familiar with computers?"

"Nope. I've never used one."

"Oh my! Well, it's very easy. Do you know how to type?"

"Yeah, I took typing in high school."

"Here, let me show you." She took him into the room and booted up her computer. "Here's an example. What is the name of one of the persons you have as a claimant?"

Ernie recalled the name from one of the files of someone he had not seen yet and was going to see tomorrow. "Jeffrey Anderson. City of Lomita."

Zelzah typed in the details. "Here he is. He has been insured with Majestik for seventeen years. You can see his place of employment. He's married to a Mary, and he also has his two vehicles insured with us. A Chevy truck and a Toyota. He had a claim filed by his wife seven years ago, when someone hit her car when it was parked. You can see the details of his and her driver's license, social security numbers, and dates of birth."

"Wow, you can find out all about him! Is this information available to everyone at Majestik?" Ernie asked.

"Most of what I just showed you is. It's all voluntarily supplied to us by the insured in his application, from what the insurance agent obtained from him, or from previous claims where he or his wife had to fill out forms with that information, which we put in the computer for later. But Mr. Bradford and I have access to additional information bases."

"Does it take a long time to learn how to use this?"

She wanted to get on with what she had in mind for the evening, and so she had an alternative idea. "I tell you what. Why don't you come over Saturday and I'll teach you?"

"Great!" He jumped at the idea. As she shut down the computer, he asked, "Why don't I take you for a ride on the motorcycle as well? Would you like that?"

Her eyes lit up. "That would be fantastic! Let's go to lunch somewhere and make a full day of it." She could see he was curious. "Why don't I show you the rest of my little place? There isn't much left to show."

"Okay."

"Here, this is my bedroom," she said, leading him to the door, but she did not go in. She walked to another door. "And, this is an extra bedroom that I made into a gym to keep myself fit."

It had a workout bench, an exercise bicycle, a running machine, and a flat screen TV on the wall in front of the bicycle and running machine so she could watch when working out. On the wall was a dumbbell rack.

Curious as to the weight of the dumbbells, he picked the lowest ones, the twenty-five pounders, and moved his arms about in all directions as though to exercise with balsa wood.

Her eyes opened like a large-eyed lemur. "My God! I only use the fives and eights. Those big ones came with the set, or I wouldn't even have them." Ernie set them back in the rack, a bit embarrassed at making a show without meaning to. Zelzah stepped in closer and put her hands on his chest. "You are very well built," she said, her voice deepened to husky with primeval desire.

She looked into his eyes, put her arms around his neck, and pulled herself up to his mouth, kissing him long and passionately.

He was only a bit responsive, still out of his league. In close, he noted the fragrance of her expensive perfume.

She found him responding slowly and decided to go on further, forgetting the usual foreplay. "I want to do it in here." She kissed him again and then turned her back to him. "Take off my kaftan."

Assuming a "kaftan" was what she wearing, he pulled it up and off. She kicked off her slippers and slipped out of her black bra and thong underwear. She turned around once to the left, once to the right, showing her wares, a coquettish mating ritual.

Stark naked, even though he was still dressed, she stepped back, pulling him to the workout bench, and sat facing him. She then helped him out of his clothes. When faced with his sex, she complemented his size with, "Hmmm, nice!"

While he was still standing, she took him orally. When it was clear he was ready, she moved him back, got up and went to a drawer, and produced a black, four-foot long whip. It was braided entirely of leather, such that it tapered down to single strand to the tip that was a few inches long and shaped like a stingray's tail. It was obviously new, as it had the odor of new saddle leather.

She handed it to him. "I've not had a chance to try this yet and have been wanting to." She then turned, dropped to her knees, and lay down on her stomach on the workout bench, her derriere toward him. She pressed her stomach down, raising herself invitingly.

Side-stepping outward on her knees, a half inch each time, she worked her legs open to expose herself to the taker as though indifferent to whom it was.

"Warm me up, honey."

Ernie, startled, tried to comply and began whipping her lightly.

She put one of her hands under herself on her sensitive spot. "Harder! Harder!" she yelled out. Soon she lapsed into complete fantasy and yelled, "Hey, loggerman, fuck me like a trophy Canadian bull moose!"

∽∾∽

Ernie motored toward the Polynesian in a cotton candy fog that settled in like a protective blanket over the human activity of western Los Angeles County. The fog moistened his clothes as though to cleanse off the events of the day. As he neared the Polynesian, close to the ocean, he became engulfed in the sea moisture, reminding him of the coast in Washington State.

Refreshed, he took a deep breath. He thought of the events of the day, concluding with Zelzah. *I wonder what sex is like for a trophy Canadian bull moose?*

CHAPTER 25

Dan Doty entered Maxwell's office in the FBI building. "I think I have something regarding my brother, sir."

"Tell me."

"A week before his murder, Dave had gone to Las Vegas for the day, returning the same evening. His wife did not even know about it. I only found out by going to the travel receipts, which took a month to come in, and then quite a stack to go through before I found one for Dave. He got a regular open return ticket. The amount was below the amount that he needed for authorization. Since he did not have to explain why he was going there to anyone, he didn't bother, and thus he lost the safety net of having someone around here informed, not to mention the lost evidence."

"Okay, so what was he doing there?" Maxwell demanded, looking impatient.

"Dave had several stacks of things he either was working on, that were dead and going cold, or were otherwise not yet organized as they were too new. You know, like a single call that comes in from an anonymous informant giving a tipoff—you write it down in pencil or pen and it goes nowhere but you don't throw out the notes for a year."

"Yes, I know what you mean."

"I found some handwritten notes from Dave's desk that may be a lead. They were put in a box with things from his desk after the funeral. He had the name and number of an IRS auditor. I called the auditor and was able to reconstruct what had occurred. The auditor is a Russian immigrant hired by the IRS. His name is Dmitriy Bobrova."

Maxwell snorted. "We're hiring Russians now?"

"Well, at least one," Dan said, smiling at the comic relief, then went back to business. "There are a few shortages of labor. For example, America is always bringing in Philippine women for nurses as no one here wants those jobs, and they train them here free and get them green cards as nurses. After they get their license, they work here and send a good deal of their money back home. They look for husbands, and they usually divorce the husband later if they find one, just using him for a cash cow. Now it seems that the IRS has been a bit hard up for field auditors. This man is an immigrant from Russia. The Russian auditor said on his application that he was an accountant in Russia, so when he got his green card, he got a job at the IRS.

"He was doing a random audit of certain aspects of a major hotel/casino in Las Vegas called the Equator. From talking to him, I got the impression that he was full of piss and vinegar, but really was not that smart or well informed. He gave me the impression that he was out to bust fat capitalists who he assumed were living high on the hog at the expense of the proletariat."

Dan went over the differences in the crap table tallies with Maxwell and planted the suggestion that money laundering might be involved.

Maxwell was skeptical. "But that can't be all that unusual, can it? Some mistake? Some section of the casino that did not get its tally into the accounting room timely?"

"The difference was three million dollars in cash!"

"Wow! Money laundering?" Maxwell was catching on.

"Bingo!"

Maxwell leaned back in his chair. "So what happened with the auditor?"

"The auditor was used to corruption in Russia, having worked in St. Petersburg. Over there, the mafia is so strong, that he would be killed if he was to threaten to reveal something like that. And, when I talked to him, he was somewhat afraid of that here as well, based on movies he had seen about gangsters. He said he was so happy to be here in the United States, that he did not want to end it by being killed. In fact, when I asked him what was the best thing he liked about living in America, he answered, 'Warning shots.'"

Maxwell broke out in laughter so hard he nearly fell off his chair. "That's a good one!"

"Apparently, he's happy lifting himself from the proletariat to the fat cats," Dan mused. "So, scared, he said nothing about it to the accountants at the casino, and just concluded his audit over the expenses deducted, leaving the casino a clean bill of health. But when he returned, he decided to report the discovery to the FBI, and the call was routed to Dave, who followed up on it."

Maxwell sighed. "So far, we have a Russian with no experience in the US and who has a fertile imagination. If we get a warrant from a friendly judge, and it is tested, as it will be, in court over probable cause, how is it going to look with just that? The judge would probably conclude the warrant constituted an unconstitutional fishing expedition, and all the evidence obtained by it would be suppressed as tainted fruit from a poisonous tree of unlawful search. And then we'd lose our case."

Dan shrugged. "He had access to the bank statements, and he found that there were several banks that the Equator used. In one of them, he noted wire transfers to the Drensder Bank in Grand Cayman. He did not get copies, or ask for them, as he got scared at that point. But he said the transfers appeared to be substantial."

Maxwell raked a hand through his hair. "Well, there is no law against transferring money out of the country. If it was in the bank statements, there is a record of it and it cannot be hidden. What do you have as the purpose of the transfers?"

A degree of excitement quickened Dan's delivery. "I was able to find that the Equator owns, or is a major stockholder in, several other investments. It owns three car dealers for example, one in Reno, one in Tahoe, and one in Las Vegas. I was able to find out that it sells extended warranties for new cars that it sells at the agencies and for some other agencies as well. Those are a complete rip-off to the car buyer. There are so few claims that they are mostly all profit. The Equator may own or control one of more of these companies in Grand Cayman or in other small countries in the area such as the British Virgin Islands where I understand there are offshore insurance companies, but that ownership or control is not reported here in the US."

Maxwell continued to question the evidence for search warrants. "So the transfers to the Grand Cayman company are for purchases of extended warranties for new cars sold in Nevada, for insurance that is not a good deal for the buyer. That's still not illegal. Is the Equator handling the monies and transfers?"

"Yep. I think that Dave smelled a rat, and went up to Las Vegas to check on it. I think he suspected, as I do now, that the management of the Equator brings in drugs from Columbia, and from sales in the US there could be millions to launder. Large sums, like the three million the Russian saw, are placed in the money taken in by the crap tables. Handling large sums of cash is easy for a major casino, unlike clandestine transactions in a warehouse where everyone brings machine guns. The money from the crap tables is put in the count room of the Equator, very safely, as they are super protected from robberies. Then, to get rid of it or some of it so as not to create taxes, one method could be for the Equator to send it to Grand Cayman to purchase offshore insurance for the extended warranties. This may be done in part by sending the money to the offshore accounts for extended warranties that may not exist or which are represented for more than they were sold for to the car buyer. For example, they might send money for hundreds of policies that were never purchased, or for more than the actual cost to the car buyer. This is a neat way to get money out of the US. Once it is in Cayman, it can then be left there or taken elsewhere. The payment to the offshore insurance companies is deductible here for the premiums and therefore gives the casino a deduction for all policies purchased. Claims are made directly to the offshore insurance company or companies, and we have no access to those records. The offshore companies are paying very little on claims, and the result is huge profit with no tax.

"There may be other methods of getting rid of the drug money as well, but I don't know yet what that might be. As for large revenues from the crap tables, there are big time gamblers that play craps, and the deal with the casinos in Vegas and the IRS is that there are no 1099 forms issued to crap players, unlike some of the other games.

"There is a lot of money involved here. I'm pretty sure that this is why Dave went to Las Vegas. It's our only lead. He might have gone to the Equator. He might have gone to a suspect Nevada bank involved. I want to follow his footsteps, as best as I know how. If I'm right, whoever was involved might have ordered Dave's death to keep him from taking it further."

"Okay, so what exactly do you want?"

"I want you to authorize Kanno and myself to go up to Las Vegas and interview those banks to see if my brother was there."

"That's a sufficient connection for me," Maxwell agreed. "But let Kanno go alone so we don't look like we were conducting a vendetta. We should get more evidence. Kanno will have to see what he can get. Maybe then we can see about going for search warrants.

☙☙

Two days later Kanno walked into a major bank in Las Vegas, one of two of the banks that the IRS auditor, Dmitriy Bobrova, told Dave Doty about, according to the notes from his desk that were found after he was killed. He walked past the tellers to the bank officers in the rear, where a receptionist addressed him. "Yes?

"I wish to see the manager."

"Who may I say is calling?"

"Special Agent Bill Kanno, Federal Bureau of Investigation."

He gave her his card with the FBI seal on it, which she took very slowly, as though it might be infected with plague. It was intimidating for a bank receptionist to be addressed by the FBI.

Regaining her composure, she got up, pulled her tight skirt down into place, and went to an enclosed office in the back, obviously the manager's, closing the door behind her. Shortly she came out and led Kanno to the office of Arnold King, Manager. He looked to be about fifty five, five feet nine in height, and had a large, barrel-chested midsection with his stomach hanging over his belt. He wore a banker's two piece suit, gray, with a non-descript tie.

King rose to greet the FBI special agent. "Hello, Mr. Kanno. Please have a seat. How can our bank be of service to the FBI?"

The two sat, and Kanno smiled politely. "Thank you for seeing me without notice. I'm following up on another agent's investigation. His name was Special Agent Dave Doty." He passed Dave's picture across the desk. "Do you recall him coming here recently?"

"Yes, I do. He wanted to know about one of our major accounts. I told him that I could not reveal information without a search warrant, and he started threatening me with a federal audit of our bank to find out what he wanted if I did not cooperate. The last time auditors were in here, the staff time alone cost us a fortune just to assist and provide the records and information, so I told him what he wanted to know."

"What did he want?" Kanno asked.

The expression on King's face completely changed, and his lips tightened. He leaned forward in his chair aggressively. "I thought you said that you were following up on the same investigation. And you tell me you don't know what Special Agent Dave Doty was looking for? What's going on here? You go get your warrant! I'm not going to risk losing a major account to side up with the law on some government fishing expedition. If you have enough information to get a warrant to see the bank's records, then be my guest. Otherwise, good day to you."

But Kanno was good at this game. "Mr. King, Special Agent Dave Doty was murdered recently. While we do not believe at this time that you had anything to do with his murder, the end result of this investigation may bring about a number of charges in federal court. The charges may include counts of RICO, that is, if you have forgotten, Racketeer Influenced and Corrupt Organizations. That comes under Title IX of the Organized Crime Control Act of 1970, commonly known as RICO. Under a RICO indictment, it is entirely possible, and usually the case, to name any banker who is knowingly involved in handling money used in the charged criminal activity. If you withhold evidence, you may also get the additional charges against you of obstruction of justice. When you get out, as a felon, you will not be welcome in the banking business—or any legitimate business."

King blanched. He rocked back in his chair and looked at the man sitting across his desk. After a pause, he nodded. "Very well. I'll cooperate to the extent that I believe I must. But like I told the other agent, you cannot take any copies of records from here without a warrant. If that is not agreeable with you, then I'll call the bank's lawyers now and let you deal with them."

"That'll be fine."

"What is it that you want to know?"

"First, I want to know what Doty asked you when he was here about the Equator or its activities."

"He wanted to confirm a large cash deposit on a certain day into the Equator's bank account and also to confirm that wire transfers were made to the Drensder Bank in Grand Cayman. He did not have the exact amounts or dates, only approximate ones. I looked up the information, and confirmed that there were transfers from the Equator to the Drensder Bank, but I refused to give him the amounts or dates without a warrant. I also told him, like I'm telling you, if you want hard copies of the transfers you must get a warrant."

"Did Doty inquire into any other activities of the Equator?"

"No."

Kanno stood abruptly. "Thank you very much, Mr. King, for your cooperation."

"Can I assume now you won't try to drag me in on some RICO charge?" King asked, barely veiling the sarcasm.

"If we have no reason to believe you are involved, we certainly would not seek an indictment against you. I'll report that you have cooperated. I thank you for your time."

Through the clear glass portion his office wall, King watched Kanno walk through the bank and out the front door to the street. As soon as he was outside, King picked up the phone and quickly dialed a number. "This is Arnold King at the bank. I wish to speak to Mr. Manelli. It's important."

❧❦❧

The partners of the management group, Manelli, Indelicato, Innocenti, and Bastini, sat around the conference table in their wood-paneled meeting room at the Equator. The door was closed, and Manelli opened the meeting. "It looks like the hit Fiorello made on the FBI man Doty did not put a complete end to the evidence trail on our money laundering business. I got a call from King at our local bank today. Another FBI agent named Kanno came in with similar questions about the wire transfers to Grand Cayman. He may be on to our bringing in cash into the casino through the crap tables. King said he only confirmed that there were transfers, but he would not give any details."

"Do you think we should stop or slow down the transfers to Cayman for the extended warranty insurance?" Bastini asked the group, putting out his hands, palms up.

"Oh God, no!" Innocenti said. "That would show up in the books as a suspicious change. The change would make a no-ticeable trail for auditors."

"I think you are right, Fiorello," Manelli said, chewing on his lower lip. "But the problem did not go away when we hit the FBI guy."

"Sal, how does that car business thing work again?" Indeli-cato asked. "Do Mrs. Gunther's tax men and auditors know about the transfers to Grand Cayman?"

"Well," Manelli answered, "all transfers from the bank here in Nevada are shown in the statements we give them. That way we're covered. All she and her auditors know is that we buy auto extended warranties from the Grand Cayman Insurance Company and that it is profitable. They do not know that the Cayman company is not a real insurance company. But it is sort of like one. Money is taken in from new car buyers for extended warranties. That is financed along with the purchase of a car and we get the interest.

"The extended warranty could be for five years or fifty thousand miles, for example, additional time and miles on a car that has a three-year warranty limited warranty, and cover whatever the manufacturer does not cover, with exclusions, of course, for perishables like tires and wipers. We have an office there that is shown with Grand Cayman as a Grand Cayman Insurance Company, but no one knows that we four own it. Claims have to be made there, which is always done by mail. We have two people there who handle and settle claims.

"Those policies are such a rip-off that the business is very profitable. There are almost no claims on new cars for eight years as they are built so well, and if there is a problem the dealer normally fixes it. And the government requires smog related items which includes the entire drive train to be repaired by the manufacturer or dealer for fifty thousand miles. But in the rare event that a claim is not covered, we have the offshore office pay it so as not to cause complaints.

"But we pay so few, it is hugely profitable. In fact, it is so profitable that we tell the sales managers of the car dealers that they can sell the extended warranties for whatever they can get with the approval of one of our guys here in Nevada or in Cayman who knows about cars. If seven hundred ninety-nine dollars is asked for by the dealer in a sale, but three hundred ninety-nine is offered by the car buyer, the dealer is usually told to take it. And the portion of the interest paid on the car financing that is for the warranty also comes to us.

"Since the insurance is a Grand Cayman company, the US cannot audit it or find out anything about it. All the US or Nevada government can get is what we give them, as they cannot audit a Cayman company's books. There is huge profit generated, but it does not show up as profit for the Equator on its books. We create phony books there to show many more claims paid which we keep as profit for ourselves. We use that for tax free distributions to ourselves out of the country, and for buying drugs.

"We take in our drug profits, realized here from sales in the US, by showing the cash as having come through the crap tables. We put it into the count room and send that money off to Cayman for policies that were never actually bought, or we show them as having a much higher premium than was actually paid. But we do show on the books the purchases of insurance."

"Can't all the details be easy to find at an audit?" Indelicato asked.

"Easy? No," Manelli said. "There are many sales and each one is an individual sale. In order to see if all the insurance policies that are shown on the books as bought and paid for and for the reported price are correct, a group of auditors would have to get hold of every person who bought a car from the agencies where there was a sale of an extended warranty. Then the address of each buyer of each warranty would have to be found, and the car agencies are not going to give that up easily, as we own them. If the buyer lists were obtained, each individual buyer would then have to be located and contacted to see if he's willing to help. Many would be hard to contact. In most cases, the car buyer would have financed the car, and while he might be aware of some extra insurance, he probably does not know the actual cost as it is built into his monthly payments without being itemized. But to track down and contact the purchaser of each extended warranty, and get him to talk and show his warranty papers, all to see if it correlates to the records at the agency would be a huge task, taking an enormous staff. And if the records are demanded, we can produce a policy in his name, even if he does not have it, and say it's a mix-up in paper work. The policies are such a rip-off that it's like money in the bank.

"Unknown to Gunther, we then funnel money easily from Cayman to ourselves out of the US, or send to Columbia for more drugs. The drugs are brought in by the Columbians, some in submarines off Florida, and some through Mexico across the border, and sold here. We take some of the cash profit, but there is so much that the majority is laundered through the crap tables. So, it looks legit from here, and Mrs. Gunther's auditors have no reason to question the investment as it shows profit. Naturally, they don't have access to the transfers out of Grand Cayman, and our arrangement there allows us to control the statements," Manelli continued. "I think we should continue, and just take another careful look. If we stop, the lack of payments for offshore insurance will stick out on the books big time. And don't forget about our over-paying several vendors and service companies for the hotel that we own or control. If we stop paying those vendors and service companies we secretly own here, as that too would leave a trail of paper evidence—more specifically a cut off in expenses which would stick out at an audit. We can still launder money through the crap tables, as this drug money and the warranties are our cash cow.

"We might want to be careful not to send large sums at one time to Cayman, and instead keep the sums smaller than before. That will make it harder to audit. We should take a new and closer look at the books and procedures, to make sure we don't have any loose ends. So far, almost no one but us knows what we do, as only we have access to the tallies of numbers before the accountants get them. But if we stopped complete-ly, it would rock the boat."

Indelicato looked around at the others before speaking. "There is another risk here, long term. If the feds get onto our laundering money by the crap tables, which is not only done by us, but maybe by other casinos, we would be really hurting our regular business if the deal with the IRS is changed. The Nevada casinos' deal with the IRS not to require reporting of winnings from the crap tables could get revoked if the feds decide to disallow it. Can you imagine the high rollers coming in with their girlfriends and playing craps if they were to get reported for winnings on a federal tax form 1099? No one with money would touch the tables. It would leave a record of where they were—their wives could find out where they were, and also the IRS would have an income record. If that were to happen, we might as well take out the high-roller crap tables!

So, hitting the FBI man was worth it. By the way, Sal, does the banker King want another payoff?"

Manelli winced. "Yeah, the greedy fucking bloodsucker wants another twenty-five grand for tipping us off." He changed the subject. "This shows us all the more reason why we have to get the deal with the Indians. No problem like this will ever arise with the Indian reservation activities, and we can launder all the money we want to there. It'll be heaven! We have to have it."

Innocenti seemed eager to speak at this point and introduced a new topic. "I have obtained some information on the president of Majestik Insurance that may be helpful. I have found out who his regular hooker is. It only cost fifteen grand to find out. I'm going to approach her and see if I can influence her. Maybe we can get some extra assurance that Bradford will make the loan."

"Nice work, Fiorello," Manelli complemented.

The other two smiled and nodded in agreement.

Manelli then looked about the men to summarize the action to be voted on. "So, are we in agreement? We continue the crap table laundering, but not huge amounts until we decide differently. We stop large transfers to Cayman, keeping them smaller. We continue the over payments on vendors and suppliers so as not to rock the boat. We will take a new and closer look at the reporting system of cash in from the crap tables to make sure we don't have any leaks or weak spots if they come in with warrants or tough IRS auditors. We pay King his twenty-five grand. Fiorello's expenses are approved. Fiorello goes to work on his plan to get something on Bradford, using his discretion on how much to spend. Vote."

Indelicato nodded.

Bastini nodded.

Manelli nodded,

Innocenti smiled with satisfaction. "I'll get to work on it."

CHAPTER 26

Ernie pulled up to the home of the claimant Jeffrey Anderson, in the city of Lomita, a homeowner with a long, picket fence partly blown down from the storm. This was the one that he had checked up on at Zelzah's computer, and he felt embarrassed for having done so.

The fence came up right along the driveway and ran all the way to the back of the lot, which was an unusually narrow one, fifty feet wide, but three-hundred feet long, with a cedar fence on either side. On the driveway side, a section of the cedar fence had blown over. The owner had phoned in the claim before the earthquake, so the damage to the fence could not have been caused by the quake. The owner was seventy-five, according to the computer records Ernie had searched at Zelzah's.

Ernie went up to the old fashioned front porch and rang the doorbell. "Sir, I'm from Majestik," he announced to the elderly man who came to the door. "Here's my card. I'm here about the fence. I saw it from the drive, but I'd like a closer look. Will you show me and explain what happened?"

"Well, how about that? Finally someone comes out! This is welcome attention." The old man came out of the small house, and, with some difficulty, came down the several porch steps step at a time, apparently due to bad knees. He led Ernie to the side and back to show him the damage. He pointed toward downed cedar pickets from the fence lying on the ground. "All that blew over in the storm. I had the fence put in eight years ago on both sides and the back. Before it was a chain link fence that was pretty well gone with rust. The cedar fence held up until this storm. A big tree in the back obscured most of the back section of the cedar fence, but there was no apparent damage there or anywhere except to the front section where apparently the high wind had less obstruction to prevent damage.

"Young man, I'm sorry, but I have to tell you I'm pretty mad! All I got from your company was a letter from a Jessica Bloom saying that I get nearly nothing. I got an estimate for three thousand eight hundred dollars to fix it, but she told me that since the fence is on the property line, that she would only pay half, even though I paid for the whole fence! Then she said that since the fence has a maximum life of fifteen years, that she would cut that in half again to depreciate it. Cutting the three thousand eight hundred in half to nineteen hundred, then in half again to nine hundred fifty, and after the five hundred dollar deductible, I end up with four hundred fifty dollars! What bullshit! It'll cost me three thousand three hundred fifty dollars just to repair the damn fence." He started breathing hard as he thought about how Jessica Bloom and Majestik were cheating him.

Ernie could see the man working himself up and became a bit concerned.

"I paid for the entire fence, not just half," the man explained. "Just because I put it on the property line with the neighbor's consent doesn't mean that I should lose the benefit of insurance. They took my premiums hungrily, but when I make a claim, they try to cheat me!"

"I'm sorry you feel that way, sir," Ernie said. "I will not try to cheat you."

Anderson peered at him as if he was an eccentric. "Are you by any chance new to the insurance business?"

"That's true."

"Okay, I understand. It's nothing against you personally. I can't fix it myself, as I have a detached retina, bad knees, and a bad heart, so I cannot do anything strenuous."

Ernie thought Anderson was going to have a heart attack if he was not calmed down soon. "Is the repair company close by?"

"Yeah. It's just a fellow who does general contracting—it's

not really a company. He does odd jobs around this neighborhood."

"Call him, and see if he'll come over."

In a half an hour, an older, white Chevy pickup drove up. It had dents and showed wear. Out came an energetic young man. "Hi, Mr. Anderson."

"This is Ernie from the insurance company."

Sticking out his hand, the young man said with a smile, "Hi, I'm Mark Applegate."

"Ernie, from Majestik." He looked over at the partially downed fence. "How come this fence is going to cost three thousand eight hundred dollars to fix? It looks like it could be done in a day."

Applegate pointed at the fence. "You add up all those cedar pickets, then the four-by-fours to hold them have to be set in concrete, and you have to put out quite a bit of money. That'll take at least three days. Then the pickets have to be painted white, easily another day. When I don't make two hundred a day, I can't pay for my expenses, especially since I have to take the time to bid and to go collect materials. I'm lucky when I get paid three or four days out of five, and there are lots of slow times. Then I've got a helper, a Mexican. My helper gets ten bucks an hour, and I buy his lunch. I need to get ten per cent profit to pay for the tools, saw blades, and such."

Ernie glanced at the fence again. He looked at Anderson then at Applegate. "Why do you need to replace all the downed pickets? It looks like most of them that came down just blew off and are still good and usable, and they're already painted white. I tell you what. You go over and get the replacements for the broken four-by-fours, a ninety-pound sack of quick-set concrete, and replacements for the broken pickets, and come back with them and the tools. I'll put up the pickets with you. That'll only take the rest of the day at the most, and then you can come back tomorrow and touch up with paint and clean up. Since you only have to paint the few new posts and pickets, touch up the others, and clean up, you can be finished tomorrow early. I'll pay you for two full days work."

Applegate shook his head. "I haven't got much in my account right now as things have been a little slow lately."

Ernie sighed. "I'll go with you and pick up the materials. I have a company checkbook. Let's go."

Anderson stood back, taking it all in, speechless, as Applegate and Ernie got into Applegate's pickup and drove off.

The two returned in an hour with all the materials, and Ernie took charge of putting up the posts, using Applegate as a helper as well as his tools, which were in a metal box in his truck bed. Anderson brought out a chair to the side of the house to watch the show, and his wife came out for a while, bringing her husband his medicine. She also brought out iced tea for everyone. Applegate was no match for Ernie's skill or speed with lumber. Within three hours they had put up the four-by-fours that had fallen or broken, set them in quick drying-cement, and replaced the broken pickets. By dusk they were done. All that remained was the paint touch up the next day, which Ernie concluded that Applegate could handle.

He slapped Applegate's back. "Now, even though you may not work a full day tomorrow, I'll pay you for two full days at your two-hundred-a-day rate, plus the ten percent for your profit as promised. I'll give him an insurance company check, like I used for the materials, made payable to Mr. Anderson and you for the amount of four-hundred-forty dollars. I already bought the paint and disposable brushes, which you can use tomorrow. I want you to do a good job. And I want the place cleaned up completely when you've finished. When it's done, he can endorse the check and give it to you. But I don't want any sloppy painting. And you clean up good. Agreed?"

"Sure."

Anderson gave his silent assent by not objecting to what he heard and still seemed spellbound at what he'd witnessed. Ernie opened his file on the seat of his motorcycle and filled in the release form. He wrote out one of the company drafts and handing it to Anderson. "Here's a check for four-hundred-forty dollars, and you must sign this release and settlement form. You will give the check to Applegate when he finishes and cleans up, okay? The repair will have cost you nothing."

Anderson signed the form, took the check, and shook Ernie's hand vigorously. "That was fucking amazing! I'm going to write the company about you."

CHAPTER 27

Evette's pager rang in her purse at the salon where she having her nails done. Like most hookers, she did not respond to calls unless it was on the call back. She assumed that if she had the number of the person calling, it provided identification of the caller and a measure of security, which, in reality, was false. She looked at the number in the pager and called it on her cell phone. "Yes?"

Innocenti hesitated. "Evette Evil?"

"Yes."

"This is Fiorello. I have been referred to you. Are you available now?"

"Yes. Where are you?"

"I'm at the Wilshire Hotel. Room 426."

"I can be there in an hour. Will that work out for you?"

"Yes, that'll be fine."

"Honey, I charge three hundred fifty dollars, plus tip."

"Fine."

❧❧❧

A tall, sexy woman, wearing a long, lightweight, tan coat that wrapped around in a double breasted fashion with a belt pushed the doorbell of room 426 of the Wilshire Hotel. Innocenti opened the door.

"Fee-rello?"

"It's Fiorello."

"Sooorrrrry, honey. Fee-o-rello."

"And you are Evette?"

"Yes, honey."

"Come in."

Walking in, she took off her coat and laid it over a chair after setting down an oversized purse with a shoulder strap, which carried her specialized equipment for the desires of customers who utilized her specialty. This first timer had not advised her of what he desired, but her reputation, name, and referral base was largely for the same type of service. The coat off, her long, sensuous figure showed. Her thighs were exposed between her black, knee-high leather boots and her leather mini skirt. A black leather vest revealed cleavage where it was fastened in front with a chrome chain. Her breasts were enlarged by a plastic surgeon, and the effect of the outfit was that she was gorgeous and race-ready for rough loving.

Innocenti sat in a chair and took in the show.

She sat on the arm of the couch. "Could I have the money now, honey?"

"Sure." He had the money ready in his shirt pocket, and handed it to her.

"Thanks, honey." She put the money in her bag then stood in front of him, modeling herself by turning around and raising her skirt high enough to reveal that she wore no underwear. A scent of perfume was noticeable as she exposed herself. After showing her heart-shaped backside, she said, "Honey, have you been naughty and need a little discipline?"

She went to her designer bag and pulled out a braided leather whip. She reached over with the out-stretched whip so that the handle rubbed the inside of Innocenti's thigh and over his sex.

Not responding to the show, Innocenti scowled at her. "I'm Fiorello Innocenti. I want you to do me a favor. If you do it right, you'll get ten thousand dollars."

"Say, what is this?" Evette said, jumping back. She headed for her coat to be ready to leave in a hurry.

"Sit down, Julie!"

Her face dropped. She stood still, gripped with fear.

"Sit down," Innocenti said this time in normal voice.

She sat down on the bed with her heart pounding. Was it a

bust? "How do you know my name?" Her act as dominatrix had vanished, Innocenti having taken over completely as the dominating one.

"You are Julie Bailey, youngest of two daughters of Phil and Valerie Bailey of Salt Lake City. Their other daughter, your sister, Iris works as a cocktail waitress at a casino in Reno called the Jackpot. You live in Marina Del Rey."

"You're police!"

"No. I'm one of the managers of a casino in Las Vegas, and also the Jackpot in Reno where Iris works."

"You're part of the mob!" Her voice broke in fear. "What do you want from me?"

"You are seeing Robert Bradford every week at this very hotel. You're going to do me a favor."

"I don't wanna get involved in anything."

"You already are, Julie. And we can get to your sister Iris."

"Are you going to do anything to my sister?"

"You just do me this favor, and no harm will come to anyone. Understood?"

She hesitated. "What do I have to do?"

"All I want you to do is next time you get a call from Robert Bradford, you call a number and tell the man that you are coming over here, and what time. Make sure that the appointment is at least an hour and a half away. He'll check in with our connection at the desk, and be given a room number that the clerk will make sure is assigned to Bradford. He'll then come at once and set up a camera in the room up there on the cabinet." He pointing to the armoire against the wall, with shelves and drawers, and a pull-out flat screen TV in the center.

"All of the rooms of this type have the same cabinet and layout. Your session will be videotaped. The mini camera will be on top, and not noticed. You make sure that he is in view of the camera, so we get him on tape. That's all you have to do. If you do it well, you will get ten thousand."

"Fuck you! He pays me five hundred, and I'll lose him over this." She got up, and went for her coat and bag to leave.

Innocenti moved surprisingly quick to block her exit, stopping her with his hand on her throat, lifting her off the ground with just the strength of his arm.

She became very frightened as though a pit bull was about to rip her throat out.

When Innocenti relaxed his hand, she backed up and sat back down on the bed. An eternity of several moments passed.

Innocenti relaxed his expression somewhat, having achieved compliance. "Bradford will tire of you soon, anyway. And I'm not asking. This is something you are going to do. Or he won't want to see you any more with scars on your face. And your sister will also have a similar problem."

Very afraid of the mob, Evette concluded he would do what he threatened and, as a prostitute, she was not one to go running to the police for help. "When do you want it done?"

"The next time he calls. All you do is call this number that I'm going to give you and come to the room you are told to by the desk clerk. You just make sure that Bradford can be seen from the top of the cabinet where the camera will be when you get him in the room. It will be just like this one, and everything else will be taken care of. When you finish, you will get a call within a day and you will be told if everything went as planned, and how your money will be delivered to you. Got it?"

"You leave my sister alone. And I want my money right after I do it."

"You have made a movie before, and you only got twenty-five hundred for the whole movie. I have it. It's named *Mistress Discipline*. So you're no newcomer to films. You will be paid right away, within a day after if you do it. And you can keep the three-fifty."

CHAPTER 28

In his apartment at the tropical Polynesian that night, Ernie read the in the next claim file. Majestic insured Derrick Cameron. Cameron brought a lawsuit against Linda Conners.

She told him that she was going to sue him, and he told her to go ahead and gave her the name of his insurance company Majestik, who she then wrote.

> *To: Majestik Insurance Company:*
> *This is to notify you that I have a claim against Derrick Cameron for sexual harassment.*
> *Unless the lawsuit against me by him is dropped, I will sue.*
> *I was economically forced to have sex with him, which is against the law.*
> *Linda Conners*

There was also a letter in the file from Jessica Bloom to the insured Derrick Cameron.

> *Dear Derrick Cameron:*
> *Majestik has reviewed the claim made by Linda Conners for sexual harassment. From the evidence presented, and from my phone conversation with you, it does not appear the claim arose in the course and scope of employment at the insured premises, which is a requirement of a sexual harassment claim.*
> *Accordingly, Majestik must deny coverage.*
> *However, Majestik will reconsider the matter if you*

present further evidence that the alleged harassment occurred in the course and scope of employment.
Sincerely,
Jessica Bloom

Ernie felt a sense of foreboding if this claim was not solved. Next in the file was an internal memo:

It appears the company division that was updating policies really dropped the ball on this one. When Majestik started adding sexual harassment claims as exclusions some years ago, the insured was supposed to get an updated policy. Apparently, the company slipped up and did not send him one. The general liability of the building insurance insures all liability unless it is excluded. This includes sexual harassment since it is not listed as excluded in this older policy. Because this is a commercial policy, unless the harassment did not occur at the premises or not in connection with work, it is covered. The claimant in this case contends the sexual harassment was in connection with work, but the insured denies that it was.

The policyholder, Cameron, has never had a claim except auto. Majestik also insures his residence, mountain cabin, two cars, a pickup, and his boat at the marina. But the insured has sued the claimant for money he says she owes him, and she threatens now to counter sue for sexual harassment. This is the sort of thing that often occurs, a claim brought as a counterclaim that would not have been brought otherwise.

Underwriting has been notified on the fact that he has an older policy, and they will update his policy at the anniversary so as not to make it appear we are changing the policy mid-term. The policy renews in four months. However, coverage under the existing policy will continue for this claim as the event occurred during the policy period. I will deny the claim and hope that the insured will drop his claim against her. Or, possi-

bly, the claimant may lose interest and will not file a counterclaim. The claimant must first file a complaint with the Department of Fair Employment and Housing or the Equal Employment Opportunity Commission within one year and get a "Right to Sue" letter. Then she can bring an action against the insured. But any lawyer she goes to will know this.
Jessica Bloom

There was an answering letter to Linda Conners.

Dear Linda Conners:
This is to inform you that the nature of your claim is not one within the scope of employment as it did not occur at the workplace, which is a requirement for a sexual harassment claim. You were not on the payroll of Mr. Cameron, and your only relationship with him was a personal one, which is not considered sexual harassment in California. Therefore Majestik is compelled to deny your claim.
Sincerely,
Jessica Bloom

Ernie sat back and could see the foreboding future of this claim. *I should check this out. This looks like a lawsuit waiting to be born. Once it is filed, like an unwanted child, it will not go away until it runs its course. The girl has been sued by a policyholder, and if she goes to a lawyer, they will file a counter suit for sexual harassment, and then the thing will get grow like cancer. Once that is done, she and her lawyer will not let the claim go for little or nothing. What is it with Jessica Bloom? She never goes out to meet the people in the field to fix these things, and they fester like an open wound. No wonder a lot of the claims end up as lawsuits.*

ᜡᜡᜡ

Ernie pulled up to the office of the contractor and real estate developer Derrick Cameron. Inside, he announced to the attractive, but older, receptionist, "I'm Ernie from Majestik Insurance. Here is my card. I'm here to see Mr. Derrick Cameron."

"Does he expect you?"

"No. I came without an appointment."

"Are you selling insurance?" she asked.

"Nope. I'm here about a claim. I'm the field representative from his insurance company, Majestik."

"Just a moment." She got up and went down the hallway. Reappearing, she smiled. "Mr. Cameron says he is delighted that someone from the insurance company finally came out, and he will be happy to spend as much time with you as you wish."

She led Ernie through a hall to a large office with a big desk behind which sat Derrick Cameron. He was healthy looking, in his late forties, tanned, and dressed in cotton slacks with a short-sleeved shirt. Against a wall below a window was a draftsman's desk topped with blueprints. On a table against the other wall was a miniature three-dimensional real estate housing development with green trees, streets, and houses with red tiled roofs. It looked to Ernie like something that would be fun to put tiny model trains on.

"Come in, please." Cameron got up and shut the door, indicating the matter was not one for the usual construction team to sit in on or interrupt.

"This claim is pure horse shit!" he started in. "I had to pay for her rent because I co-signed for her apartment, and when she wouldn't pay it back and refused to talk to me, I had my lawyer sue her ass. Now the bitch says she'll counter-claim against me for sexual harassment to try to beat me out of my money."

Ernie studied Cameron to size him up. "How did you come to co-sign for her on her rent?" he asked matter-of-factly.

"I met her at a bar at Hermosa Beach. She was out of work and getting evicted the next day. So the next morning, I took her to an apartment that she wanted to move into, but because she had bad credit, they would not take her unless she had a co-signer. So I co-signed for her and she moved in. But she never paid the rent. After fourteen fucking months, I was able to get her to move out, but only when I absolutely refused to pay any more rent."

"Did you actually pay the rent?"

"I had to, in order to keep my credit rating up. I do work that requires bonding, and I cannot afford to have a bad credit report. I paid every month for her for fourteen, fucking months straight. The rent was a thousand a month"

Ernie decided to approach the subject differently. "Were you having an affair with her?"

"Well, I was screwing her, if that's what you mean. But that started the first night I met her. I took her to my boat in the marina and porked the bitch senseless. Nice piece of ass. In fact, she likes it in the ass."

"Was she working for you?" Ernie asked, wondering if the office policy was supposed to cover that. If there was sexual harassment in the course and scope of employment, then it could come under the coverage for sexual harassment. If it did not occur during work or at work, then the claim would not be covered.

"She wasn't on the payroll. But she did some type some reports for me."

"Where did she type the reports?"

"At the apartment, and also on the boat once or twice on the way to Catalina."

Now I see the problem, Ernie mused. *She* was *working, but not on the payroll. Her pay was free rent. But he says it was a loan. Most likely she said she would pay it back, but never had the capacity to do it. This is one of those messes over insurance coverage.*

"Was there any sex here in the office?" he asked, thinking the question relevant to whether or not there should be coverage under the policy.

"She would come by and give me head. Boy, that bitch could really gargle balls, you know what I mean? She sucks dick like a Shop Vac! Here, I have some pictures of her you can have."

Cameron took pictures out of his desk, which were taken in an apartment with a naked girl doing things to herself with various objects. The picture on top utilized a green cucumber. Another used a larger, purple eggplant.

Having sex at the office only made things more complicated, Ernie realized, but did not say aloud, not wanting to say too much just yet. "Were these taken at the apartment?"

"Yeah. But I didn't take them. She took them herself. She sent them on to me to try to keep me from getting pissed off about paying her rent. She set up a still camera, as well as a video camera on a tripod, and posed for them. Here's the video she took of herself as well," he said and passed a digital memory stick to Ernie. "I made a copy already. She uses various objects on herself in the tape. There are no other people involved—I guess she wanted me to think that everything was exclusive for me."

Ernie took the pictures and the memory stick video for his file. "Have you been in touch with her since you sued her?"

"Yeah, she called and tried to get me to drop the suit. I told her that I would take time payments, or she could work it off, or whatever. She said she'll repay, but I haven't seen a single cent. I don't think she ever will. Fuck her."

Ernie sighed. "There may be some question as to whether or not this is an insured event. You realize that the insurance company will not pay if it feels the event is not included in your coverage?"

"What do I pay insurance premiums for if you're going to deny any claim?"

"Please, just give me a chance to work on it, and I'll get back to you."

"Okay."

∽∾∽

Ernie rolled up on his motorcycle to the apartment of Linda Conners. When he knocked on the front door, an attractive girl came, who looked to be about twenty-eight.

"Yes?"

Ernie recognized her from the photographs, even with her clothes on. "Hi. I'm Ernie, from Majestik Insurance. My card. I'm here about your claim against Derrick Cameron. I see that you do not have a lawyer as yet, and therefore I can still talk to you. You have been sued by Mr. Cameron and are threatening to file a cross-claim for sexual harassment. I would like to find a way to resolve the claim if you would care to talk to me."

"Come in," she said, standing back just enough to allow him entrance. "This is quite a change. I got a letter from someone named Jessica Bloom, and all she did was to tell me the claim was denied. I have an appointment with an attorney next week. You must be new or something."

"Yes. I'm a temporary field representative. Jessica Bloom did not get out in the field, and now she's on maternity leave. I'm taking over this claim, so you can take it up with me. Can you tell me about the problem so I can try to fix it?"

Relieved, she sat down and motioned Ernie to a seat. She opened right up. "I met Derrick at a bar in Hermosa Beach. When we met, I was out of work, behind in rent, and being evicted. Since I have bad credit, he co-signed for me at a new apartment so I could have a place to live. I was going to start paying the rent, but I never could get enough ahead to pay it. He told me not to worry about it, so I didn't. After a year, he said he wouldn't pay any more, so I had to move out. I was there another two months, and then I moved in here with two other girls. Now my rent is way less."

"What's all this about sexual harassment?"

"Derrick would come over and sleep with me all the time. That's why I never took on a roommate over there. And he liked it when I was available, so I didn't look for work. So he got the benefit of me and the place, and now he wants me to pay for it. I don't have the money to repay him."

"Are you still seeing him?"

"Fuck no! I broke it off when I had to move, but he still wants me. I think he sued me just because he is pissed off that I won't see him anymore. Anyway, he's married."

"Why do you think you have a sexual harassment claim if you were providing him with pictures and a descriptive video?" Ernie said, wanting to let her know that he had the porno pictures and video.

"Because he was paying the rent, and I was doing him good. He liked the pictures and the video. He said he got off on them when I wasn't around. His lawsuit is really to get more of it."

Ernie decided to get down to the point. "What are you looking for?"

"I just want him to drop the lawsuit against me."

"Did you do any work for him at the apartment?"

"Do you mean for his job? Yeah, when he'd come by, sometimes, after we would sleep together, I did some help organizing papers for him on his bids and by typing reports. He would bring over a briefcase and work for a while in the afternoons. He said that it was a chance to get things done as no one could bother him. Why?"

"I have an idea," Ernie said. "Did you have any other income last year?"

"No, I didn't get a job until after I moved out. I'm now working as a secretary at a real estate office. I got off early today. You were lucky to catch me."

"If you helped him in his work, would you mind making a declaration to that effect, and considering the rent as your pay?"

"Well, that is sort of what it actually was, apart from the screwing."

"Let me step outside, and call Cameron on my cell phone to see if I can work something out. I won't be long."

"Okay."

Ernie went outside and walked down the block out of earshot. He rang up Cameron.

"Mr. Cameron, this is Ernie. I'm nearby Linda's apartment. I may have something. Did you do some work over at her apartment that she helped you with?"

"Yeah, that's true. She's good with numbers and helped with some bids I was working on. Why?"

"She had no income last year. What if I get a statement from her that she took the rent money as her pay for helping you, and you send her a federal form 1099 for the amount, which makes it deductible to you as a business expense for outside help. Twelve of the fourteen months were in the last calendar year, so you can deduct twelve thousand dollars. It would then become income to her, but since she didn't make any more money, the rent at one thousand dollars for twelve months, or twelve thousand dollars earned in one calendar year, after deductions, will still keep her in a no tax bracket. That way you get the deduction for the money and get something out of it. Anyway, even if you continue to sue her and win, you can't collect as she is judgment proof—broke, that is."

"Say, that's a brilliant idea! At least that way I get something for my money. I wish I had some a hustler like you working for me. Interested?"

"Oh, no thanks. I'm a logger and only here for a while. Now, I'll see if Linda agrees, as it will become reportable income to her. I'll settle with her if that is okay with you then."

"Shit, why not? Go for it!"

Back inside, Ernie said to Linda, "I can settle everything this way. You sign a statement that you did work for Cameron's company at the apartment, and that you got the rent as the compensation. He will send you a federal tax form 1099, the form for independent contractors, and report it as income to you. You'll have to go to a tax man, unless you can do it yourself, and file a tax return. You take whatever deductions you can, and you will have no tax to pay, or almost none. You will have to agree to back Cameron up at any audit that might occur, saying that you worked for him. But that is honest and true since you actually did do work for him there. As it was off his business premises and done on your furniture and not at specified hours, it should be okay that he did not take deductions from your pay, and you were thus paid correctly as an independent contractor. He'll drop the suit, and everyone's happy. Plus, if you accept, I will give you an insurance check today for one thousand dollars in case you have any tax to pay, and to pay for the accountant to do your taxes. You are responsible for filing your own tax return, and for any excess taxes you might have to pay—but I don't think there will be any unless you neglect to file. So you must go to a tax person as soon as you get the 1099 form from Cameron and file a return to avoid interest penalties in case there is any tax to be paid. If you have no tax to pay, you can still keep the thousand, or any part of it that is left after taxes. What do you think?"

She got up quickly and kissed him on the cheek. "Wow, fantastic!"

"Okay, I'll put this problem to rest." He wrote up the statement for her to sign, that she took the rent money as pay for her assistance to Cameron's business as an independent contractor, and a separate settlement agreement on one of his forms. He made sure that he got her social security number and a mailing address so that Cameron, on the other end, would to be able to get the deduction for payment to an outside contractor and so his accountant would know where to mail her 1099 form. He wrote up a separate release for her as to her sexual harassment claim as well.

"Where do I sign?" she asked, as she cast a flirtatious glance his way.

"Here and here." Ernie pointed. "I'll take these to Cameron and get his signature, which, if you see here—" he said, pointing to a clause, "—requires him to dismiss the suit, and you to settle and waive any claims against him."

She signed the agreement. "Fine."

Ernie gave her a copy and wrote out a check to her for one thousand dollars. "Once I get Cameron's signature, I'll mail a completed copy to you, and get him to send you a 1099 form showing the rent as income. He'll dismiss his lawsuit, and you two can go on your own ways. I'll also include in the mailer some pictures and a video of you that I got from Cameron."

The mention of the video caused her no apparent embarrassment. "Instead of mailing the pictures and video to me, why don't you bring them back later today and take me for a ride on your motorcycle? I'll have roommates here later, but we could go to your place if you want."

This is trouble waiting to happen, Ernie realized. "I'm sorry, but after I go to see Cameron, I still have to try to make one more stop today. A lady has a big coral tree down in Pacific Palisades, and that is the sort of thing that I do best. I may be able to handle the tree yet today. Maybe another time."

"Anytime."

As Ernie drove off with the *chuga chuga* rumble of the big V-twin engine making its distinct sound, he could not help but smile about what he had heard from Cameron. '*Sucks dick like a Shop Vac!*'

☙❧

As Ernie walked up to his sliding glass door at the Polynesian, his chainsaw in hand with coral tree sawdust all over it as well as himself, he smelled like a freshly cut coral tree, since he had just cut down one in Pacific Palisades.

Three gorgeous girls in bikinis—two blondes and a brunette—were swimming in the Torrid pool. They were obviously good friends, splashing about.

"Wow! Is *zat* a real chainsaw?" one said.

Proudly, Ernie held it up. "Yep. It sure is."

"Why don't you join us in *za* pool?"

"Maybe in a while if you're still there. I have to do some work just now."

Inside, he put his saw on the coffee table, wiped it clean of the soft coral wood, and then ran his sharpening file across each of the cutting teeth. After a quick shower, he then focused on the next file—claim number 4400326. It was a case where lawyers were involved, and there were legal papers. A girl named Michelle Jones of Van Nuys, age seventeen, was badly burned and scarred. There were several pictures in the file, before and after. She had been a beautiful girl, and now was something out of a horror movie, with scarring and discoloration on her face. Her life had definitely changed. The report said she and her parents had lived in a rented townhome that burned, the cause of which was a fire in the adjacent townhome. The two townhomes shared a common wall, and the fire spread to her unit. Majestik insured the next door unit where the fire started for fire loss and liability. Michelle Jones, alone that night as her parents were out, was asleep in her bedroom on the second floor, trapped, and badly burned when the fire swept through her townhome.

Inside the file was a bill to the neighboring townhome from an electrical business named Marlow's Electric. The bill was for fixing a plug at the insured townhome for sixty dollars for the service. The bill was six months old and stated, *There is a problem with the wiring. It is not up to code and is a fire hazard. Recommend you have it fixed before it causes a fire.*

An investigator for Majestik had obtained it by checking with other townhome owners as to what electricians were known to have been used by them for electrical problems. The name of Marlow had been provided. The investigator contacted Marlow and was told about the bill. He went to him and got a copy. The repair bill and its warning clearly showed that the insured, if the owner had not heeded the warning of the faulty wiring, he would be negligent and the insurance company liable to the poor girl next door for her nearly fatal burns. It was a one million dollar policy. As Ernie looked at the poor girl's picture, he thought that she might have been better off dead than having to live with such serious burns.

"Yaaaaaaah," a girl's loud voice came from the pool.

Ernie's thoughts were disrupted by the noise. He got up, went to the glass door, and looked out. The three, gorgeous, German girls were still in the pool.

One of the girls saw him, and shouted, "Hi! Come in!"

Time for a little rest and relaxation, he conceded.

Once in the pool, one asked Ernie in her German accent, "'Vere are you from?"

"Sedro Woolley, Washington"

"What do you do?" another asked.

"I'm a logger, but I'm here in LA working temporarily for an insurance company."

The three looked at each other for someone to interpret "logger." One told the others, *"Holzfäller."*

"Wow! A *holzfäller!*" one said. "I always vanted to meet a *holzfäller.*"

"What do you all do?" Ernie asked.

"We are hostesses for Lufthansa. That airline puts us up here ven we have a layover in Los Angeles. We don't fly out until tomorrow afternoon. Vant to party with some nice German girls?"

"Sure!"

"*Willst du mit mir voegeln?*" one of them asked.

"*Ich bin geil,*" another said.

Ernie had no idea what they were saying, but figured that it related to something fun. "I don't speak German, but I think it is party time! I have some jug wine in my refrigerator. Does anyone want some?"

Inside Ernie's apartment, he tuned to a music station on the flat screen TV, and poured the wine. One, who seemed to be the leader or dominant one, took off her bikini and stood in the room with her legs a foot apart, facing Ernie who sat on the couch watching. The other two followed suit and took off their bikinis. Those two kneeled down, one in front of the girl standing, and the other in the back. They both went down to the floor with their heads, and one began to lick her leg very slowly in the front by starting at her big toe. The other girl did the same, but began licking at the back of the leg, starting at the heel. They both licked very slowly up toward the top of her legs, one in front, one in back.

Ernie thought, *Are they lesbians? Bisexual? Exhibitionists? Whatever, one thing is clear—they like to put on a show.*

But the show was only beginning.

CHAPTER 29

rnie looked out his glass door at the palms in the morning light. His eyes wandered down to the pool area, the turquoise water shimmering in the bright sunshine. He recalled the party.

He opened the door to the balmy morning and took several deep breaths. "Ahhhhhhhhhhh."

The company cell phone gave off a little beep. Opening it, he saw that there was a single message on the screen,

This is Judy Canton, secretary to Don McAteer. Please come to the main office on Wilshire today at 10:00 a.m. regarding file 4400326, claimant Michelle Jones. The staff attorneys want to meet with you about the file. Bring the entire file with you. Keep no copies.

❦❧

When he got off the elevator on the fifth floor, Ernie was somewhat surprised at how modest the attorney's office area was at Majestik. He always thought attorneys made lot of money in the big city. He was asked to go to a meeting room at the end of the corridor. The in-house attorneys had only little cubicles with five foot high separating partitions to work in like beginning secretaries. Their cubicles were not on the outside wall with windows, but separated from the outside wall by offices for more important people and a hallway in between those offices and the cubicles. The effect was that the cubicles were dreary.

The cubicles were staffed with young attorneys, busy doing their own typing. It looked like a sweat shop—the only things missing were the sewing machines and illegal aliens sewing.

The meeting room was on the outside wall and had one window. Two of the walls had bookshelves and law books. In the center was a cheap conference table with an artificial wood-grained top, with chipped spots. There were three young lawyers in the room, two men and a woman, all in their mid-twenties. The woman and one of the men were leafing through papers on the conference table, and one was putting papers into a paper shredder at one side of the room as fast as it would take the papers, which was slow as it was a cheap model.

"Hi, I'm Ernie."

"I'm Jason," said the one who was shredding papers. "This is John, and she's Carmen."

They acknowledged Ernie, but the shredding continued, and there were no handshakes. Carmen had long blonde hair with the curls showing three inches of dark roots. Ernie looked at her hair, and mused, *She looks like a hobo, like someone who lost everything and could no longer afford to keep up the bleaching. Would Marilyn Monroe have had dark roots if she'd gone bankrupt?*

Carmen's figure was exaggerated unattractively by her tight navy blue skirt cut above her knees with her heavy thighs and bulging rear stretching its seams.

The men had their suit coats off, and both men had the silly dress suspenders that Ernie had seen on yuppie businessmen in movies. The suspenders were connected by little spring clips. He concluded, *Those are so weak they wouldn't hold up anything you could work in, let alone do so with a few good tools in your pockets. They're just for show.*

"Did you bring the file?" Jason asked.

Ernie held up the file. "Yep. The one about the burned Jones girl, 4400326?"

"That's the one. Lemme see it." Jason took it, looked at the cover, passed it to Carmen, and went back to shredding documents. Carmen set the file down on the table and began leafing through it.

Ernie looked at the shredder. "What are you all doing?"

Jason continued shredding and looked up at Ernie. "This is called *discovery*. Are you familiar with it?"

"Nope."

Jason was a novice attorney and eager beaver, happy to explain his notion of his own expertise. "This claim has now been given to a lawyer. Michelle Jones, the girl who was burned, has made a claim through her lawyer that the fire that burned her started next door, caused by negligence of the next door neighbors. We insured the owners of the townhome next door. The owners next door, who we insured, were originally a couple but the husband died of cancer. Before he died, they moved out and rented their unit to a Korean couple, both of whom smoked, and who both smoked after dinner and then went for a walk the evening when the fire started.

"We have stated to the Jones' attorney that the fire was caused by the Koreans, claiming it was started by a cigarette that was not extinguished when they went for their walk. The Koreans were interviewed and admit to smoking after dinner, but deny they started the fire. The fire department investigator concluded that the fire had some minor attributes of an electrically caused fire, but there was not enough evidence to actually determine for certain that it was an electrically caused fire as so much was burned so badly that any evidence was destroyed.

"The Jones family and their attorney have not been able to come up with any evidence for the cause of fire, except the possibility of the Koreans smoking. If the fire was caused by faulty wiring, and the owners, who we insured, knew about that but did not fix it, Majestick would be liable to the girl. If the fire was caused by the Koreans, then she can only recover against them if she can prove they started the fire with their cigarettes. But the Koreans are not insured by us and have no insurance at all. They don't own anything, and so the toasted girl cannot recover against them. Screw her, anyway.

"Our fire investigator asked around and found someone that used Marlow's Electric for electric repairs and who knew the insured man that died of cancer. He said he got the referral for an electrician from the man who died of cancer, and the referral was Marlow's Electric. The investigator contacted Marlow, found out about the repair, and got a copy of the bill for a repair that was done six months before the fire, just before the Koreans moved in. The investigator sent us the repair bill which was put in the file. However, by an internal mistake, the entire file was sent to Jessica Bloom instead to us in the legal department. So, that is how you got it.

"The husband of the couple that owned the townhome died of cancer, and his widow does not know about the bill. The deceased husband paid Marlow in cash for the repair so the widow has no record. Marlow wrote in his bill a notice to the owner that there was faulty wiring that needed to be repaired. He was there to fix a bad plug, and no one told him to repair the faulty wiring. So he put it in his bill as a notice, but did not fix it. That bill is notice to the insured owners that they have to fix a hazardous condition, and the failure to do so is negligence that would be an insured claim. So we can't let them, or anyone, find out about that."

"I don't understand," Ernie said. "Why wouldn't the insurance apply even if the Koreans started the fire with their cigarettes? It wasn't Michelle's fault. The Koreans were tenants of an insured townhome."

"Hah! We got them there!" Carmen announced proudly as she continued looking through the file for the bill. "The owners of the townhome, before they rented it to the Koreans, used to occupy it as their residence, and that's when they bought our insurance as occupying owners. They moved out six months before they rented it out, but never changed the insurance to a policy that is for use by landlords. That is a different policy. The husband fell sick with cancer, and most likely his wife is so upset with everything that she never changed the policy to that of owners who rent their property. His wife just kept the same insurance policy in force, thinking she still had insurance, not knowing the difference between an owner's policy for those who occupy the property and one for those who rent the property. Our owners' policy excludes negligent acts of renters unless the policy is a renter's policy for someone renting the unit, which costs a bit more and has different terms. The faulty wiring was in the walls and was not something that the Korean renters caused. So the fire is not attributable to the renting Koreans and we would be liable to Michelle Jones if the widow knew of the notice from Marlow. Even though it was the husband who got the notice, the knowledge is imputed to the spouse who survives her husband.

"Since the owners did not change over to a policy for coverage including acts of renters, then if the Koreans started the fire with their cigarettes, there is no coverage."

She smiled proudly. "The bottom line is that Majestick is denying coverage. Not only are we denying coverage to Michelle, but also to the widow for the loss of her townhome. Great, isn't it? God, it's fun to be an insurance lawyer!"

Ernie was puzzled. "But why can't the widow just take the electric bill to the court and ask the judge to hold Majestik liable for the claim? Isn't there a legal procedure for that?"

"Yes," Jason answered, "She could win only if she knew about the electrical problem, as then it would not be caused by the tenants. She could put together a claim against Majestik for what is called declaratory relief, asking the court to determine that Majestik is on the hook for the liability as it was not the tenants' fault, and she would probably win.

"So as long as Michelle Jones and the widow don't find out about the Marlow bill, both Michelle and the widow have no claim to bring as they cannot prove it was not the Koreans who started the fire. That's why we wanted it from your file, to shred it."

Ernie's jaw dropped. "So you're leaving the widow without insurance for the loss of her townhome since it was rented as she did not have insurance to cover negligence of renters? And the Jones girl cannot make a successful claim against the widow for her burns?"

Carmen raised her head, as though getting ready to receive a medal. "Here it is! The bill from Marlow's Electric." She held it up like a trophy for all to see.

"Great!" Jason exclaimed. He took it from her and put it into the shredder, his eyes gleaming as the paper was torn into little strips.

Ernie heard the grinding noise of evidence being shredded. "Why shred it?" he asked.

Carmen looked at him with a rather condescending smirk. "The girl's attorney has sent us what is called a 'request for documents,' asking for all maintenance bills for the townhome where the fire started. We have to give him everything he asks for in a verified response. That means someone has to swear that what we are giving is complete, accurate, and all we have. If her lawyer got hold of the electric bill, he would find out about the electrician and contact him. That would kill us in the case and we would then be liable to the girl. The widow would find out, and we would have to pay for the loss of her town-home as well. This way we escape both very large claims. There is a million alone in personal injury coverage, and actu-al cash value loss coverage for the widow's townhome. That's a lot."

"Why do you call it *discovery*?" Ernie asked with a frown. "It should be called *destruction of evidence*."

"That's just our little joke," Carmen said, smiling and proud of herself and her accomplishments. "We do this all the time. We have even had to request more shredders, we do so much of this. Sometimes they overheat and break down as we regularly destroy so many boxes of paper."

"What do I do about the file now?" Ernie asked.

"Since it has gone into possible litigation with a lawyer, it's transferred here," John said. "Just leave it here, and we'll take over."

As Ernie rode away from the Majestik building, he felt dirty. *Ugly bunch, those insurance lawyers are. I feel sorry for the burned girl and the widow. And now I'm part of it, as the messenger with the evidence.*

❧❧❧

His next stop was in East Los Angeles. This was definitely Spanish town. The businesses' signs changed to Spanish, and the eating places all had Mexican foods listed as specials. The address turned out to be a dilapidated apartment building. A parking lot on the back side had space for his motorcycle. Ernie wondered if his bike would be safe there as he got off to go inside. He looked around, and no one was eyeing it. He had to go inside, so he had little choice and left it in the parking area and went inside.

Inside, he could smell the strange odors from cooking what he determined must be Mexican cuisine. There were barefoot children making lots of noise in the hallway running up and down. He knocked on the apartment door of Ms. Martinez. "Hi, I'm Ernie, from Majestik Insurance. I'm here about your auto accident."

"*Ola. Venga.*"

Ernie did not understand Spanish but he did understand body language. She motioned him in. The television was on, and set to a Spanish station with a daytime entertainment channel. "Did you get the car fixed yet? My picture shows the door damaged."

"*Si. Pero el coche no está aqui. Ah, la puerta. Mi novio tienne el coche hoy. Tengo el recive. Aqui está.*" She produced a piece of paper, and handed it to Ernie, after telling him, he assumed, that her husband had the car that day.

The paper she handed him was from a repair shop, showing repair to the right front door, in the amount of six hundred fifty dollars. It showed that it was paid. Ernie had in his file two pictures of the damage to the front door on the right side in his file.

"*Vea la puerta delantera.*" She pointed to the right front door in the picture that Ernie had in his hand.

"My file shows that the insurance company is liable to you for your damage, less the deductible of two hundred fifty dollars. The repairs are six-hundred fifty dollars, so I can give you the money now if you want. I can give you four hundred dollars. He wrote down the numbers and showed her the calculation. She seemed to understand. Ernie handed her a release form, which she signed.

"*Bueno.*"

Ernie wrote her a draft for four hundred dollars.

She smiled. "*Gracias.*"

As he went out to the parking lot in back, trouble was rearing its ugly head. Four Mexican gang types were surrounding his motorcycle. They all had shaved heads, baggy, home-boy pants that were not full length, and tennis shoes. All wore T-shirts and three had plaid, long-sleeved shirts over the T-shirts that were unbuttoned except for the top button at the neck. Apart from the difference in colors of the shirts, they might have been in uniform. As he approached, he could see that they all had tattoos, and many of them were blue made from ballpoint, meaning they were likely done in jail. All had funny little patches of whiskers at different spots about their mouths or chins.

The more aggressive one, who Ernie determined was the leader, looked at him as he approached. *"Orale Vato.* Nice ride. "

"Thanks." Ernie pretended not to notice any sign of trouble, put the file and materials in his saddlebag on the opposite side of his chainsaw, and mounted the motorcycle, hoping to leave without trouble.

"You like eeet? I like eeet too," the leader said. He turned to one of the others and said, *"Lo llevamos."*

The leader moved in and stood over the front wheel, putting it between his legs. He took out a pistol from the pocket of his loose pants and stuck it just inches from Ernie's face. He held it sideways, idiot style. It was obvious he was no marksman, not knowing how to hold a gun. The gun was a semi-automatic, the make Ernie could not identify, but the barrel looked to be a 9 mm. Even though the punk did not hold it correctly, he was awfully close—so close Ernie could smell his breath. Ernie could feel his own pulse rate increase as he mentally planted his feet and made the decision not to lose this fight.

"Eeet's mine now," the leader said. "Get off."

Ernie got off and stood back a step. *Show no moves yet.*

The leader came around the handlebars and got on the bike, which he was now claiming as their spoils. With the gun in his hand, he sat on the bike. He put his hands on the handlebars as though driving it. He then moved the gun to his left hand, freeing up his right hand so he could simulate revving the motor by twisting the throttle. With the gun in his left hand, he rested it on the left handgrip to simulate riding the motorcycle with both hands. He made a noise like an engine and bounced up and down.

One of the others opened the leather saddlebag top to examine the chainsaw that stuck out. "Check theeees out!" he said, as he held the chainsaw in different positions as though to be cutting something with it.

"What the fuck man, you a fucking gardener or something?" one of the others said, laughing and making fun by calling his friend a gardener.

The others joined in wild laughter like howling monkeys.

"Sheeet no, man!" The embarrassed gangbanger dropped the chainsaw to the pavement, and it hit with a thud.

Ernie winced. Dropping his chainsaw was another mistake. For Ernie, it was like dropping his baby. This was his tool for making a living. Although the odds were four to one, he made an instinctive choice. Instantaneously, far too quickly for any of them to react, he cocked his meaty fist and threw a punch at the "gardener's" head, the one who had dropped his saw. He put all his body behind it. The problem for the gangbanger was that Ernie aimed it for the back of his head and, to hit the back, Ernie had to go *through* his face first. And that was nearly what he did. In this manner, the absolute maximum force was brought to bear on the gangbanger's face, and no last-second flinch by the homeboy gangbanger was going to save him. It was such a powerful swing that, had Ernie missed, he would have fallen over forward. A resounding *crack* could be heard, and the gang member's nose broke in several places, his cheek bones fractured, and his front teeth cracked. Blood splattered everywhere as he slammed backward to the ground, flat on his back. He was no longer an immediate threat—or *any* threat.

The pistol was the danger. Ernie grabbed the gun, together with the left hand of the gangbanger who was sitting on his bike, and twisted the left hand with the gun in it up and behind his back so hard and fast that the hand was up at the gang member's head, with Ernie carefully keeping the barrel end of the gun pointed up and away from himself as he twisted the arm.

Crack! was the sound of the gangbanger's shoulder dislocating.

"AGGGGGGGH!" he yelled, his face contorted in pain.

The pistol came easily out of his hand. Ernie took it away from him and put it in his pocket, twisting the gang member's arm behind him with his other hand. Holding the twisted arm up high with one hand, Ernie put his other one around the man's throat. Ernie then picked him up and off the motorcycle, flinging him over the gas tank and on to the ground. The gangbanger landed on his back, his head hitting the pavement. Taking advantage of the moment, Ernie then showed them that logger boots have better uses than homeboy tennis shoes. He dropped kicked the jaw of the man he'd just thrown on the ground, kicking him so hard under the chin with his logger boot that his jaw fractured, his teeth broke, and he was knocked senseless.

Two of them were now immobilized, but two remained and appeared menacing. Ernie took out the gun he put in his pocket and pointed at the remaining two, who were moving in to gang up on him. One now had a knife in his hand. Ernie had no idea if the gun worked, was loaded, or if it had a safety on. He took a chance and fired a shot just ahead of the feet of the one who looked most aggressive, and who was approaching quickly. The bullet ricocheted off the ground and hit him in the lower leg. He hobbled back a few paces to check his wound. The remaining uninjured one stepped back with him. After a distance of several paces, they stopped to reconnoiter and to see if they had the courage to attack. They stood there, wondering how brave they actually were.

Ernie put the gun in his pocket, turned around, picked up his chainsaw, and examined it. It appeared to be undamaged, and so he decided to let those two go if they left. As he was inspecting it, the first man, who was on the ground, rose up slowly to a sitting position. He held his bleeding nose and mouth with one hand, holding himself up with the other. The leader who was on his back, lay there on top of his own twisted arm, now dislodged quite painfully out of its shoulder socket, and he was unable to move it. His face was also bleeding.

Ernie fired up the saw with a strong snap of the starter rope. He revved it a few times. "Good thing for you that you boys you didn't damage this, or I'd have to really hurt you. It's time to teach you pieces of shit a little respect for others and their property."

Ernie revved it again and then expertly flicked the tip of the thirty-two inch bar outward, digging a notch out of the cheek of the first man who was on the ground. The gangbanger yelled out and more blood came. Ernie then gave the other one on the ground the same reminder scar. "You boys like tattoos, so I geeve you a leeeetle mark to remember today. It make you tough, man," he said, mimicking their prattle.

He looked to see if the other two were going to charge. Seeing Ernie mark their leader and other friend with the chainsaw gave them momentary bravado of revenge, and the one who had not been shot started moving in slowly, this time brandishing a knife of his own. The one with the wounded leg came in as well, just behind.

Ernie motioned with the running chainsaw in front of him, holding it with both hands, willing, waiting, and wanting the gangbangers to move in for their final confrontation with life. But after a few steps, the two lost their courage against the chainsaw—an equalizer they did not want to challenge. Ernie moved forward a few steps, ready with his saw, and they both turned and ran as cowards, abandoning their fallen friends bleeding on the ground.

He shut down his saw, put it in the saddlebag, fired up his motorcycle, and rode off. He rode for a mile before he looked for a storm drain and slowed just enough to toss the pistol into it. As he rolled on, he upshifted gears and concluded, *God made man, but the chainsaw made them equal.*

CHAPTER 30

M r. Bradford," Zelzah said over the phone. "Two of the gentlemen from Las Vegas associated with Chief No Cloud—Mr. Manelli and Mr. Innocenti— are calling from a car. They have just left the Santa Monica airport and want me to confirm your meeting with them in thirty minutes. I assume you wish me to?"

"Oh yes. These are the men from the Las Vegas group who are going to run the casino for the Chockpaws."

Zelzah returned to the incoming line. "Everything is on as scheduled. Mr. Bradford is expecting you."

The elevator took the two men to the top floor. They were shown to the executive suite where Zelzah was waiting for them.

She rose. "Please follow me. Mr. Bradford will see you now."

"Mr. Innocenti and Mr. Manelli," Bradford said as a greeting. "This is a pleasure. How nice of you to come over from Las Vegas. Do you have your own jet?"

This last question was his way of sizing them up. The really big companies had a Gulfstream, the new big one costing over sixty five million, and smaller companies an older one or a cheaper Cessna Citation X at twenty- three million. Had they only a turboprop Beechcraft King Air, he would not have thought too much about them as a big time outfit.

"Yes. We have a Cessna Citation X," Manelli said.

Hiding any sign of distain, Bradford smiled. "Oh, I have heard about those new ones. I heard they are fast. What'll it do?"

Manelli puffed out his chest. "It'll cruise at Mach .92, or

about six hundred miles per hour, and it'll go three thousand miles."

"Say, that is something," Bradford said. "A Gulfstream only does Mach .80. You could go from New York to London fast in that one—not to mention all the saved time not having to go through the terminals, security and all." To high salaried people like Bradford, one of the main privileges was not having to wait, and the idea of a private jet enamored him greatly. But he could not buy one for the company, as the conservative insurance company image did not fit with a private company jet.

However, he could charter one whenever he wanted to, and he had an arrangement with a company at Santa Monica airport that provided him with a jet and pilots. However, his work seldom called for travel that far, and so the fantasy of owning one was just a dream.

"We've even got special call numbers for the plane: N88888," Manelli told him with a smile. "You know how superstitious gamblers are. We have lots of Orientals at the casino, and eight is a lucky number for them—sometimes we have the jet pick up a high roller somewhere to bring him over. They think they are riding on a lucky plane. For the hotel, we took out the fourth floor by skipping it and calling it five. Four is unlucky to the Chinese. In Cantonese, it sounds like death. Thirteen is unlucky to many Americans. So we have a hotel with no fourth and no thirteenth floor."

That friendly story brought laugh from Bradford who, experienced in management, appreciated all the strange things that could be done to be more effective at a business. The story was a good way to break the ice and get more comfortable, and Manelli seemed to be good at that.

"On to business," Manelli continued. "As you know, our group manages the Equator Hotel in Las Vegas as well as the Jackpot in Reno. We are going to run the casino and the hotel for Chief No Cloud if he can raise the money to build it. Since your generous company is considering the loan, we wanted to get together with you and provide whatever assurances might be needed, in order to make sure that you know that it will be a successful venture. We have a very good track record in Las Vegas and Reno, and also off shore."

"Yes, I have heard of your success in such businesses," Bradford said. He wasn't exactly sure who the group consisted of but he was afraid to ask, in case they were somehow connected to the mob. It did not matter to him at this point. *Just so that son-of-a-bitch Lewis loses.*

Manelli nodded. "We have determined that the success of the venture is largely dependent on the attraction, that is, the draw. In other words, if enough is spent, it'll be a big success. If not enough is spent, it won't get the reputation to draw the high-roller crowds needed to make it go big. It'll only draw a lower class clientele—like Laughlin compared to Las Vegas. But, done right, this thing will be more of a vacation holiday where people can enjoy things other than the casinos. There is flat land in an excellent spot for a private airport for the rich, and also for air shuttles in from elsewhere. In the daytime they can shoot skeet, trap, and sporting clays; ride horses; golf; go river rafting; tennis on real grass courts; take scenic hikes; and have a first class holiday. For conventions, we cannot be interfered with by regular police and can give the business men what they desire."

Bradford's eyebrows rose involuntarily. Then he changed the subject to conceal his prurient interest. "Did you say real grass tennis courts?"

"Yes, I did," Manelli explained in the Italian manner, waiving his hands about. "Of course, a few of the winter months, they won't be open, due to cold and occasional light snow. But for most of the year, they will be open and usable, just like Wimbledon. Most people have not so much as tried real grass courts. They are like night and day compared to playing on hot concrete, a real luxury."

"Very appealing," Bradford complemented.

"If we don't do it big-time enough, it will get mediocre reviews, and never be a big success," Manelli continued. "But if we go big-time, it should get rave reviews and really work. So we want to let you know that we hope you will consider a loan that will not require the Indians to only put up a modest project, less than what is asked for. If it's done as proposed, we are quite sure it will be not only a huge success, but compete in some ways with Las Vegas in that there will be no controls over much of the activities, and so it will draw in businessmen and gamblers like flies."

Bradford understood. "Yes, I've been to a few of those huge, extravagant hotels in Las Vegas, and I understand that a draw is necessary. What is it that you believe is necessary?" He already knew what it was, but played up to them very well.

Manelli shifted in his chair. "As the prospectus says that we had made for Chief, which you have, we would like Majestik to loan to the Chockpaws one hundred fifty million. Our group will put up the operating capital, estimated at ten million at opening time, and as much more as might be needed. With sufficient money, the place will be spectacular, make the news, travel agencies will distribute brochures, and conventions will be scheduled there. If done well, it will draw in the crowds, generate the talk, and be a success. We have some big name friends in the entertainment industry who owe us favors, so we can get some in up there and we think we can make it a big success. If it goes as well as we plan, we have left room for the hotel to expand later to twice the size." We also plan some private bungalows for people that do not want to be seen, such as movie stars, extremely wealthy business men, and possibly some occasional guests seeking privacy like the Saudi royal family or a movie star recovering from plastic surgery."

Bradford realized how important it could be to get some big name entertainers as a draw when Manelli said it, and remembered how Frank Sinatra got his break-through from the mob many years ago. There was little question in his mind that this group could perform from what he could ascertain. But he still had his own agenda. "I have studied the prospectus that you gave the chief, and it seems to me that it would be a success. But I have to budget things carefully. If that crusader Lewis wins the election, we're going to have to make major cutbacks in investments across the board. I do not anticipate being able to loan the money in that case."

In actuality, he could, but he had to stick to his story in order to ensure that the chief would stand behind the plan to contribute twenty million that was going toward defeating Lewis. Even though these people from Las Vegas did not know about the twenty million, as far as he knew, he wanted to ensure that the group was unified. Should they learn of it, they would certainly make sure it remained quiet in order to get the loan funded.

"What if Lewis doesn't last the race?" Innocenti asked in a cocky tone.

Manelli shot his vicious partner a stern look but, veiled as it was with silence, it conveyed the message well. *Shut up and let me do the talking!*

Bradford paused at the fearsome man's comment. Could he possibly mean what that sounded like? But skilled at handling meetings, Bradford showed no emotion and maintained his composure. "I would say that would be a miracle. But I'm from Missouri. I need to be shown. If he drops out of the race, I'll make the loan at that time, ahead of the election. Or, if he loses, then I'll make the loan. How will that work for you?"

Manelli sighed. "Very good. Let's hope for the best. In the meantime, let us know if you are coming over to Vegas, and we will see to it that you have everything you need."

"Thanks, I'll remember that." Bradford wondered if they could really set up something special for him, something that might make a considerable difference from the usual Las Vegas *comp* where he would get a free top floor suite and show tickets for him and his wife.

The meeting concluded, the men all shook hands in accord and left.

Zelzah, just outside, got up from her desk. "Is there anything I can arrange for you gentlemen?"

"No, thanks," Manelli said. In the elevator with no one else present, Manelli turned to Innocenti and snapped, "Jesus Christ, Fiorello! Why the fuck sugar-coat it? Why didn't you just tell him we're going to kill Lewis?"

Innocenti twisted his face in discontent at being criticized.

Manelli shook his head. "Let me handle these delicate matters." Then he smiled at the ferocious man, so as not to anger him too much, and added a small joke. "Fiorello, sometimes you have the finesse of a Tyrannosaurus rex."

When they left, Zelzah went inside to see if her boss wanted anything, predicting he might. "Can I fix you anything, sir?" She always, unless asked otherwise, spoke in her ultra-formal way. It was a good habit in case anyone was listening, and she was a master at the appearance of perfect decorum.

Bradford revealed his thinking to her. "That guy Innocenti scares the shit out of me. He suggested that Zachary Lewis might drop out of the race and I think the method he was suggested was that he would kill him. Shit, I might be responsible for setting it up. I could get involved in an assassination. Jesus! Fix me a martini. No mix."

"It's a bit early. Are you sure?"

No response in this situation was a *yes*. She returned to her desk and pushed the button on her phone that transferred all calls to a subordinate, who was instructed not to interrupt for any reason. At his bar, she made a shaker of vodka and ice, and poured the first in a frozen martini glass.

He downed it quickly. Seeing that he wanted more, she made his second. Two meant he was ready for more than just booze as he could not work effectively with an alcohol high and he would not likely be doing any more work that day.

He downed the second, and it was time.

They shared a common interest in sexual arousal which made her duties less onerous. She knew him well, including his specialized hookers, the latest of which was Evette Evil. Not only did she cover for him in his endeavors out of the office, but she also provided occasional relief for him in the office, and the relief was mutual. She helped him out of his clothes, took off her high heels, and lifted up her skirt all the way to her waist to free up her legs. She dropped her stylish pantyhose and stood before him. Using her feet, she moved his legs apart. She stood back a stride. "Ready?"

"Go for it!"

She drop kicked him like a pro football kicker punting on a fourth down.

He grunted loudly in pain, collapsing against his desk. He shortly regained composure and stood for another.

Zelzah complied, and he did the same. He regained his composure again and moved over a few feet so he was in front of a chair facing the desk.

She sat in front of him and brought him explosive release, followed by her own.

CHAPTER 31

Saturday, Ernie mused as he woke, remembering when he was a kid and used to watch cartoons on Saturdays. Saturdays were very special to him, indeed his special time. But, when he grew up and became a logger, when there was work and the weather permitted, he had worked many Saturdays. He retained only misty, pastel-colored memories of childhood, but they were happy ones.

The room at the Polynesian had a flat-screen TV. He leaned over to the nightstand and found the remote, and scrolled though the channels available until he found a fascinating documentary on poisonous snakes.

He later went to his sliding glass door and looked out at the pools. A red-haired girl in her late teens was sitting on the side of the pool with her legs in the water. She slid in as Ernie watched, and then turned and saw Ernie and smiled at him invitingly.

Then he remembered. *This is the day I'm to take Zelzah for a ride! And, she is going to show me how to use a computer. I wonder if I can get the hang of it in a day. Nah. Seems unlikely to learn a computer in a day. Oh well, it'll be a start.*

⌘

"Come in, honey! I'm so excited about going on a motorcycle! Will these do?" Zelzah said, looking at down her jeans, new, but pre-faded. She had on shoes with straps and a tight tank top.

Ernie wore his wool outfit. In his hand, he had an extra half-helmet he carried in the saddlebag. "You'll have to wear this. And for the shoes, you'd do better with boots. I don't want to get you burned from the pipes or from the hot air passing over the engine. Do you have any?"

"Of course. I didn't know. I'll be right back—won't be a minute." She hurried off to her wardrobe. In a short time she came back wearing tall, black leather boots with high heels. "Okay, I'm ready."

"Bring a light jacket. If you get too warm, you can put it in the saddlebag."

"Where're we going?"

"I've heard of a place called the Rock Store in the canyons where motorcyclists meet on weekends. It's probably a good place to go and see other bikers and bikes. It's above Malibu, and inland. We'll go in by the inland route, and come back along the ocean."

Ernie fired up his motorcycle, and the roar reverberated loudly off the garage walls as they pulled out, setting off an alarm on a BMW parked in the garage, its lights flashing and its horn beeping.

"Wheeeeeeeeeeeeeee!" Zelzah shrieked in excitement and at the alarm going off on the BMW.

Off they went. The first few leaning turns nearly petrified her, but she lost the fright after a few miles when they didn't crash. The leaning right and left on the curves in the winding canyon roads brought back her memories of amusement park rides as a young girl. Zelzah squeezed Ernie's hips affectionately with her thighs as they roared through the canyons. Once in the canyons, the only other traffic on the winding canyon road was other motorcycles.

Younger men on Japanese and Italian road racing bikes were going faster than Ernie and passed him, but that was of no consequence to Ernie. The riders on American motorcycles waved to each other with a small hand movement of the left hand taken off the handlebar grip and a stylish pointing down with the index finger as they passed if coming from the other direction. Observing that salutation a number of times, Zelzah felt the warm camaraderie of a club that she had no idea existed.

After a spirited and exhilarating ride, they arrived at their destination. It was a wooden, log cabin structure sitting back on the hillside to the south overlooking the road. Parked in front were hundreds of motorcycles, and a bizarre group of people. It was definitely a happening. Some were leaving, some coming, and most just parked. People were walking about, checking out the more interesting or novel bikes, and chatting. Up on a wooden porch a man was barbecuing beef for sandwiches, and selling beer and wine to the orchestra of outdoor speakers from some prerecorded music that seem to appeal to bikers. There was a strong, aromatic smoke and odor of Mesquite wood used for the BBQ coming from the smoker. Much to Zelzah's surprise, a small per cent of the other American motorcycles were driven by girls, and most of them had worn only a scant leather vest with nothing underneath which did not extend down to the waist, and fastened by chrome chains in the front in a most suggestive way. They all seem to wear leather pants, very low-waisted, leaving much of the stomach and back exposed.

"This is an amazing place!" Zelzah said, enthralled. "This is so much cooler than the places I go."

Choppers, road racers, show bikes, a motorcycle with a side car, and paint schemes that varied from wild colors to pornographic-painted illustrations on the gas tanks made the show.

After wandering about, Zelzah said, "Are we going to eat here?"

Ernie shook his head. "I think it might be more fun to press on, rather than hang out here. I think we've seen enough. The ocean is not far away on my map, and we can ease on down this road and come onto Malibu, and eat somewhere on the ocean. I think a nice ocean climate and view would be nice. What do you think of that?"

"Sounds wonderful! I know of a place on the water we can go to."

They mounted up, and motored down the hill until the ocean came into view. Ernie pulled over for a moment at a rest stop, still high above the sea. The vast panorama of ocean spread before them sparkling like diamonds in the morning sun.

"I always love the sight of the ocean," he told her as he gazed about, mesmerized by the view.

"Me too." And she squeezed the insides of his thighs with her hands, and then put a hand on his sex and squeezed it as well. Ernie fired up his engine, and down the windy road they went toward Malibu.

On Pacific Coast Highway, Zelzah recognized the place and pointed. "It's that one."

Ernie turned into a restaurant right on the Pacific. Although the lot was packed, when Ernie pulled up to the entrance for directions on where to park, the carhop, a fan of motorcycles, guided them right off to the side of the door where there was enough space for his bike. The royal treatment made them feel important.

Inside the place was jam-packed. "Look how they look at us with these helmets," she said as they walked in. "This is the most fun I've had in ages. They think we're really cool, and so do I." Her professional office demeanor, so full of propriety, was completely gone, and her usual pale face was bright and full of color, not only from the sun but the emotion of the experience.

Seated inside, Zelzah looked at a drink menu, and said to the waiter, "I'll have a Margarita, blended with salt on the rim."

Ernie held up two fingers. "Two."

Zelzah sighed in delight as the waiter walked away. "You've shown me a new world. Riding the motorcycle is such fun, and you make me feel safe. Have you ever had a crash?"

"Well, a girl I drove home from a party last year on a Saturday night and I fell over at a stop light at midnight. We were laughing so hard that we had a hard time picking up the motorcycle to get going again. She blamed it on the amount of alcohol we drank. But I discussed it with the boys at the chainsaw store on Monday, and everyone there concluded that it had to be due to unusual gravitational fluctuations in the area."

"*Unusual gravitational fluctuations!*" She shouted it and laughed so loudly that others stared.

CHAPTER 32

Salvatore Manelli, Fiorello Innocenti, Fabrizio Bastini, and Gaspare Indelicato met in their private conference room at the Equator.

Manelli opened the meeting. "Fiorello and I met with Bradford. He says he will lend the one hundred fifty million to the Chockpaws for the project, but only if the insurance reform candidate Zachary Lewis loses the election. We've got to get into this Indian thing," he said. "This has got to be our future. These Indians don't know how to do shit except drink, let alone run a hotel or a casino. They need us. We need them. The only police will be from the Indians, or whoever we hire. They'll be ours. We'll have our own police force! We can fix games, fix fights, fix the machines, run hookers, sell drugs, and do whatever we want." His face was flushed at the very ideas he was espousing. "As the government cannot come in, we can do what we want. As long as we make the Indians money, they won't give a shit. They won't even know much about what we are doing. This has got to be a dream come true."

Indelicato cleared his throat. "But it won't happen unless Majestik puts up the money, which they won't do if Lewis wins. And he's supposed to be popular. Isn't he going to win?"

"I've heard he's now neck and neck, and he might just win," Manelli piped up. "Bradford said that if Lewis drops out of the race, he will lend the money at that time."

"I saw in the news that the Chockpaws paid for an ad for the opponent," Bastini added. "There is no way they would do that on their own, and they sure as hell don't have the money. I think No Cloud is a straw man funneling money Bradford put up to defeat Lewis. Also, he gave a million to No Cloud for the engineering much too quickly."

"So much the better," Indelicato said. "It shows a commitment."

"Do you think I should assist Lewis in dropping out of the race?" Innocenti asked.

"For the one hundred fifty million dollars, and the future of our operation, are you fucking kidding?" Manelli said, emphatically.

Indelicato frowned. "But if we hit Lewis, how do we know that Bradford will come through with the money? If he gets Lewis out of the race, what incentive would he have to loan the Chockpaws the money? He might think it a better idea not to, as he would have what he wants with Lewis out of the way, and could just write off the million he gave No Cloud.

"I'm working on a little insurance of our own to make sure Bradford keeps his word," Innocenti said. "I've been in touch with his hooker and hope to get a video of him real soon."

"Good thinking, Fiorello," Bastini said. "But as to the idea of hitting Lewis, we must think carefully about the risks of killing a gubernatorial candidate. There is bound to be a lot to do about it. Is it worth the risk?"

"It may not become a federal investigation, since it is a state matter," Indelicato said. "But the FBI usually finds a way to make it one. Also, it would be a mistake to hit him in a public arena, with the public watching on TV. There would be an enormous outcry by the news media and all. What are our chances of killing him and making it appear like a genuine accident? It might work if it appears to be an accident, and not one that is televised. The hit must be impossible to trace."

"How can we get in close?" Bastini asked. "This guy has got to be running all over the state campaigning, protected by state police, and in big crowds. He probably has a schedule of public appearances, but his leisure time has got to be minimal and maybe unscheduled."

"We should put in a campaign worker, to get in close," Innocenti said. "Then we can find out about where he will be so we can get to him."

"Good idea," Indelicato said. "We need to know where he will be and when."

"I think I may be able to arrange something," Manelli said. "But, Fiorello, this is a political hit. It may bring in the FBI. It can involve itself by just claiming use of mails or interstate phone calls—and if they get involved, they can turn on the heat big time. I don't think you should do this thing yourself. The odds of getting caught hitting a political figure are high. Why don't' we get an outside hitman?"

Fiorello's black eyes blazed to life. "We just increase our chances of getting caught by hiring it out. I prefer to do my own hits. If it's to be done, I'll do it. But I may bring in Vinnie to help." He referred to a friend of his from way back, someone with unique skills.

"Let's vote," Bastini said. "Do we hit Lewis, and do we let Innocenti do it with Vinnie?" He raised a hand. "Yes."

Indelicato nodded. "Yes."

"Let's do it," Manelli said.

Innocenti's expression showed satisfaction and determination. "I'll do it."

The meeting was adjourned.

CHAPTER 33

Zelzah opened her condo door with Ernie in tow. "I'm really exhausted, much more so than with my workout sessions." She took off her boots, peeled off her sweaty clothes and put on a robe. "It's only 4:00 p.m. I had promised you that I would show you how to use the computer. Do you still wish to learn?"

"Oh, yeah."

"I tell you what. Why don't I set you up to practice, and I'll run out for some shopping for dinner here for later?"

Hearing no complaint, she led him to her computer room, and sat him in front of her computer. It came alive, and she started typing something on it at an alarming rate of speed, as her nimble fingers were second to almost none on a keyboard. Her thin fingers moved so quickly that Ernie was dazzled.

"Wow, you sure can type."

Zelzah, aware of her speed, ignored the praise. She turned it over to him. "Okay, you know how to type, so just type in the name of the person of one of your next case assignments, and see what comes up. Or, you can type in the Majestik file number. Go on, try it."

Ernie typed in the name of a claimant that he had not been to yet and the screen came up with details and information. The name of the claimant, her address, and a host of details came up on the screen. "This is really cool," he said, entranced with the power of the machine, forgetting for a moment that he was delving into the personal history of someone who bought a Majestik policy.

"Now, if you want to print out the information, all you do is move the mouse here and click it. Here, see?" she said as she clicked a print icon, and the data began printing out on a nearby, expensive, forty-inch-high, high-speed color printer/scanner. "If you want to make a copy of something, you just take one of these—" She showed him a small box of new flash sticks. "—and put it in the slot here. Then just click this C for copy, and what you select will be copied onto the flash stick. Now, if you get bored with that, just click here," she said, showing him another place to click. "This is immediate access to the Internet and then you can go into one of the chat rooms and chat with other people from whatever part of the world you want." She led him into a chat room to illustrate. "Okay?" she asked. "I'll run to the store for some things for dinner and be back in an hour. Have fun."

She was not worried about security, as Ernie would not have the access code to get into anything sensitive. She, and only she, other than Bradford himself, had unrestricted access to Majestik information.

Ernie could not remember the names of any other claimants that he had not yet settled. He wondered if the computer database had information on anyone he knew personally. Doubtful. *Oh well, why not try?*

The first person that came to mind was Lilly in Sedro Woolley. He typed in her first name, Lilly and, before he could type in her last, the screen flickered. A completely new list of options came up. *What on earth did I do?*

He stared at the screen, wondering. Then suddenly he remembered the big oil painting in the lobby of the insurance office, and the names below the portrait of the old couple

Matthew and Lilly Bradford 1920

Lilly must be the name of Bradford's grandma. It's the code word for Bradford and Zelzah to get into their secret system!

The options looked good. The first entry on the screen was stated: *Things to do.* Clicking that, appearing was a typed memo from Robert Bradford to Tom McGinn, Senior Staff Attorney.

Tom:

I want you to put together a loan agreement from Majestik to the Chockpaw Indians. The package will lend Chockpaws one million dollars at prime rate plus two per cent due in payments not to exceed four years.

There is a second stage to the loan, which is a building loan of one hundred fifty million dollars. This will only be lent if Zachary Lewis does not win the election, but don't put that in the document—just make it such that Majestik has the sole discretion whether or not to make the second stage.

This initial million will be for engineering, plans, and the like, looking toward the development of a hotel, casino, and facilities surrounding it. If I don't go through with the second stage, the first one million will be forgiven and changed to a deductible charitable contribution.

If I go through with the second phase, I want a very tight builder's control on it, with someone with building experience that we will put in place at the location to approve contracts and expenditures in advance. I don't want those drunken Indians deciding how to spend our money.

The drafts will come through our office here and one of our men will have to countersign just as we do will large payouts on our insurance business.

This should be like some other loans we have done, except that I doubt you can figure out a way to foreclose, as the land is Indian Nation property, but I leave that to you. Write in it that the Indian Nation consents to jurisdiction on our state courts, but I don't know how enforceable that is.

The Chockpaws have some government contracts, which might be assignable to us. Give me a ring or drop by for questions. Your input will be appreciated as usual.

On another matter, I am also giving the Chockpaws a charitable donation of twenty million dollars which

*we will also control, but that is a sensitive matter. I will
explain when I see you.*
    Robert Bradford, President

The next entry was to Alan Waterman in accounting.

    Alan:
    *I want you to prepare to lend one million dollars to
the Chockpaw Indians as soon as Tom McGinn tells you
he has the papers all signed. There will be a builder's
control set up over it, to protect against foolish spending and liens. Also, I want you to show an advance to
the Chockpaws another twenty million dollars for a donation to the Tribe. This will not be turned over to the
Chockpaws, except in name only. I want it put in the
books as in the name of the Chockpaws, but the only
signatory on a special account where it will go will be
you. It will go to the committee to defeat Lewis for governor, which of course is controlled by his opponent.
This account we keep under tight wraps.*
    Robert Bradford, President

Ernie gaped at the amounts of money involved. He scrolled
down the screen, looking for a way out, viewing the topics. A
topic came up called *MM.* He clicked it. As it opened up, the
screen name changed to *Money Maker.* There was much following that, dealing with the handling of claims, which he did
not take the time to read.

*This would be a good one to copy for handling of claims.
No doubt that would be something that is helpful and that I
should have. But how to copy it?*

"Take out a flash stick from the drawer," Zelzah had told
him. He took one out and put in in the slot as Zelzah had
shown him, clicked the C to copy the MM file.

*Got it. I could use this instruction file on claims to learn
how to handle claims. Now, if I only had a computer. Oh well.*

He put the flash stick in his pocket. Deciding he had
enough of work, he changed into a chat room. He conjured up

his typing skills from high school and began talking to a girl in Kuala Lumpur, Malaysia. He found himself typing faster and with more ease as he chatted with her. The chat rooms, he concluded, would be good places to hone his stale typing skills from high school.

After half an hour of chat, the door opened, and Zelzah came in with two bags of groceries. She leaned into her computer room and said in velvet-edged tone, "Hi, lover."

"Hi, Zelzah."

"Have you figured out the computer yet?"

"Well, I'm getting the hang of it." He told the girl that he was talking to in Malaysia that he had to go, and she told him how to say that she would see him later in the Malay language, *jumpa lagi.* "I'm talking to a girl all the way over in Malaysia on the Internet. How cool is that?"

"Very cool!" she agreed and went to the kitchen.

Ernie followed her. "I'm getting a little burnt out on the computer. I think I'm getting cross-eyed. It's been a long time since I typed."

"Why don't we have some wine while I make dinner?"

He stayed in the kitchen chair, sipping the wine, while Zelzah put seasoning on a prime rib and put it in the oven. "It'll be an hour and a half until dinner. How about a shower? Together?"

The shower proved to be a delightful way to wash away the dust of the day. She stood in front of him in the shower and decided it was time for sex, but she required her type of arousal. She took his hands and put them on her nipples. "Squeeze hard!"

She put her arms around him and jumped up, wrapping her legs around him. He moved her back so that the two of them were leaning against the wall, the shower pounding down on them.

"Harder," she said loudly and repeated that command as he pushed into her.

He was not sure what part of her she was referring to, but he was fairly certain that the neighbor in the next condo was being well entertained.

☙

"How do you find the prime rib?" she asked as he sampled it. "I put a seasoning rub on the top."

She had obtained a large cut, assuming he would eat a he-man portion. She was right. When cooked medium rare, she then cut it, making his three times size of the cut for her, and he found the large piece just right.

"Delicious."

"Tell me more about logging. I never even dreamed I would meet a real logger."

"Well, it has its down side as well as the up side. I got laid off because of a spotted owl. There is a lot of hardship created to keep territory open for several critters a lot of people don't know a great deal about."

Zelzah frowned. "But how can anyone want to take a habitat away from a little animal and make it extinct?"

She rang his bell, and he started with, "Zelzah, you sound like so many uninformed city folks. No matter where you look, there will always be some little critter going extinct practically every day—butterflies, insects, birds, fishes, things that crawl underground, and other animals, by the thousands. And new ones always come along. Nature changes things, and always will. Change is nature, and nature is change. Without change, we could not exist. Those places where we log are for the most part not even accessible to people. Otherwise people would have cleared them for farming years ago. They are on steep slopes, long distances from roads, and uninhabited. There are all sorts of critters in the forests, and there will always be. The logging operations plant new trees, three to four for every one cut. The new trees are healthier varieties, and grow faster. The concept that cutting trees for lumber is bad comes from people who don't know. And because the government won't allow controlled logging in many areas, forest fires destroy many more trees each year than are logged. And, people seem to forget where two-by-fours come from for their houses when they vote against logging. It drives the price of houses up."

Zelzah realized that she was out of her league. "What sort of problems do you face up there because of the preservation of animals?"

"You'd be surprised. The activists have enacted laws prohibiting anyone from making any noise that might bother such things as spotted owls and marbled murreletes. Then there are the new laws on logging near streams as they think that has created a problem with the salmon. They just don't know."

"I've heard about the marbled murrelete. I read somewhere that it is nearly extinct also. It's a fishing bird, isn't it?"

"Yes, it is. It lives primarily in rocks, but occasionally on an old growth tree. It gets up in the morning and flies out to sea to fish. It flies very fast. It comes back in at night and sleeps. It has a funny way of landing as it flies so fast. It is a very up-tight bird, acting sort of neurotic all the time. Anything makes it jump. I think the thing has bred itself into something that doesn't belong anywhere, anymore."

"But I read that if you take away its nest, it will die, and it is nearly extinct, isn't it?" Zelzah asked.

"Let me tell you just how bad it is. If you see a marbled murrelete leaving a tree in the morning, and you go cut down that tree, an amazing thing happens about dusk. It only knows to fly right back to the exact same tree that it was living in. It heads for the tree at seventy miles per hour, as it is one fast bird. When it gets to where the tree was, it goes into its ritual dive toward where its nest used to be, picking up speed. But now, the top of the tree is gone, and only a stump is left near the ground.

"Not hitting the nest, it gets going so fast that it loses control, building up speed to nearly a hundred miles an hour as it goes on down and crashes right into the tree, its long beak driving right into the stump. The long beak sticks into the wood deeply, like a long nail, and the bird just sticks out of the stump, very dead. It is a horrible sight."

"My God! That's horrible! No wonder they have those laws to protect them," Zelzah said, defending her obvious favor of any law to save any animal.

"Bought it, didn't ya?" Ernie said with a huge smile. "See

what I mean? People are so ready to believe anything about animals."

Zelzah's horrified expression morphed into a big grin. "You are terrible! You had me believing you!" She began to sock Ernie playfully as she realized she had fallen, hook, line, and sinker for the yarn.

CHAPTER 34

L et's test it," the electrical technician said to the hotel assistant manager. Standing on a short stepladder, he then aimed the lens of the miniature video camera hidden on top of the armoire that held the pull-out, flat-screen TV, refrigerator, and shelves in front of the bed in the suite at the Wilshire. He turned it on, went into the area of the expected activity on the bed, and moved about to act the part of a subject. He then looked at his laptop screen to check the positioning.

"The camera has a wide angle lens and should be able to pick up just about any activity in the room. It needs a tiny adjustment here on the angle. There, that should do it. There is no need to focus as it is always on wide angle. It'll do just fine. The on switch is activated by a tiny motion sensor, so no one has to touch it."

"They're on their way over now, so let's haul ass," the assistant manager said.

Fifteen minutes later, Bradford and Evette Evil, entered the room. The tiny, concealed video camera activated itself by its miniature motion sensor.

"What do you feel like today, honey?" Evette asked.

He started taking off his clothes. "The full treatment."

Evette opened her large bag, carried by a shoulder strap, and began taking out her special equipment.

ഇരു

"I have examined the tape, and it's perfect. Here's your money," Innocenti told Julie Bailey in the café. He then handed her a wad of hundreds in an envelope totaling ten thousand dollars.

"I don't want to get into trouble over this," she said, counting the bills in the envelope.

"There'll be no trouble. And your sister Iris is doing quite well at our casino," he told her, his grin evil.

"Is there anything I can do for you today? I can make you really feel good for only three fifty." She put the fat envelope in her purse. She couldn't resist soliciting a wealthy potential customer even though she'd already had a record payday.

"No, but thanks, good looking. I'll keep you in mind for sure. Maybe another time."

"Anytime." She walked out of the café.

CHAPTER 35

"My name is Maria Manelli," she told the lady at the desk. Maria was pretty, dark-haired, olive complexion, twenty-two, and slightly overweight. She was offering her services to the Southern California campaign office of Zachary Lewis for Governor.

"Have a seat please," the woman told her. "My name is Doris. How do you do?"

"Very well, thank you."

"Are you here to volunteer?"

"Yes, I'm a very strong supporter of Zachary Lewis, and I'm between semesters right now at school. I want to join in and work on his campaign. I don't need any salary or pay."

"We have lots of work for Mr. Lewis's supporters. We have to get the word out on his proposed legislation and platforms. You can start at once if you like. There is a station set up today at a mall, and we have several people passing out materials. You could start out by helping out there. Here's a form for you to fill out. We need your name, address, and a number to contact you."

"Wonderful. I wonder if I could get a schedule of Mr. Lewis's scheduled appearances so I can plan to attend rallies?"

"Yes, in fact, it's right here." Doris handed her a printed schedule of rallies and public appearances already scheduled. "So, now you can go on over to the mall if you want and help out there."

"That'll be great," Maria said. "Should I come back here tomorrow? I'd love to work in the headquarters."

"Yes, that'd be good. We could use some help here, and then we will find something for you to do."

"I hope to be able to meet him personally and get to work close to him. I just think he's super."

"We all think he's wonderful, and don't worry, you'll get to meet him soon."

"I'm so excited! I'll head out for the mall. See you tomorrow."

While driving to the mall, Maria pressed a speed dial number programmed in on her cell phone. A long distance number rang and a man answered. "Hello?"

"Hi, Daddy. It's me. I just left the Zachary Lewis campaign office."

"How'd it go, sweetheart?" asked Salvatore Manelli, in Las Vegas.

"A piece of cake. They asked me no questions, and I start today. I already have a copy of his appearance schedule. I'll send it to you today."

"Nice work. Stay with the campaign, and see what you can do about getting close to Lewis. I want to find out about his leisure time."

"Sure, Daddy. Love you."

CHAPTER 36

Ernie approached Berth C-26. He walked along the pier toward a forty-six-foot sport fishing boat on the Long Beach boat dock called the *Hookup*. The scent of the sea filled the air. In the harbor, the odor was not completely fresh, but still very much an ocean smell. "Hi, I'm Ernie from Majestik."

"I'm pleased to meet you," Dwight Winger said. "Come aboard."

Ernie walked along the gangway to the finger, the floating walkway alongside the boat. He mounted the movable boarding steps to meet the owner.

"Welcome aboard," Dwight said with a big smile. "Care for a drink?"

"Got a beer?"

"Sure," Dwight said and went to get a beer for him, but Dwight did not join in. "I'm very pleased that someone has finally come out about the claim. I got a letter from a Jessica Bloom stating the items claimed were not depreciated, and I would have to depreciate everything to settle the claim. I wrote back for directions and never heard anything further."

"Well, I'm here. Tell me about it." Ernie sat down with beer in hand across from Dwight.

"I use this boat for charter fishing. I had out a group of three for marlin fishing between San Clemente and Catalina. My fisherman got a one hundred seventy-five pound marlin and was reeling him in, when an eight-foot mako shark came up behind the boat after hearing the sound of the marlin being landed. Mako makes one of the best fishes for eating. The fishermen wanted him, so we chummed for him and brought him back up to the boat. One of them fishermen got him to take bait, and the fight was on. After he tired, we got him up close to the boat. I gaffed him with a flying gaff with a break-away hook. I always let the fishermen do everything, as that way they get to enjoy the experience. With the fish still in the water, I handed him my baseball bat, so he could kill him. He went to the shark in the water and beat him on the head. You have to kill a big fish like that before bringing it into the boat, or it can become big trouble. He beat the shark, and it went still. It looked dead. But it wasn't, which we did not realize as it was completely still. So I hooked him and brought him into the boat. There were some other sharks visible and if we left him in the water and towed him in, they would have eaten him on the way in. The fishermen wanted him to eat."

"I can guess what is coming," Ernie predicted.

"Yep. The shark turned out not to be dead, and all of a sudden he was about to bite into one of the fishermen's legs. He had the fisherman cornered and was flapping up a storm. One of the others actually got injured just from the flapping. So I picked up a 10 mm Glock that I have for shooting such fish in the water, went up beside him, and emptied the magazine in him. That killed him dead. I had bought the 10 mm Glock, as it has some serious power and will operate when wet—in fact, it'll operate under water."

Dwight went to a drawer, and pulled out the weapon to show Ernie. "Have you ever shot one of these puppies?" He handed it to Ernie, but only after he took out the magazine and locked the slide back to show it was unloaded. Ernie could see he handled guns well.

Ernie took the pistol from him and examined it. "Yes, I have. A friend of mine bought one when the caliber first got popular, and we went out shooting. I remember that when we shot it at two hundred yards it had only less than half the drop of a .45. I can see how the holes got punched in the boat. This caliber would punch right through a shark and then the boat.

"Well, I never figured on using it inside the boat," Dwight replied. "I bought it to shoot sharks in the water that were try-ing to get game fish when we reeled them in. The 10 mm cartridge is very effective for shooting sharks. But shot in here," he said, pointing to the deck, "the bullets went through the shark, down through the deck, right on down through the hull, and punched holes in the bottom. A couple that hit a motor did not go through, but the rest did. I went down in the hull when I realized it, but couldn't patch all the holes successfully as there were too many. By the time I got down there the water was already several inches deep. The pumps went on automatically, but the incoming water overwhelmed the pumps. We headed for shore at top speed, which is normally twenty-five knots, but the water flooded one engine, and then the boat would not plane. Pretty soon the second engine went dead, and we had taken on two feet of water in no time. We were nearly scuttled when the coast guard arrived, a mile out at that time. The coast guard put its big four-inch hose pump inside until the crane arrived, which kept us afloat. There is only one crane in this area on floats, and the sons-a-bitches charged me thirty-nine thousand dollars since it was a Sunday, for double time for the union rules.

"My God," Ernie exclaimed. "Thirty-nine thousand dollars for a crane! How long did you have the crane in use?"

"Four hours, until we got into the maintenance dock, and they pulled the boat out of the water. Figure that! They have a monopoly. That works out to ten thousand dollars an hour for a crane that probably didn't cost new more than a hundred thousand. And that thing was really old. I wish I had that concession."

"So what was left to settle on the claim?"

"The crane company billed the insurance direct and got paid. So did the dry dock repair place, except for the five thousand dollars deductible that I paid. The engines had to be overhauled, the transmissions the same, and the electronics as well. Salt water was in everything. That was one hundred twenty-nine thousand seven hundred fourteen dollars. But that place did not fix everything in the interior. Not fixed was the refinishing of the cabinets, replacement of some furniture items, the upholstery, carpets, and all the personal stuff that got ruined when it was soaked with seawater. That cost me twelve thousand one hundred forty-three dollars, and I still have a few things left to fix. I sent in a list, and you should have it. I have my original here."

"I see it in my file," Ernie said, finding it. "So Bloom said you have to depreciate the items?"

"That's what the letter says. How do you depreciate refinishing cabinets? They were fine before the water was taken on, and afterward, I had to replace some and refinish the rest. I got nothing better out of it. I had a perfectly good rod and reel that got knocked overboard in the excitement. I just bought them last year, and have the receipt for it here. Water got in the electronics, and I had to send those over to get fixed."

"Mind if I look at the cabinets and the things you fixed?"

"Help yourself."

Ernie walked about the boat with him, with Dwight pointing out what was repaired. Finally, Ernie said, "I tell you what. I have ten thousand dollars in authority. I can give you a check, which is actually a draft, for ten thousand dollars at this time in exchange for a release. If you want more, I have to turn it over to another level, and it goes out of my hands. I can't say when you will ever settle, as I'm only a temporary adjustor here for ninety days. I can show depreciation of some of the items since you spent more than the ten thousand dollars to get everything fixed."

"Ten thousand would be wonderful! I'll take that in a second," Dwight said exuberantly. "When can I get it?"

"How about now?" Ernie smiled and began filling in the blanks on the form release.

Dwight signed the form, and Ernie wrote him a check for ten thousand dollars.

"I really appreciate having someone competent come out. Say, do you like to fish?"

"I'll say," Ernie responded excitedly. "I'm from Washington, and we have a lot of good fishing there."

"Did you just recently move here?"

"I'm only here as a temporary field representative for ninety days."

"Have you ever done any ocean fishing?"

"Yeah, a few times."

"I tell you what. I've been out of business for several months, as you know, and no one paid me for that. So I can't take just you out fishing alone. But next time I get a day charter, I'll call you to join as my deck hand to help out with the boat. How about that?"

It was only an invitation to be a deck hand, but it was better than nothing. "Great. I don't mind helping out with the boat. I can only go on a weekend."

"As soon as I get a one-day charter on a weekend, I'll give you a call."

"I'll come for sure." And with that, Ernie walked off the boat dock back to his motorcycle to go to his next assignment, another boat claim, nearby, in a boat yard in San Pedro.

The next boat claim was regarding a forty-five foot Bayliner. Ernie recognized the boat as it was built in Billingham, Washington. The memo he had from Bloom said there was no coast guard report on the damage and therefore she denied the claim.

Ernie drove right on into the crowded boat yard since he was on a motorcycle and able to go around the two foot space beside the wooden arm that was intended to keep out motorists—not motorcycles, something those in charge had not figured on. The claimant, Eric Carson, was prearranged to meet him at his boat.

The boat was on cradles, out of the water. The cradles were in turn on a special boat yard trolley on rails so the boat could be moved around in the yard. The boat looked very big out of the water, up in the air, and had its name painted on the transom, *Tanqueray.* The bridge of the boat was missing, and the rear deck was full of rubble. It looked like it had been hit by a helicopter gunship with a machine gun in the war zone.

"Are you the owner, Eric Carson?" Ernie asked the man in a suit who was standing near the boat.

"Yes. Who are you?"

"I'm Ernie, from Majestik. My card."

"Since when to insurance men drive motorcycles?" Carson asked, eyeing Ernie's bike.

"Don't you like motorcycles?"

"I love them," Carson said, with a smile. "I used to have a Honda, but I crashed twice so my wife made me give it up. Actually the motorcycle got totaled in the last accident and I never got another one. But I miss it and I've thought of getting another one now and then. I really like yours."

"Majestik is giving me mileage to drive my bike. Not bad, all in all," Ernie said. "So what happened with the boat?"

"Well, Majestik has denied my claim until I get a coast guard report of the incident. I told them I will get one, but I just haven't gotten around to it yet."

"So tell me what happened."

"I dock at Alamitas Bay. I took the boat to a restaurant to meet a friend that also has a boat in Long Beach. We met at a restaurant in Long Beach on the water where you can dock your boat just outside. To get there from Alamitas Bay, I cruise inside the breakwater for about thirty minutes. We had dinner, and afterward, I headed back home. I was cruising at about twenty five knots. I was up on the flying bridge, alone.

"Inside the breakwater was moored one of those big orange barges used for hauling rocks in from the quarry on Catalina Island over here to the mainland to build wave break walls. There is a lot of that sort of building going on all the time with the various shoreline improvements at Long Beach and Terminal Island. The barges are one hundred fifty feet long and fifty feet wide. They are open and built out of one inch steel and really heavy. They are anchored inside the rock wall breakwater, when not in use, and moored with a one inch braided steel cable to a buoy the size of a car, which in turn is tied to a huge concrete weight on the bottom."

The story was getting more interesting to Ernie, and he listened intently without interrupting.

"This one particular barge was empty, and so it was fifteen feet out of the water where the steel cable was attached to it that went to the big buoy, a hundred and fifty feet away. That meant the cable tied to its front or bow was nearly horizontal. There was a little wind, from the west, such that the barge was pulling on the steel cable leeward of the buoy. I did not see the cable, and my boat went right into it just below the flying bridge at twenty-five knots. The tight steel cable went right smack through my boat, shearing the boat in two, like a hot knife through butter. The cable sheared the bridge of the boat right off and carried it back to the aft of the boat where it fell right to the deck. I was in the captain's chair up on the flying bridge at the secondary helm, above the main one in the main cabin. The whole flying bridge, including the helm seat with me in it, went to the back of the boat where everything fell onto the rear deck! The steel cable holding the barge continued right on through the boat, but it went right underneath me. That's what all that rubble is in the stern of the boat."

Ernie was in shock. "And you lived?"

"I hardly even got a scratch. I did get knocked out, I figure, for about twenty minutes, based on how far the boat drifted. The steel cable cut off all the controls, sheared all the electric wires, and the motors shut down. The boat was adrift. The shortwave radio would not even work."

"What did you do with the boat?"

"None of the electronics would work, so there was little I could do. I couldn't use the main radio, and the only radio that worked at all was a battery powered portable, with a receiver only—no transmitter. So, I put out the anchor, and went to sleep until the next morning. Then I put my dingy in the water, and went to shore at Shoreline Village, where I called the same friend that I met the night before. He lives on his boat near Shoreline Village. We came out to my boat with his and towed it in to the boat yard here."

"This is an amazing story. You were traveling at twenty-five knots, and ran into a nearly horizontal steel cable that sheared your boat in two, and you didn't even get hurt?"

"That's right. Given the fact that this is a gas boat, powered by two, 450-cubic-inch Mariner Chevys, I was lucky that there wasn't an explosion or fire. That is always a risk in gas-powered boats, as the engine compartment can fill with fumes and blow."

"Have you obtained a marine survey from the boat yard yet as to the damages?"

"Yeah, right here." Carson took several pages stapled together out of his briefcase.

Ernie looked at the estimate from the boat yard. It seemed to provide for the depreciation and things the insurance company would require. "The total here is seventy-two thousand eight hundred dollars. The amount the insurance is to pay is only fifty-nine thousand four hundred eighty dollars. Some things are upgrades, is that right?"

"Yes, some of the things cannot be fixed, and so new items must be purchased. Like the radio. The new one is better with a state of the art global positioning satellite receiver. The repair estimate from the boat yard here has only included the value of the old one at the time of loss. It seems they do this insurance work all the time."

"You will have to come up with the difference. You are aware of that?"

"Actually, these boats are under constant attack from the salt water, the sun, not to mention wear and tear," Carson said. "I'm going to spend extra on it since it is already in dry dock. It was time for painting the bottom again, which has to be done every year and a half or so, and you will notice that is not included in the survey. That alone is normally seven thousand dollars, but will only cost me about six since it is already out of the water."

"Can I please look at the inside the boat?"

"Sure, that is why we're here, isn't it?"

The two of them climbed up the cradle, up into the boat, which was quite high when out of the water.

Ernie looked about in amazement. "Good Lord! The flying bridge looks like someone took it off with a giant chainsaw."

"At twenty-five knots, that one inch steel cable had the effect of being pretty sharp."

Ernie went to the kitchen and bar and noticed the complete absence of any liquor, liquor glasses, no mixes, and there were no drinking accessories. It was entirely too suspicious. He walked out the door and went to the bow, where there was a dingy on top of the boat, used for shuttles to and from shore. The dingy had its name painted on the transom *Olive.*

A boat named Tanguerey? A dingy named Olive? No liquor aboard? Something is wrong here! Ernie looked back to the area where there used to be a flying bridge. He then walked back to Carson. "I think I know what happened. You were drunk on your ass, and you passed out. When the accident happened, you came to and worried you were going to get busted for drunk driving of a boat. So you threw all the booze as well as all drinking accessories overboard. You did not call the coast guard so you would not get busted for drunk driving, the same charge as driving a car. We have the same thing up in Washington. You then went and got your buddy."

After a few moments of silence, realizing he was discovered by someone who knew what he was talking about, Carson winced. "You got me!"

Ernie laughed. "Hah!"

Carson grinned. "Everyone who has seen this cracks up, laughing. When I brought in the boat the next morning the guys here at the yard could hardly stop laughing."

The image formed in Ernie's mind of the cable cutting right through the top of the boat less than a foot or so below its passed-out pilot, and then carrying the bridge as well as him, still passed out, to the back of the boat and dumping the bridge with him in it right onto the rear deck. "I'd give anything to actually see the cable cutting the top of your boat off with you passed out above it in the captain's chair."

Ernie started to laugh at the idea and the image of it happening in his mind. Then Carson started to laugh, and in no time the laughter got infectious.

Finally, when the laughter subsided, Ernie said, "The insurance coverage cannot be denied based on drinking, but the company will surely cancel your policy if they are informed that you were drinking."

"Yeah, I know," Carson said. "Bummer."

"I can't settle this claim myself as I only have ten thousand dollars of settlement authority. But I'm going to write it up as checked out by me as okay to pay. After that, it is out of my hands. But the insurance company will probably pay what I, as the field representative, recommend, having seen the boat in person, and verified the reasonableness of the estimate, the marine survey. I think your claim is just and fair."

"What about telling them that I was drinking?" Carson asked. "Kennedy got away with it at Chappaquidick."

"Majestik will probably re-evaluate you anyway, since you had a claim," Ernie replied. "I see no reason to put something like that in your folder. Most all of you people who have a part-time luxury boat go out to have a couple of shooters. Who am I to judge?"

Ernie took another look at the sawed-in-two boat and started to laugh again at the at the thought of the steel cable cutting the boat top neatly off at twenty-five knots with Carson, drunk and passed out, flying backward with the flying bridge. Carson joined in, and the laughter continued.

CHAPTER 37

I'm so happy to finally have lunch with each of you," Zachary Lewis told the group of five young people sitting around him at a big table at a café. Candidate Lewis had come to his southern campaign headquarters and took a lunch with some of his local staff. He decided to take a small group of the younger workers to a nearby café for a sandwich. Nothing fancy, but it was personal time with the staff, which they very much appreciated. Especially Maria Manelli.

"You all have been working so hard on my campaign, it is the least I can do. Don't think for a moment that your contributions of time and work go unappreciated." He looked at Maria. "You're new, aren't you? What's your name again?"

"Maria Manelli," she said with a big smile.

"What have they got you doing?"

"All sorts of odd jobs like passing out literature at gatherings. But I'm between semesters at school and can devote all my time to your campaign. I hope to work at the headquarters."

"Well, since you're full time, maybe we can find you something more important to do. What would you like to do?"

"Maybe I could work as an assistant to your appointments and scheduling secretary Doris? She seems to be overloaded at times and can seldom so much as take a break."

"I think she could use some help, so I'll ask her. I expect she'd like that very much. You could help her coordinate schedules with so much going on, and things are going to get even busier as the election draws near." He looked at the others, and asked them collectively, "How's everything going with you?"

Everyone murmured, "Fine," honored to have lunch with the popular candidate.

"I'll remember each of you when we win. If any of you hard-working people need assistance after the election, be sure and come and see me."

☙❧

"Daddy?" Maria asked from her cell phone.

"Hi, sweetheart," Salvatore Manelli said to his loyal daughter.

"How are you, Daddy?"

"I'm fine. How'd it go?"

"Perfect," Maria jubilantly reported. "Lewis has put me on as assistant to his appointments and scheduling secretary. I should have his entire schedule and know where is going most of the time."

"I heard he's a big sport fisherman," her father said. "I'm especially interested to learn of any fishing plans he may have. Let me know if you hear of any, and as soon as you do, okay?"

"I will, Daddy." She was raised in the traditions and family values of the old school, of traditions past, and fiercely loyal to her father and family.

"Nice going, sweetheart. Is there anything you need?"

"No, I'm fine. I have your credit card."

"Okay, darling. Take care."

CHAPTER 38

Whiplash?" Ernie asked the claimant, Samuel Weinstock. "Is that the injury you are claiming twenty-five thousand dollars for?"

Ernie had his file from the insurance company and sat across from Mr. Weinstock, a young entrepreneur in his early thirties, owning his own business. It was a company that made aftermarket leather seat covers for new cars that did not come with leather. Weinstock had turned in a claim from an auto accident he had where he was rear ended six months earlier.

Weinstock's desk was a mess, full of papers, files, and junk, all full of dust. The factory was just a short distance away though a large opening in the wall, and dust seemed to be everywhere.

"The chiropractor's bills are over seven thousand, five hundred dollars. The damage to the rear of my BMW was two thousand, five hundred, forty dollars. I paid that out of my pocket. I heard you are supposed to get three times your medical bills for your injury plus the expenses."

"It's a leased BMW?" Ernie asked.

"Yes. This is the third one I have leased. I turn them in every three years."

Ernie recalled how his prejudiced uncle used to say back home that leasing a truck or car was the same as putting a Jew between you and your vehicle. This, he used to say, was based on the principle that if you have money, you buy if you really need it. If not, don't. He shook his head, trying to forget that horrible statement about Jews. "You got a form letter from Jessica Bloom, I see, denying your claim. It says that you slammed on your brakes in front of someone else and then you were hit in the rear. If you had not been following too close, you would not have been hit in the rear. Therefore, you were at fault as well. She further contends that you have not substantiated your claim by the necessary documentation."

"I've since sent in the medical bills, but no one has contacted me until now."

A girl stuck her head in the door and said in a worried tone to Weinstock, "Sammy, it's a leather supplier. What do you want me to say? We don't want him to cut us off."

"Just shmooze him. Tell him I will have something for him in a few days."

She left and he focused his attention back to Ernie.

"I see you have not paid the chiropractor, yet you have bills here for a visit nearly every other day since the accident. Is he collecting his bills only as a lien on a successful recovery?"

"Yes, he was good enough to wait until I recover on my claim to get his bill paid."

Ernie looked at the report in the file. "According to the police report, my insured behind you bumped into you after you slammed on your brakes hard to avoid hitting someone ahead of you who was already stopped. Is that what happened?"

"Yeah, this car ahead of me, and several ahead of him, all came to a sudden stop. I stopped in time behind the one in front of me, but the car you insure, the one that was behind me, ran into me."

"Our insured couldn't have hit you too hard. At the excessive prices of BMW parts, if he hit you even slightly hard it would be fifteen thousand dollars, not two thousand, five hundred, forty." Ernie began to doubt the validity of the claim. "According to the picture, all it did was ding the bumper and break a taillight. There was no body damage to your car at all. How do you claim twenty five thousand five hundred dollars for a light tap like that?"

"Do I have to go to a lawyer?" Weinstock asked cautiously.

"You may do as you wish, of course. But I tell you what I'll do today. I'll pay for the bumper. I'll give you that now. And if you want to settle the personal injury claim, I'll give you a check today for an additional five thousand dollars. That's all I think it is worth. Otherwise, I'll turn it over to the Majestik legal staff since you're going to go to a lawyer."

"But my chiropractic bill alone is seven thousand, five hundred dollars."

"Sorry, it's just too much. Why don't you call him up and see if he'll cut his bill to two thousand, five hundred for you? Then you can split that and get your money today. I doubt if you made all of these appointments it shows on this list here." Ernie looked at the bills, again, cocking his head, doubtfully.

"He would charge me if I skipped an appointment," Weinstock said defensively.

He probably only went to a few of them, Ernie thought. *Otherwise, he would not been able to keep the manufacturing plant going.* "Well, that's my offer. And it's now, and I'm here, checkbook in hand."

"Will you excuse me while I call him?" Weinstock asked.

"Of course. I'll be outside."

"Thank you."

Ernie went to the disorganized, dusty reception area, and sat on a sofa across from a table with a bunch of out of date trade magazines.

In a few minutes, Weinstock opened his door. "Come on back in." Inside, he sighed. "The chiropractor will discount his bill, and so I'll accept it today. I figure if I go to a lawyer and pay him a third, I probably won't come out any better. Anyway, I could use the money now."

"Good!" Ernie got a release ready and handed it to him while he wrote out the terms, and made a draft from his company field checkbook.

Driving away on his motorcycle, Ernie shook his head. *There's another side to the insurance business. Whiplash in a leased BMW with a dinged bumper? A yuppie injury, mostly to the car.*

∽∾∽

Not far in miles, but slow in heavy traffic, was the area of the next claim, Monterey Park, nearby San Gabriel, the heart of the new Chinatown of Los Angeles. Ernie motored between the vehicles on the freeways at several times the speed of the cars nearly stalled in the lanes.

Arriving at the address, he parked his motorcycle in the driveway of the Chinese household. The claimants were a couple named Chang, who had agreed to meet him at their newly acquired home, which, oddly, was itself the subject of the claim. Majestik insured the previous owners, a husband and wife, but the husband died, so the wife was now the only insured.

The Changs were making a claim against the previous owner regarding the purchase price of the house, claiming they were defrauded as the house was not worth anywhere near what they paid for it, due to non-disclosure of a material fact.

In the drive was parked a silver Mercedes, one of the mid-sized versions, fairly new. The Mercedes looked a little bit expensive for the value of the home, but then Ernie remembered that Asians were into fancy cars as status symbols or as a business tool for giving the impression of prestige and success. *An American motorcycle has more prestige*, Ernie thought, as he parked his in the drive beside the silver Mercedes—but he had yet to see a Chinaman on a motorcycle. He suddenly remembered what bad drivers the Chinese were and moved his bike to the other side of the Mercedes so the Chinaman would not back over it if he left first. Removing the correct file from his saddlebag, he approached the front door.

A Chinese lady, five feet tall, answered his knock, wearing pink Capri pants that stopped just below the knee, a white Western-styled shirt covering her nearly flat chest, and rubber flip-flop slippers. She had a typical Chinese flat backside, rendering her pants baggy in the seat.

She said something in Chinese. Behind her was a cute, little Chinese girl holding onto her mother's leg, looking up at Ernie and his strange Caucasian face.

"I'm Ernie from Majestik Insurance. I'm here about the claim. My card."

She took the card and disappeared inside, the youngster in tow, leaving the door ajar. Her Chinese husband then came to the door in suit pants, white shirt and tie, no coat, still chewing something with rice, as it was coming disgustingly out of his mouth.

He was obviously the person Ernie was supposed to see and was having lunch.

The man motioned him in. "Yes, insurance."

Ernie was invited to sit. The wife politely took the child off for the men to discuss business. A strong odor of Chinese food emanated from the kitchen.

"I understand this is a claim about your house," Ernie began. "Majestik insured the former owners who sold you the house, and apparently the husband of the couple died while still living in the house. Is that correct?"

"Yes! No one will buy this house now with bad luck of death! House have no value!"

"I understand you are making a claim for two hundred twenty-five thousand dollars. Is that so?"

"Yes. Price I paid three hundred twenty-five thousand dollars, less price can sell for, only one hundred thousand dollars."

Ernie sat forward in his chair. "Tell me more."

"Cannot live here. Owner die of heart attack before we bought it. When we saw house, house empty. No one say owner die. House have bad *feng shui.* Cannot live here and cannot sell."

"Isn't *feng shui* about luck?" Ernie asked.

"House cursed with death!"

"Who was the realtor who sold you the house? Didn't the realtor tell you that the former owner died here, and aren't realtors responsible for doing just that?"

"Realtor my sister-in-law. She not know of death at time of sale."

Naturally, they are not going to make a claim against the wife's sister, Ernie concluded. "You had no idea of death of the owner when you bought the house?"

"We not know."

"Don't the Chinese normally bring out a *feng shui* man when they consider buying a property?"

"Yes. We hire *feng shui*, but *feng shui* not discover death as too soon for spirit to settle in and bring bad luck."

"Then how did you learn of the death of the owner?"

"Neighbor tell us."

Ernie could hardly believe what he was hearing. But then, this *was* the big city. *Better stay cool and come up with a solution.* "Okay, here is what I want. I want you to have your *feng shui* come over here. If you can get him over in an hour, I'll go to lunch and then meet him here. Otherwise, we'll have to make it a later date."

"Okay," Chang said and left the room to go to the phone to call him. He returned after a few minutes. "He be here one hour."

"Good. I'll go to lunch, and return in an hour. Is there a restaurant around here nearby?"

"Chinese?" Chang asked.

☙❧

At a nearby Chinese restaurant, Ernie phoned in to the office at the number McAteer gave him for assistance. McAteer himself answered, to Ernie's surprise. McAteer loved to be personally involved in claims, Ernie found out, and jumped at the chance to assist in defeating any claim.

"Mr. McAteer, this is Ernie, one of your temporary field men."

"Yes, I recall you. How's it going?"

"Oh, fine. But I have a question. A Chinese couple bought a home and found out later that the husband of the couple who owned the house before died in it. The buyers now claim it is bad luck and the price fell on the house, at least in the Chinese community. Majestik insured the former owners. What's the deal on that?"

"I'm glad you asked, Ernie. This could be considered as fraud, which would be not an insured event under the home-owners' policy. Non-disclosure is one kind of fraud. There is a fairly new statute in California that knocks out the liability of the owners or a realtor for an undisclosed death that occurred if the death was over three years prior to the sale. If it occurred within three years or less, it has to be disclosed by the sellers, and in that case, if it was not disclosed, we could be liable, unless it was a matter of fraud. I recall the code section. It is California Civil Code 1710.2. But check and see if the realtor disclosed the death. If the sellers, who would now be just the wife since her husband died, disclosed it, then she is not liable. If the realtor was told, and the realtor did not disclose, then the realtor is liable. If there is a dispute as to who told what to whom between the realtor and the seller, since we insured the seller, we can counter sue the realtor and we can get out of paying anything if we win. The seller and the seller's realtor are supposed to disclose any material fact to a buyer that might affect his decision to buy the house.

"The other thing you can do is to deny coverage based on the fact that the seller, who is the wife, committed fraud if she did not disclose the death. If the widow did not disclose her husband's death, we can deny coverage based on the contention that we do not insure fraudulent acts, and that concealment of a material fact is a form of fraud. There is usually a form that realtors use that asks the sellers to disclose any material fact that might affect the prospective buyers' decision to buy the property. The disclosure should be in that. However, if the sellers' realtors filled out the form, then we are on the hook as their realtor was their agent, and we can only collect in a counter suit and then only if the realtor has assets or insurance. It means a lawsuit."

"Okay, thanks. This one occurred within the three years."

"Well, see what you can do," McAteer advised.

Ernie considered what to do. Majestik could deny coverage to the widow, if she did not disclose the death, and also counter sue the realtor for not disclosing if the widow did disclose the death to the realtor. But that meant defending the claim of the new buyers, providing a defense to the widow but telling her Majestik won't pay, and counter suing the realtor for not discovering and disclosing a material fact of the death in the house. The thing could go on for years. *Maybe there's a better way.*

Ernie returned on his motorcycle to the Chang house with the taste of monosodium glutamate lingering. There was another car parked in front of the house on the street, another silver Mercedes sedan, a few years older, but this one had minor dents in all of the fenders. *The feng shui must be a pretty lousy driver*, Ernie surmised. He parked his bike safely on the street, well out of the way of the Kamikaze driver of the dented Mercedes.

As he approached, Chang came to the door. "*Feng shui* Mr. Lee here," Chang told him, leading Ernie to him for the introduction, as though he was to meet Jesus on the cross. Ernie approached a small, frail, man in his sixties, known as the *feng shui* man.

"So you inspected the house and found no evil spirits, did you?" Ernie asked him. He realized that he was being sarcastic with this concept.

The man began talking in Chinese, as though he had no idea what Ernie was talking about. Ernie felt that the man was simply hiding behind Chinese as a language, as it would be nearly impossible to get along in Los Angeles without some English.

On a hunch, Ernie said, "I would like to talk to the *feng shui* outside for a few minutes."

Taking his file with him, he beckoned to the *feng shui*, and the frail little man followed Ernie outside. The *feng shui* man was nervous.

Outside, Ernie led him to the side of the house, as though to look at it, to an area where the others could not see them. Towering over the Chinaman, Ernie reached down to the man's shirt, grabbed a handful of it, and picked him off the ground, up over a foot, to Ernie's face. "Listen to me, you piece-of-shit fraud. You speak English just like I do. You were supposed to be able to tell if the house had bad luck. You inspected this place and told them there was no bad luck here, for which you charged them money. You couldn't find an evil spirit if one bit you in the ass. I'm going to expose you and ruin your business unless you help me. I'll put your name on the insurance computer system as evidence of fraud. Then I'll run an ad for a year in the Chinese newspaper as well with your picture. If I have to defend a lawsuit, I will have our lawyers file a counterclaim against you which will expose you for not being able to detect a bad spirit. You'll never get hired again."

Lee's eyes opened wide as Ernie held him up in the air, an inch away from his face. "If he learn I miss the death, I lose face and get no more business."

"Now that we are communicating," Ernie said, putting the man down. "Here's what you are going to do. You'll find a way to tell Chang and his wife that the circumstances of the previous owner's death are such that his spirit does not bring bad luck to this house."

Lee, still shaking from the scare, appeared completely terrified. "What you know of death of former owner?"

Ernie looked into his file and thumbed through the papers. "It looks like he died on the eighth of the month, six months ago, of a heart attack while in bed. He was taken in an ambulance to the hospital and pronounced dead on arrival. His widow sold the house after that to the Changs."

Lee thought about it for a moment and, losing his accent, asked, "Did you say he died on the eighth of month?"

Ernie double checked the paper. "Yes, the eighth."

Lee's expression changed, and a look of relief came over his face. "Eight is a very lucky number with the Chinese. I know what to do. I know. I know. I know." He began walking back toward the front door, repeating it.

Ernie did not know just what the *feng shui* had in mind, so he followed several paces behind.

They sat again and this time Ms. Chang joined them in the living room. Lee began carrying on in rapid Mandarin, and there was conversation back and forth. Ernie had no idea what was going on, but Ms. Chang showed an expression of great relief. Finally, Mr. Chang turned to Ernie. "Mr. Lee say the former owner, Mr. Hsing, died on the eighth of the month. That is a very lucky number for the house, and because of that, his spirit will never haunt house and, instead, only return and bring good luck. That is why Mr. Lee did not detect any bad luck when he examined house. Good thing, or we have to move."

"Well, It looks like you're in luck," Ernie said, relaxing. "I guess that you'll be able to stay here, after all. I'll consider the matter settled. May I shake your hand in hopes that some of your good fortune will rub off on me?" he asked, pandering to their superstitions.

"Yes," Mr. Chang said. "I guess we have good luck here." He rose and shook Ernie's hand. "Thank you for coming."

Ernie pulled away on his bike, taking extra care in the area due to the Chinese drivers, and approached the freeway ramp. *I think I'm getting the hang of this insurance business. You just have to know how to motivate certain people and have good feng shui.*

⌘

Ernie turned off the freeway ramp on the never-ending greater Los Angeles freeway system to his next stop. The address was a single-story building, and there was a one hundred fifty foot flagpole outside.

The building was identified as a machine shop by a small sign. Inside, Ernie counted eight people working on lathes, mills, and drill presses. The few workers there all speaking in a language that Ernie did not understand. A man saw him and motioned him to a small office inside the shop to get away from the noise of the machines.

"Hi, I'm Ernie from Majestik. I'm here about your claim."

"How do you do," the man said, holding out his arm and then shaking Ernie's hand with gusto. "I'm Ferenc Horvath."

"I see in my file a flag was damaged by vandals."

"I came from Budapest. I'm so proud to be an American. They gave me my citizenship just last year, and so I made a big flag to show my appreciation for this wonderful country. I love America."

"Is there an insurance claim over the flag?"

"Vandals jumped the fence and brought down the flag at night. They tore it up, and sprayed graffiti on the building. It was terrible! The shredded remains are in the back room." Horvath led Ernie to the back room where there were metals and other materials stored. On the floor was a large pile of the remains of the previous flag.

"I got a letter from a lady named Bloom denying the claim. Do you think the insurance would pay me for just the material? I don't have much money yet, as I'm still paying for the machines. I painted over the graffiti on the walls the next day with my son, so I don't need a claim to have it repainted."

"How much did the flag cost?" Ernie asked.

"My wife sewed it," he proudly announced. "It took a long time to sew. The material was over two thousand dollars. I swore I would always fly my new country's flag over my shop, and to go to fight in a war for America if called on me."

Ernie was puzzled. "I have to call in on this one. I don't know. Give me a minute." He walked outside, away from the Hungarian, and called the programmed-in number to the insurance office where the experienced personnel were supposed to be on hand, and where McAteer himself might answer the phone. This time is was not McAteer. It was one of the sleeze-bag attorneys.

"Hi. This is Ernie, one of the temporary field representatives."

"This is Jason. What's up?"

"I have a man here who put up a monster flag up outside his building. He has a small commercial building and business we insure. Some gangbangers jumped the chain link, took down his flag, and tore it up, and then sprayed the building with graffiti. Is the flag insured?"

"I need a claim number to document the call," Jason said.

Ernie read off the claim number to Jason, realizing that now he was creating a record that would end up in the file.

A minute later Jason returned. "The answer is no. There's an exclusion for banners, and that's a banner."

"Well, this big flag was permanent. How can Old Glory be a sale banner?"

"Fuck that asshole! Just tell him it's a banner and excluded," Jason said. "I'll make a note that I told you to deny the claim in the computer and it will be added to the file later. Anything else?"

"No. That's all." Ernie clicked off the phone. *What a bunch of cheating bastards! And now they've made a note of my call—I should have just settled it. I can't pay for the flag, now that it's in the company computer. If I write a company check and include the cost of the flag, the company accountant won't co-sign for it and it'll bounce.*

This poor guy gets vandalized, and the company won't even help. Calling Old Glory a banner! Those pieces-of-shit attorneys.

Ernie walked slowly back in the door to the machine shop to Horvath. "Show me where the graffiti was sprayed."

Horvath walked him around the building and it was obvious where he had rolled on new paint over gang insignias as the single coat of paint did not completely hide the graffiti.

"Mr. Horvath, the insurance company tells me that the flag is classified as a banner, like a sale banner, and is not insured. But I tell you what I'm going to do. If you'd had the building painted professionally to cover up the graffiti, you would have had to spend about one thousand, five hundred dollars. And I see you have business interruption insurance, for which you probably had a claim, with the down time in dealing with the graffiti and the flag."

"What's that?"

"Just go along with me on this. I'm going to make it one thousand dollars for business interruption. With your deductible of five hundred, that means I can give you two thousand dollars. That should help cover your losses."

"Oh, thank you. So the flag is not insured? I don't know about these things. They did not tell me that when I bought the insurance. The agent knew about the flag, because he was here and saw it. I leave it up twenty-four hours a day. At night, I shine a light on it as required by law. I want it always to fly over my shop."

"Did you take it down in the big storm recently?"

"Of course. Do you think I would leave such a beautiful thing out in a big storm?"

"What have you done to prevent it from happening again?"

"I put razor wire all over the top of the chain link fence."

Horvath pointed to the nasty-looking razor wire that had sharp barbs everywhere, rolled about the top of the chain link fence.

"That should slow those no good gangs down," he said. "America is too soft on criminals. They should see how bad it is back in Hungary. They should ship them there for a year for this. They would do well to get a job and then at eight dollars per day."

"Can I have use of your office to make a call?" Ernie asked.

"Sure. Now, if you don't mind, I will go back to work. Just call out when you finish. I have some work to get done. I work six days a week, only taking off Sundays for church. I am open from six to six every day, and sometimes I work late. I'm going to make the business a success."

"I can see that." Ernie followed him back into the busy little shop.

And he will make it a success, he concluded.

"Just wave or shout when you need me."

Ernie reached for the dusty phone book on the owner's desk. He found a number and rang it up.

"American Veterans Association," an elderly man answered.

"My name is Ernie, from Majestik Insurance. I have a situation here that might be of interest to you all. Can I explain?"

"Sure. I'm retired and come in here most of the time. I'm in administration."

"Have you ever seen that huge American flag flying over the 91 freeway?" Ernie asked.

"Sure. How could anyone miss it. There was an article about it in the paper when it first went up a while back. An immigrant from Eastern Europe, I think. I would like to meet him and shake his hand. What a flag!"

"That's the one. Well, the owner had some bad luck. Vandals ripped up the flag, and the owner is looking to the insurance company to pay for the material for the replacement. He says the material was two thousand dollars, which seems about right for enough material to cover most of a basketball court. The man is from Hungary, and his wife sewed the flag. She is going to sew a new one, and that will probably take some time. My insurance company says a flag is not covered, but I am giving him a contribution for his overall losses. Would your association be willing to contribute?"

"I know of some of the members who will personally pay for that flag, even if the association can't. Give me his name and address, and someone will come out to see him. I wish I could come too, but my diabetes and arthritis have both been getting pretty bad, so I doubt I can."

"I'm sure it would also make a good article for any paper you publish, and make the new American very proud to have his picture in the paper," Ernie said.

"Yes, we're always looking for any interesting news such as that. I'll make sure the photographer comes out too."

Ernie gave him the man's name and address. "Thanks, very much. I'm sure that assisting in flying Old Glory over the freeway will be something that your association can be proud to be part of."

He waved at the owner through the glass window of his office and got his attention. Horvath shut down the machine he was working on and came back to the office.

"I'll give you a draft for two thousand dollars for the graffiti and for business interruption. You have to agree and sign this release." He handed the man the release which he signed. "Now, I have given your name to the American Veterans Association. Here's the phone number. Someone will be contacting you. I think they will buy you the material for a new flag, and they want to put your picture in their newspaper. Your enthusiasm in being an American is of interest to them, and I suspect that you may end up with some new friends and get some referrals from vets or their contacts who need machine work. Their paper alone might make that happen."

Horvath seemed deeply touched, and his eyes watered.

"I'm most thankful." With both hands he shook Ernie's. "The other person from the insurance, Jessica Bloom, denied the claim. Why did you handle it differently?"

"Well, from what I have seen so far, Jessica Bloom did not come out to any of the claim sites to find out what they were about. But, anyway, sir," Ernie said to change the subject so as not to criticize his employer, "I must be off."

"God bless you sir, you are very helpful. I'm proud to be here in America with such wonderful people."

Ernie handed him the check. "Welcome to America."

As Ernie pulled out, he thought, *Why do those low life insurance lawyers have to cheat everyone? Calling Old Glory a sale banner! Those little shit lawyers never served in the military nor do they give a shit about America, that's for sure. Well, I did what I could for Horvath. Welcome to America, friend.*

ℭℭℭ

There was one more claim he had in mind to handle that day, and that was en route on the way home if he had time. It was 5:30 p.m., and there wasn't much time. But he was willing and able, if it could be done. It was a small apartment building of sixteen units, two stories high. The claim was from the owner of the building, a widow, who maintained an office in one of the front units.

Ernie walked up to the office just as Ms. Elniff, the owner, was about to leave. "Hi, I'm Ernie, from Majestik, about the water damage claim."

"Oh, I wasn't expecting you."

"I did not know if I could make it today, but since I could, I just came by. Can you show me the damage?"

Ms. Elniff went back inside to get some keys. She returned and closed the door to the office. "This way." Along the short walk she described the claim. "This is a flooding problem that came from a broken water line. The line broke on the upper floor and did quite a lot of damage to the unit below. Fortunately, the tenants below had moved out just the day before, or they would no doubt be making a claim as well for furniture damage."

She led Ernie to a vacant apartment on the first floor and opened the door. Inside the air was rancid, full of moisture and mold smell. Water damage witness marks were on the walls in one section where water had come down from above, soaking the walls, staining them. The water also stained the rug, which had begun to mold.

Ernie opened a window to let fresh air in, and then another in the kitchen to get some cross-flow ventilation to curtail the growing of mold. It was an average unit, and the damage appeared to be limited to new carpeting, painting, and also some new linoleum in the kitchen that had curled up from being soaked in water.

"Ms. Bloom wrote me a letter denying the claim, based on her statement that such damage must have come over time from lack of maintenance. But it all happened in one day, so she's wrong. I'm glad you're here. Maybe you can help me?"

"I guess the question is, where did it come from?" Ernie said. "That will determine if it was insured or not."

"There is no doubt that it came from the unit above. They had flooding in their bathroom."

"Are there tenants still living above at this time?" Ernie asked.

"Yes, there's a couple living there. They've been there now for a year and a half and seem to be quite nice. They're not married." She walked outside and looked up. "It looks like someone is in now. The lights are on."

"May I go up and interview them? I have to determine that this was a sudden event before it is insured, as opposed to gradual water damage over time that would come under maintenance."

"Sure. I'll introduce you, and I'll then go put some things in the mail and come back."

Ms. Elniff led Ernie up the stairs to the upper apartment and knocked.

An extraordinarily wide and heavy woman, about thirty years of age and actually quite pretty, came to the door. She had the absolutely hugest breasts that Ernie had ever seen.

"Pam, this is Ernie from the insurance company. Would you mind talking to him about the water damage claim? I'll run to the post office and be back in an hour. Do you mind?"

"Not at all," Pam said. "Please come in." She had to move her massive chest away from the door so Ernie could pass.

"I'm from Majestik. If the damage occurred slowly from leakage, it would not be covered. But if it occurred suddenly, as in an accident, it would be. Can you provide any information for me?"

"Of course," she said. "The water came from our bathroom. Come and I'll show you." She led him to the bath. "The toilet broke off, and the water pipe feeding it broke and flooded the area below the bath in the apartment below."

"How can a toilet break off?"

"Why don't you come over to the table and sit down." She led him to the dining table and showed him to a seat. "I'm going to have a glass of wine, as I just got off work. Would you like some wine or a beer?"

"Well, okay. Wine." Ernie wondered what was it about the story that required him to sit down just to hear it. When she returned, she sat across the table.

He tried, but failed, not to stare at her huge tits that rested on the table in front of her like watermelons on display at the market. "So, how did it happen?" he asked, looking around at the walls as though there was something interesting there to see.

"My boyfriend is a mechanic. He'll be home in a while. The night it happened was a Saturday night, a week ago, He drinks quite a lot on the weekends—that's an understatement. We had gone to a bar where he got plastered. I drove us home."

Pam sipped on the wine, as though looking for liquid courage to continue. She maintained a very pleasant, yet concerned expression. "He had decided that he wanted me in bondage. He really likes that. He bought some real handcuffs to put on me. When he does that, he then does things to me. I enjoy it, But, you know, it seldom seems to get him off as he gets too drunk or passes out. But I guess it's the idea that counts."

Ernie leaned back in surprise at the boldness of the testi-monial. He wasn't sure just what to do or say.

"So he had me get naked, and he put the handcuffs on my wrists, behind my back. He then put me in bed, and he got on top of me to put things in me. He suddenly realized that he had to go to the bathroom, and so he got up and cavorted to the bathroom. He pulled down his pants, and sat on the john, where he immediately passed completely out."

Ernie wasn't sure if this was leading to the water story or not, but decided to listen politely as she continued.

"There I was, in bed, completely naked, with my arms handcuffed behind my back, and my boyfriend on the john passed out like a zombie in a catatonic stupor. I managed to get up, and I went over to the bathroom to see if I could wake him. He was completely gone, and the heat lamp built into the ceiling light was on and making his forehead sweat as he sat there, pants down, leaning his head against the wall."

"So where did the water come from?" Ernie asked, trying to hurry this bizarre story along, as it seemed uncomfortably embarrassing.

"I'm coming to that." She seemed reluctant to hurry through the details, as though they were important. "I had my hands handcuffed behind my back, and could not get him to come to by shouting, although I tried. So I turned around and tried to shake his head with my hands but it wasn't easy with my hands behind me. What happened next is that I slipped and fell over and on top of him and the toilet, and my fall broke the toilet right out of the wall. The water line came loose and that is what flooded downstairs. It was only a small water line to the toilet, but it was on for quite a while."

Ernie sized her up at about two hundred eighty pounds, and forty was in either tit. She could definitely break a ceramic toilet. The story seemed credible. *How to write this up?*

"Couldn't you have stopped the water from coming? Water lines to toilets have a shut off valve and the lines are only a small, three-eighths-inch water line that could not do very much flooding in a short amount of time."

She leaned forward, which only made her tits appear larger as the table pushed up on them. "When I fell, I hit my head and was knocked out. We lay there for a while before we woke up. He had to take my handcuffs off first and had to search for the key. Water was everywhere. We finally got the water line to the toilet turned off, but by that time it had run a while. We pretty much cleaned it up here, but it was Sunday morning and we could not find Ms. Elniff, so the water that dripped down through the floor stayed in the lower unit until Monday. I guess we screwed up the unit below us pretty good, huh?"

Ernie blinked. "That has got to be the most unusual story I have ever heard!"

"I hope you don't have to tell anyone."

"No, I guess not. This is certainly a sudden claim and would be covered by insurance. Thank you for the wine. I'll be going now." He got up and went to the door. She got up to see him out, lifting her huge tits off the table.

Just as he was about to leave, she looked at him intently. "Can I ask you something?"

"I guess so. What?"

"I discussed what happened with my girlfriend, and she thought the whole thing was a little weird, the handcuffs and all. Do you think so too?"

Ernie shrugged. "It's not for me to judge others."

Then she asked another question. "What is it they call that when your boyfriend likes to tie you up and do things to you with objects? Isn't there a name for that?"

Ernie looked at her for a long time and, just before he turned to walk out, he answered, "Foreplay."

CHAPTER 39

T his is excellent salmon," Mrs. Zachary Lewis told her hostess, Mrs. John Poladian. "What do you call this sauce?" she asked, referring to the maroon sauce surrounding the salmon prepared by one of the finest chefs in Los Angeles.

Mrs. Poladian grinned with satisfaction that her food was going over well. "That is called red curry sauce," she told the wife of her distinguished guest. "But I don't want to fool you. We did not make it here. I had a well-known chef bring it in and finish it off in our kitchen here. He's in the kitchen now. That way it was a sure thing."

Mrs. Lewis showed a bit of surprise. "Oh, Dorothy, I should have known. You always have the finest dinners."

Mrs. Poladian had a famous chef pre-make everything and bring it along to the house as culinary delights from his famous restaurant.

A servant stood back from the table at a relaxed form of attention in the event a plate was to be picked up, a water glass filled, more wine, or any request.

"I'm so glad you like it," Mrs. Poladian said. *She should like it,* she thought, *considering what it cost to bring in that chef.*

Another guest, Steven Addison, turned to Lewis. "Zackary I see the insurance industry has spent more against you in California than the Republicans and Democrats did combined in the last presidential election."

"We have reasonable reliable feedback on that," Lewis said. "Whenever it comes out that an insurance company is funding the ad against me, it has almost no effect. In some cases, a negative effect. They have to state the name of the organization that is running the ad, and people find out no matter what sort of clandestine name they come up with for some new committee to elect so and so, or to defeat so and so, or some proposition. People are simply fed up with the crooked insurance companies, and the companies have no credibility. I intend to put a stop to these insurance company shenanigans, which I think are criminal. The people see that and believe that I can do it."

George Papac, another guest, rubbed his chin. "What is all this about some Indian Nation coming out against you? They reported twenty million dollars in contributions to your opponent."

"We have been looking into that," Lewis said. "It seems that the Chockpaws have been preliminarily funded to put up the engineering for a new hotel and casino. They have been submitting various engineering plans to the state and federal government to bring in power and utilities in contemplation of a new hotel and casino. They want to run some major power over from the nearest dam. They have some big plans, which mean big money. We suspect that their money is coming from one or more insurance companies."

"Well, enough about politics," Poladian, the host, said. "Zachary, you and I should take off a day to go fishing like we used to."

No stranger to politics and contributions, Poladian's company had already contributed a million dollars to support Lewis thus far in the campaign. It was a private dinner party for Lewis and a few close friends at Poladian's expensive home in Rancho Palos Verdes. There were four couples, including the candidate and his wife. Each of the other guests, as well as the Poladians, had made hefty contributions to the candidate's campaign. The dinner was a way of acknowledging gratitude for the contributions, such closeness to the candidate becoming valuable if Lewis won the election.

"I've been running like crazy with this campaign," Lewis said, looking at Poladian. "And I miss the fishing trips we used to do. But say, didn't you sell your big eighty-footer?"

"Yep, I did. I got tired of all the maintenance and sold it last year. Even though I had everything done and a full time crew chief, I still had to go there to meet people at the boat for this and that. Having the engines serviced, fixing the electronics, repairing something, continuous varnishing of the wood trim, in addition to the dry dock painting ever year and a half, all took my involvement."

"Isn't that what the crew chief was supposed to take care of?" Lewis asked.

"I found out he was having parties on the boat and fired him. Then I had another fellow for a short while, but he quit. I got so fed up with it all. But, to be truthful, I have mixed feelings now about not having it. On one hand, I am glad to get rid of the pain of maintaining it. On the other, I miss it. But I can rent us a wonderful sport fisher, and everything will be done for us. The boat will be in order, the bait already on board, rods and reels provided, everything! It is so much easier renting than owning."

"Well, you sure had a nice boat. We had some nice times on it," Lewis said, recalling some of the cruises and outings they had together. "Remember when we anchored next to the Queen Mary at the Fourth of July and lay back and watched the fireworks from up close that the City of Long Beach shot off from next to it? That was really a show. And the fishing! I miss that."

"I tell you what," Poladian said. "You just say when, and I'll rent us a sport fisher for a day. We will go out early, and be back before cocktail time. Let's go for marlin. What do you say?"

"That would be wonderful. I'll be back down south here in…" Lewis paused, trying to remember his schedule. "Let's see, next week. How about Saturday after next?"

"I'll set it up," Poladian said. "The Yacht Club has names of reliable charters and I'll rent us one for the day. You'll need nothing except your hat. How about you two?" Poladian asked the other two gentlemen.

"Sorry, John," Addison said. "Charlene and I are going down to Cabo San Lucas that weekend."

"I don't do well at sea, as you know, John," Devan said. "But you all go and have a good time"

"I'll set it up," Poladian repeated. "I'll confirm everything with your appointments secretary. It'll be like old times. We'll have a blast!"

"Oh my," Ms. Addison said, changing the focus of attention. "Look at this dessert!" The chef himself came into the room, pushing a dessert cart, the dessert having been prepared by the chef's pastry chef, in advance. The chef wore his tall toque blanche and white apron as he came out with the last part of his gastronomic extravaganza.

CHAPTER 40

Three men stood atop the hill, alone in the morning under a partly cloudy sky. The two from the Equator came up in the jet to see the progress. No one else was anywhere near. There were no trees on the hilltop, only brush. Surveyors' stakes marked the virgin ground. A new dirt road had been cut with a dozer blade for access for the surveyors and engineers. Four-wheeler tire tracks were everywhere. This was Sunday, and none of the activity of the previous week was happening on this day of rest.

Chief No Cloud, the third man, pointed, "In through there is where the power will be run from the nearest hydroelectric plant. Since we own the land, we can run the power lines above the ground and don't have to go through no governmental agencies for permission. I learned that from talking to the power company."

He was proudly showing off his newfound knowledge on the subject that he had just learned from talking to the engineers he had hired in the past few days. "And over here…" he said, pointing in another direction, "is where we'll put the world-class golf course with water and sand traps, and rough areas of trees. Golfers like the trees, as it gives them a place to take a piss on the middle of the course. We'll have another course over there." He pointed. "People who want to ride horses can take a ride on several long trails. The new airport will be put on our own land instead of using the strip that you landed on which is not on our reservation. That way we control it, and nobody can tell us that we are making too much noise. I was thinking about having a small airplane there with someone to give lessons. Maybe even a glider and a tow plane in addition—what fun the guests could have taking a glider ride. We can initially bring in fuel trucks for aviation fuel, but later we should put in storage tanks, and some kind of hanger for maintenance and things like spare tires for jets. It's going to be something, huh?"

"I'm very impressed with the way things are shaping up," Manelli said. "I'll tell my other partners that. I think we are going to have a first class operation"

"Many thanks for what you have done for us," the chief said with a big smile.

"Sure," Manelli said. "As soon as the loan comes through, we will have to start working up training programs for members of your tribe who want to work in the hotel. I'm especially keen on using only your tribe members for the police. We want some of your young men for that job, and it is always good to have a few females too for making arrests of women. We want to control all police work without outsiders. We will have to see what other jobs at the hotel and casino can be filled by your tribe. We usually get pretty girls for dealers, which we will bring in. There will be many jobs for maintenance, so any good mechanics and handymen from the tribe will have work if they want it."

"I'm sure you will have to bring in some outsiders," the chief said, silently admitting to the lack of talent available in the tribe. "I'll try to fill as many positions as possible from the tribe. But tell me, I hear that Zachary Lewis is doing much better and may win. I'm afraid that we won't get the money from Majestik, so maybe we're all going nowhere. Do you really think our project is going to happen? "

"Relax, my friend," Manelli responded. "We have it all together."

The chief, ignoring the cryptic remark, turned away, walked a few steps, and stopped. He looked up to reach the spirits, moved his shoulders from side to side and up and down like Ray Charles on the piano, and gave a chant.

After the takeoff noise subsided in the Citation en route back to Las Vegas, Indelicato grinned. "This is all too fucking great. Imagine, our own police force. This'll be like having our own country. It's perfect. A cash cow the government cannot look into. This will be heaven."

"Absolutely," Manelli said. "Now we need to make sure we get the insurance company loan."

CHAPTER 41

Captain Dwight Winger?" John Poladian asked over the telephone.

"Yep, that's me. Call me Dwight."

Poladian sat behind his heavy oak desk in his study. The room could have been in an exclusive English men's club, with its rich wood paneling, and bookshelves that climbed to the ceiling filled with the classics and expensively bound books. Then there was the trophy area with its big game heads adorning the wall. Also mounted was a huge stuffed blue marlin that he had caught off Baja, Mexico, years earlier.

The chairs were over-stuffed green leather, and on the wooden floor there was a huge oriental rug.

"Your name was given me by the Yacht Club as a responsible captain who does well at finding the big ones. Is that true?"

"Well, I do fairly well, but you know fishing," Dwight told him, being cautious not to boast too much about a venture as risky as big game fishing.

"I want to hire you for the day, the Saturday after next. I want to go out early, and return the same afternoon. I hear the Marlin are biting. Do you know where to go?"

"I sure do! We should leave at 5:00 a.m. It'll take about an hour or an hour and a half at speed to get to a good spot. How many in your party?"

"Only two, myself and an important person. I want everything to be prepared in advance, all bait already on board, reels ready, ice, the works. Can you do that?"

"That's my specialty. You won't need anything. I just got my boat out of dry dock, and don't have a deck hand at this time, but I'll get one. Although I can do without, I prefer to have a helper to handle bait, the lines, and to help get any fish we catch into the boat."

"Yes, we would like an extra helper," Poladian told him, being as pampered and wealthy as he was.

"No problem. It'll be two thousand, five hundred dollars for the day, including everything. Is that acceptable?"

"That's fine. But I want you to check out where they're biting and do your best to make sure my guest has a good time. As I said, he's a VIP."

"You got it. Send me a deposit of five hundred, and I'll call you to confirm that I have received it. I look forward to seeing you at 5:00 a.m. at Berth C-26, Long Beach. I'll get the bait in advance. Here is my address and phone," Dwight said, providing the details.

He was used to entertaining important guests. On occasion it was a TV personality, someone from the movies, or other person who did not want to let on that he was coming, in order to avoid the paparazzi. Dwight thought about a deck hand. *Maybe that insurance fellow Ernie will be available. This Mr. Poladian sounds like he is used to having extra help. His guest must be some big shot.*

∽∾∽

"Doris? This is John Poladian."

"Oh good morning, Mr. Poladian," Doris said. "Mr. Lewis told me to expect your call to book the Saturday after this one. Did you need to speak to him? I think he's in his car. I could put you through to his cell phone."

"No, no, no need. Just tell Zachary that I have everything arranged for the Saturday after next. I'll come for him at 4:30 a.m. in the morning. We'll be going to Long Beach, Berth C-26, to go out on a sport fisher boat owned by a Dwight Winger. The boat is called the *Hookup*. Tell Zachary to be ready for some fun. We're going for marlin!"

"I certainly will, Mr. Poladian. And I know he will be looking forward to it."

Doris motioned for her new appointments assistant, Maria Manelli, to come over to her desk. "Put down on Mr. Lewis's calendar a fishing trip for marlin, fishing all day Saturday after next. The boat is the *Hookup*, owned by Dwight Winger, Berth C-26, Long Beach. Keep the plans private."

"Okay, got it," Maria said. She booked out the entire day for that Saturday on her big paper calendar, and made an additional entry in an electronic calendar that she could tie into the northern office by Internet to coordinate Mr. Lewis's schedule, and which could be used for contact if there was an emergency. She also made a note of the details of where he would be on a small piece of paper, which she put in her purse, which was not part of her job.

☙☙☙

Ernie's cell phone beeped as he was looking at a house in Malibu that had damage from the high winds.

"Ernie? This is Dwight Winger. Do you remember me? The boat owner that you helped out in Long Beach."

"Sure, Dwight. How's it going?"

"I got my first charter booked today since the dry dock repairs. It's for the Saturday after next. It's for two people, and I think one may be a big shot or somebody well known. They specifically asked me to have a deck hand, so if you want to help out, you can come along. You won't be able to fish on this trip, so I'll still owe you that one. But I can offer to pay you $200 as a deck hand. We have to see to it that these fellows are well taken care of. We will be back in the late afternoon. Interested?"

"Sure. I'd love to come along. And no need to pay me. I'll be happy just to come along and help out. What time?"

"They are going to be at the boat at 5:00 a.m. So you should be at the boat at 4:00 a.m. Is that okay?"

"Sounds perfect," Ernie said. "I'll look forward to it. I'll be there at 4:00 a.m. to help you get going."

"I'll go for bait the day before, so we'll be ready to go," Dwight said.

"What are you fishing for and what do you use for bait?"

"Marlin is the game. I'll go out by the floating bait dock where they sell squid. The bait that gets spilled draws in mackerel, which I can catch for good bait for the Marlin."

"Sounds great."

"Good. See you then."

◌◑◑◌

"Doris, I'm going to take a short break," Maria told her. "I think I'll just walk around the block once to get outside and for a little exercise. Is that okay?"

"Sure," Doris said. "I'll mind the fort."

Outside, and down the block, Maria took a cell phone out of her purse and called a number. "Hi, Daddy."

Hi, sweetheart," Manelli said. "Have you got some news?"

"Zachary Lewis is being treated to a day of marlin fishing the Saturday after next. He's leaving Long Beach Berth C-26 at 5:00 a.m. on a boat called the *Hookup*. It's owned by Dwight Winger. His host is John Poladian. As far as I know, only the two of them are going on the boat, and they will fish and return in the late afternoon."

"Nice work. Let me know if there is any change."

"Sure, Daddy. Love you."

◌◑◑◌

Manelli called for Innocenti to come to his office. Innocenti happened to be in one of the hotel restaurants having lunch, and came right away.

"Fiorello, we got the tip. Lewis is being taken out fishing Saturday after next, out of Long Beach Berth C-26, on a boat called the *Hookup*, owned by Dwight Winger. His host is John Poladian. Only the two are going, plus whoever is on the boat. They're leaving at 5:00 a.m. the Saturday after next, and returning in the afternoon. Let's go for it!"

CHAPTER 42

Ernie pulled up to the Cresta View Townhomes. The complex was walled but Ernie noticed that it would be very easy to scale the wall several yards away out of sight of the guard. No doubt the guard gave the residents a sense of security, although a false one. At the entrance was a guard gate, with an unarmed security guard in a blue police-styled uniform standing in a tiny booth next to a gate crossing. Entry could be by a card in a slot in a machine, or if you had none, the guard would lean over and address you.

"Yes?" the unfriendly guard asked.

"I'm Ernie from Majestik Insurance. I'm here to address a board of directors meeting at six this evening. I'm expected"

The guard looked at the clock behind him, which displayed 5:50. He then looked contemptuously at Ernie's motorcycle. "No motorcycles allowed."

"I'm from the insurance company about a claim and have been invited to the board meeting," Ernie said, miffed. It had been along ride over just to address the claim with personal service, only to be met by such rudeness. It quickly reduced his patience and filled him with a sense of indignation. "Would you rather I left and told the insurance company I was denied access to the meeting and the insured property, and that such failure to cooperate with the insurance company, a condition of making any claim, is the reason why I'm denying insurance coverage?"

The not-so-bright guard's expression changed to a concerned look, as he realized that he better take this up with his employers. "I have to call. Can you stand by for a moment, sir?" He abandoned his cocky expression and tone for one of marginal manners and dialed a number on the association's phone. "There is a man here from Majestik Insurance for the meeting. But he's on a motorcycle. What should I do?"

He was told something on the phone and then he turned to Ernie. "All right." He put down the phone and leaned out. "You may come in. Here's a temporary parking permit to go to the board meeting, which you should display on the motor-cycle." He wrote a pass from a pad of stickers. "You can park in the guest zone next to the clubhouse with this. Go around to your right, and you'll see the clubhouse. That's where the meetings of the directors are held. Remember that the speed limit inside is five miles per hour."

He handed Ernie a sticker for his motorcycle and pushed a button that raised the gate. Ernie said nothing and rode on through toward the clubhouse. *What sort of concentration camp is this? No motorcycles? Five miles per hour? Parking stickers? Minimum wage guards? Too many rules!*

Inside the clubhouse were five men, their average age in the mid-sixties. They were a ridiculous sight. The five stooges? One wore a straw cowboy hat, who Ernie would remember as Mr. Cowboy Hat. Another had on bright lime green pants, white shoes, and a lime-green-and-red-flowered golfing shirt. He would be Mr. Golfer. Another wore shorts, rubber shower thongs, and a T-shirt with a cartoon figure of the Road Runner and the Coyote. He would be Mr. Road Runner. Yet another had on shorts, and wore a black shirt with brightly colored pictures of different mixed alcoholic drinks emblazoned on it. He would be Mr. Cocktail. Still another had on a cotton pullo-ver sport shirt with the wording *Cresta Views* sewn on the chest, as though living at this concentration camp was prestig-ious. He would be Mr. Cresta Views.

They were standing, talking to one another, but stopped when Ernie came in. They stared at him as though he was an alien from outer space. The alcohol smell was pungent, and so strong that it reminded Ernie of being in a confined area with escaping fumes of an explosive.

"Hello. I'm Ernie, from Majestik."

No one smiled. No one introduced themselves. They had

been forewarned by the call from the guard and watched him arrive on his motorcycle outside the glass sliding doors. It was obvious that none of them liked motorcycles, motorcyclists, or for that matter, hardly anyone who was not one of them. They took seats behind two oblong tables put together end to end, sitting behind them to form a row of justices like in a real appellate court. A row of folding chairs faced the appellate bench. Clearly this was how this board addressed members who had been fined—to hear them come in, sit and face the tribunal, humble themselves and plea for mercy, such as asking to have their fine reduced. It was no doubt the only power these losers ever had in their uneventful, doldrum lives.

If they had on the black robes instead of the comical outfits, the setting would have very much resembled a court out of some old movie from a long time ago. These buffoons were definitely on a power trip.

Mr. Cowboy Hat sat in the middle. Ernie guessed that he must be the president, and he was the first to speak. "Since when does the insurance company send out representatives on motorcycles?"

Ernie kept his cool. "Due to the huge number of claims because of the big storm last month and so many trees down, I was hired as one of a hundred temporary field representatives. Here's my card." He ignored the initial question and handed the card to Mr. Cowboy Hat.

Mr. Cowboy Hat rudely did not rise to lean over the table to reach the card, let alone to shake hands, so Ernie laid it down on the table in the middle. After a pause, Mr. Cowboy Hat reached out and picked up the card slowly, as though it was infected with something, then turned it about, looking at it from different angles, as though a close examination of it would reveal that Ernie had something wrong with him. He then laid the card on the table in front of him.

This added indignation told Ernie it was time to equalize the situation. "Shall we discuss your problem, or would you rather talk about motorcycles?"

Mr. Cowboy Hat looked at Ernie like it was time to mete out punishment for insolence, but then he must have realized that he had no power over Ernie as he was not a townhome owner pleading for mercy, such as he was used to dealing with. He then got visibly red in the face and it looked for a moment that he actually might get physical with Ernie. "Listen to me, you son-of-a-bitch—" He stopped himself, clearly realizing this was an insurance claim and they needed help as they were about to be sued.

Mr. Golfer must have realized that his drinking buddy was not handling the situation well and intervened. "Very well, let's discuss the problem. We got a letter from a lawyer representing Janice Mattley, saying he's suing the association and we directors personally on her behalf, so we sent it on to Majestik. We got a letter from a Jessica Bloom denying the claim. We sent a copy to the association lawyer, but we haven't met with him yet."

"You are aware that Majestik insures Ms. Mattley as well, aren't you?" Ernie asked, taking control.

Mr. Golfer nodded. "Yes, the articles and bylaws are set up where the fire insurance is provided for everyone by the association as each townhome shares two common walls with other townhomes. So, any additional insurance for liability, personal property inside, and other risks for each townhome owner is easy to sign up for and cheaper through Majestik since it is already insuring for fire. And, the association itself is insured by Majestik, as well as we directors for errors and omissions. So, as far as we know, all the members have Majestik."

Ernie looked at Mr. Golfer's silly lime-green-and-red-flowered shirt and had to restrain himself from laughing. The man looked like a drunken Christmas tree. "Do you have a copy of your articles, bylaws, and the rules in question? I also want a copy of all recent statements sent to Ms. Mattley, and all communications between you and her."

Mr. Cowboy Hat had regained some of his composure. "I prepared a copy of those for you as you said in your call to the office that you wanted those at this meeting." With insolence, he pushed a manila folder across the table toward Ernie.

"Is the insurance company going to cover us?" Mr. Road Runner asked.

Cool and calm, Ernie shrugged. "I'm here on a fact finding visit, and your policy requires your cooperation. I'll be back in touch with you over what the company is going to do and what it is not going to do in a few days. Now, my notes show that you are foreclosing on the townhome of Ms. Janice Mattley. She's still residing here, correct?"

"Yes, she is," Mr. Cresta Views answered.

"She's a trouble maker," Mr. Cocktail said. "She has to be taught a lesson."

Ernie looked at the group and thought that these were indeed clowns. "Did she not pay her homeowner's dues?"

"She paid her dues until six months ago, at which time we had to start refusing them and we sent them back," Mr. Cowboy Hat answered.

"You sent them back to her? Why?"

"Because she stopped paying her fines along with the dues. Our association lawyer told us to refuse her dues unless her check included all the money due, including the fines."

"You got legal advice like that, and now you are being sued? Did you just pay a lawyer to say what you wanted to hear?"

Mr. Cowboy Hat bristled. "Listen, smart ass. We follow what our lawyer tells us to do. Our lawyer told us that if we accept the dues, we might have to sue her in a separate case for the fines. So her monthly statements now include the fines and charges. This way, since we can foreclose over unpaid dues, we can also foreclose over the fines as well as they are just added into the monthly dues. We don't have to file a separate lawsuit. We simply hire a foreclosure service and set up a sale of her townhome in ninety days unless she pays the full amount. And, this is what we did. We saved a lot of legal expense that way. Also, that way, we got to add in the foreclosure charges as well as the lawyer's bills and it is up to her to hire to lawyer to contest the charges, whereas we just add them, and whatever we want, in her monthly statement. What could be better? That'll teach that bitch!"

Ernie had gotten him to admit he was foreclosing over fines. Keeping his cool, he wanted to confirm what he heard.

"How much are you foreclosing for? Six months of overdue monthly dues?"

"Nineteen thousand, eight hundred dollars," Mr. Golfer answered,

"What?" Ernie blurted out in surprise. "How much are the dues?"

They looked at each other. The directors of the association did not even know how much the dues were. Finally the man in the cartoon T-shirt answered. "I think two hundred fifty dollars per month."

"You're foreclosing on her for nineteen thousand eight hundred dollars. How can that be?"

Mr. Cocktail shrugged. "She has lots of fines. Under the rules, the association can fine a member for violations of the rules. This woman refused to follow them. She has accumulated fines, late charges, and interest on the fines. And now, the foreclosure charges, interest, and legal fees are added in."

"What's she fined for?" Ernie asked.

"A number of things. Here's a list," Mr. Golfer said and handed Ernie a list, adding, "She's a trouble maker."

Ernie looked at the long list and noted that there were fines without descriptions of what they were for. "There are many descriptions missing."

"Don't worry, she did them," Mr. Golfer said. "They may not be taken down, but she did them."

Ernie looked at the list carefully. "It looks like the majority of fines are for tennis court violations, at one hundred fifty dollars each. For each fine not paid there is a fifty dollar late charge. Then there is a one and a half per cent interest charge per month on each monthly statement. There is also a late charge each month in addition. How do you get fined playing tennis? Miss the ball?"

Leaning forward aggressively, Mr. Cowboy Hat said, "You think you are funny, don't you, smart ass? I don't. She's separated from her husband, and he keeps their kids who are young teenagers. They come over here to play tennis, and she lets them play as though they lived here. That's a violation, each time. Non-residents cannot play on the courts unless they are playing with a resident member. Period."

Keeping his cool and trying to get whatever information he could, Ernie asked "Why can't she let her own kids play on the tennis court? Is it that crowded?"

Mr. Cresta Views shook his head. "No, only a few people play tennis. Her kids play more than anyone. But rules are rules."

"You must be joking!" Ernie sat forward, and started to become animated. You fined her one hundred fifty dollars each time she let her own children play the tennis court, of which she owns a part of?"

"Say, whose fucking side are you on, anyway?" Mr. Cowboy Hat asked.

"Majestik insures both the association and Janice Mattley," Ernie reminded him. "I'm not out here to take your side or hers, but to find out facts about the claim, and you must cooperate under the policy terms. Otherwise the company will deny coverage."

That seemed to silence him, Ernie observed, satisfied with the comment. *They sure don't like me. First, I'm an outsider. Next, I ride a motorcycle. Then I'm not drinking with them. This group would dislike any outsider.*

They have their own little government like in some storybook of times past. It's no wonder they sit around here and volunteer for the non-paying position of director, as it is the only power these cretins ever had, or will have, and they haven't the foggiest notion of how to use it justly. They probably seldom leave their little fiefdom. I wonder if they have their liquor delivered?

"There are thousands of dollars here for tennis court violations. Now, what is this about trashcan violations?"

"That's what I do mostly," Mr. Cresta Views said. "I go around on the night before the trash pickup day, as well as on the day itself, and check to see that the members put their trashcans exactly where they are supposed to. In the event that they are not where they are supposed to be, I write up a ticket."

"I wrote her up on a couple of those also," Mr. Cocktail added.

"How far out of place does the trashcan have to be in order to get a ticket?" Ernie asked.

"It doesn't matter," Mr. Cresta Views answered.

"Even a few inches?" Ernie asked.

"Rules are rules," Mr. Cowboy Hat announced with a raised voice.

"If a can was out a few inches, why didn't you just move it yourself if you were there instead of writing a ticket?"

"We don't know where you come from but that is not how *we* do things here," Mr. Golfer answered.

"But now you are about to be sued," Ernie pointed out. "How many others have you fined in the last year for trashcan violations?"

They looked at each other for an answer, and no one seemed to have it. "There have been others," Mr. Roadrunner finally said.

"How many?" Ernie repeated.

"Well, there may have been a few, but I can't remember them now," Mr. Road Runner said. "Oh yeah, I remember. That one guy who was renting and used to work on things in his garage, which is a violation. We busted his ass for that and for trashcan placement. That's about all. He finally moved out. A guess we taught him to fuck with us! The owner, who rented to him, had to pay his fines since he didn't."

Ernie could hardly believe what he was hearing. "You fine someone for working in his garage? It looks like you fined Mattely for that at least once."

"Definitely," Mr. Cowboy Hat answered. "The garages are for parking of cars, not for activities."

Ernie looked at the list of Mattley fines again. "What is this about 'leaving garage door open'?"

"If a member drives in from the store and forgets to close his garage door for more than fifteen minutes, he gets fined," Mr. Cocktail answered. "Mattley left her garage door open on several occasions. I remember writing her up."

Ernie cocked his head. "How can you fine someone for

working in her garage or for leaving her garage door open?"

"Because here at Cresta Views we only have garages for parking of cars," Mr. Cocktail answered. "We don't allow people to use their garage for a workshop and using tools like saws, or for working on their cars or other projects. Also, they will leave the garage doors open if you let them, and that is unsightly. We allow fifteen minutes to unload a car and that is all."

"If a garage door gets left open, why don't you or one of the guards just tell the person to close it?"

"We don't go around reminding people of rules they already know about," Mr. Cocktail answered. "The guards and any director can cite a member. If there is shown a violation in the record, it occurred."

"So each of you can go out and cite someone for a violation. You just write it up and then what?"

Mr. Cowboy Hat leaned forward again and showed more irritation at having to educate the insolent interrogator. "The violation is given to the management company, and they put the fine on the owner's next month's billing. There is also interest added in if not paid by the next billing cycle, and late charges. Otherwise, these guilty people would simply not pay their fines."

"So eventually, if the person doesn't pay her fines, you turn over the unpaid claim to a foreclosure agency, a recorded foreclosure of the person's townhome is commenced, and then the person has a foreclosure on her record, ruining the person's credit rating?"

Leaning back with a smile, Mr. Cowboy hat said, "You got it."

Ernie shook his head in amazement. He looked farther down on the long list of fines. "What's this about an overnight car with no sticker?"

Mr. Cowboy hat turned to one side to the others and exhaled, too angry to answer.

Mr. Golfer answered. "In order to have an overnight guest, you must apply for a sticker at the office to one of the directors, whoever of us is on duty that day. If you don't, and have a guest with a car in a guest spot over night with no sticker, the guards are instructed to cite the member who had the guest."

"How would the night guard know whose guest it is from a car with no sticker on it?"

"When you live in a place for years, you know what's going on," Mr. Golfer said.

"Why don't you just give the members a stack of guest stickers so they can use them if they have an overnight guest?"

Mr. Cowboy Hat snorted. "If you start doing that, then they pass out the stickers to friends, and you lose all control."

Ernie was amazed. *This is the ugliest bunch of people on earth. I'm guess I'm dealing with the perfect lifestyle of the directors and the majesty of the sovereign government of Cresta Views.*

"So, in the case of Ms. Mattley, her fines include late charges and interest, and now you are foreclosing on her home?"

"That's right. We can't allow someone to not pay fines at the expense of others," said Mr. Cowboy Hat, ever so righteously.

"What did you intend to do with her home after you've foreclosed on it?"

Silence filled the room. All of the directors looked at one another, dumbfounded. None had an answer to the question. It was obvious that they had not even considered that question. They were just out to get her. After the eternity of nearly a minute of dead silence, Mr. Cocktail shrugged. "We haven't considered that yet. We expect her to pay her fines."

"How many others have you foreclosed on for non-payment of fines?"

Mr. Cresta Views answered, "We filed a few liens, but the owners paid them right away. This is the first that has gone to foreclosure."

"What if she doesn't have the money for the fines?"

Mr. Cowboy gritted his teeth. "That bitch has it coming. She can just go get a loan and pay the fines."

"Have any of you directors yourselves ever received a fine

in all the years you have been here?" The question was a load-ed one and would reveal a good deal to Ernie.

They all looked at each other, and then Mr. Cresta Views spoke. "My wife had a loaner car two years ago when hers was being fixed after an accident, and she got one for not hav-ing a pass on the car by one of the guards."

"What happened to the ticket?" Ernie asked, although he already knew the answer.

"The office saw it was mine, and gave it to me instead of the management company. I tore it up since it was a loaner car."

"And none of the rest of you ever had a ticket?"

They all exchanged troubled glances and no one spoke, which was his answer and an admission by silence.

"So now she has gone to a lawyer, and because you are try-ing to take her home, she's filing a suit against the association, and each of you individually?"

"Yeah! Can you imagine the gall of that diseased cunt?" Mr. Cowboy answered.

"I think I'll take advantage of the fact that I'm here, and go and take her statement. I'll call you soon. I want each of the director's names, residence addresses, and phones, since you may be sued. I'll need to verify who are directors and who are not for the insurance coverage." Ernie was stretching the truth a little, as he wanted to be sure he had each of the five stoog-es' names who he was confronting that night. He had not fig-ured out what to do yet, but he would need their names for the insurance coverage and file, so the question was a proper one to ask. And he might need the names to do something to solve this mess.

Reluctantly, and after a pause, Mr. Cowboy Hat got a piece of paper and wrote down everyone's name and address. They still did not introduce themselves, and it was uncertain who was who of the group from the names. Handing Ernie the pa-per, he warned, "If you talk to her, you can expect her to try to lie her way out of the situation. She owes that money and that bitch will make up anything to avoid paying what she owes."

Ignoring the further slander, Ernie put the piece of paper in his pocket. "I'll contact you as soon as I can—probably early next week."

He remembered a movie with a witch-hunt group running a town in early America. *It must be like that to live here, with this bunch of idiots fining you for their idea of your sins, hoping you will come to plead with them to eliminate or reduce the fine—which would give them a sense of power they never had elsewhere in life.*

He left the clubhouse to go find the townhome owner Janice Mattley. He meandered about the property on foot until he came upon her unit. All the curtains were drawn as though she was hiding.

A fiftyish woman with a tired looking face came to the door, but only opened it up to the length of its chain lock. "Who are you?"

"I'm Ernie from Majestik. Here's my card." He passed it through the narrow opening of the door. "I'm here about your letter to Majestik, and also your claim against the association. Can I please come in?"

"Well, I have a lawyer now. I don't know if I should talk to you."

"That's up to you. But I may be able to help."

"Oh, all right, come in." She took off the chain lock and opened the door. "At least you're not one of them. "

"I understand that the association is foreclosing on your townhome for nineteen thousand eight hundred dollars in unpaid fines," Ernie said, as he followed her to the kitchen table where they sat.

The table was filled with notices, papers, letters, townhome rules, and things obviously relating to the case.

"Is it up to that now? Last I heard it was seventeen thousand nine hundred." She began to weep. "I don't work. I live off what my husband gives me for support. He pays for the payments, dues, and utilities, and I get eight hundred a month from him in addition. That's all I have. I have no way to deal with these people."

"Why do you believe they are after you?"

"I don't know. That man, Stanley, who golfs all the time, is the one that started it. I have not been too well in the last few years, and have been on medication. So I thought my boys would be better off at their father's as I wasn't always able to make them meals. But they do stay over once in a while, especially on weekends."

Ernie took that to mean psychological problems, but he wasn't positive. He figured that Stanley must be Mr. Golfer.

"Stanley said that since my boys don't live here full time, that I couldn't let them play tennis when they come to see me unless they are playing with me. I thought that was ridiculous as hardly anyone even uses the tennis court, and there was no rule in the conditions, covenants, and restrictions that limited the court to only those living here full time. So the boys went ahead and used the court if no one was on it. Stanley then started fining me when they did, and he had the guards report it if any of them saw my boys playing, which would be a fine also. There is also a sign-up sheet to reserve a court. Since I would occasionally reserve the court for them knowing they were coming over, they used every time my name appears on the sign-up sheet as a violation. In many of those instances no one used the court at all."

"Did they know the boys stay here part of the time with you?" Ernie asked.

"Sure. But when I pointed that out to Stanley, they made a new rule, because of me, that only full-time residents can use the tennis courts. A full time resident can take a guest to the court but only if accompanied by the resident. My boys want to play by themselves, not with me. They don't think it is cool playing with their mom, and they are both better than me. But, as I said, they stay here on lots of weekends, when their father is away, and on some holidays. They are not guests. They're my boys!"

Ernie put it into a hypothetical example to help him understand. "So under this new rule, a person could own a townhome here and just stay here once in a while because he had another place elsewhere. Then if he tried to play tennis when he came here and stayed at his townhome, he would be in violation of the new rule that restricts use of the tennis courts to

full-time members unless accompanied by a full-time resident?"

"Exactly," Mattley said. "But I don't know of anyone like
that who has a townhome here and doesn't live in it, unless it
is rented out full time. They tailor made the new rule just for
me."

"I can't believe that can be legal," Ernie said.

"You don't know these people!"

"I'm beginning to." Ernie looked at a number of fines on
the list that stated *Trashcan*. "Now what is all this about the
trashcan out of place?"

"Oh, that's when one of them claims your trashcan is not
exactly where it is supposed to be. But I always put the can
where it is supposed to go. These tickets are mailed to me days
or even a week or more after someone writes the ticket, so
there is no way to determine if the can was out of place or not.
I think in many instances they just made it up, since I have not
been paying the fines, to make things tougher on me."

"Do you have any idea why?"

"They need someone to go after, like a hammer looking for
a nail. They are retired or semi-retired. They have no ability to
run such a place, but they are the directors and have always
been. They have proxies for voting from many of the owners,
and with those they have a majority and vote themselves into
office each year. No one else even wants the job. As directors,
they are in charge of a fairly good-sized pot of money, as there
are two hundred eighty nine units. At two hundred fifty dollars
per month from each owner for dues, you can see that it quite
a lot—that's over seventy two thousand dollars a month. And
if they need more, they just declare a special assessment.
When they want to hire a lawyer to write me a letter, it gets
paid for out of the dues.

"But if I have to hire a lawyer, I have to pay for it. I had to
give the lawyer three hundred dollars just to look at the facts
briefly and to write them a letter. He wants a five thousand
dollar retainer before he files an action. He says he can file for
a preliminary injunction to stop the foreclosure, for damages
for my emotional distress, and for a permanent injunction to

stop the actions of the directors. He said to see the suit through a trial would cost fifty thousand dollars or more. I don't even have the five thousand. I don't know what I am going to do!"

She began to cry as she thought about her predicament. "I'm afraid to go out now. I'm on medication, and because of all this I have had to increase it."

That statement confirmed to Ernie that her medical problems were psychological. "Before I go, let me ask a few questions. What about these 'garage door open' fines?"

"They have a rule that you cannot leave your garage door open more than fifteen minutes, which they consider enough time to unload your car from the grocery store or shopping. What happens is the directors, or some of them, meet at one of their townhomes and get liquored to the gills. Then they get mean, and those that can still walk sometimes go out for a walk around the property and write up tickets against whoever they want to harass. I think they make up a lot of the fines. I don't leave my garage door open unless I am unloading my trunk, and then only for as much time as it takes to unload it, as the garage door is too close to the trunk to get groceries and things from the trunk—so the garage door has to be open to unload.

"But as to whether the garage door is open for fifteen minutes or less—it is their word against mine. I can assure you that those bunch of drunks don't wait for fifteen minutes with a watch to see how long my garage door is open. And you cannot work on anything in your garage, especially if you want to have the door open for light and air while you are doing it.

"You can't even empty your vacuum in the garage or get fined. Oh! You should see what they do about the pools. There are two pools. Because the directors are old and mean, they do not like kids at all. So they designated only one of the pools for kids and have a rule that anyone under eighteen must be accompanied by an adult at that pool. But that pool is only designated open for minors Mondays through Fridays, from nine to six, and on weekends it is for adults only. So the only time minors can swim at all is with an adult and then only during school days when they are in school. It's incredible. I just keep my kids out of the pools altogether."

"What is all this about parking violations? A lot of the fine money is because of that," Ernie said, looking at the sheet of fines.

"Most of that is for cars that I had nothing to do with. They make most all of that up. If they see a car overnight here without a pass on it anywhere near my unit, they attribute it to me and write me up."

"Can't you have any overnight guests here?" Ernie asked.

"I try to," she said. "I've been separated from my husband for two years, and he is living with a younger girl. It's over."

"Don't you have passes here to give to a guest for his car if his car is to be outside overnight?"

"That is their most fun game! They have made a rule that overnight guests must have a pass. But to make it fun for them, the overnight pass can only be issued on that same day. So, if you want an overnight guest, you must go for a pass that same day. You can't get some in advance and just give one to your guest for his car. The only people that can issue the pass are the directors themselves. There is normally one director at the office during the day, but not always. And, they are never there past 4:00 p.m., as that is cocktail hour. So if you want an overnight guest, you must know it in advance, then go to the office and see one of those horrible men and tell him what you want.

"Can you imagine? You have to go to see one of those men and tell him that a certain man is coming over to see you and spend the night. You have to give his name and identify his car. What great fun they have finding out about your affair and treating me like a whore!" She began to sob. "I cannot go through with it. I have had an occasional guest, but I will not go over there anymore and face those horrible men!"

"According to this sheet, you must have had quite a few callers!" Ernie said, looking at the number of different cars on the sheet. Each citation had the car model, sometimes the color, and sometimes the license."

"That's not true! I have only had two different men over

since my husband and I separated two years ago. One has been over twice, the other four times. I'm not so pretty anymore." She hiccupped a couple of times. "They will charge any stray car they want to as going to my unit, which puts me in a position of going over to one of their board meetings and pleading my case. Do you understand? I'd have to go over there, sit before all five of those lecherous drunks and tell them that the cars that the guards or one of them cited as visiting me is wrong—and I have to admit to exactly how many times an actual caller came. There are others at the meetings as well, and it is like going over and revealing your sex life, or what little I have of it." She began to lose control, crying.

Ernie looked at the sheet again. "What's this parking violation on Christmas Day last year?"

"Oh, that one. There are strict parking rules about where to park. They sent out a flyer in advance before Christmas saying that the parking rules would not be enforced on Christmas Day. On Christmas, my boys were here. My ex-husband told me he got a Santa Claus outfit somewhere on loan and would put it on and bring over presents for the kids on Christmas. They are a bit old for that, but it was still a nice thing to do. So he came over on Christmas Day, with the outfit on, bringing some gifts for them. He did not bring me anything. He parked in a no parking zone nearby as there were so many guest cars here that day there was no regular place to park. After he delivered the gifts and spent some time with them, he then left. On his car was a parking violation, and it was assessed against my unit and me."

Ernie almost came out of his seat and raised his voice. "The bastards ticketed Santa Claus?"

"You really don't know these people." She began to cry again, this time sobbing hard.

"I'm not quite sure how to handle this, but I'll see if I can come up with something," Ernie told her, trying to reassure her in hopes of stopping the crying. "I'll try to find a way to consider it an advantage that Majestik insures both sides, instead of a conflict. Let me have your phone number please, and that of your attorney. I'll get back to you shortly. I'll do something, but I'm not quite sure just what yet." He walked back to his motorcycle, which was still by the clubhouse where he left it. As he approached it, he saw a ticket looking piece of paper on the handlebars. It was an association ticket, chargeable to the townhome owner. It said at the top: THIS IS YOUR NOTIFICATION OF A VIOLATION.

There were several lines from the middle to the bottom, where the issuing person could write in what the offense was. It was written in someone's hand.

Unauthorized motorcycle visitor at Janice Mattley's.
Add-on Rule 101.9
Officer 14

"The bastards!" Ernie shouted. He lost his diplomacy. He mounted his motorcycle and rode it at a high rate of speed, instead of the five mph posted speed limit, to the guard gate. There was no parking place at the gate, but Ernie pulled his motorcycle right up next to the guard shack in the narrow road, obviously a place where no one was supposed to park, and dismounted as though getting off a horse to go to battle.

The guard saw him and hurried out, shouting, "Hey, you can't park there! Get that thing out immediately or I'll—"

He didn't finish his sentence because Ernie walked into his belly, the thing sticking out the most on the lackluster guard, knocking him backward and over onto the ground. The guard was not expecting that at Cresta Views, as that had never happened, and he got very scared, very quickly. He rose up slowly.

"You'll what?" Ernie demanded, poking a forefinger of his powerful right hand into the center of the guard's chest, hurting him, and pushing him back until he was up against the guard booth. "Go ahead and do whatever you're going to do now, asshole. And you are going to eat this ticket before I go." He stuffed the ticket into guard's mouth.

When Ernie backed up a few paces, and it appeared that he was not going to punch him, the guard took it out of his mouth. "I didn't write it. Don't hurt me!"

"Where's the piece-of-shit-limp-dick coward who wrote it? Get him here now!" Ernie was more than just a little heated up.

The guard looked at it. "That's Dennis Cummins. There are two of us on tonight. One relieves the other for breaks, and in the meantime, we are instructed to go around and look for violations. We only follow instructions."

"Get Dennis Cummins here *now*," Ernie barked.

The command scared the guard, and he knew it was not subject to negotiation.

The frightened guard started to turn to the hut to radio the other guard when he saw someone coming on foot and pointed. "There he is!"

The other security guard, also without a gun, came walking up toward the gate.

These minimum wage guards were not allowed to carry guns, Ernie figured, sizing up his opponents.

As the guard approached, Ernie showed him the ticket, glowering at him. "Did you write this ticket, dickhead?"

Cummins looked at it. "Yes," he said meekly.

"Can you back it up, punk?" Ernie challenged to see if he wanted to take him on. "You can have your buddy here join in on your side if you want. I'll turn the two of you into the grease spots that you came from in two seconds." He leaned forward and took a step in closer, hoping Cummins, or even better, the two of them, would accept the challenge.

"Hey, look man," the now-worried Cummins said. "Gimme a break! I get minimum wage and have to buy my own uniforms. I don't want to fight anyone. I haven't even been to guard-training school. I work this night shift job because it was the only job I could get. I've only been here for four months, and I'm leaving next week, as I finally got a decent job. I was told to write the ticket—it wasn't my idea."

"Who told you and when?" Ernie demanded, now calming down. He knew the guards had sensed the outcome of any confrontation.

"The president, Mr. Freeman, just a little while ago. I got a call at the guard shack, where I was taking a coffee break, and was told to cite the motorcycle as visiting Janice Mattley without a guest pass."

"I have a guest pass!" Ernie said, pointing to his motorcycle, with the guest pass stuck on it.

"But that is to go to the board meeting, not the Mattley residence."

Ernie's jaw dropped. Here he was on their insurance claim, and they fine him—or her, to be more precise. It would be assessed on Mattley's monthly fines. He cooled himself down as he realized he was about to slap the guard around and *that* conduct Majestik would not like. "I think I'm just beginning to get the picture." He realized there was no reason to get tough with the minimum-wage guard who was just following orders. "Does Freeman wear a cowboy hat?" he asked, trying to figure out who Freeman was, as the directors never introduced themselves.

"Usually, in the evenings," the guard said. "When he walks around the complex. He drinks a lot. But they all do. He's bald, so that may have something to do with the hat."

"Who is the golfer with the silly clothes?"

"That's Stanley," the guard told him.

Ernie checked his list to make sure that he had the right directors identified.

"What is your opinion of Janice Mattley?" Ernie asked, probing.

Without hesitation, Cummins said, "I think she's a really nice person, and it is really shitty what they are doing to her."

"Both of you give me your home phone numbers and addresses," Ernie commanded. "I may need you as witnesses. And, as long as I'm here, I have a recorder in my phone, and I want both of you to give me a statement as to what happened tonight and as to how the board treats her."

"I'm glad to help," Cummins said. "I'm leaving here anyway, so I don't care. This place is weird!"

The other guard said nothing, but did not refuse.

ເຈເຈ

As the morning light reflected off the Torrid swimming

pool into Ernie's sliding glass apartment door, he sipped coffee behind his round coffee table, his chainsaw resting on top of it. The night before he finished reading the relevant parts of the Cresta Views Association Articles, Bylaws, Rules, and the new Emergency Rules which had the new tennis restrictions, and looked at the statement of fines from the management company that looked like some department store's bill to someone with a big spending appetite and no money to pay. There were notices of foreclosure, and dates certain by which she had to pay the fines or lose her townhome. He pondered the words of the insurance policy that insured those lunatics at the association. The insurance policy appeared to have been written to confuse. The more he looked, the more ambiguous the policy sounded. On the one hand, the company insured the woman. On the other, it insured the association and the directors. *What to do? I better call in on this one.* He reached for his cell phone, and dialed the programmed in speed number set by the company for the help line.

"Hello, McAteer here."

"Oh, good morning, Mr. McAteer." Ernie was surprised once again that what he thought was such an important person would be on the phone line personally again. He realized that Majestik had some very effective means of cutting down claims, such as access to the senior person in claims who one could talk to.

"This is Ernie, one of your temporary field representatives. I have a situation."

"Yes, I remember you. You just called the other day about the death in the Chinese home. How did that one come out?"

"I resolved it, sir, and we did not have to pay anything. But I have a situation here. Majestik insures a townhome owned by a woman, and it also insures the association and its directors for errors and omissions in managing the association. The association is foreclosing on her unit, and she has been to a lawyer. So we insure both sides of a dispute. What should I do in a situation like that?"

"We do that a lot where we insure both the owners and an association. If we get the association policy, we usually get all or most all of the members. We give them a break on the premiums since it's altogether. What's the claim about?"

"The association passed new rules that were aimed at her to prevent her from letting her boys, who live primarily with their father elsewhere, from using the association tennis court when they come to see her. Because she ignored the new rules, they have put enormous fines against her for that and other ridiculous reasons and have put her townhome into actual foreclosure for a claimed nineteen thousand, eight hundred dollars in fines. So, naturally, she went to an attorney and is now going to sue them. The fines against her must be illegal, and now she has emotional distress and is taking medication as she is desperate and losing her home. It's sort of a deadlock, and Majestik insures both sides. What does Majestik do in a situation like this?"

McAteer answered, with all the seasoning that made it clear why he was the most experienced. "We got burned last year on a deal like this one. We denied coverage to a townhome owner, and he sued us over failure to provide a defense, and won. The owner claimed emotional distress from wrongful conduct of the association. The claims against the owner were outside the scope of legitimate fines, but the court found that a claim could be sustained against us for not providing a defense since the damages for emotional distress might have come within coverage, depending on the outcome as to what the jury found as to the cause.

"In a case like this, we can provide a legal defense under what is called a reservation of rights, which means that what happens afterward is still open, but we just finance the lawyer for her. Since there is a conflict of interest, as we are on both sides, we have to allow her to hire her own lawyer and we have to pay for him. However, we usually only have to pay the rates we pay for lawyers, which are a third of regular rates for regular lawyers, although that may change under some new case from an appellate court. Another good trick that may work is to see if you can buy her out of the claim. You might try offering her and her lawyer a fixed sum of money and get her to waive her right to make any claims against Majestik.

She will then probably have to sell and move out, but it gets us out of the fight. Try to keep us from getting into the middle of a pissing match. It could cost us a bundle. You might try reasoning with the association, but you will probably have a hard time getting their attention if they have been living this way for very long. I have already given a memo to underwriting to work on an exclusion for these types of claims in new policies. You know we try to avoid insuring against any real risk we can."

"Okay, thanks. I'll see what I can do."

"Call me if you need me. That's why I'm here," McAteer assured Ernie. "Use your ingenuity on how to settle it if you can. If they are not listening to you, see if you can get their attention."

"Thanks, I will."

The call ended and Ernie pondered the situation. *Naturally, they will exclude in new policies any genuine risk that comes up. Just buy her out, send her to the wolves. That's the insurance company solution. But it's not mine! Use my ingenuity. Get their attention.*

The words rang in Ernie's head as he tried to think of a solution—his way.

ↄⱸↄ

The next day, Ernie pulled up to the building of Janice Mattley's lawyer. File in hand, he went in to the receptionist. "Hi. I'm Ernie, from Majestik to see Mr. Stowe about Janice Mattley. I phoned this morning."

"Oh yes, Mr. Stowe is expecting you. Would you please follow me to the library?" And she led him into a small library with wall to wall books.

He sat at the long table, and within minutes, Mr. Stowe came in. Ernie stood to meet him and shake hands.

Attorney Stowe was in his mid-fifties and had a very pleasant manner. He looked seasoned and had an authoritative presence.

"How do you do, Mr. Stowe? I'm Ernie from Majestik."

"Which side are you here on?" Stowe said, chuckling. "Majestik insures both my client and the association."

"Perhaps you can help me find a way to resolve this," Ernie replied. "Can you enlighten me as to what the association is doing wrong from your legal point of view?"

"The directors, by themselves, and on behalf of the association, are acting beyond the scope of the articles of the association and the conditions, covenants and restrictions, or CC&Rs. They have enacted rules to limit the tennis court that treat her boys as guests, and further that the boys cannot use the tennis court in a manner consistent with other members or members' children. The CC&Rs that are recorded and set forth rights of the property owners, contain the right, and that of her family, to use the tennis court as a common area, and which constitutes a right of the owner of the property that cannot be taken away by some rule enacted by the board. The CC&Rs grant the right to use the common areas to all members and their families. The new rules of the board go beyond what the directors have the power to do under the articles. This constitutes a taking of a property right that she was given in the purchase of the townhome. The term in law is called *ultra vires*. It means beyond the scope or power. The result is that she now about to lose her home, through no legitimate fault of hers, and has emotional distress. She is seeing a psychiatrist and taking medicine."

Ernie liked the attorney who did not seem to be an ambulance chaser. "So what can you do to stop it?"

"I can bring a lawsuit against the association and its directors and can get an injunction against the foreclosure with damages. But it will be very time consuming and take a good deal of money. She doesn't have the money to do it. And the association has infinite money from the dues to put up a fight, and that they will do, as it would be a challenge to their life style. But I'm also making a demand on Majestik to provide her with a defense against the claims of the association, as under her policy of insurance the claims are not excluded as the actions taken are beyond normal fines provided by the articles, which would be excluded. There was an appellate case just last year on that, and Majestik lost that very point," Stowe told Ernie.

He must know about the case that McAteer mentioned to me. "Yes, I'm aware of that," Ernie told him. "I have a proposal for you. What if Majestik were to hire you to defend her? Now, before you get carried away, it would just be for a fixed sum, like ten thousand dollars, and a buy-out under the policy so that the fixed sum would be all you and she would be entitled to. You would have to see her case through to a conclusion on her behalf. I'm authorized to provide some limited assistance financially."

"Well, if I have to take on a five-year cause for a token fee, forget it," Lawyer Stowe said. "But if it would be simply to take measures to put this matter to rest for her, I would do it, and even contribute time or work at a reduced rate. I think what this association is doing is very nasty business, and it has to be stopped. But it may be very difficult to get the attention of the board, as this is a situation that's a lifestyle for those board members, and to get them to compromise would be making them change their ways of doing things."

"The claims manager at the insurance company said the same thing. Getting their attention is the trick. I may be able to do something. I'll work on it. In any event, I'll get back to you. Can I assume that the Majestik proposal may work with you on the buy-out if the matter does not have to end up in trial?"

"Yes you may," Mr. Stowe said. "Your visit is very encouraging. It's unusual to see an insurance man extend himself like this."

Ernie shook his head as he rode off. *Everyone agrees that, in order to get that group of mean old farts at the association to listen, I'll have to get their attention.*

CHAPTER 43

Innocenti and an old friend from Waterbury, Connecticut, Vincenzo "Vinne" Lunati, drove down at night to the marina where the *Hookup* was docked "We have to make this look like an accident, so there is no major investigation," Innocenti warned him. "If it comes out there was an assassination of a candidate for governor, the FBI will get involved and we could get busted."

"I have been working on it since I spoke to you," Lunati said. "And I think we can pull it off. But first, I have to check out the boat to see what equipment it has, and what I can do. There are lots of boating accidents, and I should be able to make the hit look like one."

They parked in a guest area, not too close, so no one would remember their car later on as in proximity to the berth of the *Hookup*. They walked toward Berth C-26 at the Long Beach Marina. Lunati was a regular for certain kinds of work for Innocenti. By coincidence, he had worked in a boat repair yard on the East Coast when he was a teenager, but it was his technical skills that made him good at a multitude of situations. Lunati was especially handy, working with most types of tools, electronics, and his hobby was flying radio-controlled model airplanes.

Most all boats were already berthed at their slips and only a few people who lived aboard were around. Lights showed on just a few boats.

"Okay, Vinne, *andiamo*." Innocenti whispered. "We probably won't find a better time."

The two of them climbed up and vaulted over the big iron security gate. Once on the gangway, they walked toward Berth

C-26 as though they belonged. Nobody paid any attention to them.

Once at the *Hookup* they slowed and looked about. No one living on a boat on the C gangway was in sight, and so they entered the boat. Lunati lifted the floor hatch to the engine room. Each of them had a flashlight. Two big, V-12 diesel engines occupied most of the room. They could not stand up straight due to the low ceiling.

"See?" Lunati said, pointing with his flashlight to metal, rectangular parts on the bottom behind the transmissions. "These are the shaft logs. The propeller shafts go from the engines through these on out the bottom of the hull. They have bearings and seals inside. There is one for each shaft from the transmission from each diesel. There is a lower part below the boat as well as the upper part in here."

He moved his light beam from one to the other. Twelve bolts secured each to the hull to hold the driveshafts in place. The bolts were stainless carriage bolts, put in from the bottom, and secured with stainless nuts inside the boat. Lunati traced wiring from the generators to the batteries, and on to the various locations he was interested in.

He shone his light on a five gallon, plastic gas container bungeed just off to the side of the opening to the compartment used for the gas motor on the dinghy. "There it is."

He got down on his knees and crept forward toward to the bow of the boat, and then returned.

Having finished his inspection, he looked at Innocenti. "Let's get out of here. I have what I need."

❧❧

Lunati walked into a model shop. Radio controlled airplanes, electric, gas, and gliders, hung from the ceiling. The newest ones were the electric, multi-rotor helicopters.

"I want one of the latest frequency-hopping RC radios with servos," he told the clerk. "I also need a dozen solid rocket ignitors for model rockets for my son."

He was presented with a radio kit, one of the latest frequency-hopping radios that came with transmitter, receiver, receiver battery, and motorized servos. "How long with the receiver battery last when not in use but turned on?"

"I'm not sure, as no one leaves the switch on when not about to fly the plane." The clerk then estimated. "I'd guess four to five hours."

The clerk produced a package of rocket fuel stick ignitors, which were thin strips of copper with gunpowder coating that ignite the solid rocket fuel used in model rockets.

"Perfect. These are what my son uses," Lunati told him, trying to avert suspicion, although he had no son. If the FBI was to later contact model shops for information of recent purchases after the boat incident that Lunati was going to create, the clerk should not think to mention him buying normal parts for a son.

His next stop was a building supply where he bought a gallon of two part epoxy and a six-volt lantern battery that weighed two pounds, but which would last several days as opposed to four to five hours. His project did not have to fly like a model plane, and weight was not a factor.

✃✃✃

The following morning Innocenti sauntered into the garage of Lunati. The early morning fog blanketed the house with soothing quiet. The garage was a sight. There were four roll-a-way tool boxes filled with tools. There were welders of all sorts, a plasma cutter, drill presses, band saws, a table saw, chop saws for wood and for metal, belt and disk sanders, and a plethora of other tools. It was a tool fan's paradise. There was very little room for people, and it was clear that Lunati could make just about anything. Elaborately made radio-controlled model airplanes, his hobby, hung on the ceiling, as other space was all used up by many different kinds of tools and building supplies.

The six-foot wide wooden bench that Lunati was sitting behind had his digital soldering station which was in use, a super accurate electronic testing meter, a rack of very small screwdrivers, and specialized electronic tools. A steaming hot cup of coffee was on the bench.

"That smells really good, what is it?" Innocenti took in a deep breath, hinting that he wanted some.

"Freshly ground Jamaican Blue Mountain, the best. It's still fresh and on the kitchen counter if you want some. The expresso machine next to it is working if you'd rather." Lunati loved the best coffees. He was engrossed in soldering a connection and so did not get up to get his boss coffee.

Innocenti went to the kitchen and took a cup from the cupboard, heated it with hot water from the tap, and then filled it with the freshly dripped Jamaican Blue Mountain coffee. He returned with a cup of the delicious brew with its fragrant aroma, and pulled up the only additional bar stool that Lunati had for a guest. There was no room for another guest with all the tools.

The coffee was so smooth, he downed half cup in no time, the caffeine honing his razor-sharp criminal mind. "What has the wizard conjured up?"

"I've got it all worked out. Check this out." Lunati put a rocket ignitor, wired to a special switch he had made up with a nine-volt battery, on the bench. He had fastened the switch to a regular model servo. The transmitter and the receiver both sat on the bench. "When I actuate that channel on the transmitter here, it will actuate the motorized servo, which will turn on the electric switch and the 9-volt battery will ignite the rocket ignitor. Watch."

Lunati pushed the stick on the transmitter for the channel in use, and the servo attached to the switch, and it opened the circuit for the nine-volt battery to ignite the rocket ignitor. The rocket ignitor began to glow, almost to a fire. "See? Pretty cool, eh?"

"Okay, explain," Innocent said.

This is a radio control transmitter and receiver used in model aircraft. It has quite a long range. When I actuate each channel, that channel will in turn actuate the regular motor servo that is normally used for flight controls on a model airplane, like the elevator. But instead, I have it hooked up to an electric switch that will activate the rocket launcher, which is that little wire that you see glowing. It normally ignites a solid rocket fuel pod in a model, but I will have it igniting other things in the boat. I will mix epoxy with rifle loading gunpowder and paint it in various places. It will be painted on wires that I wish to burn through on the boat. Another will ignite gasoline that will be in the engine compartment. Another will ignite gunpowder that I will paint all around the inside of the hull. I will also use one of the motorized servos to turn a petcock to let gas into the engine compartment. What we do is come down the night before, around midnight, and set everything up. Two of us can do it in an hour. We undo the nuts on one of the shaft logs with a portable electric drill. Those nuts are on carriage bolts coming up from the bottom. We remove all the nuts on the carriage bolts on only one shaft log, so it will not look like a hit in case they bring the boat back up from the bottom for an investigation. We leave the bolts in, and put silicone on them to hold them in place so they don't just fall out right away.

"We mix my special paint and put it in all the right spots. We exchange the five-gallon gas tank for mine. I will place the radio receiver in a good spot, set all the ignitors where they need to go, and paint the ignitors on the wires to the bilge pumps, the exhaust fan motor, and also the main wire out of the battery. I will also paint one ignitor where it will ignite the gas on the engine compartment. With the remaining special paint, I will paint that around the front of the hull underneath to the bow, close to the top of the hull so it will blow the top right off the hull.

"The next morning, once fired up to go fishing, the diesels will vibrate, shaking the shaft logs nuts loose. Some will fall out. The skipper will make turns, especially when out at sea when they see their game fish which is marlin. Those turns of the boat under power will torque and twist the shaft logs. The bolts without nuts will come out and then water will come in the holes. There are twelve carriage bolts on each shaft log. Since we are only going to do one of the two shaft logs, there will be twelve holes. Eventually, enough bolts will fall out so that the shaft log will lift up on a turn or sudden torque of the motor, and then the water will come in big time."

Innocenti looked puzzled. "Won't the shaft log come loose and come up inside the boat right away and sink the boat before it gets far enough out to sea?"

"Nope—won't happen in a short while. Typically, the skipper will keep the motors on slow inside the breakwater. Then he will hit them full throttle to get to the fishing spot. He won't turn the boat with the throttles on full unless and until a marlin is spotted. Several bolts might come out quickly and let water in the holes, but there are four, high-capacity bilge pumps in the engine compartment that can keep up with that amount of incoming water."

"So how can we be sure that the shaft log will come loose when out to sea?"

"When it is loose, tight turns chasing a fish will make it happen from the torque. I'll cut some, but not all, of the original sealant around the edge of the flange inside the boat with a knife, and the vibration of the engine and the turns will work it loose. It'll vibrate loose and come up a bit, and let water in. The shaft log can't come up too much as it is on the shaft, but it will come up enough to do what we want. Water will be coming in like gangbusters."

Innocenti was still skeptical. "Won't the loose shaft log make a noise that the skipper will notice?"

"Nope. The noise those monster diesels make combined with the other noises will be too much to be able to hear one of these coming loose when at full throttle. And the shaft and prop will still be turning. But anyway, I'll make sure there this boat is going to take on water. Wait'll you hear the whole plan." He grinned. "We'll be in a chase boat, within radio range for the radio controlled transmitter. I'll make the bilge pumps inoperative when out at sea, by one of these remote controlled servo hooked up to a rocket launcher which will ignite my special paint on the power lines coming to the pumps. I'll use another to cut the exhaust fan on the same channel. "

"What kind of special paint?" Innocenti asked.

Lunati smiled, reached under his bench, and produced a ten pound can of gunpowder used by sportsmen to make their own rifle shells. "I will mix this with a gallon of two-part epoxy and use that to attach the ignitors to the wires. It's a sure thing."

"Wow," Innocenti said. "That is really clever."

"This is the transmitter, and this the receiver," Lunati continued, holding them up. He produced the lantern battery he had bought. "This big battery will last several days with the receiver in the 'on' position, unlike the small one that came with the radio kit which is only good for a few hours. So we can be sure it won't go dead on us." He then held up one of the model rocket ignitors. "When I actuate the servos, they will ignite the rocket launchers and burn right through the wire to the bilge pumps and the one to the exhaust fan with ease in just a second."

"What does the exhaust fan have to do with this?"

"This boat has an exhaust fan to blow out any gas or diesel fuel fumes to prevent an explosion in the engine compartment. Most boats like this one have one. The engine compartment can become a sort of bomb if fumes are allowed to stay in it. I have something to create gas fumes as well. There is a dinghy on the bow on this boat, and, like all of these fishing boats, the dinghy has a gasoline outboard motor. There is a five-gallon plastic container of gas in the engine compartment, bungee tied to the side of the hull, which we saw. When a skipper like Winger can't tie up to shore in a crowed place like Catalina, he will tie to a mooring some distance from shore, and use the dinghy to go back and forth. He always needs gas for the little outboard, and that is why he has that five-gallon red plastic tank we saw. Gas is different from the diesel fuel in that it is more flammable and more explosive."

He reached under the bench and produced a five-gallon plastic gas container that was red exactly like the one in the engine compartment they saw in Winger's boat. "See this pet cock and mechanical servo I added?" He pointed to them on the bottom of the red, plastic, five gallon container. He hooked up a battery lead to the servo. He actuated his model airplane transmitter sitting on his bench, and the mechanical servo turned the pet cock to the open position, then back to closed, several times, Lunati grinning at his own prowess.

"With the help of a few small air holes I drilled on the top, the gas will pour out quickly and on top of the water in the engine compartment. Gas is lighter than water, and so it will stay on the top. It's the fumes of gas that burn and explode, and so it will be ready to let go when actuated with another of my actuators for the rocket fuel which will be placed with the gunpowder paint in the engine compartment. The boat will be taking on water, and the pumps dead. The exhaust fan will be dead. The skipper will notice the rear of the boat low in the water. He'll look in the engine compartment and notice the bilge pumps not working, and also smell gas. He'll go to the fuses and try the fuses for the bilge pumps and the exhaust fan. When he finds them not working, he'll then call in an emergency."

Innocenti's eyebrow raised. "Do we want him to call it in?"

"Absolutely! After he calls in the emergency for sinking and gas fumes, which we monitor, I'll hit another servo which will be painted with the gunpowder paint to the electrical lead out of the batteries which will cut all power to the boat including its radio. He won't be able to make further communications. I will then actuate the servo that will ignite the gas in the engine compartment, aided by being attached to special paint that I will paint next to the top of the compartment, and the explosion should cause enough damage to make the engines inoperable. That way they cannot hit the throttles and try for shore.

"Then we move in quickly. "There will be three of us nearby in the chase boat. Those on the fishing boat will think we are there to help and will not be defending against us. Two of us get on board with guns, and hold the candidate, his host, and the skipper at gun point while we tie them up with special dissolving rope. You go under the boat with the air saw and make the hole around the shaft log larger to be sure it will be sinking fast." He produced an air powered saw with a five-inch blade. "I have a small, gasoline powered air compressor and will have it on the speedboat with an air hose to power the air saw. You will cut around the shaft log to make it a bigger hole for more water to come in. You should be the one for that as I remember that you are a good swimmer. Those on board will have a twenty-pound barbell attached to their special ropes. We throw them overboard with hands and feet tied, and the weight tied to the special rope. They'll sink to the bottom fast.

"The coast guard will come to the distress call, but there will be nothing there. They will later determine the boat, which will have already sunk when they arrive in the coast guard cutter, sank due to a gas leak in the engine compartment and an explosion, which is a common occurrence. The ropes will eventually dissolve with no handcuff or ankle scars, and the bodies will float to the surface in a day or two. When they float up and get found, autopsies later will show they drowned. No one will be the wiser."

Innocenti, acting the doubting Thomas as he figured he would be the one expected to come with pistols blazing if things went wrong, asked a pertinent question, "How can you be sure your enlarged hole in the bottom and the explosion with the gas fumes will be big enough to sink the boat before the coast guard arrives? Maybe it will be just low in the water when they arrive, and suspiciously no one is on board—like a ghost ship?"

Lunati grinned. "Well, I have a backup. After I paint the gunpowder epoxy on the ignitors, I will paint the rest, which is most of it, all around the inside of the front of the hull near the top. When we finish tossing the men overboard and leave to a safe distance, I will hit the final servo and it will blow up most of the ten pounds of gunpowder in the front of the boat. Compressed by the enclosure, it should blow that boat to smithereens!

"Now, come in to the kitchen. I want to show you my ropes."

In the kitchen, on the table, were three foot lengths of newspapers rolled tightly up. Lunati gave one to Innocenti. "Pull on it."

Innocenti tried to break it by pulling on it. It did not come apart.

"These are what we use to tie the wrists and ankles of those on board," Lunati told him. "They will each have a twenty pound barbell attached, and the weight will pull them down fast. The newspaper dissolves and comes loose, and the bodies later float up to be discovered perhaps a few days later."

"Vinnie, you are the cosmic madman. You always outdo yourself and everyone else."

Lunati grinned at the praise and dubbed his masterpiece with a name. "The perfect crime." Then he asked, "As we need three, I want to call Tony Sandino for the third, if that is okay."

Innocenti knew Sandino, who was very big and very tough and who would be perfect for the third man. "Yeah, call Tony."

CHAPTER 44

In his apartment, Ernie called an animal shelter in San Diego County. He wanted to find one at least two counties away from Los Angeles County to reduce the chances of getting caught.

A lady answered. "Yes, may I help you?"

"I'm looking for a family of skunks. I have a large ranch, and I want to put a family there as I'm studying their habits. Do you have any?"

"We sure do, and would we like to get rid of them! Just a few days ago, a mother and four offspring were brought in. The offspring are fairly large. They'll be euphemized unless the zoo or someone picks them up in a few days. You want them, they're yours. Anyone taking these gets them without the usual charges. I'll even waive the modest charge for rabies shots."

Five. Just the number I need. This will save me from having to call anywhere else. Perfect! "Yes, I want them. I'll be down today. My name is Pete Simpson," Ernie lied. "I'll rig up a cage for the special handling."

"You'll need that," the lady told him with a laugh.

Ernie next called a truck and trailer rental yard he had seen close to where he lived. He said to the man that answered, "I need to rent a pickup for two days. Do you have one?"

"Yes, we do."

∽∾∽∾

Later, Ernie pulled up in front of the San Diego County Animal Xhelter in a white rented pickup with a huge sign painted on each side that read *Rent Me*. In the back was a large Sky Kennel that Ernie bought second hand at a pet store, and a smaller animal cage as well. He had covered the cage wires of the Sky Kennel and the smaller cage on the front and the sides with cardboard so no one would notice the animals while he was on the road. He left the top open for air.

"Hi, I'm Pete Simpson," Ernie told the lady. At least she would not have his correct name in case any inquiry got as far as San Diego County.

"You're here for the skunks?"

"Yep, that's me."

"No one ever takes skunks. Even the zoos do their own breeding and, of course, they remove the scent glands. Are you going to do that?"

"We're going to try not to, as we want to observe them without removing their main defensive weapon. They're going to a large ranch, and about the worst that will happen is one of the dogs may get sprayed."

She seemed to be going for it. "Just fill out this form here," she told him. "Normally we have a charge for dogs and cats, which are spayed or neutered and given shots, but we don't expect people to take skunks, so we don't bother," she said, chuckling. "Frankly I'm glad to see them out of here. They would have been put into the chamber to put them to sleep right away, but no doubt they would have sprayed up the place as much as they could, especially if they got scared."

Ernie wrote down the false name he was using, as well as a false rural route address in Santa Barbara County.

The lady put on a yellow rain jacket and led him to the skunks. The jacket was obviously designed to be hosed down after dealing with strong smelling animals. Together, they put his Sky Kennel in front of the metal cage after putting some food inside to lure the skunks in. The young ones followed their mother, once she decided it was safe. They walked very slowly without fear, having not had too many other things scaring them, especially people.

Once they were inside, Ernie closed the gate, followed by some commotion and, of course, the inevitable odor of the skunks spraying. Ernie and the lady moved away for a while and returned when the odor had subsided a little to put the Sky Kennel in the back of the pickup.

"Thanks," Ernie told her. "Since you have on the rain slicker, would you mind setting a water bowl in the cage?" He handed her a water bowl that he had brought along.

"Sure, why not? I'm really glad to see those fellas go. I'd rather have to deal with a poisonous snake or a rabid wolf than these things!"

෪෪෪

Ernie didn't return directly to his apartment, once he got back to town, as he didn't want anyone to see or smell his special cargo. Instead, he took a longer route back, taking in the new scenery, and stopping at a twenty-four hour diner. He parked his rental truck at the far end of the parking lot, in the back, where there were no other cars, so the smell of skunk would not be noticed. However, the skunks seemed to have settled down in the Sky Kennel after the initial scare, and the odor was not nearly as strong as it had been earlier. Sipping coffee, he took his time so as not to arrive too early at his destination.

The calendar showed it would be a moonless night, which was why Ernie chose it. It was pitch black when he left for the townhome association at 11:45 p.m. He wore newly purchased black jeans and a black shirt, bought for the occasion to be stealthy at night. And they were cheap so he wouldn't feel too bad when he had to dispose of them after he finished. He pulled over the rental truck on a quiet side street nearest Cresta Views. The townhomes were all dark, save for a few night lights. He put on disposable rubber gloves, both to prevent leaving fingerprints and also to reduce the smell that would get on his hands.

He took the Sky Kennel with the skunks and the smaller cage out and carried them to the shrubbery surrounding the Cresta Views perimeter. *Some security.* He chuckled. *These people put in an expensive guard gate, which has to be staffed around the clock, which is three shifts daily of people, plus someone else for days off and for relief for breaks for the gate guard on the grounds, and all they end up with is a way to keep out friends. And to limit motorcycles, which is a crime against nature.*

He went to a large cluster of high bushes, just a few yards from the boundary, and hid the Sky Kennel there. He put the smaller cage up to the larger one, opening to opening, with some food and water in bowls in the back, and waited. Two skunks wandered in together. He had only wanted one at time, but two would be okay, as that would cut the time down to restock the small cage. He closed the gate on the two of the offspring, which were two-thirds the size of the mother.

He had the addresses of the directors written down on the sheet of paper they had given him at the meeting, and had planned his event down to a "T."

As it was a warm night, many of the owners had left one or more windows open in the two-story units. *It's funny. When I evaluate a claim for Majestik, I have to take into account the new codes which require dual pane windows, and insulated everything to some new standard. Yet here in this warm LA, everyone leaves one or more of those expensive dual pane windows open for ventilation. More government people making laws that don't work.*

There it was, the first of the directors' townhomes. Ernie looked around for an open window. Would there be one? Yes! There was one in the family room on the ground floor. Ernie pulled the screen out just enough to ease it off of the hooks, but not enough put a dent in its aluminum frame. The screen then came off.

He reached in, took a skunk by the back of the neck, and tossed it in through the open window. He could tell it was scared and spraying, but making no noise except a little hissing. Perfect! The smell was so strong that it seemed caustic.

Carefully and quietly, he replaced the window screen by bending it just a little so it would snap into place without any permanent bends. Once it was back in place, Ernie was off to the next director's house.

This one had no lower windows open—only an upper bedroom window. Stashing the cage with the skunk in the bushes, he looked carefully down the front of the unit and, seeing the coast was clear, went to the front door. There was a dead bolt in addition to the regular lock, so no credit card was going to work to force the door. What to do?

The garage door was a double-wide, wooden type that had the Southern California type of hinges which swing the door up and out from the bottom, as contrasted with the type in the north where it snows and the door goes up and back on tracks so as not to be blocked by snow drifts.

The door was out of adjustment, and also somewhat warped which was typical. One of the bottom corners was sticking out several inches. He pulled on it, and it moved enough that he could crawl in underneath. He found a single car inside, a Chrysler. The door to the townhome from the garage was locked—this person liked security. He checked the driver's door on the car. It was unlocked and it opened. The driver's window was down several inches. This would do. The skunk smell, by all rights, should total the car, as there would be no way to get the smell out of the fabric interior. Of course, a crooked insurance company like Majestik, would only pay to have the interior cleaned so the smell would linger for a year or two.

Ernie went back under the door and to the bushes for the skunk. He brought the cage to the driveway in front of the garage, got down on his back, and slid under the end of the garage door with the cage in hand. Once in the garage, he grabbed the skunk by the back of the neck, opened the door of the Chrysler, and put in the skunk. The skunk started spraying like crazy, and it was nearly all Ernie could do to overcome the odor and continue.

He knocked softly on the window a few times to rattle the skunk, and the animal sprayed big time. Ernie could smell it at once, even standing outside the slightly open window. Taking the small cage, he went back out under the door, and returned to where he'd left the Sky Kennel.

Once he got back to the skunks, he put the small cage up to

the gate again. Initially, the mamma showed her teeth and hissed, but after he stood back and waited five minutes, she came out and walked to the food in the small cage. The two remaining offspring tried to follow, but Ernie closed the gate before they could.

Big Mamma has to be for the president, the cosmic asshole, Mr. Cowboy Hat, Ernie concluded. Moving to the president's street, carrying the small cage, Ernie heard someone. Oops! There was a security guard on foot making rounds!

Ernie quickly ducked behind some bushes. The security guard walked by slowly, a flashlight in hand. He pointed the light at the bush Ernie was hiding behind but didn't notice anything.

When he was gone, Ernie moved quietly out of the bushes and darted across the road. The president's townhome had no lower windows open. But the front door had no deadbolt. Ernie stashed the cage in the nearby bushes, took out his pocket knife, stuck it into the tapered door latch, and wiggled it until it opened. When he retrieved the skunk cage, Mamma was at the back, making noises and showing her teeth—a nasty one she was. There was no way she was going to allow him to pick her up.

Taking the small cage to the front door, he pushed it open just the width of the cage and put the end into the opening. When he lifted the gate on the cage, Mamma bolted from the cage and raced into the dark interior of the house. Three!

Back at the Sky Kennel, Ernie got the last two skunks into the small cage together.

The next one was for Mr. Golfer. Ernie stooped behind the bushes across the private interior road in front of Mr. Golfer's townhome. There was a street lamp nearby, adding to the risk. The townhome shared a wall on either side with the neighboring ones, as it was not a corner unit. Ernie went around to the back side, some distance away. A swimming pool was behind the townhouse. He crept around the pool and crouched down low, below the windows, until he came to Mr. Golfer's unit. There was a kitchen window overlooking the pool area, and it was open!

Car lights! Ernie ducked flat on the ground behind some bushes as the car approached. Someone was coming home late. The car passed him, without stopping. Ernie breathed a sigh of relief that he was still unnoticed.

Back in business, he got up and crept to the kitchen window. He eased the kitchen screen off, lifted another skunk out, and put him inside the kitchen, right on the counter. He put the screen back in place. It did bend a wee bit in the process, but he was able to straighten it so the dent did not show.

Observing the last unit, he saw that it was a corner unit, and there were no open windows. He left the cage in the bushes and went to the front door. It was dead bolted. The garage door was tightly shut. Ernie checked to see if it was loose, but no such luck. A puzzler. He had to get the skunk inside to get the full effect—all of the directors getting hit at the same time. He peeked into the living room through the picture window and saw a night light on in the hallway—and a fireplace in the living room.

Scanning the neighborhood, he noticed that all the units had fireplaces, or so it seemed from the many chimneys. This one, being a corner unit, had a galvanized rain down spout fastened to the side of the house. Would it hold him?

Ernie went to it and pulled on it. It didn't move. When he was younger, he'd entered several logging contests where the contestants had to shimmy up a hundred-foot pole, cut off the top with a chainsaw carried up on their waist, and came back down in a race. So, going up the down spout was something he could do, even though it had been some years since he had entered one of those contests.

He loosened his belt and took it off half way, putting the tongue end through the handle on top of the small cage, so that the cage hung from the middle of his back at his waist, then put the belt back on. With both hands free to use to hold onto the spout, he pressed his cleated boots gently against the side of the house, the skunk spraying wildly, and easily climbed up. At the top, he grabbed hold of the gutter and then the roof edge, pulling himself up.

He crept over to the chimney and looked down. He could

see ashes. The nightlight from the hallway shone into the living room and reflected off the fireplace. He took the cage and held the door open over the chimney, certain that the drop to the bottom wouldn't harm the little fella. He didn't want to hurt it, but he'd been on several raccoons hunts—he figured they were about the same as skunks—and seen them jumping in and out of tall trees, to and from branches high off the ground, with no problem. Ernie estimated the distance to the bottom of the chimney was not even as high as most of those branches, so he was sure the skunk would be fine. Pissed but fine.

He shook the cage. The skunk slid out and fell down the chimney, landing on the cold ashes, which exploded in a cloud of black dust. The creature shook his head, looked around, and scurried into the living room, clearly a little shaken and spraying the place for all he was worth. Ernie could smell the obnoxious fumes drifting back up the chimney. *That makes five!*

He put the cage back on his belt and began moving quickly down the rain spout. *Car lights!* A car turned the corner and started down the road. Ernie jumped the rest of the way to the ground, dove for the shrubbery next to the house, and lay motionless. The car drove on by without stopping.

After slipping back to his truck, Ernie drove some distance until he saw a twenty-four hour grocery store. He drove around to the back and found an enormous dumpster next to the delivery ramp. He got out, quietly chucked the cage and the Sky Kennel into the dumpster, got back into his truck, and drove off.

He then went to a twenty-four-hour wash-it-yourself car wash to hose off the skunk smell from the bed of the rental truck, so that when he returned it the rental agency, hopefully, no one would notice. He had to do it three times trying to get most of the odor out, but it refused to go away completely.

He went to the back of the property, behind a big green dumpster, and changed out of his skunk-infested black clothes into his regular jeans and shirt. He discarded the contaminated clothes in the dumpster.

At the Polynesian, Ernie took an extended shower, contemplating what he had done. Even after half an hour in the shower, breathing the moistened air, he still had the overpowering odor in his nose. He then went outside to the laundry to wash the second set of clothes he'd worn that evening. To further subdue the odor, he jumped in the pool to soak, assuming the chlorine would kill what was left of the odor.

The evening was a success.

ℰℭℰℭ

Ernie's recollection of what he'd done the night before came immediately and distinctly to him by olfaction when he awakened. It was 9:40 a.m. But the odor was still present, even after all he'd done to get rid of it. Why? Was it in his lungs? His skin? Hair? He got up, made coffee, and sat at the coffee table, which was adorned with his chainsaw, overlooking the Torrid pool. Today he would return the rental truck, take the rest of the day off, and go soak in the chlorinated pool water. He wondered if the smell would ever go away.

ℰℭℰℭ

At the Polynesian, after reading a few more files, he decided at 3:30 p.m. to try soaking in the Torrid pool to see if inhaling and soaking in chlorine would help rid him of the odor.

While he was there, his cell phone rang.

"Is this Ernie?" a woman asked.

"Yes it is."

"This is Ruth from claims at Majestik. We had a nearly hysterical call today from some irate board member of Cresta Views Townhomes about a problem with skunks in the complex. I checked the computer, and there is already a case number on another claim on that insured, with the claim assigned to Jessica Bloom. I called for her and found that she is on maternity leave, and that you have taken over the existing claim file. Is that correct?"

"Yes, I was already out there on another claim," Ernie told her. "I'm very familiar with the place." He exaggerated a little as he wanted to be sure the new claim was assigned to him.

"Well, since you're familiar with the insured, the new claim will be assigned to you as well. You go ahead and take it."

Perfect! Ernie thought with a smile as he put down the cell phone. The game was afoot.

CHAPTER 45

It was evening when Ernie opened the sliding glass door of the clubhouse and walked inside for his 6:00 p.m. appointment with the "noble" Board of Directors of Cresta Views. They were all very excited, standing and talking to one another. Spotting Ernie, they stopped talking and took seats at their "justice" bench arrangement they made out of the two oblong tables, end to end.

Mr. Cowboy Hat, now known to be the president, Mr. Freeman, sat in the middle. Mr. Golfer wore a different golfing outfit, but just as silly as the last one. Mr. Cocktail had a Hawaiian styled shirt with flowers. Mr. Road Runner had on a colored T-shirt with Porky Pig on it. Mr. Cresta Views wore another pullover, also with the name *Cresta Views* sewn on it, but a different color.

Mr. Cresta Views is so proud of where he lives, Ernie thought, *he must have the name sewn on all of his shirts. Maybe he has underwear and condoms printed with it.*

Being a director there was probably as close as he—or any of them, for that matter—ever came to managing anything. Ernie moved over to the row of seats in front and sat down. He could detect the slight odor of skunk, which he realized was coming from the board members themselves, as he had gotten rid of any traces of it on him.

The skunk smell overpowered the smell of alcohol, but it was clear that they had not missed cocktail hour.

Mr. Cowboy Hat broke the silence. "I take it you have heard about the attack on us?"

"All I have heard is that there is some problem with a skunk. What happened, did a skunk get into something?" Ernie asked innocently, claiming it was *a* skunk, so as to divert suspicion away from him.

"It wasn't *a* skunk! Each of us had a skunk put in his house! " Mr. Cowboy Hat shouted. "There were five of them!"

"Not me," one said. "Mine was put in my car. My car is ruined!"

"Yes, well, all but one of us had a skunk put in his house," Mr. Cowboy Hat corrected. "This was a deliberate, premeditated attack on the board of directors. We have now hired a service that provides armed guards to patrol the complex at night. There is no telling what might happen next!"

"Do you have a police report?" Ernie asked, as cool as a cucumber.

"Yes, here."

Mr. Cowboy Hat passed a several-page document to Ernie. It was a form from the local police department, with sections filled in with block print by a policeman. There was nothing much in it, other than a description of what occurred with each of the five directors.

He noticed that it clearly stated that there was *no forcible entry.* It said that an animal control officer was dispatched, and caught three of the skunks. The skunk in the car, once let out, got away, as did one from one of the townhomes when the door was opened to let it out.

"Our homes are a fucking disaster!" Mr. Cowboy Hat exclaimed. "All of the furniture, drapes, carpets, and cloth materials are full of skunk odor. We think that everything will smell of skunk for months or maybe forever! Is Majestik going to replace our rugs, drapes, and furniture?"

Ernie stifled a grin. "From the police report, there was no forcible entry into any of the five residences. That means that someone had keys or access, or that the homes were unlocked. If you look at the policy, you will see that forcible entry is necessary to make a claim for damage to the interior, such as in the case of vandals or burglers."

"*What?*" Mr. Golfer practically yelled. "What the fuck do you mean, it's not insured?"

"Take it easy," Mr. Cowboy Hat told him in a normal

voice. This time it was Mr. Cowboy Hat who was calming Mr. Golfer.

"Fuck 'take it easy,'" Mr. Golfer shouted. "My fucking house smells like skunk and you tell me to take it easy? I'm staying in a fucking hotel. I can't even go in my own house!"

This is going much better than I had hoped. Ernie savored the pleasure, hiding his feelings of euphoria at their reaction.

One of the others spoke more calmly than Mr. Golfer. "We have a catastrophe. I took the drapes to a cleaner, and they refused to clean them, stating it would ruin their fluid and any other clothes being cleaned. So I had to put them in the dumpster. We each had a furniture cleaner with one of those trucks, that brings warm water and cleaning solution in from a hose, scrub the furniture and the carpets but the it only reduced the smell a little bit!"

"I can't even get in my car!" another said. "The whole interior is ruined. It's a total!"

"Is your car insured with Majestik?" Ernie asked.

"Yes!"

I've got their attention. "Please be calm. I'm only a field representative and do not write these policies," Ernie said, to make it appear he was powerless.

"Someone has clearly gone after us as a board," Freeman said. "We're not safe!"

"Could this be retaliation for your policies about parking, use of the common areas, and issuing tickets and fines?" Ernie asked.

"Obviously," Mr. Cowboy Hat admitted. "Someone is trying to get us. We have made a list of suspects. We think it is definitely one of the fucking renters. They have no respect for property or authority. We have contacted our attorney to see if we can ban owners from renting thier units."

"Isn't renting out a property a right that comes with ownership of the property?" Ernie pointed out.

"That's what our attorney said. But we told him that's not acceptable," Mr. Cowboy Hat retorted. "We are thinking of getting a second opinion from another lawyer."

"Trying to ban renters sounds to me like more of the same

thing that caused somebody to come after you in the first place," Ernie informed them, wondering if these cretins would ever get the message that they had to respect owners and their rights.

"I, for one, am resigning from the board," Mr. Road Runner announced. "I don't need this shit. There's no pay, and I'm retired. I've had it."

That's only one member. The bylaws allow the board to select their own choice of replacement until the next election. They'll simply put another of their cronies on the board. He also recalled that the bylaws provided that one board member need not be an owner. *This is a good time to take over.*

Ernie straightened in his seat. "You are quite a problem now for Majestik. With this big problem of foreclosing on Ms. Mattley's townhome, with us having to defend her, and now this new claim for skunks, Majestik will cancel your policy. And, if that happens, when you try to get insurance with another company, you will be asked about prior claims or if you have been canceled and, in any case, they'll find out. Once a new company hears about all this, and the ongoing case against Ms. Mattley, no new company will insure you. Also, with the main policy cancelled, the owners will no longer be entitled to their twenty-five per cent discount on premiums on their individual policies."

"Jesus Christ!" two of them said in harmony.

Finally, I struck a note. Ernie smiled within. *Perfect.*

The board members looked at one another, never before realizing that they had any problem with their secure living conditions. It had been the feeling of great security that led them to take such oppressive action against Janice Mattley. Now they had been hit with the skunks and were about to lose their insurance.

"What can we do?" Mr. Cowboy Hat asked, showing a sign of humility for the first time.

I have their attention. Cowboy Hat's tone is finally contrite and free of arrogance. Time to move forward with the proposal. "Majestik insures Janice Mattley. The company has decided that it has to provide her with an attorney to defend against your claims of foreclosure, as the claims are beyond the power and scope of your articles and bylaws, and you have caused her emotional distress by your wrongful conduct, which is insured."

"You mean Majestik is going to pay for her lawyer to sue us?" Mr. Cowboy Hat asked in disbelief.

"Not exactly," Ernie said. "Majestik is not hiring her lawyer to sue you, but only paying to defend her against you foreclosing on her townhome."

Mr. Cowboy Hat got even more animated and slammed his fist on the table. "But isn't that the same thing? That bitch's lawyer will be getting money from Majestik enough to cover his fees, and so it is the same as you paying her to sue us! She can't afford an attorney on her own, which we counted on. Now that cunt has a free lawyer!"

Ernie did not react to the desk pounding, as to him the man was as intimidating as a mosquito. "You could look at it that way. But Majestik has an obligation to defend the claim against her. This situation that you have put Majestik in is why you are going to lose your insurance." He really had no idea if Majestik would cancel them or not, but his proposal seemed to be working.

"So what can we do to keep that from happening?" Mr. Cresta Views asked. "We never thought that the Majestik that insures us would be paying Mattley's lawyer when we foreclosed on her. If this sort of thing gets out—and it surely will if our insurance is cancelled and everyone's rates go up by twenty-five per cent—we'll look like shit to the members."

Ernie knew then it was time. "Here's my proposal to put an end to the lawsuit before it starts and to save your insurance. You rescind the rule about the tennis courts as it applies to someone's immediate family, whether or not they reside here, which of course includes Ms. Mattley's boys. Include renters and their families too. Since you will be rescinding the rule, you also rescind all the fines and charges against her for all tennis court fines. Rescind the rule prohibiting activities in the garages and not allowing garage doors to be open. The rule about trashcan placement goes, too. Each member will be given, in advance, a packet of fifty non-expiring guest passes and as many more as he or she wants to give to his or her guests for parking. And, since this will be a settlement with Ms. Mattley, you will rescind all other fines against her as well. You will refund to her any fines, including any charges you assessed against her that she did pay. You will sign a notice of rescission of the foreclosure, stating the foreclosure was a mistake, which will be notarized so it can be recorded with the county recorder to leave a record and at least try to repair her credit. And you will agree not to fine her again for any reason—"

"*What?*" Mr. Cowboy Hat interrupted, nearly shouting. The idea of admitting a mistake, losing face to her, and giving up the ability to fine her was ridiculous and would be an end to his power. He glared at Ernie. "Fuck you!"

Time for a little respect from this cesspool of genetic trash. Ernie leaned forward in his seat and tilted his torso aggressively toward Mr. Cowboy Hat, which frightened the man into leaning back in his seat.

Ernie forced himself not to get too aggressive. *I must be careful what words I use because if I curse at them, they will repeat that to Majestik. Also, I can't hit any of them.* "You put a ticket on my motorcycle," he told Mr. Cowboy Hat. "Now you interrupt me. I don't like you and think you are incompetent and ignorant as a director. Is that clear? Maybe I should just forget about all this and let you do what you think you have to do. Maybe Lloyds of London will insure you for some fantastically outrageous premium. It would serve you mean-spirited incompetents right." He shifted his gaze to the rest of them.

Mr. Golfer looked at Mr. Cowboy Hat. "Maybe we should listen."

Ernie took advantage of the fact that one had said he was resigning. "If you do as I suggest, I can make a better report to Majestik and recommend that your insurance not be canceled. In order to carry out the amendments to the rules, I want you to select Ms. Mattley's attorney to fill the board vacancy left from the one of you who is resigning until the next election, but not less than a year from now. The bylaws provide that one member of the board need not be an owner, and so it's legal. He will only participate in the changing of the rules to put an end to all the fining, and then he will be gone, although he might want to stay on a year to be sure. Majestik will pay him to see that through and then be done with it. Do you want that, or do you want to go hire your own lawyers while I hire one to defend her? And by the way, I don't give a shit how much it costs to defend her."

They seemed to realize that this was a catastrophe they could not eradicate with fines as they were used to doing and began to talk to one another in soft voices.

Ernie stood, interrupting the process. "Why don't I step outside while you discuss it, and also to make sure no asshole tickets my motorcycle?" *Darn, I used asshole. Diplomacy, diplomacy.*

There was no audible response, but the five men stood up and began talking to each other in a manner that did not include Ernie. He went outside and walked toward one of the pools and the tennis court to get away from them for a while.

After fifteen minutes, deciding that the cretins had had enough time, he returned to the clubhouse. The five were seated, but their seats were moved about such that they could talk to one another.

When they saw Ernie come in, they got quiet, as though to hide their secrets, but they did not look at all happy. Ernie took a seat across from the lot of them, enjoying himself immensely.

"We have a question," Mr. Cowboy Hat said to Ernie on behalf of the sorry-looking group. "What about the damage from the skunk vandalism? Will that be paid?"

"We need a complete settlement here," Ernie said. "And there really is no damage. The smell will leave, eventually, and since you feel that the action was taken against the board, you can consider it against the association itself and pay for the cleaning from the dues you collect."

Of course, Ernie knew the smell would not leave for a very long time, as he knew forest creatures much better than these geriatric drunks. But the idea of them smelling like skunk for several months was too delightful.

They looked at each other. Finally, Mr. Cresta Views said, "That's a good point. The action was taken against us as a board. We could pay for it out of the dues, by our majority vote as directors. We can take it from the amounts we have been saving up for roof replacement in several years. No one will notice or give a shit as usual. We have a bunch of proxies."

"Then I can consider the matter settled?" Ernie asked. "I'll contact Lawyer Stowe and ask him to monitor the rule changes as a lawyer and act as a replacement board member until he deems it no longer necessary. You'll follow his suggestions to the letter as to the rule changes and adopt what he tells you to. You'll rescind all fines against Janice Mattley, and you will agree not to fine her again for anything, unless the association pays for her fines. You'll sign the rescission of fines and of the foreclosure, refund any fines and charges assessed or collected from her, and sign any other documents that Lawyer Stowe will prepare, which will contain an apology. I'll notify the insurance company that the matter is settled, conditioned on your compliance, and tell them not to cancel your insurance coverage. Lawyer Stowe and I will have papers to you within a few days. Agreed?"

They looked at each other and mumbled, and then Mr. Cowboy Hat said in a sheepish, defeated voice, "Agreed."

"And," Ernie added, to rub in salt into the wound, "you will tear up the ticket you put on my motorcycle, and further agree to allow motorcycles in Cresta Views. And, you will get rid of the rule on the five mile per hour speeding limit and change those signs to 'Please Drive Slowly,' since it is hard to drive a motorcycle at such a slow pace."

"Actually," Mr. Cocktail said, "I was thinking of getting a motorcycle myself. Maybe a nice little Honda."

The others gaped at him in disbelief.

CHAPTER 46

Dwight Winger sang a tune as he walked down the gangway to C-26. There she was, his trusty sport fisher, his pride and joy. It was a few minutes before 4:00 a.m., still dark, and the birds were soon to get up. There was no other activity on the gangway yet. There was no evidence apparent that anyone had been on the boat the night before.

"Hey, Dwight," he heard from behind him as he neared the boat. He could see someone at the gate, but could not recognize him in the dark.

"Is that you, Ernie?"

"Yeah. Let's go fishing!" Ernie shouted back.

Dwight walked back to the gate and let Ernie in.

"Is everything ready?" Ernie stood ready to assist.

"Yeah, I was down yesterday and took it out for fuel. I went and caught some mackerel for bait. All the systems are in order. Bait, rods, and reels, are all ready. I stocked up with refreshments. When I tell you, cast off the lines."

Ernie grinned. "Aye, aye, Skipper!"

Inside the boat, Dwight went down into the hold to do a visual check and looked about with a flashlight. He didn't notice anything suspicious. The red five-gallon gas container that had been switched, the tiny radio control receiver, and the other additions Lunati and Innocenti put in place the night before were well camouflaged.

Back at the helm, Dwight did a systems check on the circuit breakers. All were functioning properly. Everything was in order, or so it seemed. He paused to look at Ernie. "Nice deck shoes!" he joked, making fun of Ernie's logger boots. "Hardly the normal deck shoes."

Embarrassed, Ernie felt the blood drain from his face. "That's all I have. But they are rubber soled." He lifted one boot to show Dwight the bottom, revealing the black rubber cleats. "So they won't damage the deck or anything."

"Yeah, okay, those are fine." Dwight went to a drawer and took out a knife in a sheath. It was a good sized one, with a seven-inch blade. "Here, you'll need this for cutting the lines and things to help the guests."

"Thanks." Ernie opened his belt, putting it through the loop in the knife's scabbard.

At 4:45 a.m., the sky was still dark. "Why don't you go on over by the gate and wait for our charter?" Dwight said to Ernie. "I'll go ahead and unhook the water line, power line, and phone."

"Who's coming?" Ernie asked.

"Somebody named John Poladian, and he said he would have an important guest. Who, I don't know. Sometimes celebrities or the rich don't want anyone to know when and where they are going. The guest is probably someone like that, a movie star or a rich person. Or, maybe it is Poladian's girl-friend." He chuckled at the idea.

Ernie laughed and walked up the gangway toward the gate. He looked at his watch. It was 4:50 a.m. The charter should arrive any minute.

As he approached the gate, a shiny, silver Rolls Royce limousine pulled up. The uniformed driver opened the rear door for John Poladian and Zachary Lewis, gubernatorial candidate for the State of California.

Stopping just behind was a state police car with two uniformed officers. They exited and came up to Ernie at the gate, as though he was a threat.

"Are you Dwight Winger?" one of the officers asked Ernie.

"No. But I'm his deck hand. Why?"

"We are state police in charge of Mr. Lewis's protection as a gubernatorial candidate. If you are going to be on the boat with Mr. Lewis, we would like to see your identification."

Ernie was a little taken back. His initial reaction was to refuse, but then he was only a deck hand and he dared not cause a scene over Dwight's important guest. "Sure." He took out his billfold, removed his Washington State driver's license, and handed it to the officer.

"Why don't you have a California driver's license?" the officer asked.

"Because I'm a resident of Washington. Perhaps the candidate would prefer that I not go, and he can bait his own hooks, and bring his fish into the boat if he catches one," Ernie said, pissed off and becoming sarcastic.

The officer appeared to be trying not to show any reaction. "If you are to be aboard, taking part in the candidate's safety, we must check your record. Do you consent to that?"

"Sure, go ahead."

The other officer went over to the police car and called up the National Crime Information Center on the car's computer.

In a few minutes, while the Rolls Royce driver was getting the candidate's things out of the trunk of the limousine, the officer came forward and said to his partner. "He's clean."

The state policeman handed the driver's license back to Ernie. "Thank you, sir. Is that Mr. Winger?" he asked, looking at Winger on the boat in the modest light afforded by the rising sun.

"Are you going to take my word for it? Maybe he's a Muslim terrorist," Ernie snapped, angry at being treated like a nobody.

"We have already checked his background, sir. I'll just go identify him," the officer said. He walked down the ramp toward the boat to identify Winger.

Poladian walked up to Ernie. "Are you with the Dwight Winger boat?"

"Yes, sir. I'm Ernie. I'm acting deck hand today. You must be Mr. Poladian."

"I'm John Poladian. This is Zachary Lewis." Poladian held out his hand and shook Ernie's.

Lewis broke into a big smile and approached Ernie, his open hand ready to shake, too. "Hi, Ernie," he said with his usual exuberance. "I'm so excited about going fishing. It's been quite a while. I can't wait!"

"Let me get your things, gentlemen," Ernie told them. He lifted their big cooler from the trunk of the limo, which was too heavy for just sandwiches. Ernie guessed it must be full of ice and booze as he carried it toward the boat. He was right.

"Did you wish for us to be here for your return, sir?" the state cop asked Lewis.

"No. You boys just go on, and I'll be fine. John here will call for his car and give me a lift home. Thanks."

Dwight fired up the *Hookup*'s big diesels when he saw the guests arrive. The motors made their muffled sounds, burbling exhaust into the water.

As Ernie brought the heavy cooler aboard, Poladian and Lewis came up the small, white stairs on the gangway that led to the deck of the boat. They went inside the stateroom from there to put down their things.

The *Hookup* was ready. Ernie knew he would enjoy the day, even though he wouldn't get to fish himself. That was for rich people.

Dwight came to greet his two guests. "Hi. I'm Dwight Winger, your captain."

"John Poladian," said the man who had hired him. "How do you do, Captain?"

"Fine, sir, and how do you do?" Dwight said, shaking his hand.

"Just call me John, please. This is a fishing trip and we're going to be friends. And this is Zachary Lewis."

"The candidate!" Dwight exclaimed, a little surprised.

"None other," Lewis said. "But call me Zachary please."

"Yes sir, Zachary," Dwight said, shaking his hand. "I know you'll enjoy the trip. I intend to show you where the fish are."

Lewis gave him a big smile. "Great!"

"How does marlin sound for today?" Dwight asked.

Lewis beamed. "That's what I was hoping for."

"Great. We have to go out to sea about an hour and a half. I'll go up to the flying bridge to maneuver out of the harbor now. Make yourselves at home, and Ernie will show you around." Dwight nodded toward Ernie who was standing by to cast off.

Dwight went up to the flying bridge and looked down at Ernie. "Let's go."

Ernie cast off and climbed aboard. Dwight engaged the big diesels in reverse, expertly backed out of the slip, put the transmission in forward, and motored out at the obligatory five miles per hour through the *No Wake* area to head for the high seas.

As his VIP guests looked up to begin the experience of the day, there was just a tinge of morning sky as the sun came yawning from the east. Poladian and Lewis stepped up to the flying bridge to enjoy a better view of the beautiful sunrise and the excitement of the sea.

"Everyone set?" Dwight asked, as the boat was past the five mile per hour zone and he was ready to hit the throttles.

Receiving their nods, he eased the throttles all the way forward, and the big diesels accelerated the boat hard. In no time at all, it was planing and doing twenty-four knots as they headed for the place where he calculated the marlin would be, an hour and a half to two hours out to sea at full throttle.

As they cruised past the breakwater, a speedboat with double, two hundred fifty horse outboard motors, began to follow, but discreetly and at a distance. The low profile of the speedboat made its intended stealth much easier to accomplish.

Down in the *Hookup*'s engine room, the carriage bolts, that came up from the bottom of the boat into one of the shaft logs, shook from the vibration of the big diesel engine and the spinning propeller shaft that went through it. Several of the carriage bolts worked their way loose and fell out the bottom. Water came in through the small bolt holes. The four bilge pumps handled most of that by sucking out the water, but a bit of water was on the bottom as the pumps worked to remove it.

After almost two hours when the boat approached the fishing spot selected by Dwight as the best place to fish, seven of the bolts had fallen out completely, but the shaft log was still in place. The four big bilge pumps, which had been activated automatically by the water coming in, were able, barely, to handle the water squirting in through the bolt holes.

When they reached the spot that Dwight believed to be

where the marlin were, he stopped the boat and began to set up the fishing gear, unaware of any problem.

He looked at his new deck hand, "Ernie, I am going to go with lures rather than mackerel this morning. As soon as I get these outriggers ready with lures, you go up on the tower and look for marlin fins."

"Aye, aye, Skipper. Them that die'll be the lucky ones," Ernie said, mimicking Long John Silver in the classic movie, *Treasure Island.*

Dwight set out lines with lures to attract marlin and then fired up the diesels and engaged the propellers as Ernie watched from the observation tower.

Below the hull, another bolt fell out of the shaft log. Water was coming in the bolt holes, but the bilge pumps were still able to handle that amount.

This is great, Ernie said to himself, up on the lookout tower, spotting for marlin. They had been fishing for only fifteen minutes, when he thought he saw something. *What is that?* He put his hand over his brow to shade his eyes. *Is that a marlin fin?*

"Ernie, change to mackerel," Dwight said.

Running down to the deck, Ernie pulled in the lure lines, slid mackerel onto the hooks, and put them back out. Then he went up to the tower once again.

"Marlin!" he yelled out, pointing to the starboard side of the boat.

A marlin fin was pacing the boat, running parallel to it, his eyes on the bait. Dwight saw it from the flying bridge and acknowledged that to Ernie.

Ernie came down from the lookout tower. Poladian had declined to use his rod, turning over the fishing experience to Lewis, in case there was only one catch.

Dwight sped up to get ahead of the marlin and turned hard to go in front of him. Unbeknownst to him, turning the boat put a sideways torque on the loosened shaft log. Just as Lunati predicted, the remaining carriage bolts fell out and the shaft log shifted, allowing more water in.

"He hit!" Lewis shouted, wide eyed with excitement.

His reel spun away, whirring loudly as the big marlin pulled out the line. Then, suddenly, the fish jumped straight up, completely out of the water, dancing on its tail—a dream come true for a fisherman.

"It's a big one," Winger exclaimed. "I'd say two hundred fifty pounds."

Poladian moved in, standing just behind Lewis in the fishing chair, to encourage him on as he fought the big marlin.

From a half mile away, Innocenti, Lunati, and their helper Sandino were ready and moving in slowly. Lunati turned on the transmitter and activated the servo that ignited the power lines to the bilge pumps and the engine compartment exhaust fan in engine room of the *Hookup*. It worked perfectly and the pumps and fan went dead. He then actuated the mechanical servo to turn open the pet cock on the gas container, and gas began to pour out and pool on top of the water already in the bottom of the engine compartment.

Innocenti made ready with the compressed air powered saw hooked up to a gasoline fired air compressor with a yellow air hose.

Sandino and Lunati checked their pistols. Tony Sandino had a formidable appearance in size, shape and expression, and his choice of weapons was also formidable. He wielded a six-and-a-half-inch barreled, stainless Smith & Wesson 500, a fifty caliber, five-shot revolver, the largest handgun made. With ammo it weighed four pounds. It was so large he had to wear it over the front of his chest in a chest holster. Apart from being able to blow a hole in just about anything, the other advantage was that he could use it as a club. He also carried another unusual weapon as his backup on his belt, a small Smith & Wesson called the Governor, an unusual revolver that shot both .410 two and a half inch shotgun shells as well as .45 long colt bullets interchangeably. He always loaded it with alternating rounds, a .410 shotgun shell, then a .45 long colt, and so on. That one was not legal in California, but neither was murdering a candidate for governor. Lunati, by contrast, brought a more practical weapon, a Glock .45 semi-automatic.

Sandino collected the homemade newspaper ropes and positioned the twenty-pound barbell weights to off load them to the *Hookup* while Lunati motored the speedboat in closer, waiting for the right time to strike.

With the diesel motors running and the propellers turning, the boat did not immediately lower much in the water as the prop thrust held the back end up. As they continued chasing the fish, the loose shaft log finally gave way, coming up inside the boat enough to allow a lot more water to come in. Lunati had designed it perfectly.

Dwight could feel by the sluggish handling that his boat was low in the aft. He looked and could see the aft lower than normal. It made him suspect a leak. Thinking it might be the circuit breaker to the bilge pumps, he beckoned to Ernie. "Take the helm. I want to check the engine room, as I think we may have water coming in—probably the circuit breaker for the bilge pumps is not on."

Dwight ran down to the main cabin steering station where the circuit breakers were. All were in the "on" position, as though nothing was wrong. He could not be sure if they were working, due to the noise of the diesels. He went to the back, just ahead of the fishermen, and lifted the hatch. Water! The pumps must not be working. He hurriedly climbed down into the engine room to investigate. He could also smell gas, which was odd on a diesel boat. He looked over to the red, plastic gas container, and it was empty. The exhaust fan was silent.

In the meantime, Lewis continued to fight the big marlin from the fishing chair, having the most memorable experience that he'd had in many years, unaware of any serious problems yet.

Dwight left the hatch open to vent the compartment, rushed back up and onto the deck, and hurried over to the ladder to the flying bridge where Ernie was steering the boat. "Ernie we've got a problem! We're taking on water and the bilge pumps are not working. And, I smell gas! The gas can for the dingy must have cracked. I better call the coast guard. We're in deep shit. I left the hatch cover off to vent the engine compartment."

He decided it was time for a distress call and dialed the

emergency frequency on his radio. "Mayday Mayday Mayday! This is Dwight Winger, skipper of the *Hookup*, a forty-six-foot sport fisher. There are four of us aboard. We are between Catalina and San Clemente Islands. We are taking on water and will scuttle soon! We also have gas in the hold! Send help at once!"

Dwight then gave his location more exactly from the global navigation system, which he had not done in the first message. He then repeated the message again. Like a good skipper, he gave details of the problem in the mayday so that the coast guard could be more prepared when they arrived, and to alert other vessels if in the vicinity.

"This is the coast guard," came the response. "We have your message. We're about forty minutes from your position and en route."

A half mile away in the speedboat, Lunati was listening on the emergency channel as that was to be his signal to proceed. "Okay, they made the call."

He moved another control on his transmitter, and that one activated the electronic servo that burned through the wire to the batteries, cutting off the electric power to the *Hookup*, which included the power to the radio.

Lunati moved anther control on the transmitter, the one that actuated the ignitor in the engine compartment from the gas fumes, creating an explosion, damaging the stern of the boat and rendering the engines inoperable. But because the experienced captain left the hatch off the engine compartment, it did not explode the boat, but just created a huge explosion damaging most everything in the compartment and rendering the engines inoperative.

"My God!" Dwight shouted at the explosion.

Lunati went to full throttle and the three hitmen began to close in on the *Hookup*. Innocenti fired up the gasoline powered air compressor and made ready to dive with the air saw.

Winger, having radioed his mayday call, jumped down into the damaged engine compartment with a flashlight. He saw the shaft log up from the bottom and water coming in like gangbusters. He dashed back out, and yelled to Ernie, "Let's try to put the shaft log back in place to keep from sinking."

Lewis still had the marlin on the line, and continued to fight him, even though the boat was disabled. He was unsure what to do.

"Can you go under the boat and put in bolts in the shaft log, while I get above it in the compartment and fit nuts on the bolts?" Dwight asked Ernie. "That should keep us from sinking."

"I'll give it a try," Ernie volunteered. "Give me a mask, quick!"

Dwight ran forward and untied the dinghy. He pointing to it and told Ernie, "If we go down, make sure our guests get into it." He hurried down to his lower drawer in the salon where he kept extra bolts and nuts. He dug out a handful of different sizes, picking ones that would most likely fit in the holes, then fished around for nuts that would fit them. "Go underneath and I'll align the shaft log," he said, handing Ernie the bolts. "Try to get these in. You put one in, and I'll put a nut on it from inside. I'll hand tighten only until we get a few in place. We can tighten them later."

"I need a mask," Ernie said, putting the bolts in his pocket.

Dwight got him a mask. Ernie figured he didn't have time to take off his boots, so he jumped overboard, boots and all. With the boots and the weight of the bolts in his pocket, he was not very buoyant, but he wasn't sinking, either.

Dwight got a mask for himself as he needed it to see below the water in the engine compartment which was rising rapidly. He took his flashlight, the nuts, and hurried down into the engine room.

Ernie bobbed up after jumping in, took a big breath, and swam under the boat to have a look. There it was, the shaft log slightly out of its hole, as it had worked up the driveshaft. He waited for Winger to put it back into place, and then Ernie tried to get the first bolt in. It refused to go in easily, and he fought with it until finally he got it through. Dwight grabbed it with his fingers as best he could against the water trying to push it up. He was able to start a nut on the first bolt, and screwed it several turns. The shaft log was now somewhat back in place, but the other bolt holes were not lined up and the water was pushing it up.

Ernie went back to the side of the boat for air, took a huge breath, and went back under to try to get another bolt in. Both Ernie and Dwight believed they might just save the *Hookup* from going under at that point.

Poladian and Lewis saw the speedboat approaching and assumed it was just a friendly group of boaters who had noticed their stern was low in the water.

With Dwight in the engine room, and Ernie underneath, they were both unaware of the approaching boat.

The speedboat came up next to the *Hookup*, and Sandino tossed up a rope around the deck railing.

Lunati and Sandino, pistols in hand, jumped aboard and held their pistols on Poladian and Lewis, like Somalian Pirates. Innocenti went over the side of the speedboat, the five inch air saw in hand, tethered to the yellow air hose. He took a big breath and went under the *Hookup*.

Poladian and Lewis stopped what they were doing, leaving the fish on the line and swimming about. "What's this?" Poladian demanded.

"Hold still and you won't be shot," Sandino said, holding his revolver out. "Put your hands behind your back."

Poladian did not comply with the command to put his hand behind his back, and Sandino then used the four pound revolver for its alternate use, that of a club, and hit him over the head with it, nearly knocking him out. Poladian changed his mind about complying and put his hands behind him, unaware of what was in store. Lewis got out of the fisherman's chair. The marlin had pulled the rod away smartly over the back of the boat, and swam away, still hooked up to it.

Sandino held his huge revolver on Lewis and Poladian and motioned them to the side of the boat. Lunati tied their wrists and ankles with the dissolving rope.

Unaware of the attack as his head was under water in the engine compartment, Dwight stuck his head out of the engine compartment for air. Sandino pointed his huge pistol right at Dwight's face. "Get out."

Ernie had just come back under the boat from the other side, having taken in a big breath of air, and had managed to get in the second bolt. Holding his breath under the shaft log, he waited for Dwight to grab it and put on a nut.

But Dwight was not responding as he was then being escorted out of the engine compartment at gunpoint. He was lined up with the Lewis and Poladian and tied by Lunati and Sandino.

Under the boat, Ernie heard the whirring noise of the air saw and turned to see a man coming at him. At first, he first thought the coast guard had arrived.

Innocenti expected there might be a deck hand, but had not expected to see someone underneath trying to fix the shaft log. Seeing the man, he moved in aggressively with the air saw, tethered by the yellow air hose to the pump in the speedboat. Swimming rapidly toward the man trying to fix the shaft log, he charged forward, without fear, attacking with his air saw whirring at five thousand rpm, followed by little bubbles of air after the pressurized air spun the saw.

Completely surprised to meet someone trying to kill him, Ernie was startled and instinctively backed up, but not fast enough. The assailant struck Ernie in his side, and the spinning blade went through the skin to his ribs. But fortunately for Ernie, his jumping back had kept the saw blade from cutting deeply into him and severing his ribs.

Ernie pedaled back a few more feet, blood coming out of his side. He then knew it definitely was not the coast guard, and this would be a fight to the death.

The assailant moved in for another hit, lunging hard. Ernie was vertical in the water, his feet and arms apart, still not quite ready for a fight as he was under water and short of breath.

His attacker was then nearly horizontal in the water, holding the saw out in front of him for the next strike. As he got very close, Ernie got ready with his logger boots and, as hard as he could under water, kicked the saw. The thick rubber cleats on the sole of his boot hit the saw blade. The blade stopped, imbedded in the thick rubber sole of Ernie's logger boot. Ernie continued with the kick and drove the air saw and its blade up and into the bottom of the boat, where it stuck. It was no longer spinning, and until the hitman could get it out, his weapon, and advantage, were compromised. Ernie pulled his boot off the blade but the blade stayed stuck in the boat.

He recalled the fishing knife in his belt, took it out, and lunged at the hitman.

Innocenti pulled back his upper torso to get away from the incoming knife, but hesitated letting go of the saw which had become his weapon, thinking it might break lose and he could use it again.

Ernie moved in hard and fast and stuck the seven inch knife all the way into the hitman's stomach. For good measure, he gave it a twist to the right and to the left.

Ernie pulled it out and got ready for another attack. Just as he was about to move in for the second strike, something happened behind his assailant, off to the side of the *Hookup*. Ernie heard a loud splash. A twenty-pound barbell came over the side of the boat, followed by Poladian who made a bigger splash.

His arms and legs tied to the barbell, Poladian went right on down, deeper and deeper, much too fast for Ernie to do anything about it.

In front of him was the hitman, who was pedaling backward, very hurt, holding his bleeding wound with one hand, blood turning the surrounding water crimson red.

Ernie had been under water, trying to get a bolt in for some time before the attack and he was out of air. He went back to the other side of the *Hookup*, opposite the assailant's boat, and came up for some much needed air. Blood was coming out of his rib area and it was very painful. He assessed the situation quickly and, not deterred, went back under to finish off the hitman.

When he got back past the centerline, the assailant was no longer there. Ernie followed the blood and saw the man climbing into a speedboat. Ernie swam toward it.

Another loud splash sounded off the same side of the *Hookup* where Poladian was thrown overboard. Ernie saw another barbell going down, and this time Dwight was tied to it.

Ernie swam hard for his friend, but the captain was fifty feet below him and sinking fast by the time Ernie got near. Dwight was gone, like Poladian.

A third barbell splashed into the water. This time it was so close to Ernie that it almost hit him. He instinctively reached out and grabbed the person tossed into the water. It was Lewis!

Ernie found himself holding on to the gubernatorial candidate and going down very fast.

He wrapped his arms tightly around Lewis's midsection as they descended down and down, the water becoming darker and colder. Gathering his wits, Ernie realized there were precious few moments to do anything if he and Lewis were going to survive.

Against the current of water as they descended, he crept down Lewis's body toward the rope fastened to his ankles and the barbell weight. He finally reached the rope and thought of the knife.

The knife was gone! He must have dropped it when he grabbed for Lewis. Taking the newspaper rope in between Lewis's ankles and the barbell weight with both hands, Ernie ignored the pain from his wound and began to pull as hard as he could. But the newspaper rope was still not completely saturated with water and was still strong.

The water now was dark as they descended, and the change in temperature was considerable. With all of his might, he pulled on the rope and it finally gave way to his strength. The weight descended even faster away from them on its journey to the bottom in two thousand, five hundred feet of seawater.

Ernie and Lewis began to float upward, but the rate was too slow, and Ernie knew that Lewis would drown. He kicked hard to increase the assent.

No one left on board, Lunati and Sandino returned to the speedboat to join Innocenti. As the coast guard was on its way, they had to hurry. Lunati disconnected the air hose, having to leave it behind. Lunati fired up the two huge outboard motors and off they went toward the shore. As they were speeding away, Lunati used his one remaining move—the ten pounds of gunpowder that was mixed with epoxy and painted inside the hull of the *Hookup*. When he thought they were at a safe distance, he hit the remaining servo, igniting the nearly ten pounds of gunpowder.

BOOM!

It literally blew the *Hookup* into two halves. Lunati had overdone it, using too much gunpowder. He was very pleased with his handiwork and proudly shouted to his companions over the motor noise of his speedboat, "Yessiree, I just blew the living shit out of that sport fisher mutherfucker!"

The explosion was so big that, even though under water, Ernie and Lewis were knocked several feet to one side by the percussion which hurt their already suffering ears. Ernie had no idea what that was about, until he saw the two big diesels that used to be in the engine room sinking fast, tied together only by metal fuel lines. The two monster diesels just missed him and Lewis as the motors sped down into the deep abyss.

Finally, the front half of the *Hookup* came down in one piece, although slower than the two diesel motors. First the shadow of the boat covered Ernie and Lewis. Ernie looked up to see it coming straight down, directly on top of them. If it hit them, they would go down with it. Ernie kicked as hard and fast as he could to one side, holding on to Lewis who was not moving and couldn't help. Just a foot away, the front half of the *Hookup* went down right past them.

In the speedboat, Innocenti lay back, holding his bleeding stomach. "There was a deck hand underneath, putting bolts back in the shaft log. I nicked him with the saw, but he got me with a knife."

"I bet the explosion got him," Lunati said.

"Dunno," Innocenti groaned. "Shit. If he's alive, there goes the perfect crime. He's a witness."

"But he didn't see me or Vinnie. Did he see you?" Sandino asked.

Innocenti groaned in pain. "I was wearing my mask. I don't know if he can identify me or not."

In the water, Ernie continued to kick his way up, and finally, after what seemed like an eternity, broke the surface. He took a huge breath. Lewis did not seem to be taking in air. Ernie saw the dinghy not far away. *Trust Dwight, the good skipper he had been, to untie the dinghy, just in case, and now it's needed.* Ernie, with Lewis held in the lifeguard hold around the neck, kicked over to the dinghy. He crawled over the side and then pulled Lewis in, which would be no small job to someone less strong or determined.

Lewis came in on his stomach. Ernie pushed on his back, to get the water out of his lungs, then rolled him over to his side and got more water out. He then put Lewis on his back and administered CPR as best he knew how.

Suddenly, Lewis coughed out seawater and took in air. The candidate was alive! Ernie's ears hurt, he was short of breath, his side ached severely, and it was bleeding. And he had received quite a shock from the explosion. Feeling safe in the dinghy, and with Lewis breathing, Ernie rolled over on his back and passed out.

The next thing he knew, he was being awakened by the extremely welcome sight of a coast guard man holding out his hand to lift Ernie up into a big, white, coast guard cutter with its red stripe.

CHAPTER 47

I can't believe it!" Bradford shouted in front of his home entertainment center, as the Saturday evening news broke a story of the gubernatorial candidate nearly being killed in a boating incident.

His wife, Barbara, was in the kitchen with the maid, designing dinner. She hurried into the living room at the shouting. "What's the matter, dear?"

"That son-of-a-bitch Lewis was on an ocean fishing boat, and there was an assassination attempt. The boat actually sank. Two of four people went down in the ocean and have not been recovered yet. But the news says that Lewis was saved by a hero named Ernie who works for Majestik. I can't believe it. Our man saved the bastard! Who is that son-of-a-bitch? I'll have his ass."

Barbara sat in front of the big screen trying to hear more of the news over her husband's ranting. "Did the news say how it happened?"

"Apparently, our employee is some kind of hero, saving the candidate with some heroic dive down deep in the ocean. I still can't believe it. All he had to do was to let the fucking crusader die. I have a suspicion those mafia types who came into my office were involved."

"Won't it help the company's image that he was rescued by a Majestik employee?" his dutiful wife asked.

"What good is *image* when the way we do business is *ruined*? This will probably increase his chances to win the election." He went to the bar to make a drink and calm down. He wished he had Zelzah, at times like this, sitting in front of his desk. He made a martini with straight vodka leaving out the vermouth and went to the phone to call Zelzah at her condo. His wife had no idea how much personal care Zelzah provided him. Or, perhaps, she did not want to know.

"Hello?" Zelzah asked.

"It's me. Did you see the news about Zachary Lewis?"

"Yes, sir."

"I want you to find out just who that guy was who works for Majestik and saved Lewis. Monday morning will do. Okay?"

"I'll have it for you, sir."

"Okay. Thanks. See you Monday."

He hung up the receiver and sipped his vodka, wishing Zelzah was there. Maybe a call to Evette would be in order? No way. He was already drinking and didn't want to drive. In his position a drunk driving charge would ruin him, and his wife would be suspicious if he called for a car without telling her in advance that he had to be at some function. He would call in his wife for a hand job—that would have to do."

"Shit," Zelzah shouted out in her condo. "I wonder if I should tell him I know Ernie?"

∽∾∽

"We're FBI. I'm Special Agent Doty, and this is Special Agent Kanno," the man in the suit said, introducing himself and his Japanese American associate in the hospital room. "How is the hero?"

Ernie lay in the hospital bed, his chest wrapped in bandages where he had been sewn up. The wound was still very painful. "Fine," he lied.

"We'd like to ask you about what happened yesterday on board the boat," Doty said.

Ernie groaned at the pain. "We lost the marlin."

Doty and Kanno both laughed. "We see you're in good spirits. It's our pleasure to meet a real hero."

"What's going on? I'm just trying to make a living. I have never met anyone from the FBI before."

"We have jurisdiction in this case under Section 7 of Title

18 of the US Code," Doty said. "The incident was a crime against US nationals, against a US-owned vessel, and the vessel departed from and would have returned to a US port."

That didn't mean anything to Ernie. "How's Zachary Lewis?" He'd had no word yet on the man's condition.

Doty smiled. "He's quite well. He suffered broken ear drums from the extreme water pressure at the depth he went down to, as well as hypothermia from the lack of oxygen and cold water, but is otherwise doing fine. The doctor said that they're operating on his ear drums, and most of his hearing should be restored. He's in this hospital as well, in a different wing. He's being guarded by a division of the California Highway Patrol that now guards the governor and candidates and by one of our men. One such state policeman and one of our men are also outside your door, and keeping reporters away until you instruct otherwise."

Ernie sighed, struggled to sit up, and recounted the events for the agents as best as he could remember them through the fog of the painkillers in his brain.

"I take it you did not get a very good look at the man who came after you under the boat?" Doty asked.

Ernie shook his head. "He had on a face mask. Medium large in size. I didn't see the others at all."

"You say you stabbed the man underneath the boat with a knife. How deep did you stick that knife in his belly? If you stuck it in deep, he'll need hospitalization."

"I stuck it in pretty good I think. I remember turning the knife. It was pretty long, maybe a seven-inch blade. I gave it a twist or two."

Doty nodded. "If that is the case, he will definitely need hospitalization. We are already systematically checking out every knife wound hospital admission in the area, and we will eventually expand the search if nothing turns up here."

"Since hospitals have to report such wounds, maybe he has found some doctor to treat him at some location other than a hospital," Kanno suggested.

"I take it that it was an attempt to kill Lewis, right?" Ernie asked.

"There doesn't appear to be any motive as of yet for anyone to want to kill John Poladian," Doty said. "As far as for the boat owner, Dwight Winger, the only people who wanted him dead are his two ex-wives."

Ernie burst out laughing. As his rib cage moved with the first part of the laugh, a searing pain hit him as the wound over his rib cage stretched.

"Sorry," Doty said, as he saw the expression on Ernie's face change from a laugh to a grimace.

After a few moments, the pain subsided and Ernie felt he could talk again. "Who would want Lewis dead?"

"Since he's not an elected official, only a candidate, we don't feel that it's likely to be a fanatic, undertaking a political assassination," Doty said. "Therefore we're looking into possible suspects that might have an interest in seeing that he not get elected. From your description of the shaft log coming loose on the boat, the explosion in the engine room, and the final explosion that blew up the boat, it sounds like there was a carefully planned and well-orchestrated effort to make the boat go down with no evidence left so it wouldn't look like anything other than a boating accident. The newspaper ropes you describe, the men coming in quickly in the speedboat, the air saw—it all sounds expertly planned."

"It sounds to me that the only thing they did not count on is you," Kanno added. "Do you know of anyone that would want Lewis dead?"

"No. I didn't even know Lewis was one of the passengers until he came. Dwight didn't know either. He only knew about Poladian and, even then, Poladian was someone he had never met. He was a referral through the Yacht Club. All Dwight knew was that Poladian was bringing an important guest."

Ernie thought of Dwight Winger, and what a nice guy he was. The reality of the deaths he had witnessed began to overwhelm him, and he got mad. He felt like he had to get up and go do something about it. He sat up and turned to get out of the bed. As he did, he felt a sharp pain again over his ribs where the wound was.

Giving up on the idea, he lay back.

Seeing the painful effort, Doty sighed. "Please stay in bed. If we're making you upset, we can return. The doctor said you'll be here a few days."

"I don't think I'll stick around here very long," Ernie said. "I don't care for this."

"I'll leave you my card," Doty said, taking out his card and putting it on the table beside the bed. "This number works twenty-four hours. I can be reached though the operator who answers it wherever I am. If, for any reason, you can't get immediately get through to me, you can also ask for Special Agent Kanno.

"Please call me if you have anything to add, or if anything comes up. In the meantime, we would like you to keep us informed of any change of address, so we can call on you, if need be, as a witness. We'll probably want you to come down and look at some mug shots."

"I don't think it will help, but I'll come. The man had on a swim mask."

A commotion broke out in the hallway outside the door. "What's all that?"

"That's the press. There's a reporter and a camera man out there. I told the state policeman to not let anyone see you. It's up to you if you want to see them or not when we're gone. Lewis has said you're a hero.

"I don't want to see the press," Ernie said, feeling shy about going on TV or making a public statement. "I'd appreciate it if I could be left alone for a while." He just wanted to lie back in peace to let his wounds heal and think about the good men who went down around him at sea. He wondered if he could have done more.

"Call us if you can add anything, and we thank you. We will tell the policeman to keep reporters out when we leave," Kanno said, as he and Doty walked out.

The image of the man he fought under the boat formed in Ernie's mind as he went to sleep. He could see the puckered face in the swim mask, and he would dream about it.

❧❦❧

Across town, Fiorello Innocenti lay on the operating table of a plastic surgeon, as the doctor examined the stomach wound with skillful hands. The plastic surgeon, unlike most other specialists, had his own operating room, used for cosmetic surgery, and thus there was no hospital involved to report the knife wound to the police. Innocenti had lost a good deal of blood and was very weak. But he had not dared to check into a hospital, as every hospital would be on the lookout for such a patient on request from the FBI, and the hospitals were required by law to report such injuries. Instead, he just waited until evening when he could get into the plastic surgeon's office after the staff left. When he said he was one of the illusive owners of Exotic Productions, the doctor volunteered to stay late for him. The doctor told him that he would have no anesthetist or nurse on duty as it would be after hours. That was fine with Innocenti—no witnesses. The doctor knew something must be up, but the company was a good client to have and so he agreed to meet Innocent at the office.

"It is a pleasure to finally meet one of the owners of Exotic Productions," the doctor said.

The nearby Exotic Productions sent over young girls for huge breast enlargements regularly. The company dealt in porn videos, porn publications, and provided young girls with huge breasts to topless bars, some that it had an interest in, and some that it did not. It paid for regular breast enlargements on an average of one girl every week. The breast enlargements sought by the performing girls were so large that it usually required two operations, and sometimes three. The resulting size was sometimes freakish. But it was a constant source of good income, and the doctor gave them a special price for volume. He hadn't known who were the actual owners before, as porn businesses had several layers of insulating companies to cloak who the real owners were.

But when he got the call from Innocenti, announcing that he was an owner, the doctor knew it was a special patient.

"I appreciate your seeing me like this," Innocenti said, grimacing in pain.

"Your company has brought me quite a lot of business, so

it is the least I can do. I'm glad to finally get to meet you personally. I actually did not know your name." Shaking his head, the doctor washed out the deep wound. "You know, you have to go to a hospital. The knife wound is deep, and I suspect that the intestines have been nicked. If so, there will be peritonitis."

"What's that?" Innocenti asked.

"Inflammation of the peritoneum. Think of it as a serious infection. Your temperature is up a little already. If the intestines have been cut, contamination will seep into the stomach cavity, and you will be in serious trouble soon. If any organ has been cut, other complications will follow. This wound needs to be opened, under a general anesthetic, and explored. Since this was done under sea water, contamination is certain. The procedure is to open the wound, repair any damage, and then leave the wound open for a while and irrigate the area. Then later close it."

"So, go ahead," Innocenti said boldly. "Let's do it now."

"I would if I could. But I have several problems here. I'd need an anesthesiologist for openers. I could not monitor you while operating. Also, I would need some form of assistant, like a nurse. That means witnesses. And I don't have the kind of instruments needed to operate on a lower abdomen. This needs to be done in a hospital. If something goes wrong, you could die. And I'm not exaggerating."

"Doc, if I check into a hospital, it'll be reported, and I can't have that," Innocenti said. "What can I do?"

"You could check into a hospital here under an alias, but depending on who is investigating anything, that might not work. Who's looking?"

"The FBI," Innocenti muttered, wincing again.

"Holy shit!" the doctor said in a very startled voice. "Then your best chance is to get to someplace like New York at once. There, simply go into a hospital and say you've been attacked by a mugger in the street. They have several of those every night, and it won't be made into something big."

"How long can I take to get there without medical attention?"

"The sooner the better, but if you can get right over there on a private or charter jet, you'll be all right until you get there. You'll probably check into the hospital in about seven or eight hours, and I doubt that any complications will arise before then. I can give you some massive antibiotics. Do you have a way to get to New York? It doesn't have to be New York, but the bigger the city, the more routine it will be to have a stabbing, and thus fewer enquiries."

"Yeah. We have our own jet."

"Can you trust the pilots?" the doctor asked. "I doubt that you can conceal your pain the entire trip."

"Both," Innocenti answered. "We can trust the pilots, but I'll not let them know. You never know what might happen if the FBI came around and scared them. I'll act like I'm not well and am going to use the bed in the jet. I'll have them drop me off in New York without letting them know."

Not only did the partnership have trusted pilots, but its success thus far was largely because so few people knew about its highly profitable activities, a different concept from the families of the past from New England. Innocenti doing his own hits, as opposed to hiring contract killers, was just one example. But still, the pilots could not be hired for life as most aspired to get a position on a jumbo jet, and not letting them know would be better.

"Call for it at once," the doctor said. "Then go directly to a hospital there. I'll get you the names of some hospitals in a moment."

"I cannot have any record of this visit. You understand the need for patient confidentiality, don't you?" Innocenti asked, making light of the concept.

"Oh yes, very much. I do famous personalities all the time, and the fact that they have even been to a plastic surgeon must not be let known. You can trust that no one will know you have been here."

"I not only want you to tell no one, but I don't want you to make any record of the visit," Innocenti said.

"I'm required by law to make post-treatment notes for my files," the doctor replied in a worried tone. Offending Innocenti seemed worse than crossing the path of the FBI. It was a true dilemma.

"You'll make an exception in this case. There is to be no post-treatment notes, and no file on me at all. Is that understood?" Innocenti said, even though weakened from the loss of blood, he was still in control of his senses and his business.

The doctor remained silent as he put tape over the bandages on the wound. He wondered about the comment and what he would say if the FBI came to see him. The lack of response from the doctor as he completed the bandaging Innocenti's wounds made the silence of the room more intense.

"Doctor, can you call in my friend now?" Innocenti asked, referring to Lunati, who had accompanied him to the doctor's office as Innocenti could hardly walk.

The doctor went to the door, as the limited procedures he could perform were now complete. "Mr. Lunati?" the doctor said through the door. "He would like to see you now."

Lunati walked into the operating room where Innocenti was now sitting on the table. "Vinnie, show the good doctor why he should not keep any record of today's visit, and how much we appreciate his service."

Lunati reached into his coat pocket and took out two stacks of hundreds, each ten thousand dollars, a total of twenty thousand. He put them on the operating table while the doctor was putting instruments in an autoclave.

"Doc, this is for you," Innocenti said. "There is to be no record, no file, and no visit here today. If I need you for a complication, I'll call on you. Agreed?"

"Very well. But if there is a complication, it may very well require hospitalization."

"I really appreciate this, Doc."

"Now, if you don't get to a hospital soon," the doctor said, "you may not be around any longer. So off with you to New York. Here are antibiotics." The doctor handed Lunati a bottle of pills for his friend so he would not have to go to a pharmacist and leave a trail of evidence. "And when the medication I have given him wears off, he may need these," he said, handing him another bottle. "This is for pain. You can bring him back here after you return for me to check up on him."

"Doc, you have great bedside manner," Innocenti said. "Whenever you need a favor, any kind, you call me. I won't forget."

The doctor was moved. He imagined being owed a favor from a mafia man—the kind of favor that was hard to get elsewhere. His imagination went wild thinking if someone sued him for malpractice, he could have them killed. "On with you to the Big Apple so you can suffer a knife wound there."

"We appreciate it," Lunati said. "I'll phone for the jet to get him to take him to New York. I'll have it pick us up at Van Nuys as that is the closest airport."

Lunati and the doctor helped Innocenti off the table, and he walked out carefully. In the car on the way to the Van Nuys airport, Lunati asked Innocenti, "What do you think we do next? Can we still kill the candidate?"

Innocenti nodded. "Of course. We have our futures tied up in this. Just because that deck hand, Ernie, screwed up our hit does not mean we quit. It all would have gone smoothly, except for him. I don't know if Lewis can identify either you or Sandino, but if so, we might have to get both of you out of the country. As for identifying me, I had a diver's mask on under water, and the only person that might identify me was that Ernie. I think we should take him out. I'll have you stay with me until I get to a hospital where you can drop me off and disappear so you won't be questioned as a witness. As soon as I can get out of the hospital, I want you to get me back home."

CHAPTER 48

Bradford glared at a file on Ernie he requested from Zelzah. It contained Ernie's one page settlement documents with the signatures of the claimants, and a notation of the amount of money paid out, and little else. Zelzah also included several newspaper articles describing the event at sea, including quotes from Lewis describing Ernie as a hero. "How in God's name did we ever hire some backwoods, trailer trash, piece-of-shit logger to go out and settle claims when he's never worked a day in insurance in his life?" He waved the file at McAteer. "He actually lives in a trailer outside of bumfuck, Washington."

McAteer had already looked into the matter and was ready to address it. He never dared bullshit Bradford. "Well, it seems that there was a new arrangement with cooperating states to take people off unemployment rolls. We had requests out for one hundred temporary adjustors, and we had contacted our state unemployment department looking for them. With the other companies in California hiring local, unemployed adjustors as quickly as we did because of the storm, the local adjustors with experience were quickly taken, and so we looked outside the state, at your direction. We were given his name from the State of Washington. Apparently, the Washington State Unemployment Department certified that he was an experienced field representative, which was mistaken for an experienced insurance field adjustor. Your instructions were not to be concerned about checking the backgrounds of the temporary adjustors, since they were only to be hired for ninety days, and all of our competitors were grabbing them up fast. He called my office, and there was yet a further mix-up with my secretary talking to him. She understood that he had experience in handling of claims following storms with *fallen* trees, whereas his experience was in *falling* trees. He never misrepresented anything to anyone, as far as we can tell."

Bradford was not moved. "The son-of-a bitch saved Lewis. That country bumpkin pigfucker doesn't know what the insurance business is all about. Fire his ass."

"Well, although the story will die down in the news, it might come back strong if we fire this man who is a now a hero," McAteer warned. "It might make him a martyr if the news decides to contact him and make firing him into a story. Since he is not in our business, he might get on some TV show and reveal what he learned from my indoctrination class and come off like a whistle blower. Those talk shows are hungry for stories. We had only offered him ninety days employment. Don't you think we should let him ride that out and let him go with a nice letter?"

Bradford's blood pressure was rising. "Fuck him!"

"There's more," McAteer continued. "From what I've been able to find out about his claim handling in the short time he has been with us, he's the most efficient adjustor we have. He does no office paper work—in fact, he never went to the field office at all except one time to pick up files from one of ours named Jessica Bloom who went on maternity leave. He has yet to have a single document typed. Instead of his files getting several inches thick with paper, he goes out in the field on every case, and the case is somehow settled then and there with no letter writing, no legal expense, no lawsuits, and almost no money. The only paper in any of his files is the required release form filled out by hand on location. In fact, he may be the most effective adjustor who ever existed. Several people have called or written in to compliment his performance. Apparently, he completes a file in record time and then just goes on to another. And, he does it all on a motorcycle. He even brought his chainsaw with him in a saddlebag and cuts up trees that have fallen on the spot. Imagine if we did not have to have all those lobotomites sitting in our air conditioned offices, dictating letters and not doing anything other than delaying and denying claims. I could replace fifty adjustors with one Ernie, not to mention their support staff, vacation scheduling, medical benefits, maternity leave and expense, attending sexual harassment prevention classes, and the like. We'll never see another like him. I'd like to offer him a full time job."

Bradford's face turned from red to purple, a condition that McAteer had never seen before. "You *what*?"

McAteer jerked involuntarily back in his seat, startled at the outburst. "Okay, okay. Sorry, boss. As you wish. I just hope this doesn't come back to haunt us." He left the office with the feeling that firing Ernie was a bad omen.

❧❧❧

With stitches in his side, Ernie walked gingerly up the few steps from his motorcycle parking spot at the Polynesian. He stopped at the mailboxes and opened his to look inside. Having not been there in a while, the box would hardly open, due to the enormous amount of advertisements. Unlike many, he was not angered at the ads, but instead looked through them for a few moments before throwing them away, with the thought that those people who sent them were spending money trying to reach people, and they had to make a living, too.

In the pile of colored brochures and ads was a letter from Majestik. The apartment manager conveniently kept a waste barrel only several steps from the mailboxes, where Ernie deposited the ads. Inside, he sat and opened the letter.

> *I regret to inform you that a mistake was made in your employment with Majestik. It was understood, by mistake, that you had twelve (12) years' experience working in the insurance industry, which is not the case. You do not have the requisite experience. I am therefore compelled to terminate your employment before the ninety (90) day period for which you were originally hired, as the position also requires that the person is to have field settlement authority of Ten Thousand dollars*

($10,000) to settle claims, and that can only be held by someone with insurance experience.

Please bring your files in to the office upon receipt of this notice. Your final pay check will be provided to you at that time. Have your expense reimbursement and mileage ready when you come, as those will also be evaluated and provided, if approved, at that time.

Don McAteer
Vice President, Operations

Ernie lapsed silently into shock. *How do you like that? All the way to Los Angeles with a promise of working ninety days, and hopes of saving up some money since an owl put me out of work. I did well by Majestik, and surely better than the pregnant Jessica Bloom whom everyone who had dealt with her complained about her doing nothing. I took over for her, an adjustor who never went out on a single claim. It just doesn't seem fair. And then too, the job was only for ninety days, so the company could have let me stay until then so I could have saved up enough to fix my truck when I got back home. Now that'll have to wait longer. Well, there is nothing to decide. This apartment costs money, and there's no more money. Time to cut the overhead and head home.*

Ernie pondered the various claims he settled and wondered if he had performed well. One stuck out in his mind. The poor girl, Michelle Jones, who was so badly burned in the townhome fire, and the crooked insurance staff attorneys who had shredded the evidence that would have gotten her recovery she was entitled to.

Then too, they were cheating the widow who owned the townhome where the fire started, cheating her out of money she needed and was entitled to. *That was dishonest, and I took part in it. I delivered the evidence from Marlow's Electric, that was required by law to be given to Michelle Jones, to those sleazy attorneys, and I had a part in destroying it by keeping quiet and taking it to those who shredded it.*

⌘

At the Majestik office front desk on the first floor, Ernie was told to wait there and to turn in his files to the receptionist as well as the company cell phone, checkbook, the packet of sample insurance policies, and other things he was provided when hired. He was also told to provide on the company form any expenses and mileage incurred on the job. He didn't have any expenses to submit for reimbursement, nor did he keep track of his mileage. He didn't bother keeping mileage on his motorcycle, as it got so much better mileage than a car and he did not want to be bothered with it. The receptionist called someone to report what he turned in, and soon a woman messenger came out of the elevator delivering his final check, prorated and reduced to that very day from his monthly promised pay.

It was all over.

He expected McAteer to come to say goodbye, but he didn't. *McAteer doesn't even have the huevos to come and get rid of me himself, the coward. If I were firing someone, I would have the decency to tell the man myself.*

A feeling of mistreatment overcame him. It was as though he was an ant of no importance to the corporate giant.

He recalled Zelzah, who invited him for dinner and showed him how to use a computer as well as the mating rituals of Majestic executive secretaries. He asked to use the in-house phone at the desk, and for Zelzah's extension.

Zelzah answered. "Mr. Bradford's office."

"Zelzah?"

"Ernie!" she cried out in surprise. Then she lowered her voice. "Listen, lover, I know what happened. It was Bradford himself. When he saw that you saved Lewis, he had you fired. But I can't talk now. Will you call me?"

"I'm heading back home. I have no job here."

"Please call me if you stay or come back."

"Okay, I will. Thanks for helping out on the computer and for the dinner."

"Anytime for you, lover. Call me."

ের৩৫৩

He left the office with mixed feelings. Officially he was fired because he did not have experience, but Zelzah said the real reason was because he saved the crusader Lewis's life. At least he was not fired for incompetency.

He headed for the Polynesian to collect his modest things and go limping home to Sedro Woolley. As the freeway on-ramps came near, he pulled over and stopped on the shoulder to ponder. The Polynesian was south. But there was something to the north that was bothering him.

He put the shift lever of the gearbox in between first and second, which is neutral, and the green "N" light lit up on the tank cluster of gauges, indicating the bike was at rest, out of gear, and he could let off the clutch lever to relax. He took off his helmet, scratched his head, thinking.

And so, too, my life is in "neutral." Put in neutral back at home as a logger, due to porridge-brained voters having their way with what they think is saving nature for an owl that has as much benefit for nature as toxic chemical waste. Lured a thousand miles from home to work for ninety days and fired for saving a candidate's life, again put in neutral. I should just go back home and consider a different calling.

What about Michelle Jones? The poor girl's whole life is ahead of her. She will have to live it with intense scars and suffering. On the one hand, if she could recover some money from the insurance claim, she could have enough money to get herself more medical attention, a little house, and maybe some things to make herself more comfortable. On the other, she could just continue to suffer as Majestik would have her do, as it could care less, as long as it saved money. In either case, the doors of opportunity in life for most people were closed to her and would remain closed.

Before being fired, I would not have considered doing something that the company would not allow and telling her about Marlow. But by not doing the right thing, I'm no better than those slimy people at Majestik. If President Bradford had his way, he would have had me let Lewis drown.

The feeling of shame overwhelmed him. Then he was jolted out of it with a scary thought, *Maybe if I stayed on with*

Majestik indefinitely, I would have become one of them. Holy shit!

He made a decision. *There is something I want to do before heading home.*

Helmet back on, he pulled on the clutch in on handlebar, and with his left boot stepped on the shift lever. The transmission made the "clunk" sound of going into first gear. One on-ramp went south, the other north. He pointed his motorcycle to the north on-ramp, in the direction of Van Nuys, remembering Michelle Jones's address from the file. *No neutral today for me.*

☙

Since the fire, the girl's parents had taken a small apartment in a crowded, inexpensive part of Van Nuys. There were so many apartments in the area, that the street in front was entirely filled with parked cars on both sides. Ernie rode up and down the street twice, wondering where on earth he could park, when finally a woman pulled out from a parallel parking spot. He quickly motored into it, backed up his rear wheel to the curb, and went to the apartment of Michelle Jones.

She came to the door herself, as her parents were both at work. There she was, not three feet away. It was a shocking sight to witness in person, her face so horribly scarred and discolored. It was a hundredfold worse to see such permanent injuries in person than from the pictures in the file. But as he looked at the girl, he could see underneath the mask of scar tissue and blotches of discoloration, a warm expression.

"Yes?" she greeted in a high, clear tone.

"Have you settled your case yet?"

"Are you from the insurance company? My lawyer said not to talk to you people unless he's present."

"It's best that you don't ask who I am. I'm here to do you a favor. Just listen and see for yourself if you like what I have to say."

Tears began to form in Michelle's eyes, as memories of the fire, the hospital, and her ruined life all flashed before her once again. Mustering her courage she raised her chin. "No, I have not settled the case," she said, her voice cracking. "The lawyer says that we have no case, except maybe against the Koreans who were smoking, but they have no insurance or money. My lawyer thinks we should drop it altogether. I have thousands in unpaid bills, and collectors are calling here all the time. I still need more medical attention, but cannot get it. Everything is pretty bad right now," she finished, tears rolling down her ruined cheeks.

Ernie handed her his handkerchief so she could wipe her tears and took command of the situation. "Get a piece of paper and a pen. Go on, do it, and stop crying."

She hesitated, regained her composure, went inside, and returned with pen and paper. "Come inside and let me write at the table."

Ernie followed her inside. "Now take this down. 'Marlow's Electric.'" He spelled the name and gave her the city. "I can't remember the street, but you now have the name and the city. You can find him easily, as he's in business as an electrician. You call Marlow yourself and go there and ask for a copy of his repair bill for the work he did at the townhome next door to you where the fire started. It was six months before the fire, and he was there to fix a faulty plug. You will find in his bill a notice and warning that there was faulty wiring and that it was a fire hazard. From that, and from Marlow, your lawyer can establish that the fire was from wiring, not from the Korean couple smoking, and, further, that the owner had knowledge of the faulty wiring. Okay?"

She was busily writing down what he said and asked for a few things to be repeated. As she did, several tears fell on the paper. A whole life changed, Ernie realized, by faulty wiring and by someone who could have but did not fix it. Now at least Majestik, that had taken premiums to insure the event, would have to pay up.

"Now, one other thing. Since I, and not your lawyer, found the evidence that will make your claim go from nothing to one million, you should not have to pay more than a five per cent legal fee, since your lawyer does not have to go out and find it and will incur no overhead, and that is fair pay. If you need help on what to say to your lawyer, here is what to say.

"Take this down. 'I just learned of evidence that will win this case. In order for you to continue to represent me, I require you to tear up our one-third retainer agreement and prepare a new one to handle my case for five per cent of the recovery. If you do not agree to that and give me a new written agreement with those terms, I will go find another lawyer who will do it for five per cent. If you will represent me for the five per cent, I will tell you how to win the case easily. With this evidence, you will demand the policy limit of one million. You will get fifty thousand dollars and I will get nine hundred, fifty thousand. However, if Majestik refuses to give us the full one million and we have to go to trial over it, you can then charge ten percent.'" He paused to let her catch up then continued dictating. "'After my case settles, what I am going to give you can also be used to contact the widow who owned the home where the fire started to ask her to let you represent her to get the value of her lost townhome from Majestik, but you must also agree to represent her for five per cent, or ten per cent if you have to take the case to trial.'

"Did you get all that? Read it back to me."

She read it back, and a few corrections were made.

"Good. Do not tell him about Marlow's bill until he agrees, tears up the one-third agreement in front of you, and gives you a new one for five per cent, or ten percent if it goes to trial, which he and you must sign and he must give you a copy. You read it carefully. Only then, if it is totally correct, and when you have the new agreement in your pocket, do you then hand him the Marlow's Electric document. If he refuses, leave and go get another lawyer. There are tons of lawyers who will take your case for fifty thousand instead of three hundred thirty-three thousand for legal fees. Do you understand?"

"Yes, but why are you doing this for me?

"Don't ask. It's better you don't tell anyone about me. If the lawyer asks where you got the tip on Marlow's bill, just tell him it's from a source that required remaining anonymous. Since you don't know who I am, you will not be lying. Once you have the bill from Marlow's, you have a perfect case and can demand the policy limits of one million dollars. Don't settle for less. Trust me, okay? Then when you get your money, I don't want you to let anyone waste it for you, including your family. I want you to use a lot of it to buy yourself a nice house in your own name. And no matter what you do in life, keep that house in your name alone for your investment. If you move out, keep it and rent it. Do you understand?"

"Yeah, okay." She started to cry and began to breathe hard. "I'm feeling excited now, and I may faint. Ever since the fire, my skin doesn't breathe too well, and when I get too excited or hot, I faint."

Ernie got excited that she might collapse. *I don't need her to faint.* "Relax and take advantage of what I'm doing for you. And do exactly what I say."

"I wish I could do something for you. Would you like a Coke? That's all I have to offer."

"No, but thanks. I'll be on my way."

She leaped into the arms of her new, much larger friend, wrapped hers arms around him, and did not let go. She kissed him on the cheek.

He was as startled as he was pleased, and then he felt the leather-like roughness of the scarred flesh of the poor thing's cheek. He lowered her gently back to the ground after she hugged him very long and hard. Deeply touched, Ernie leaned down, kissed her forehead, and bid her, "Godspeed."

A strange and wonderful feeling came over him as he motored away. He was no longer in neutral. He crowed aloud, over his motorcycle's engine noise to which no one could hear. "I just cost Majestik a million bucks and possibly the value of the widow's townhome, in addition. That'll teach 'em!"

CHAPTER 49

On his final night at the Polynesian, he sorted through all the notes and papers, like directions to the various claimants' sites, and put all of it in the waste basket as he readied for his return trip. Everything he would take had to fit into the saddlebags, and all unnecessary cargo had to go.

On the table sat his trusty chainsaw. According to the termination letter from Majestik, he was fired because he did not have ten years' experience with insurance. But he had brought his saw and used it on the job, and surely no other adjustors had a saw.

The saw, a badge of honor, was his way of making a living, and he used it on claims. Yet, as a logger, he was not good enough to keep his temporary job.

In tossing out the materials to get the apartment clean, he came across the flash stick made at Zelzah's called *MM*, for Money Maker.

Better save this. It's supposed to have good instructions on it. You never know. One day I might get a computer and I could learn something from this. Anyway, it doesn't take up any space, so why not take it?

Tomorrow is the day. Should I go straight through? What for? There's no job waiting. The only thing I have to go back to is my trailer house and sweet Lilly, and she would rather have me back in good shape rather than comatose from riding for twenty-four hours. I'll make it to Oregon, and stop there. That will be about eight hundred miles. The next day, I can ease right on into Sedro Woolley, about the same distance. That'll be a good ride. Now, time to settle up with the Polynesian manager and be ready to go early.

As Ernie walked out of his apartment, a man with a five-o'clock shadow watched him from across the street in a dark van, the industrial kind with no side or rear windows. He saw Ernie go into the manager's office, come out several minutes later, and head back toward the apartments.

The man got out of the van, went to the manager's office, and addressed the manager Wendy. "Hi. I worked with Ernie, and we at the office have bought him a going-away present. Don't tell him that I came by, as it's a surprise. Several of us will be coming over to present it. Did he happen to say when he's leaving?"

"Yes, he did. He's leaving early in the morning," Wendy revealed, not suspecting anything.

"Well, then we better come by tonight with it. Thanks."

Back inside the van, Lunati made a call. "Fiorello, this is Vinnie. He's leaving early in the morning."

"We've decided to take him out," Innocenti said. "I'll come over at 3:00 a.m. and join you, unless you call first. If he leaves before then, call me and I'll catch up on the highway. We'll hit him on the highway. We'll wait until he's out of LA before we hit him. There'll be less traffic and less police outside of town where he'll die."

∽✄∽

No stranger to early mornings, at 4:00 a.m. Ernie was already dressed in his leather chaps and riding jacket. At 4:30 a.m. it was time to say goodbye to the big city of Los Angeles. Loaded up, he mounted his motorcycle, his chainsaw in the saddlebag. The engine of his trusty motorcycle fired up briskly.

Pulling out of the Polynesian, Ernie stopped, turned around, and took a last look at the interesting apartment complex with fond memories, and bid it a silent farewell, along with his big experience in Los Angeles.

As he pulled out of the lot, Lunati and Innocenti, waiting in the van, followed. Innocenti, back from New York with stitches in his stomach, held in his lap his gun of choice for the task at hand, an Ithaca, 10 gauge, semi-automatic, shotgun called the Roadblocker. The shells were three-and-a-half-inch magnums and held twice the powder and shot of a normal twelve-gauge shotgun shell. It was fairly effective at stopping a car, which was how it got its name. It was no longer made after 1989, but this one was part of Innocenti's collection. He had two barrels for it, a full choke, longer barrel and an open choke short, eighteen-inch barrel. He fitted the quick change short one for this job, as he anticipated a close range shot. Lunati was armed with his Glock .45, but he was driving and not expecting to use his pistol on their moving target.

Ernie made his way to the freeway, heading north toward Washington State. Up the ramp he rode, settling into a lane with the fast, early morning traffic of Los Angeles. He then kicked back and rested his mind for a long ride. Behind, in the many cars in the ever-present traffic leaving Los Angles was a dark van, carrying its lethal passengers, completely unnoticed.

The trip took him out of the Los Angeles basin, climbing into the mountains. Eventually trees replaced the fast food restaurants, minimarts, strip malls, liquor stores, gas stations, Oriental massage parlors, and other commercial businesses, the absence of which was a nice sight to Ernie after living in the concrete jungle of LA. Although faint, he smelled the first scent of a forest and longed for the strong aroma back home.

As the traffic thinned, the van became noticeable behind in his rear view mirrors, getting closer, as though it wanted to overtake. Ernie changed lanes to the right lane to make it easier for the van to pass him. Already going five miles per hour over the speed limit, he didn't want to travel faster and risk getting a speeding ticket.

The van accelerated and moved over into the left lane beside Ernie. As it pulled alongside, it slowed to equal Ernie's speed.

Ernie turned to look at it. Pointing out the passenger's side window was the big bore of the ten-gauge Roadblocker. Resting on the wooden stock was the cheek of a man that that looked familiar. His cheek puffed up against the stock.

It's the same face I saw under Dwight Winger's boat! Do

something quick! Ernie grabbed the front brake lever hard and stomped on the rear brake foot pedal, slowing suddenly, changing the relative positions of the two vehicles by just a foot, and taking himself out of the sights of the big barrel that had been pointing right at him.

And, not a moment too soon. A thunderous boom and enormous flash of fire came out of the big barrel, lighting the pre-dawn darkness.

Grabbing the brakes had moved the motorcycle back just enough so buckshot was discharged ahead of him, with most of the double-ought pellets hitting the gas tank. The motorcycle, together with Ernie on it, was blown off the highway by the horrendous force of the impact.

Although most all of the buckshot hit the tank, one of them went into Ernie's left leg that was up against the tank, and another pierced his side.

As he and his motorcycle became airborne, there was nothing he could do, except ride it to the ground. The motorcycle landed and flipped over and over, throwing Ernie off and to the right. It finally came to a stop, a total wreck. Ernie lay on the ground, wondering what bones were broken. A strong pain protested from his side, and another from his leg from the buckshot. Abrasions from the tumble stung him sharply. As the shock subsided, he began to hurt more.

He moved his arms and legs. He did not seem to have any broken any bones. However, that was not much consolation, given the condition of his motorcycle. Raising himself up to a sitting position, he stared over at toward his mangled machine.

A noise from the road made him jump. *What's that? That van must have stopped and now it's backing up! The men from the boat incident are coming back to finish me off! Pain or no pain, if I don't move, I'm a dead man.*

Sticking out of the upper saddlebag on the motorcycle, now lying on its side in the dirt, was his chainsaw. Ignoring his pain, Ernie crawled quickly over to it, loosened the straps of the leather saddlebag, and removed the saw. *Still intact. It's my only weapon, and it's time to move!*

Saw in hand, he struggled to his feet, pulling himself up on a nearby sapling. Overcoming the dizziness from the pain, he bolted to the protection of the trees.

Just inside the trees, staying within their protection, he instinctively readied his chainsaw by snapping its cold motor to life with a brisk yank of the starter cord. It coughed once, spit out white smoke from oil put in the cylinder when he readied it for the return trip, and, like the well-maintained saw that it was, snapped to life for its owner.

Knowing the men would soon be within earshot, Ernie hurriedly revved it up to make it hot and ready. Its motor warmed, it would now perform if called upon. *Time to shut it down and get silent.* He shut off the saw, took off his leather chaps and coat—to eliminate the noise of the leather rubbing against itself—and laid the clothes in a pile behind a bush. Now he could move more quietly in the forest and, taking his chainsaw, put some distance between himself and his stalkers.

Out of the van came two men, Innocenti from the passenger side with the Roadblocker in his hand and, from the driver's side, Lunati with pistol. The morning light had yet to dawn as the two of them rushed into the dark trees in search of their prey.

Used to living and working in forests, which were native to him, Ernie moved about more quickly and with less noise than his stalkers. He could hear them behind him, stomping clumsily through the brush. Well ahead of them, he maneuvered around to the left, flanking them, and ducked behind some heavy brush. He controlled his breathing, remaining silent, as they approached, and they walked right by.

The older man was not very agile from his recent stab wound. His walk was clumsy and easy for Ernie to hear. "Vinnie, let's spread apart and cover more area," he said loudly.

"Keep your voice down, Fiorello. If he hears us, he may slip away."

Vinnie headed off to the left. Ernie was now directly behind him. When it appeared that the two of them were as far apart as they would get, Ernie crept in quietly until he was just behind Vinnie, his movements concealed by the noise the guy made, breaking twigs and breathing heavily. When he was just a few feet from him, Ernie snapped the starter cord of his chainsaw smartly. The chainsaw saluted by jumping to life with a ferocious growl.

Startled, Lunati jumped and then spun around to meet whatever was behind him making the frightening sound. As he turned, Ernie used both arms to tilt the saw horizontally, aiming for Vinnie's neck. Ernie's powerful swing put the high revving saw, with its razor sharp chain teeth, right through the guy's neck, as though it was a small limb on a Douglas fir.

His head came quickly and neatly off his shoulders, tumbling end over end before hitting the ground. Blood squirted out of his neck and after a few eerie moments with the headless body standing by itself, it collapsed.

Ernie shut down the saw, charged to the left, and then hustled deeper into the forest to distance himself from the shotgun-wielding Fiorello.

The sound of the saw brought Innocenti hurrying through the dark forest lit only by the stars and moon. Fearlessly, he charged toward the noise with the Roadblocker in hand, ready to blow body parts off of his prey and kill him dead. His pain from the knife wound and stitches in his stomach went unnoticed due to the adrenalin surging through his blood, and also from dose of a narcotic pain killers he had taken.

Innocenti did not see what was in front of him, and he stumbled and then fell over the body of his old friend Lunati, and landed prone on the ground. Innocenti fell such that his face was only inches from Lunati's head, which had a horrified expression on the face. His eyes bulged in shock, and the mouth gaped wide in a silent scream of terror.

The sight caused Innocenti to lose control of himself and, despite the need for silent caution, he let out a scream. "Aghhhhhhhhh."

He rose and stumbled backward, desperate to get away from the carnage that had once been a friend. Collecting himself as much as possible, Innocenti scanned the trees for any sign of Ernie. Anger set in hard and fast, as he thirsted for revenge. He'd get that son-of-a-bitch Ernie if it was the last thing he did. He crouched, both hands around the Roadblocker, creeping into the trees, stalking his prey.

Ernie could hear Fiorello lumbering through the trees and underbrush, which pinpointed his location. Wanting to put more distance between them, Ernie crept deeper into the forest, light on his feet as a Russian ballerina compared to Fiorello's noisy fumbling.

After several minutes of stalking, Innocenti realized that he could probably never catch the woodsman in his own habitat and, further, that the van was still on the roadside, parked near a wrecked motorcycle. It was time to give up the hunt. The van and the motorcycle would no doubt attract the attention of motorists, who would call the highway patrol. This was not the time for an all-out, do-or-die, vendetta.

Angry and dismayed, he turned and trudged back toward the van. As he walked, he noticed the morning light changing the sky from black to gray in the east. He got back to where his friend lay, decapitated, and paused to view the horrific sight. He picked up Lunati's Glock and put it in his pocket. He then tucked the Roadblocker under his arm and picked up his friend's head by the hair. With his other hand, he dragged the body of Lunati by the neck of the jacket through the forest to the clearing. He wanted Lunati's body, to remove evidence and also to arrange a funeral. As he dragged the body, his normally cool and composed mind heated with rage, as he thought about how he would one day get the guy who killed his old friend.

As Innocenti approached the edge of the trees he saw flashing lights of blue and red. *Oh, oh! Police!* There was a highway patrolman stopped behind the van! Innocenti dropped Lunati's body and head in the brush, before the highway patrolman could see them, and tucked the short barreled Roadblocker underneath his jacket, holding it up vertically with one hand by the butt of the stock. He then walked out of the trees toward the patrolman, who was standing over the wrecked motorcycle, looking at it with a flashlight, clearly trying to figure out what happened.

Putting on his politest manners to deal with the law, Innocenti approached the wrecked motorcycle, straightening up his posture and leaned his head back so as not to look aggressive.

The patrolman, startled by the sudden noise and Innocenti's looming shadow, put his hand on his pistol in its holster.

"Hi, Officer," Innocenti said, trying to sound like a tourist on holiday. "Looks like there has been a serious accident here with this motorcycle. I didn't see the accident, but only the wrecked motorcycle. I stopped, backed up, and got out to look around. I went into the trees a short ways to see if this motorcyclist had maybe been thrown in there by the crash, but no one's there. He must have been picked up by someone."

Not sensing any danger, the patrolman relaxed his hand away from the pistol. "My guess is that the rider must have flagged down a motorist and left with him for a hospital." He aimed his flashlight at the now-mangled license plate on the bent back fender of the motorcycle, trying to read the numbers. "It's a Washington plate."

"Poor fella," Innocenti said.

The patrolman looked at the motorcycle. "There doesn't seem to be another vehicle involved. But there is something strange here," he said as he directed his flashlight toward the gas tank. "There are a bunch of dents here in the tank. It almost looks like someone shot the tank with a shotgun."

"A shotgun? Really?" Innocenti watched the patrolman's expression as the man clearly began to suspect foul play.

Glancing at the patrol car, Innocenti saw the standard, police twelve-gauge Remington 870 pump shotgun sticking up from the floorboard in the center of the front seat area. He recalled that any cop who had a shotgun would have to qualify with it at the range, and he would be familiar with the look of the pattern of buckshot hitting a target, so he must know it was a shotgun that was used on the motorcycle.

"Can I see your identification sir?" the patrolman asked suddenly, apparently not eliminating Innocenti from being involved. The officer again rested his hand on the pistol grip of his pistol in its holster, just in case—a compromise between scaring innocent motorists and, at the same time, reducing the time to draw his weapon.

"Mine? Sure. It's in my billfold. Just a sec," Innocenti said cheerfully and walked toward the driver's door of the van parked just ahead.

Flashing police lights from the top of the patrol car illuminated the back of the van in alternating blue and red.

The patrolman sidestepped cautiously, so as to be able to see Innocenti, his hand still resting on the pistol grip of his gun. Innocent determined if he uncovered the shotgun under his coat, it would become a quick draw contest and a shootout like the OK Corral. But an eighteen wheeler went roaring by in the right lane, followed by the deafening wind noise of the wake behind it, which took the patrolman's attention toward the big rig.

Innocenti made his decision. In a single movement, he let the short barrel of the Roadblocker drop down in a swinging motion, while hanging onto the butt of the stock. He continued the swinging motion and let the barrel swing on up to the horizontal position as he turned to face the patrolman and put his open hand on the grip. The maneuver could not have been smoother if it had been done by a trained stage performer.

The patrolman's eyes dilated as he saw the movement and the gun barrel swing around to face him. In spite of his many hours of training, he froze. Although he only hesitated for a fraction of an second, Innocenti moved faster than the patrolman could draw his weapon. The last thing the patrolman would ever see was the brightness of the exploding gunpowder from the huge ten-bore pointing at his face.

The bullet proof vest he wore to protect his vital organs couldn't protect him from the ferocious mobster shooting at his head. His facial features were entirely lost, and his widow and daughter would later attend a closed-casket funeral held by the state police with bagpipes and a twenty-one gun salute to honor one of their fallen.

CHAPTER 50

Ernie awakened in a hospital. As he thought about the day before, the door opened, and in came the familiar faces of FBI agents Doty and Kanno, followed by a doctor in green operating scrubs with two attendants in tow, a young doctor in residency and a Filipina nurse.

Doty spoke first. "Doctor, this man has to be kept alone for his protection and also for the protection of others, so I want that other patient moved," he said, pointing to the guy in the next bed. "The government takes all responsibility and will take it up with the hospital head administrator directly. Any cost for the private room will be paid by the FBI. As for this room, we will have an armed man outside the door as long as Ernie is here. This man is under the protection of the FBI, from this point on, and any medical practitioner who enters will be searched, if not recognized by the guard, and will not be allowed in unless he can satisfactorily identify himself."

The doctor nodded, sighed, examined Ernie's wounds, looked at the body temperature records from the nurse, made a notation in Ernie's chart, and left the room with his two attendants in tow, leaving only agents Doty and Kanno.

"This is getting old," Ernie said to the agents. He then remembered being taken to the hospital, and then wheeled into an operating room to have buckshot from the Roadblocker ten-bore removed from his leg and side a few hours earlier.

"I just came down here for a temporary insurance job in the big city, and I end up in the hospital—*twice*. I have not even healed from the air saw wound, and now this. This insurance work is a whole lot more dangerous than logging ever was."

"We know about the highway incident," Doty said. "The

state police are conducting an investigation over the murder of their patrolman, and we are also checking the scene."

Ernie tried to sit up in his bed, but felt a sharp pain in his side where the buckshot had been removed. He then realized that he had one of those controls that moved the bed up in the back, and pushed it until his back came up enough to look forward at the men standing in the room.

"We sent in a truck and took your motorcycle from the wrecking yard to study the pattern of the shot from the shotgun that was used on you. You might also be interested to see what came out of your leg and side." Doty reached into the side pocket of his suit jacket and pulled out a small plastic bag with two copper balls inside, each the size of a large pea. Blood stained the inside of the bag.

"I just got these from the doctor who took it out of your leg and side. We are fairly certain it was from a ten-gauge shotgun. You're very lucky. If the blast had struck just a foot behind where it hit on the motorcycle tank, I would have had to identify you in the morgue."

"Agh!" Ernie exclaimed in shock.

Concerned he might have shocked his witness with his coarseness, Doty quickly tried to recover the propriety of the situation. He had seen the aftermath of much violence and sometimes forgot how discussing it with victims could be upsetting. To remove those thoughts, he put the bag quickly back in his suit pocket and said, "You must be very upset about having been shot."

"No, not that. My motorcycle is ruined."

"Special Agent Kanno," Doty said to his partner. "Here's a man that took two double ought shots from a ten gauge, a foot from taking the rest of the load, and all he's worried about is his motorcycle? Why don't we have agents like that in the FBI?" He smiled at Ernie as he turned from Kanno to face him again, looking relieved that he had not offended him.

"Where's my bike now?"

"It's at a building under lockup where we keep evidence," Kanno said. "We'll do a forensic analysis of the pattern left by the shotgun. We might even gain some evidence, if we're lucky. We do that sort of thing rather well, compared to local or state police."

"What are you going to do with my bike? If I can fix it, I need it to go home."

"Right now it is seized as evidence in a Federal investigation," Kanno answered. "We'll have to hold it for a while but, my friend, I fear it's a total. I know you really loved your motorcycle, Ernie. I'm sorry about that."

"I have insurance. I should have the card in my billfold."

"Did you get a look at the man who shot you?" Doty asked. "Maybe now we can get him identified? This, of course, assumes he has a record, and has been photographed."

"Enough to know it was the same man that I saw under Winger's boat. I got a look at his face, even though it was night. I saw more of him than when he had the swim mask on."

"So do you think you could identify him now?"

"I can't say for sure, but I'll be glad to try."

"The state police examined the woods nearby," Doty said. "They found a bloody spot with quite a lot of fresh blood. We got a specimen of the blood, and will check the DNA if the dead man has a DNA on file. But if he has does not have a record, that won't help. The one still alive must have gone back into the woods and retrieved the body."

Kanno cleared his throat. "We've been told by the state police that you told them you actually decapitated one of the men with your chainsaw. Is that right?"

"Yep. A chainsaw can put a quick end to a lot of arguments."

"Good God," Kanno exclaimed, "Don't' get pissed off at me!"

Doty took over the conversation at this point. "We think whoever's behind the assassination attempt on candidate Lewis is very worried that you'll identify him and lead us to some group behind it. That's why, we believe, they went after you again when you were not killed in the boating hit. If no one identifies anyone, we'll probably not be able to put together enough evidence to get a prosecution, let alone a conviction.

So we think he may still come after you again. That's why we have a man outside and, of course, to keep out press so we can control what's released. We hope you'll cooperate."

Ernie nodded. "I was leaving town. Do you think they were just mad because I messed up their attempt to kill Lewis and wanted to get even?"

"That doesn't add up," Doty said. "This doesn't have the aspects of a vendetta. They're worried you'll be able to identify them, or at least the one person you saw under the boat, which would lead to the rest of them. They must think that they need to get rid of you so you can't identify them for a grand jury or at trial. They know the FBI is involved, and that once we get a lead on who did it, our Seattle office close to where you live could get your testimony easily, unlike local police. So your leaving town did not matter to them—they want you dead. We think the mob may be involved, and we're working on various leads. It has to be someone, or some group, that does not want Lewis to get elected."

Special Agent Kanno had a briefcase, which he opened. He took out a flash stick. "Ernie, we went through your things at the evidence building where we took the motorcycle before coming over here. We found this flash stick. Is this something private to you? I didn't want to run it if it was something personal—I wanted to respect your privacy, given all you have been through."

"No, not at all. That is called *Money Maker*. It's from Majestik Insurance. I got it from the head guy's secretary's computer. I think it has instructions on how to act as an insurance man, but I never got to try it out since I don't have a computer. I saved it, thinking it might have some value if I ever get a computer."

Kanno cocked his head and studied Ernie. "Do you know of any connection between Majestik and the mob?"

"The closest thing that I know of that could be called a mob would be that bunch of owl lovers up in Washington that cost me my job."

Kanno and Doty broke out in hearty laughter.

"Did you need the flash stick?" Ernie asked. "I know I'll

never get another insurance job. They fired me when they decided they had hired me by mistake. I thought I did a pretty fair job, but they didn't see it that way, I guess."

Kanno looked at Doty, who shrugged, then set it on the table next to Ernie's hospital bed. "No, I guess not."

"Is Lewis going to win the election?" Ernie asked. "I don't watch news."

"The attempt on his life seems to have given him a little more popularity," Doty said. "He has moved up in the polls and is now leading slightly. The election isn't far off." Doty cleared his throat, looking suddenly uncomfortable. "Special Agent Kanno and I have an idea, and we'd like to see what you have to say about it."

"I'm afraid to ask," Ernie joked.

"Here's what we'd like to do," Doty continued with a chuckle. "We'll let it out to the press that we have a witness who can positively identify a suspect in Lewis's attempted murder, and that the witness will be able to give evidence to a federal grand jury in a very short time. This announcement might flush whoever it is out to go after you once again. It's not without risk, but it would be very valuable to us. We'll provide you with protection and a wage during the time, equal to what you earned at the insurance company for any time you're working for us. What do you think?"

"Best offer for work I have had for since the insurance deal. In fact, it is my only offer."

"*No, it's not!*" Those booming words resonated through the hallway and into the room. Candidate Zachary Lewis walked right in as though there was no FBI security.

Right behind him was a young FBI agent, looking worried that the candidate walked right past him.

"I'll put you on my staff, if you need a job," the charismatic candidate said. "I could use you as a bodyguard, since someone wants to kill me."

The young FBI agent, who wasn't supposed to let anyone in, grimaced and stared at the floor.

"Sorry, sir, I know you said no one, and I told him—but he is a major political official, and he has state police outside with him—I didn't think I should be forceful," he muttered.

"That's fine, Warren," Doty told the young agent.

Outside the door in the hall Ernie could see two uniformed California State Police, the candidate's escort, now following him everywhere since the attempt on his life.

Lewis held out his hand to shake. "How's the hero who saved my life?"

"I'm pretty good, all in all," Ernie said. "Gee, I was out of work, and now I have two offers. Things are looking up."

"I understand that you checked out of your hotel and lost your motorcycle," Lewis informed him. "How would you like to stay temporarily in my guest house? That is the least I can do for the man who saved my life."

"Sounds good," Ernie said with a relieved grin.

"We'll leave you alone, Mr. Lewis?" Doty made the statement and then turned it into a question by raising the inflection at the end.

Lewis was a little bigger than life, as a successful politician has to be, and had a charisma about him that filled the room. But then, Ernie also had a bigger than life manner. The room seemed too small for the two of them to be in together.

"Hell, no," Lewis scoffed. "Stick around. I need all the protection I can get," he said jokingly to the FBI agents but, in fact, he meant what he said. "I still don't have all of my hearing back from the damage to my ear drums, but the docs who operated on me say it will nearly all come back. That is why, by the way, Ernie, that I could not come to thank you myself sooner. I was in the hospital, until you were said to have left. Then I heard about the highway incident."

He paused and turned to Doty. "Say, do you FBI boys think there is a connection? One of you left word at my office to talk to me, but I didn't return the call yet as I have not been able to hear very well until yesterday, and I have been booked solid since I started returning calls, with the election coming up and all."

Doty answered, as he was the senior of the two agents. "Since we're all together, we can discuss a few things if we can be alone here."

Lewis went to the door. "Keep everyone out," he said to his two state police escorts. Once the door closed, he turned to Doty. "This is as good a place as any, and you have me as well as my rescuer here, another witness at the same time."

"Mr. Lewis, we're investigating leads concerning special interests groups that might have much to lose if you're elected," Doty informed him. "You haven't been campaigning against organized crime, so that doesn't lead anywhere. However, we think that organized crime may be working for some special interest group that wants to make sure that you don't win the election. Have you got any ideas for us?"

"My single most-controversial platform is insurance reform. But I can't imagine the insurance industry having the wherewithal to hire a hitman. They just specialize in cheating billions of people with dirty tricks. You wouldn't think that the insurance industry is hooked up with organized crime, would you?"

"We have no leads that anyone involved in the insurance industry is involved," Doty said. "Yet, we still think that there must be some connection. We have pretty much ruled out some screwball trying to propel himself into the limelight, like those nutty ones who go for the president. You're not in power yet, and killing you wouldn't transmit immediate recognition for the killer.

"And your platform is one affecting business, the insurance business, but we still feel that our best direction is some connection between that and the mob. Perhaps one of the big insurance companies owns some other business, or industry, that's depending on continued money from the insurance company and fears losing the support from them if you win. Possibly that business is connected to crime, or was involved in hiring the assassin to kill you. But all we have on that is a concept—no proof."

Lewis absorbed all that Doty said. "My legislation will make a big change in insurance, that's for sure. And the insurance industry is one of the largest industries in the US or, for that matter, the world. Some of the companies have more assets than some countries."

Looking at Lewis, Doty said, "That's the point. If the insurance industry has their way of doing business at stake, someone in it might very well connect with the mob to keep you out of office. Since the assassination attempt on you is still a very hot story, we can leak it out that Ernie can identify the men who tried to kill you. In order to make it credible, we will probably leak it that the FBI has someone, without mentioning Ernie's name, that can identify one or more of those involved, and the suspects will assume it is Ernie. We have to suspect that whoever wanted to kill you still wants to do it. If they hear that someone will be testifying before the grand jury in a few days, we expect them to go after him as well, and right away. If Ernie joins your campaign staff, it would be somewhat easier for us to try to cover the both of you, but you must be advised that putting Ernie near you may increase the risk to yourself. But if you agree, we will also provide a few FBI personnel for protection."

Lewis answered quickly, "This hero saved my life. I have California State Police protection, and now from you. I'm not concerned and, frankly, after the boating incident, I would rather have Ernie by my side than not. Why don't I just announce he's on my campaign staff, and take him around with me? Maybe it will flush them out?"

"That is very brave of you sir," Doty said. "With permission from both of you, I'll call a friend in the news and leak the story."

"All right with me," Lewis said. "How about with you, Ernie?"

"Sure," Ernie said.

"Will you federal boys get him one of those bullet proof vests and a sidearm, or do I have to try to get him one? You know I'm not governor yet," Lewis pointed out. He would not be able to sign for Ernie for a California Concealed Weapons permit unless and until he became governor.

Doty grimaced. "The vest is easy. But the weapon's a different matter. Can you imagine the press if he shoots an innocent bystander with a FBI issued weapon? Shit, we'd be roasted. I don't know if I can get permission for a weapon or not."

Hearing that, Ernie got pissed off and raised his voice at Doty. It wasn't that loud, but with Ernie, it was intimidating. "You asshole! I'm already the target of hitmen, and you want me to not only continue, but you want to make me bait for more. And you're worried about your fucking image or judgment if you let me have a pistol to defend myself? Fuck you and the FBI horse you rode in on. If you want my help, you'll get me, not just any gun, but one of those expensive .45s. Make it a stainless Sig Sauer, six clips and six boxes of the hottest ammo. And you give it to me, so if I don't get killed, I can take it back home with me as a present. And, I'm not going to use it and then later find some piece-of-shit, anti-gun liberal district attorney prosecuting me in state court for shooting someone when defending myself when acting as a witness for the FBI. So you deputize me for the entire time I'm working for you, in writing, and with a federal gun permit. If you want me to be your decoy, that seems like a fair risk for you to take." Ernie figured he had the bargaining power. "Take it or leave it. I've been shot at enough for one job!"

"Okay, okay, I'll do it," Doty said. "But you'll have to meet me at the range so at least I can say that you passed proficiency test before getting you a weapon permit and weapon."

"I'd love to test my new weapon as I would always do before I have to rely on it. And these pistols need some wearing in to loosen them up. I want two hundred rounds or ordinary ammo to run through the weapon to loosen it up which I will do at the range. I bet you that after three practice clips, I can best you on the target range."

Doty did not accept the bet, doubtful he could beat Ernie, and also wondering how he was going to break it to his boss that he was going to deputize Ernie under posse comitatus, making him a federal deputy by common law.

"Now," Ernie said, "Who is going to pay me, and how much?"

CHAPTER 51

Resting in the old Catholic church in Waterbury was the ornate casket of Vincenzo Lunati, made of mahogany, varnished with high-gloss lacquer. His head had been put back on by the mortician and the family did not know it had been surgically removed by Ernie and his chainsaw.

The open casket was lined in rich, stuffed, cream-colored satin. An ostentatious display of flowers luxuriantly embellished the background. In the front two rows sat the extended family, dressed in black, most of them weeping. Behind them were old friends of his from the past. On the other side, the front pew was left vacant for very special guests who would arrive soon.

In from the double doors of the funeral parlor came four very well dressed men. Each waited patiently for the others as, one at a time, they went up to the casket to kneel and make the sign of the Catholic cross over their chests to pray for their fallen. Space had been reserved in the front row on one side for these powerful men, Bastini, Manelli, Innocenti, and Indelicato of Las Vegas who employed Lunati, and who had paid for the lavish funeral in old-world respect for their fallen comrade. There would be money for the family, but since he was not married, it would be a smaller amount and given to the parents.

Following the service, the four men followed the hearse with the casket from the church to the burial site in a black limousine.

The four used the opportunity to discuss business brought up by an article one had seen in the Los Angeles newspaper about Ernie testifying before the federal grand jury very soon.

Since all were present, their rules were that they could conduct any business.

"What are we going to do about this guy, Ernie, who took out Vinnie and who can identify Fiorello?" Indelicato asked the group. "The news says that there's a witness who will be giving testimony to the grand jury very soon—that has to be Ernie. If he does, Fiorello may go down, and then they can connect all of us. Do we try again, or is it too risky?"

As Innocenti was the subject of the conversation, he remained silent in a show of decorum.

Manelli nodded. "As far as we know, the only way they can get an indictment at this time is if he identifies Fiorello. They will then connect us to Fiorello, and we all get charged with something. The bad press, even if they can't get a conviction, would cost us our management contract in Nevada with Ms. Gunther. And if we blow that, we will probably lose the deal with the Indians. So I say we kill him and do it right away, before he testifies. I hope the feds don't tuck him away in the witness protection program so we can't get to him."

Bastini shook his head. "The news says he's working for the candidate Lewis now. Since he saved Lewis's ass, Lewis offered him a job on his campaign. Sal, can your daughter Maria can tell us where Ernie will be for a hit?"

"She should be able to," Manelli said. "She told me that Ernie is traveling with Lewis as his aide and we should be able to hit them together."

"So, is it decided?" Indelicato asked. "Are we going to hit the two of them? I say yes."

Bastini nodded. "Kill both."

Manelli joined in. "I agree. Let's get them both." He turned to Innocenti.

"Let's do it and in a hurry," Innocenti snapped.

"Maybe we should bring in someone else on this," Manelli suggested. "If Ernie can identify Fiorello, the police will have his description and make it hard for him to get in close. And Lewis will no doubt have extra guards, probably from the state police."

"I have to get a new helper now that Vinnie is gone," Innocenti answered. "I'll use him if the hits involve places crowed with cops. But if I can do it myself, I prefer that. That Ernie stuck me with a knife under water and took off Vinnie's head with a chainsaw. So I have a score to settle. I want to be the one to kill him."

Manelli then said to the group, "Anyone opposed to letting Fiorello do both of the hits?"

Silence was the answer.

Innocenti gritted his teeth and the muscles tightened in his face. "Vengeance is mine."

The motorcade came to a stop at the at the burial site. The Mafioso got out for the final service where the body of Vincenzo Lunati would be laid to rest for eternity. In Heaven?

CHAPTER 52

T his is the hero who saved my life," Lewis said, introducing Ernie to his staff at his campaign headquarters on Monday morning. "And he has agreed to join the staff temporarily as my personal aide."

Staff members came up to shake Ernie's hand and complimented him on the heroics they had heard about at the campaign headquarters as well as on TV. Ernie flushed at all the attention and felt like a fish in a bowl.

He wore the wool outfit from Lilly as he was not presently felling trees. Under his jacket he sported a nifty, pigskin shoulder holster filled with a new, stainless Sig Sauer .45 pistol. The holster strap went around his neck, and down his front just to one side of the opening in his coat and became a single suspender to hold up his pants, a very stylish design. On the strap in front was a pouch holding an extra clip. The suspender model was picked out by Doty, as it fit in with Ernie's regular outfit of using suspenders.

Ernie also had a letter folded and in his billfold deputizing him by the FBI, as well as a federal concealed weapons permit. Ernie was thinking of what he was carrying, not of the attention, He'd always wanted a nice, expensive pistol like that. In .45 caliber, because of the big bullets, it only had an eight-shot clip, whereas the 9 mm used by police carried nearly twice that with a stagger clip. But Ernie, who knew a lot about hunting and weapons, preferred the .45 over the 9 mm that Doty and the other agents carried, due do the stopping power of the .45 over the 9 mm. He got six clips total as he asked for, and hot load ammo. He was also given his double - extra-large size in a bullet-proof vest which he put on when outside as he was told by Doty that he was a target. The vest was a bit uncomfortably warm in the sunny LA climate.

The staff members faded away after their meeting, but a dark-haired Italian girl stayed on to speak to Ernie.

"I'm really am so pleased to finally meet you," Maria Manelli told him innocently. "Where will you be working in the campaign?"

Ernie's ears perked up like those of a wild animal in the forest sensing danger. Doty had told him to report anyone who asked about his schedule or whereabouts. He should get her name, see what she wanted to know, and tell Doty about her. "What's your name?"

"I'm Maria Manelli. I'm working here in between semesters at UCLA. I've heard so much about you. I work on Mr. Lewis's appointments and scheduling. Where will you be working on the campaign?" she asked a second time.

Persistent. He remembered what Doty told him to say. "Mr. Lewis will have me traveling with him as his personal aide." *She wants to know my whereabouts! Could it be her? This girl? It seems so unlikely. But I must tell Doty.*

Maria decided to push it further to see if she could get something more specific to please her father. "Are you going to the expansion ceremony of the new water district in San Diego County on Friday?"

This sounds suspicious. But why not tell her? This is what I'm supposed to do. So, go for it. "Yes. We're going down to San Diego County for ribbon-cutting ceremony at a new expansion ceremony on top of a small mountain just above Vista where the water district has put in a new water reservoir tank. The head of the water company has endorsed Mr. Lewis and has contributed to his campaign."

How much should I tell her if she's the source of information to the hitmen? But then, I have to set myself up as a decoy, and report it to Doty if I am going to make something happen. I must let her know enough to bring out the assassins. Is this jeopardizing Lewis? Yes, but the best thing to do with that is to make sure Lewis knows first, and the FBI second.

"Are you and Mr. Lewis driving down to the event?"

"No, Mr. Lewis and I will be going down in a helicopter and will return the same morning."

୧ଓୡ

That afternoon, Lewis had no more appointments, so Ernie went to the FBI building to see Doty. Doty escorted him to the computer room were Doty did his research to show Ernie what he did. "Ernie, this is a very powerful computer," Doty said, as he and Ernie sat side by side in front of a monitor. "We have access to more data than any other source in the world. The CIA has more of some things, but now we exchange information with the Homeland Security program. We can connect with credit information, criminal record backgrounds, real and personal property ownership, real estate tax records, Interpol, departments of motor vehicles, Uniform Commercial Code filings, lawsuit filings, business licenses, corporate and limited liability company filings, licenses like hairdressers and car dealers, federal bankruptcies, boat and airplane licenses, telephone logs of almost anyone, and most other listed types of licenses and permits. And, of course, we can get into phones, and into most people's computers without them knowing it. You are not allowed to reveal this, okay?"

Ernie faced Doty and attempted to add a little humor, "My FBI Special Deputy Agent lips are sealed."

"Now, what is it you came here to tell me?"

"There is a dark-haired Italian girl at the headquarters who is a student at UCLA and working for Lewis in between semesters. She is Maria Manelli. She asked me specific questions about where Lewis and I would be going. She specifically asked me about an event this Friday at a ribbon-cutting ceremony at a new water tank opening in San Diego County. Lewis and I are flying down in a helicopter Friday morning, and after the event, we'll be flying back. She was all too interested in it, as far as I'm concerned. I think we should warn Lewis about it."

Doty got ready at a computer terminal. "Maria Manelli, you say? What is her age, as best you can tell?"

"Oh, can't be much over twenty."

Doty started looking for a Maria Manelli in the computer. "Wow! There are quite a few Maria Manellis. I have to narrow it down a bit. "Some say that all Italian girls are named Maria," he joked.

"Do you have access to UCLA files?" Ernie asked.

"Not legally. Those liberals at the university would never turn over their files to us voluntarily. We need a search warrant to get in legally. But I have a special program from a friend in the CIA that can hack in to it. Of course, I can't use the results on a search warrant affidavit as it is not legal. I'll check the DMV records first." After a bit, he said, "Here are the Maria Manellis with California driver's licenses. He put them up on an overhead large monitor for Ernie to see. There were fourteen.

Ernie looked at all of them, asking to enlarge a few, and finally said, "I don't see her in those."

"Well, if she's a student from out of State, she might have kept her out of state driver's license. I may have to hack into the UCLA files. But let's try the social networks first.

In almost no time he came up with a picture on Facebook and put it up on the monitor.

"That's her," Ernie exclaimed.

"Okay, now I have a handle on her," Doty said. I can start a background check easily now. It may take a little while. If you want, you could go over to the lounge area for coffee."

Half an hour later, Ernie sauntered back to Doty at the computer.

"Got it." Doty said with satisfaction, stacking printed downloads for a new file on her. "She's twenty-two. She lives at a student living quarters at UCLA. She has a Nevada driver's license. She has no criminal history. She has one credit card in her name as a permissive user of a Salvatore Manelli. He lives in Las Vegas, but I have not had time to check him out yet. She has a local cell phone, and I have her records for the past six months. One of her frequent calls is to Las Vegas, but that number is unlisted and I have not broken into those Nevada records yet. I am betting it is to Salvatore Manelli, and that will turn out to be her father. I'll ask Kanno to get me information on Salvatore Manelli." Doty smiled. "Now, Ernie, I want you to come with me in a helicopter tomorrow morning to the site of the event in San Diego. I'll find out exactly where it is for the pilot, and see what else I can find out about it from calling the water district."

Ernie grinned. "Cool! A helicopter ride."

An hour later, Ernie was back in the lounge when Doty came to sit with him. "Okay, I have some information from the water district for the event on Friday. The water district is a contributor to Lewis's campaign. There's a new water tank up on a hill that is part of an expansion program. The executives and a number of employees from the water company will be there. The executives want to get their pictures taken with Lewis. A company that does pipeline contracting for the district will have a few people there. There'll be a few county officials, and perhaps some elected people like a local mayor. A local TV station is sending over a cameraman and a reporter for the local news. Lewis will make a short speech and cut the ribbon. After picture taking and handshaking, the helicopter will bring the two of you back here. After the event, the water district is throwing a luncheon at a hotel banquet room for anyone invited and their spouses. Lewis will not be attending that. This could be a good place for a hit. Let's get down there tomorrow and scope it out to see what we need to put in place."

ᗑᗒᗑᗒ

Ernie stared in awe at the sleek, shiny, black FBI helicopter on the helipad atop the FBI building. He decided that if he could do whatever he wanted, that flying a helicopter was one of those things.

The pilot was there, doing a pre-flight check list, and saw Ernie. "Hi, I'm Chuck. Have you flown in one of these Robinson R 66 turbines?"

"No, but I did get to go up as a passenger once in the two-seater R 22. My employer up in Sedro Woolley gave me the chance to go up with a fellow he hired who has an older R 22 to scope out from above the best places to log. The pilot let me take the controls a couple of times, once we were in the air, but of course he took off and landed it. The fellow bought his R 22 when they first came out for about a hundred grand. I bet they've gone up a lot, and I bet these new Turbine-powered, R 66 models cost a bunch more, eh?"

Chuck nodded. "Oh, yes. The piston engine R 22 is almost three hundred thousand, and the law enforcement R 66 Turbine like this is over a million."

"Wow!" Ernie exclaimed. "I guess that lets me out. Say, do you think I could take the stick on the trip down to San Diego after you take off, and then up until you get ready to land?"

Chuck rubbed his chin. "Well, I'm a certified flight instructor, so it's legal—but that would be up to your passenger, Special Agent Doty. You can even sit in the right seat, as that is where the pilot in command sits in a Robinson, unlike in other aircraft. Since I'm a flight instructor, the student takes the pilot seat. And you can even log the event as a lesson."

Doty came through the door to the roof helipad, and Ernie anxiously put the question to him. "Is it okay with you if I get a lesson en route with this R 66? Chuck said it is up to you."

Doty shrugged. "Sure."

"Wow," Ernie said. "Wait until the guys back at the chainsaw store hear I got to fly an R 66 Turbine. I'll be the talk!"

❧❦❧

While Ernie and Doty were getting ready to take off in Los Angeles, in San Diego County Innocenti and his new assistant Mario Capirchio were already at the site of the water district event, scouting out the area. Capirchio was not a large man at five foot six. The multi-talented Lunati was gone, and Innocenti chose Capirchio to replace him. Capirchio owned a home and had a workshop in his garage. Although not as well equipped as Lunati's, he had most of the tools to make just about anything. By coincidence, Capirchio also built and flew radio-control models. He also liked motorcycles, and had a

Harley Sportster which is smaller than the big Harleys, as he was not that big. He was a fanatic about anything he worked on, and Innocenti loved the fanatic aspect of his personality, as he had with Lunati.

Innocenti looked around the hilltop near the huge water tank. A salmon-colored, round tank, fifteen feet high and eighty feet in diameter, it occupied a flat spot twenty feet down from the crest of the big hill. It was shaped like an upside down cake pan. "This is where we'll do it on Friday."

The two men stood atop the hill where the event was to take place. All over the hill, there were tan colored rocks jutting up everywhere, some the size of cars. To the south, the hill went down steeply half a mile and ended just before the town of Vista. To the east, there was a row of houses almost at the bottom, and then the terrain went on down to the freeway running north and south. To the north, an undeveloped hill went down a steep slope with no houses anywhere. To the west, one could see rolling hills and undeveloped land, and beyond that, on a clear day, the ocean, twenty miles away. The rolling hills were not flat enough to build houses on yet, and until the property appreciated enough in value for a developer to bring in heavy equipment to excavate building pads, including getting rid of the car-sized rocks, the property would remain undeveloped. The ground to the west was lower, and covered in large, unattractive bushes some twelve feet in diameter, growing on the unirrigated and undeveloped land. The water district had chosen the huge hill to put its water tank on, gravity being the best friend for water pressure.

Innocenti pointed to the west. "See that next hill over there? It's about five hundred yards from here. That's where we'll find a place where we can hit Lewis and Ernie with a sniper rifle."

"It's way too far, Fiorello," Capirchio said. "You can't count on hitting anything on this hill from there."

"I know of a place to get a very special sniper rifle that should do it," Innocenti said. "I'm going there today."

They left the water tank site and drove down the narrow road, partially dirt and partially paved, that meandered up and down the hill. Searching out the best place for a sniper hit, they headed west on the a road at the bottom until they came to the slightly lower hill to the west that they'd seen from the top of the water tank hill.

They hiked up the steep hill for fifteen minutes, working their way with difficulty through huge rocks, small caverns, and giant bushes that covered the harsh, dry landscape.

When they reached the pinnacle, Innocenti stopped to get his breath. He pointed over to the east. "I will hide just below here under one or two of these bushes and take the shots. There will be police. We'll have to make a rapid getaway. Once I get my targets, I'll race down the hill to the road as fast as I can to meet you. You'll wait at the bottom in a vehicle to get me out of here."

From of his pocket, Innocenti took an electronic range finder, the kind that hunters used, and focused it on the water tank. "It's just a hair over five hundred yards to the tank, and the landing spot is a bit closer, so I'll call it five hundred even."

"Can you hit them from this distance?" Capirchio wondered.

"I think I can with that special rifle I'm going to go get."

"And, even if you do, won't the police give chase and make getting away tough?" Capirchio asked.

"I'll camouflage myself so they cannot see where the shots came from and then race down the hill as fast as I can. I want you to steal a van the day before, as we'll abandon it when we're through. Put some other stolen tags on it in case cops are looking for the stolen van. We'll put my motorcycle in the back. After I take the shots and get down the hill to you, we will take the van into Escondido a few miles away, park it somewhere and then get the motorcycle out and leave on it. If anyone sees the van, they won't expect the motorcycle. We'll take the motorcycle in the van to Palomar airport, fifteen miles west, where the jet will be waiting. I'll leave in the jet, and you ride the motorcycle on up to LA. No one will suspect a jet is involved, and no one will know about the motorcycle. Got it?"

"Okay, sounds good."

"Now, I want you to take me to the Palomar airport where the jet is waiting to take me to Arizona. I'm going over to meet up with a special gunsmith."

The Palomar airport was off to the west, near the ocean, and it had regular private jet traffic there, with rich people who had houses in Orange and San Diego Counties who owned jets and used the airport and its hanger. After making their way down the hill, Innocenti and Capirchio got into the van and left for the airport. Just as they were leaving, a black FBI helicopter came over the horizon from the north.

⦿⦿⦿

After a flight of an hour and a half from the FBI building, Chuck took the controls back from Ernie, and made a good landing on the flat spot near the water tank. It was much too risky of a spot for a him to allow a student to attempt any landing, because if the helicopter were to go just a bit one way or the other, as happens with students, it's rotor blades would either smack the water tank or hit a rock, and could tumble off the side of the hill.

The three men exited the helicopter and walked about to get the lay of the land, studying the hill.

"There will be officers at the bottom of the road to check everyone coming up," Doty told Ernie. "Cars arriving will be directed to park alongside the lower road, and then the people will have to walk to the bottom of the hill where the state police will have a checkpoint. There will be minivans to take people up and down the hill. There's no place to put cars up here, so it would be foolhardy for an assassin to come up the hill and shoot anyone, as he would never get away. That undeveloped area over to the west," he said, pointing, "is the only place that could hide a sniper, but it's really far from here."

With that, they took off and flew around the area. There were open rolling hills, caverns, huge rocks, and large bushes off to the west. There was another hilltop some distance away, lower than the water tank hill, where there were places to hide.

"It seems unlikely that an assassin would hide in that area as the distance is too far to make a sniper shot," Doty said to Ernie over the headset.

He was wrong.

✃✃✃

The shiny Citation jet belonging to the Equator in Las Vegas landed in the gun lover's paradise of Tucson. It pulled up to the temporary parking ramp and its engine shut down. The pilots were to stay in the terminal after refueling the jet, waiting for a call to announce the return trip.

A healthy looking outdoorsman came up to plane when its engines shut down and its door opened with steps in the door. He approached and asked, "Mr. Innocenti?

"Yes."

"Alec Katsenes. My pleasure."

Katsenes's store had closed a little early that day when he left to fetch his guest at the airport. He had only one employee, a retired man who worked part time. But in the interest of security, as Katsenes had been forewarned that no one was to know of Innocenti's visit, he had given his helper the afternoon off.

They pulled up to the rear of the gun store in Katsenes's four-wheeler. Katsenes was known for having not only an excellent selection of rifles for varmint and deer hunters, but also an impressive array of assault weapons. He was a master gunsmith.

In the back of the shop, Innocenti looked about with great curiosity at the benches full of gun vices with cork in the vice grips, gunsmithing equipment, lathes, drill presses, tool boxes, and endless drawers and shelves of gun parts. A number of guns that were having something done to them were lying about in various stages of modification.

"Wow! This is some shop," Innocenti said, genuinely impressed. "As I told you by phone, I need a very long range rifle."

"How long range?"

"Five hundred yards.

"I can put together a .50 caliber that can do that with a good shooter."

"That's why I'm here. What have you got?" he asked, not wanting to reveal any more details of the hit.

"Well, I think I just may be able to fix you up. But five hundred yards is a very difficult shot," Katsenes said diplomatically, trying to find out what sort of shooter Innocenti was without insulting him.

"I've used hunting rifles, if that's what you're asking. I understand the principles."

"For an accurate and dependable shot at five hundred yards, you'll need the best of the best. I have just the thing." Katsenes went to a gun rack on the wall to the side of one of the work benches and picked up a completely black rifle with a thick, dull barrel, and a flat black fiberglass stock. Any beauty in this weapon was not to be found in its finish. He handed Innocenti the heavy rifle.

Innocenti took it and scrutinized it. "Tell me about it."

"This is a .50 BMG rifle."

"Doesn't BMG mean Browning Machine Gun?"

"Yes. But this's not a machine gun. It's made with extreme precision and shoots very accurately at long range. This one has a twenty-eight-inch barrel, with a one-in-fifteen twist. The gun is fifty inches long, and the action is set in a very good synthetic stock. And it does not use crude wartime ammo."

"Would it take a lot of practice to hit something at five yards?" Innocenti asked.

"That's more or less at the end of the range of the ammo before you get into something difficult. At five hundred yards, with the ammo I have, the drop is only three feet on this beauty. After that, the drop increases a great deal, and you have to take into consideration the atmospheric pressure, the altitude, the temperature, the humidity, and especially the wind if you want to have a good chance of hitting your target. Wind is a factor at five hundred yards, but it gets to be a much bigger factor after that. Now, I have two models in this one. One is a bolt action. The one you have in your hands is a semi-automatic and holds ten rounds. It costs more. The semi-auto has the big scope on it, which has been bore sighted. Which one do you prefer?"

"Well, the semi-auto sounds like a better one for me," Innocenti said, pretending to be a well-off gun nut so as not to alert the man that it was to be used on people. There were a number of gun collectors who had .50 caliber guns, mostly for bragging rights, as there was no earthly practical use for them. He hefted it in his arms. "Man, this sucker is heavy. What does it weigh?"

"Thirty-five pounds without the scope, with it, two more. Ten shells add another three pounds."

"If it was any heavier, I'd have to put wheels on it and tow it out to shoot like a civil war cannon!" Innocenti joked.

"You wouldn't want to shoot it if it was light like a hunting rifle. It would injure you. But it's not like you have to take the gun to the location on wheels like heavy artillery. The scope and the bipod detach and can be carried in a bag along with the ammo. These are the shells." Katsenes handed Innocenti a box of ten.

They were a name brand, made in the Midwest, and had long, spire-pointed bullets of 750 grains.

Innocenti moved the box of ammo up and down to estimate the weight, which was three pounds just for the shells. "These babies are heavy."

"These are super accurate. They are 750 grain bullets. Note the special shape of the bullets. Extremely aerodynamic." Katsenes picked up a small chart and read off the numbers. "These leave the muzzle at two thousand eight hundred twenty feet per second. The muzzle energy is thirteen thousand two hundred forty-one foot pounds. But get this. At five hundred yards, the velocity is still two thousand three hundred seventy-nine feet per second and the energy nine thousand four hundred three foot pounds. At five hundred yards, the drop only thirty six and eight tenths inches from a twenty-four-inch barrel. This one has a twenty-eight-inch barrel and will have about two hundred feet per second more than with the twenty-four-inch, and a few inches less drop."

"Jesus!" was all Innocenti could muster, being familiar with ammo. Most of his shooting of people had been with pistols. But even rifles he had owned were not in the same ballpark as this one. Content it would do the job, he addressed an important point of vital concern. "Does this have to be registered? I hate gun control." He'd never hinted, as far he could tell, that the gun for people and not for targets.

Katsenes was very familiar with gun lovers who would pay more just to get an unregistered gun, and there were many rich people who would do that. "That would make it illegal." He couldn't be sure this guy wasn't a fed, but the referral seemed to be reliable. All gun lovers would buy a gun unregistered if they could do so legally. He sidestepped the question and wanted to talk more to make him feel comfortable enough to consider selling it illegally. "As for use of the .50, there are quite a lot of owners out there who buy .50s for long range shooting. It's just for sport and bragging rights, as there hasn't been game on the planet that needs this big of a gun since the dinosaurs died off. As for the weapon itself, both of these guns here were put together by me from parts and do not have serial numbers or registrations. But that adds to the risk, big time."

And that translated to *price*. Innocenti was silent, holding up the most unusual rifle, contemplating the shots he wanted to take at the water company event. He engaged in gun talk to make Katsenes more comfortable. "We used to make hand loads for rifles a long time ago," he said finally. "We used once-fired brass, put in extremely accurate amounts of powder, and placed the bullets in the brass with exact measurement with a press. Would hand loaded ammo for this gun be more accurate than factory loads?"

"Nope, that's no longer necessary these days. There are factory bullets as good as what you can load yourself. Of course, they cost more, about ten bucks each. If you want a lot, the cost is less. But then, how many times can anyone shoot one of these monsters? If you shoot it too many times, you will develop a flinch when using it, out of fear of the recoil, and lose your accuracy. Hell, after a while, you might flinch just seeing it!"

That brought a big laugh from Innocenti.

"Why don't we go try them?" Katsenes offered, wanting to close the deal.

కుసిసి

The gun range was deserted and blocked off by a heavy, single-bar steel gate painted red and holding a sign.

PRIVATE GUN CLUB
KEEP OUT

Katsenes, a member, opened the lock with his key and swung the gate open. A number of sun-bleached, green paint-ed shooting benches were set up in a row and there were tar-gets marked down range at intervals. The benches had a wooden roof over them for shade.

Katsenes drove his truck down range to the five hundred yard site, and set up a target on the posts in the ground. The target was six feet square in white, and the bulls-eye one foot round in shape and red.

The two of them set up the semi-automatic .50 on a bench and, on the bench next to it, a spotting scope. Katsenes brought a small, deerskin-covered sandbag for the rear of the stock, and a bipod for the barrel, adjustable up and down. He had an anemometer to measure the wind but, except for an occasional desert gust, the wind was calm.

He set up the semi-auto rifle for his customer, sighting in the four-to-twenty-four power scope and loading the weapon. He'd brought the bolt action along as well, in case Innocenti wanted to try that one, but it did not have a scope on it yet. Katsenes filled the clip of the semi-automatic with ten rounds. "I have set it up for five hundred yards, so it should be really close." He handed his guest ear protectors. "You need these for this thing. After a few rounds, the recoil and the blast will probably make you a little dingy."

He could not say to Katsenes that this would be Innocenti's only practice shooting before the hit of two people. Most buyers would take the gun to their favorite range, and shoot there. But Innocenti had no time for that and had to sight it in carefully that day. With the barrel in the bipod, it was easy to place the cross-hairs of the scope on the bulls-eye at twenty-four-power and not move it, which would have been impossible if it wasn't resting in the bipod.

He controlled his breathing, like a seasoned sniper, and became calm. He ever so gently put his finger on the trigger, and squeezed it.

BOOM! The gun went off and the supersonic bullet found its target.

Katsenes looked through the spotting scope, turned, and smiled at Innocenti. The hole was only twelve inches below the one-foot round bulls-eye and six inches to the right. "You really know what you're doing, don't you," he complimented.

"My God!" Innocenti exclaimed as he looked through the scope and found the hole in the target, amazed at his own accuracy. "That was at five hundred yards. I can't believe it!"

Katsenes moved in beside the rifle and twisted the adjustments on the scope to raise the trajectory adjustment up and to the left. "Try another."

The semi-automatic had already chambered a round. Innocenti fired again. This time he was six inches below the bulls-eye, and directly centered underneath it.

Both of them looked through the spotting scope and found the hole.

"This is amazing! Let me see if I'm consistent." Innocenti was exuberant with his newly discovered ability at such an extreme range.

After another tiny adjustment made by Katsenes, the next shot by Innocent would have been in the lower half of the bulls-eye, but it was just outside to the left, six inches.

They both looked again. "Talk to me," Innocenti asked. "I'm six inches to the left. Is it the gun or me?"

"Mostly likely a small gust of wind." Katsenes held up his anemometer which showed the wind speed which he locked in at the time of the shot. It showed the wind at that moment. "Five miles per hour from the right where we are. I think that it may be the same at the target, in which case, a gust blew you off." He adjusted the scope to shoot just a little up, but kept the horizontal adjustment alone.

"I'll try again. What's the windage correction?"

Katsenes looked at the anemometer. "The wind is calm now. Try again."

Innocenti let off another round. Katsenes looked into the spotting scope. The shot was almost dead center. He smiled at his client. "You're dead nuts on!"

"Wow, I could do this all day long," Innocenti said. He realized he was nearly shouting because he still had his ear protectors on and peeled them off to talk normally.

Katsenes grinned. "Well, most shooters will get a little dingy after a few rounds of these powerful loads and begin to work up a counter reaction in the body to the recoil in advance of pulling the trigger which causes them to go off target slightly. You have not done that yet. But you might want to stop for now, as you may find yourself anticipating the recoil due to shoulder pain and pushing forward on the gun in an involuntary action when you torch off a round. But it looks like you don't need that much practice."

Innocenti got up, walked around a bit, and then sat back behind the weapon, and prepared for another shot, as he would not have any further chance to practice or dial in the big scope. "I'll try two or three more rounds before we go in, so I can see how that anemometer works and sight it in, as long as I am here at this long distance range."

♥ↄ♥ↄ

Later at the shop, Innocenti's shoulder hurting, he placed his hand on the weapon and patted it like it was a pet. "This is an amazing piece. How much for it, the anemometer, the bipod, the scope, and three boxes of shells, unregistered?"

Katsenes had to make a decision as to whether or not to go unregistered. "Registered, twelve thousand five hundred dollars. Unregistered, twenty thousand," he decided. "Remember, that it's for the effort of bringing in parts for a complete weapon, and making sure that they are accounted for in some fashion—a lot of trouble—and it includes the risk factor. The parts themselves are expensive, and that is the finest scope." He said it a little sheepishly, wanting to leave the door open for negotiations if twenty thousand was too much.

"I'll take it unregistered." Innocenti then became very serious, and made his expression a little frightening. "I want absolutely no record of the sale, and naturally you will tell no one—and I mean no one. You understand that, don't you?"

There was something very authoritative in Innocenti's words. "Yes, sir. You have the utmost in discretion with me. No one, but no one, will ever know of the transaction. You may count on me if there are any inquires since I am also subject to federal and state prosecution for not registering the transaction. I would lose everything if I talked."

"You got that right!" Innocenti said in a very scary tone.

Katsenes cleaned the bore of the beastly weapon and oiled the gun. He added a strap, and then put it in a canvas carrying case, to which he added a cleaning rod and patches, a bottle of cleaning fluid and one of oil, the bipod, a sandbag, his anemometer, and three boxes of shells with their ballistics chart. The bag was over fifty pounds with everything inside.

Innocenti laid out the cash, and Katsenes decided he would treat his wife to a steak dinner that night.

CHAPTER 53

Doty sat at a table in the lounge, sipping coffee. It was Thursday morning at the FBI headquarters and he was nervous. Ernie was there, having come in early from Lewis's guest house, not very far from the FBI building in LA. Kanno walked in for coffee.

"Hi, Bill, any progress?" Doty asked.

"I got hold of that IRS auditor, the Russian immigrant Dmitriy Bobrova, who was at the Equator in Las Vegas, and he told me that the place is now run by a management group. One of the group worked in management for Mr. Gunther when he was still alive. Mr. Gunther was in charge of managing the place, but when he died, this person formed a group to manage the place for the widow."

"Names?"

"The auditor could not remember, but recalls that the group all had Italian names. He was dealing with a CPA hired to interface with him and their in-house accountants and heard the names spoken at times when he was there."

"So can't you check with the gaming commission in Nevada as to who are on the license of the Equator?"

"I did. The licensee is the corporation, and the qualifying individual used to be the widow's husband, but now it is the widow Gunther herself. When he died, they allowed the qualifying person on the license to be her as she had no criminal background. The management group is not responsible to the State of Nevada on the license and are treated just like hired employees of the corporation. I did ask the gaming commission if it would allow a group with criminal records to run a casino, directly or indirectly, and I was told most likely not, as the concept of a silent partner who is a criminal is something that they check on when a license is issued, or upon any investigation. But I have been assuming that the management group consists of people with criminal records. I called the hotel and asked who the managers were, but when I did that, they just put me through to the office, and then they wanted to know my business and phone number, and said someone would call me back. If I call and say that I'm FBI, we tip our hand to the fact that we are on to them, and all the effort in setting up Ernie as a decoy may be wasted. I might just zip up there today and ask around."

"Why don't you?" Doty said. "Just ask the desk clerk or others in lower management. No doubt you can get the names. Get some desert vacation clothes—forget the gray-suit look."

"Okay. I can go on up yet today and return this evening."

"While you're here, I want to discuss the water district event tomorrow with you," Doty said. "How do you think I should cover it? I don't know if whoever it is might come or not, or if the candidate is also included in the hit. I think the best move is to be safe and have a few agents there. There will be state police."

"But if you have visible agents or police, you can't flush the assassins out, can you?" Kanno asked.

"That's true. It would be ideal if we could be invisible, but with sufficient manpower to observe anything when it starts to happen—just enough to stop it, of course. How's that for an impossible task?" Doty scratched his head, wondering how to do that and still provide protection. "Maybe I should just flood the place with agents and police and not take any chances. I really don't know what to do. There are other speaking events coming up soon, and those have to be watched as well. But we have it leaked that someone is about to give testimony to the grand jury, so I feel there's a chance that this could flush out whoever it is."

"How long is the ceremony going to take?" Kanno asked, looking at Ernie.

"The part with Lewis is only going to take about thirty minutes," Ernie replied. "It begins at 10:30 in the morning, and then the officials are going to some lunch afterward at some fancy place. Lewis will not be going to the lunch. The water district has donated a bunch to his campaign, so he is repaying them by going to the inauguration of the company's expansion project. He'll go there with me in a helicopter, shake hands, stand with the officials to be photographed, cut a big ribbon, and give a small talk for a few minutes. He'll probably speak on some support for the water company's interests and then leave. I'm going along with him, hoping to flush out who you are looking for."

Doty stopped sipping coffee and turned to Kanno. "I've been looking at a map of the area. This is on the top of a small mountain, or a huge hill, however you wish to classify the area. It's unlikely that someone might try to get into the event itself and make a hit, since the water district and the state police will set up a table at the only road going up the hill, and check each person trying to enter. We want to check any bags for a possible bomb. And it is a long steep road up the hill, so it would be impossible for anyone to get away coming back down the road if he tried a hit up at the top at the event itself. But there is a surrounding, rolling hillside to the west that is undeveloped. A person might try to shoot down the helicopter, but that's extreme and there's no guarantee of successfully doing that with ordinary weapons, unless it's a lucky shot or the pilot is hit. Anyone have any thoughts?"

Kanno and Ernie said nothing.

"I'll get some extra agents there for the event," Doty said. "So I'd better get busy as I have a lot to do before tomorrow."

"I'll be back from Las Vegas tonight," Kanno said. "I'll call you at home if I find out anything."

❦❦❦

"I'll take this one," Kanno said to the sales clerk at the small clothing store in the Las Vegas airport terminal. It was a ridiculous look for Kanno—a Hawaiian styled shirt worn outside the pants, done in green and red flowers on a cream-colored background. Doty had told him not to go in a suit, but

Kanno didn't have time to go home or shopping if he wanted to get to the Equator while the day shift was still on duty, and he feared the night shift might not know the names of the management group. He went into the airport men's room, took off his suit coat, tie, and white shirt, and put them in the shopping bag. He then put them in a rental locker and went for a taxi in his Hawaiian shirt, trying to look like a tourist. Kanno thought he probably looked ridiculous. Then again, some tourists looked the same.

Outside the passenger pickup area, there was the usual Las Vegas bustle of cars, limousines, and shuttles picking up and dropping off people by the droves. As Kanno looked for a taxi, a black limo pulled up near him with a single passenger in it—a woman in a beige outfit. The limo had the name *Equator* and its logo on the door. The chauffeur opened her door, let her out, and went to the trunk for her bags. After he passed her bags to a baggage handler, he started to go back to the driver's seat.

Kanno realized that this might be an opportunity and approached the driver before he got away. "How much is a ride to the Equator?"

"Are you a guest of the hotel?"

Kanno knew this was the query for high rollers. Those special guests had all services provided complimentary—not salaried FBI agents who had to justify expenses. "No, I'm not," he said, knowing the driver would just radio the hotel and check. "But I'm going there and will be glad to pay your fare for a ride there, if it is not too much. I have no bags."

"It's normally fifty-five to eighty-five dollars, depending on the time. But since I'm going there, anyway, I'll make it thirty-five for you if you have cash." The driver could see the man was on a budget—but an empty trip back to the hotel was pointless, and, if the guy paid in cash, he might just keep it since no one at the hotel would know he was not on a hired ride.

"Deal," Kanno said and got in.

En route to the hotel, Kanno moved up near the glass partition window so he could talk to the driver, in case he could get anything from him. "I bet you get to drive for all sorts of rich and famous."

"You bet I do. There are a lot of rich people and movie stars who come here."

"I haven't been to the Equator, but I saw a brochure. Who owns such a beautiful place?"

Luckily for Kanno, the driver was a talkative sort and proud to share his knowledge. "That's the widow Gunther. She's worth a bundle."

"Do you get to drive for her?" Kanno asked, playing on the man's ego.

"No. I started just after Mr. Gunther died three years ago, and she doesn't come to the hotel much anymore now that he's gone. She has a house in the ritzy area, and sometimes goes there, but she has her own limo and driver. It's a white Rolls. But I drive the bosses around fairly often. Sometimes one of them goes to a party, or maybe the wife wants to go shopping or something. I go to the airport quite a lot for them. The Equator has its own jet. I often take one or more of them to the jet or pick them up."

Holding his breath, Kanno popped the question. "Who are the bosses?"

"That is Mr. Indelicato, Mr. Innocenti, Mr. Bastini, and Mr. Manelli," he said, having memorized their names with the "Mister" as that was how he always addressed them whenever he drove for them.

Manelli! Kanno wanted to pump his fist in the air, as he'd won a victory, but didn't. "Gee, you know a lot about what's going on in Las Vegas," he said, keeping up the ego trip. "What interesting names. They all sound Italian. Are their first names just as interesting?"

"Mr. Bastini's name is Fabrizio, Mr. Manelli is called Sal. And Mr. Indelicato is called Gaspare. Mr. Innocenti, he's got an unusual name, Fiorello."

Kanno gave another inner cheer. *Wasn't that the name Ernie said that dead guy, Vinnie, called the other man? I think it was. Now we're getting somewhere.* "Is Sal short for Salvatore?"

"I dunno. Maybe."

"Are they a good bunch to work for?" Kanno said, thinking it was time to ask the sort of normal tourist-type questions, and, while doing so, he wrote the names down in his notebook, careful to keep both the notebook and his hands below the partition window.

"Oh, yes. If I go out with one of them for the evening, or take one of the wives shopping, I always get a nice tip. Usually a hundred."

The limo pulled up to the sheltered entrance of the majestic Equator. A man in a green outfit with white stripes on the legs and a matching hat, opened the door for Kanno.

"Well, I feel lucky today. Here you go," Kanno said, handing the talkative driver a fifty. "Keep the change." He wanted to act the part of the typical gambler, and they always tipped well—unless they had just lost everything.

Even though I have the names, he thought, *I shouldn't just get back in a taxi or the talkative driver might see me, suspect something, and report it. I'm here, so I might as well go in and look around. Maybe some additional information can be gained.*

Inside, behind the concierge desk, a young lady sat on a high chair, talking on the phone. and a young man stood at relaxed attention, apparently ready to assist. Both clerks wore hotel uniforms. To confirm the information he'd gotten from the limo driver, he headed for the young man. "I'm looking for the offices of Mr. Salvatore Manelli, Gaspare Indelicato, Fabrizio Bastini, and Fiorello Innocenti," he said, reading off the paper he'd written the names on in the limo. "They're the managers, I believe?"

"Yes, sir. Would you like me to take you there?"

Kanno was sure the concierge recognized the names, so they had to be correct—or at least substantially so. "Oh, no thanks, just point the way."

The young man stepped out, led Kanno a few feet to the opening of the casino, and pointed to the far end. "Go to the back through there, sir. It's off to the left once you get to the end."

"Thank you," Kanno said and began walking in that direction.

When he got to a hallway at the end of the casino, there was an armed guard in uniform sitting on a chair in front of a small, high desk, guarding the entrance to the corridor. There were no names painted anywhere. Above the guard was a small TV monitor.

Kanno grimaced. *Better stop the inquiry here, or I'll get noticed.*

"Can I help you sir?" the guard asked.

"Restroom?"

"Over that way sir," the guard said and pointed.

Enough, Kanno decided.

The driver had given him the names and the concierge had confirmed them. Kanno had enough to work on. Time to head back. Especially as he didn't think anyone had caught on to the fact that he was investigating these four men. Yet. Striding toward the exit door, he passed the slot machines and paused. No. He had to leave and head back to LA. As he started for the door again, he heard coins pouring out of a nearby machine as someone won a minor jackpot. He put his hands in his pockets, jiggling his change. Oh, hell, surely he could stop just long enough to put a couple of dollars in.

෴

Kanno sat in front of the FBI computer terminal at the Los Angeles office later that night. *Salvatore Manelli. The same surname as Maria Manelli. Is that the connection? Maybe they're related or is it just a coincidence? A look into NCIC records for criminal records will be the first thing to do. Italian names. Hmmm. Maybe this is a bunch of mobsters.* He accessed NCIC and typed in the name Salvatore Manelli. No one with that name came up with any felony record. Next he typed in Gaspare Indelicato. Three Indelicato names came up, but none with a first name starting with G. None of those were living in Nevada, and one was in prison. Next he tried Fiorello Innocenti. No hits. Last he tried Fabrizio Bastini. Several Bastini names had a criminal record, but none living in Nevada, and no one with the given name Fabrizio. One Pietro Bastini had a conviction for murder, but his conviction was fifty years old. *He must be dead.*

He shifted databases, accessing the Nevada DMV, checked the four names, and found all four. Each had a Nevada driver's license. Bastini's license showed nothing remarkable, but Kanno was able to get the number, and so he plugged that into the information for the NCIC criminal records search and went back to the NCIC database. Nothing. His license was changed to Nevada three years ago from Connecticut. Kanno then looked at Manelli's driver's license, and it showed that it was transferred from a Connecticut license nine years earlier. Looking at Indelicato, Kanno saw that his was also transferred from Connecticut, only three years ago. The same for Innocenti. Putting it together, Kanno figured that the owner Gunther probably had Manelli employed in a some sort of manager's capacity and, when her husband died, Mrs. Gunther kept Manelli on and gave him more control and the power to hire whoever he wanted. He then brought in friends he knew from his home state of Connecticut, that being Innocenti, Indelicato, and Bastini. Most likely, those same Italians grew up together or go way back.

No criminal records? Can these people be associated with the mob if they have no criminal records? But would Mr. Gunther, or his widow, ever hire a bunch of people with criminal records? No way. And, while they're not on the gaming license for the Equator, no doubt the licensing bureau of Nevada would not like it if felons were managing a gambling casino for a widow. No, either this whole thing is a bum steer, or else this is a new kind of mob, one comprised of men with clean records.

Kanno sat in front of the screen, thinking. NCIC only showed rap sheets. Sometimes NCIC didn't have the records, and the state itself was worth checking. Also, in an extensive background check, as an application to become an FBI agent, or for a security clearance for the military, the agency checked the state records of the state where the person came from to see if there were arrest records that didn't come to a conviction, or sometimes minor crimes, such as misdemeanors.

He accessed the directory of phone numbers in Connecticut. The government offices would all be closed at this hour, so he looked for police departments—they were open twenty-four hours and had computer access to criminal records in the state. Police departments would be listed by the city, and he couldn't think of any city in Connecticut, having never been there. *Connecticut Highway Patrol.*

"Highway Patrol," the dispatcher answered.

"This is Special Agent Bill Kanno, FBI. Let me speak to the watch commander."

"One moment, sir."

"Watch Commander Clark speaking." It was a woman.

"This is Special Agent Bill Kanno, FBI, Los Angeles office. He gave his ID number, case number, and phone number. "I want to do an extended search into any criminal records for four people from Connecticut. They have no records on NCIC. I would like to have the information as soon as possible."

"Sir, that sort of search requires a hands-on search of files, unless you only want if for the last twelve years, since only those are in the computer and are on NCIC. Other records are in archives, and someone has to go through actual files for you. That location is only open from 8:30 a.m. to 5:30 p.m., Monday through Friday, local time. It is now nearly midnight here, 23:45 hours, and no one can do it for you until morning. I can give you the number of where to call in the morning."

"Thanks." He would have to come back to the office early in the morning. There was a three hours difference between Connecticut and California. He could come back in at 5:30 a.m. tomorrow, California time, which would be 8:30 a.m. in Connecticut.

Next, Kanno called Nevada police. "Please check to see if you have a Nevada driver's license for a Maria Manelli."

"Yes, I have a Maria Manelli with a current driver's license," the female officer said.

"Check the address of her license with the current address of Salvatore Manelli."

"Yes, they are the same."

"The FBI and I really appreciate your cooperation," Kanno complimented her.

He thought he better alert Doty to what he had, and called him at home. "Dan, this is Bill."

"Hi. What've you got?"

"I have some information on the Equator," Kanno informed him. "The then owner, Mr. Gunther, died three years ago. His widow now owns the place, but is not active in management and seldom goes there. She's probably worth a bundle. The management is done by a group of four men, Fabrizio Bastini, Gaspare Indelicato, Salvatore Manelli, and Fiorello Innocenti. Manelli has been in Nevada nine years, and the other three only three years. They are all from Waterbury, Connecticut. I haven't got confirmation of details yet, but I'm pretty sure that Manelli was working at the hotel for some time before in management, and when the owner, who used to manage things himself, died, Manelli was given control by the widow. As the hotel and casino are a handful to manage for just one, he brought in his friends from Connecticut and formed a management group. Salvatore Manelli has to be the father of Maria Manelli as they had the same address in Nevada until three years ago when Maria moved to California, no doubt to go to college. But I checked for criminal records on the four, and none have any record in NCIC."

"Well, maybe they're not involved," Doty said. "Maybe Maria is just a political activist like so many at UCLA, and just wanted to get involved in government by joining Lewis's campaign."

Kanno shrugged. "Could be. I've requested an extended background search on all four of them in Connecticut, including any misdemeanors and arrests that did not result in a conviction, whatever is available. The Connecticut records are in their archives, and no staff is there until 8:30 a.m. East Coast time tomorrow when I can get a hands-on search. It will probably take a few hours after that before I get anything. It is unlikely that I will get anything from Connecticut before Lewis and Ernie go down to San Diego tomorrow to the event. I'm coming in at 5:30 a.m. tomorrow morning to call back to Connecticut and get things rolling. I assume you're leaving early by car in the morning to San Diego?"

"Yep," Doty confirmed. "I also asked the state police who provide security for the governor at political events to be there."

"Okay," Kanno said. "I'll be here in the morning and call you as soon as I hear anything that might be a lead."

CHAPTER 54

A t 4:30 a.m. the next morning while the sky was still dark, long before any FBI, police, media people, or representatives of the water district came to the location, a white van—freshly stolen by Capirchio the night before, with stolen Nevada plates not readily traceable by California cops—drove along the bottom road below the hill where the water district event would be taking place later that morning. In the back of the van was Innocenti's motorcycle, a Japanese crotch rocket.

Innocenti unfolded the multi-colored brownish camouflage net, specifically selected for the surroundings. He took out his new prize, the .50. The weapon had a strap attached to carry it down the hill. He loaded ten bullets into the gun, a full load, and there was certainly no need to take extra ammo. If he couldn't do it in ten shots, he couldn't do it all. Given the kick of that .50 canon, he could probably only get off five or so anyway. But he was confident that he wouldn't need more than two shots for the two kills.

In his bag was a folded blanket of netting in the same multi-colored camouflage pattern as his outfit, the sandbag for the rear of the gun, the bipod, and the anemometer for the wind direction. He added two bottles of water.

"My cellular phone is not getting any signal in this valley here, so I might as well leave it," he said to Capirchio. "You take off, and come back here at 10:00. They are supposed to arrive at 10:30, but if they come early, I don't want to miss a shot and I want you here when I come down the hill. If you're stopped, just say that you're looking at the area with an eye toward buying a building lot. If they ask you for you ID, you show them the phony driver's license from out of state, as they can't punch that into the regular computer terminal in a police car. After I take the shots, I'll hustle down the hill, keeping low and between the brush and rocks. You park here and we'll get over to the airport. I'll get away in the jet, and you take the bike away, leisurely.

"I understand," Capirchio promised his boss.

Innocenti lifted up the rifle and put the sling over his shoulder. On the other shoulder, he put the strap of the sandbag. He threw the camouflage blanket over the rifle and his shoulder, just in case anyone was around, and started up the hill as the sky began to lighten in a pink color toward the east.

Fifteen minutes later, he made it to the spot that he had selected. He put his things down and sat on a rock nearby to catch his breath after the arduous hike up the steep hill that towered above the road below. Innocenti watched the sky turn to light blue as he rested and decided that he'd better set up his hiding spot. Opening up the camouflage net blanket and comparing it to the color of the ground and wild brush, he felt he had chosen the style of camouflage wisely. It looked just like some natural brush and dirt on the hill. The spot he selected was between two large wild bushes, each around eight feet high. They grew into each other in the top half as the trunks were only three feet apart, making a perfect spot for him to lay down in between them. The hillside, as well as that of the next one over where the water tank was located, had many tan-colored rocks, ranging from several feet to some huge ones ten feet in diameter. Rocks in front of the bushes provided cover, and there was an opening between two of the rocks that was perfect for his five hundred yard shots.

He laid the net blanket down on the ground as there was plenty of it to go around him and the padding would help keep him from getting uncomfortable. The sandbag was set up as a pillow for the time being. He laid his sniper rifle beside him on the netting, took out the water bottle, and set it down nearby so as not to be shuffling about when the authorities might be looking for movement later on. Then he pulled the camouflage netting over him like a blanket.

The event was six hours away, so a nice rest seemed in order, maybe even a short nap. He rolled over on his back, laid his head on the sandbag pillow that would hold the barrel on his gun soon, and looked up at the sky through the camouflage netting at the occasional early morning birds flying over.

❧❧❧

"Archives," the female clerk answered with a yawn.

"This is Special Agent Bill Kanno, FBI, Los Angeles office." He gave her his ID, case number, and the main line phone number, so whoever called back could check number before releasing any information.

"Say, it must be pretty early out there," the clerk said in a friendly tone.

"It's 5:35 a.m. here in Los Angeles. But the early bird gets the worm. I'm looking for extended criminal activity of any kind on the names Salvatore Manelli, Gaspare Indelicato, Fabrizio Bastini, and Fiorello Innocenti. All four had Connecticut driver's licenses until they surrendered them for Nevada licenses—nine years ago for Manelli, and three for the others. How long will it take?"

"Well, we have a stack of requests. Are you in a hurry?"

"Yes, I'd appreciate it if you could do it right away."

"It'll still take several hours. They're arranged alphabetically, and by year. We have to go each year, and then to the right section in boxes, and look for the each name in that section. How far back did you want to go?"

"Since each became an adult."

"All right. I'll put it at the top of the stack of requests, and put someone on it. I'll call you back when I have it."

"I can't thank you enough. Lives may depend on it."

CHAPTER 55

At 7:00 a.m., Doty arrived, with six additional agents, at the base of the hill where the water district had its new water tank, and where the event would be taking place at 10:30 a.m. Uniformed state officers began to arrive.

The road up the hill had been put in a long time ago in the 1960s when there were no county standards for steepness or width of roads. The winding road led up the hill past three potential building lots. At the top was the new water tank on a lot which the owner had sold to the water district.

The road was only fourteen feet wide at some spots, and very steep in other spots as it meandered up the hill. At one place there was a fairly steep drop off to the side, going down fifty feet into an adjacent canyon. There were no guard rails.

At 7:45 a.m., a water company utility van pulled up. Two young men and three young ladies who worked at the water district's office got out and met the officers. They got out a card table and chairs from the van and set them up as a checkpoint. Those who had an invitation were on a list provided by the water district, a request from Doty since Lewis and Ernie were to be under his protection.

Cars would not to be allowed to go up the narrow, steep road to the top, as there was very little space at the top. A number of people were coming from the water district's main office in several hired vans that would pick them up and take them to the event. Those vans would park at the bottom and the people then check in at the table and catch a ride in the smaller shuttle to the top.

A local news van with a cameraman and a reporter arrived. Another privately hired photographer also arrived, wearing a photographer's vest with lenses and equipment stuck in the special pockets—he was there to get Lewis in individual photos with several big shots from the water district.

A flatbed truck arrived with a lift gate, delivering four Johnny-On-The-Job portable toilets. Two were directed to be lowered a short distance away from the card table, and the other two taken to the top of the hill.

"Okay," Doty said, taking charge. "You officers gather around." He formed them into a semi-circle around him. "As you have been informed, we are here to try to protect Mr. Lewis and also his aide, Ernie, who will be accompanying him, from possible assassination. They're arriving in a helicopter from Los Angeles County, and landing on the flat part of the hill right next to the water tank. My men have radios already, and ear pieces with a mic that pins to the shirt collar. I have extra radios here for you, already set to our selected frequency," Doty said as he passed them out from a box.

"Now I want to thank each of you for volunteering, as this is a potentially dangerous assignment. Mr. Lewis and his aide Ernie are potential targets for an assassination. They'll be arriving in a helicopter and landing very nearby to the big water tank. When they arrive, gather around them and pretend to be friendly, as though greeting them. I want a number of you stay with Mr. Lewis and Ernie always as they go to the water tank to cut the ribbon and make a speech, even if you get in some of the photographs, as I don't want them left exposed. Then follow them back to the helicopter and see them off. During the ceremony, if you see anyone on any of the surrounding hillsides, report that to me immediately and we'll hustle right over there. Lewis should not be here for more than thirty minutes, and then he'll leave.

"If you see anyone with a gun out and pointing, do not hesitate to shoot. You can read them their Miranda warnings at their funeral. I somehow doubt that will occur, since the road leading down is so narrow that we can get them at the bottom with a road block. I think if there's going to be an attempt, it could be from a distance by a sniper with a long-range rifle. Once Lewis and Ernie leave, just stick around until the traffic

leaves, and then your job is over. If anyone sees anything suspicious, call me. My call sign is 'Command.' Any questions?"

No one spoke.

"Okay. Let's mix it up with the group when they get ready
to board the buses and ride with them so not to draw attention
to ourselves. Let's see if we're successful in drawing out our
suspect. I want you all to be very careful. If you get in a chase
with the suspect, consider him extremely dangerous."

CHAPTER 56

Save for a panoramic view of the surrounding lands near-ly a thousand feet below, the hill where the water tank was situated was singularly unimportant. But to the water company, known as a district, because of its quasi-governmental status and political nature, the inauguration of the new expansion plan and use of the huge new water tank represented the completion of a very expensive expansion plan that had been underway for several years and involved public hearings to charge more for water. So to the district, it was time for a celebration, and the water tank represented a good spot for the celebration, as much of the money for improvements went into underground pipelines and other improvements not visible like the salmon colored tank. Following the ribbon cutting, there was to be a banquet brunch at a fancy hotel paid for by the district.

Candidate Lewis would have his picture taken with the executives of the district at the site of the tank, and if elected, his picture shaking hands with the executives would be behind several desks in offices at the district office displaying the perceived influence of the water district executives.

The employees who brought the card table also brought some rebar pieces five feet long and a hand sledge hammer to pound them into the ground near the water tank to hold a long red ribbon six inches in width, the cutting of which would represent the opening of the access to the water tank and inauguration of the new equipment that the district had paid millions for. A hundred fifty were expected at the hill top event, and more at the hotel banquet, with some spouses joining later at the banquet. Two more cars of regular, uniformed police also arrived, requested by Doty, directed to stay mostly at the bottom of the hill and hopefully divert attention from the taller, plain clothes men who were going to surround the candidate and Ernie from the surrounding hillsides.

Doty rode up the hill with a group of water district personnel and got out trying to look like one of the group. But, he realized that someone has to look around the surrounding hillsides, and so took the risk of being discovered and used his small, image-stabilizing binoculars to look for anyone in those areas. There was no sign of life on the hill to the west or elsewhere.

Fiorello Innocenti lay five hundred yards to the west, and eighty feet lower in elevation, in between two large, brown bushes and under a camouflage net. He watched all the bustling and preparations for the ribbon cutting ceremony. He tested the wind with his new anemometer, and found it to be dead calm so far.

Lying there for so long, he pondered the shot. Given the fact that his targets might be moving, and there might be heat waves coming off the ground, his shots might be difficult. He would probably not have the opportunity to take a second shot at the same man, and so a chest or torso shot rather than a head shot would be the best. Even with bullet proof vests, the monster 750 grain .50 caliber bullets would go right through. At five hundred yards the chance of hitting the head were not the way to go. So the chest it would be. His new weapon was a semi-automatic, and he could get the two of them, hopefully, in just a few seconds and then high tail it out of there, taking everything if possible. He would work his way down the hill keeping low and behind the rocks and the dense brush, and get down to Capirchio in the van.

There was one open spot fifteen feet wide that he would have to cross lying down close to the ground to keep a low profile. After coming down from top of the hill, he would be out of sight of the target area in a minute or two as the terrain was such that it would block the line of sight to him, where he could run standing up right on down the rest of the hill to Capirchio for the get-a-way.

It had to be done quickly, and the get-a-way had to happen fast, before anyone could locate him. The place would be buzzing with police in no time, afterward.

CHAPTER 57

I'm your pilot today, Mr. Lewis. I fly exclusively for the FBI. I'm an FBI employee, but not trained as an agent." That meant he had no gun. "Ernie knows me as we flew together to the same spot a few days ago. Ernie flew us there and back after the takeoff and before the landing. He did a very good job."

Ernie smiled as he was very proud to be complimented for flying such a complicated machine, but he knew he was anything but qualified to fly a helicopter alone. Lewis and Ernie were at the rooftop heliport on top of the building where Chuck had brought the FBI helicopter to pick them up. The FBI was providing its helicopter and pilot as part of the protection afforded Lewis. Ernie did not ask to fly after the take off as he did not want to make Lewis uncomfortable with a novice at the controls.

"Sir, there's a chance that there could be an assassin waiting to try to kill either or both you and Ernie," Chuck reminded Lewis. "I know you told Doty that you refuse to wear a vest. I'm ordered to ask you again if you will please do so, for your own safety. I have one for you, sir. I have one on. Ernie, you have one on, don't you?"

"Sure do," Ernie said, tapping on his hardened chest with the vest underneath his wool jacket. "And I've been provided with a pistol," he added, opening his wool coat to reveal the neat shoulder holster Doty had given him.

"So, Mr. Lewis, how about it? Can I appeal to you to wear a vest this morning? It could mean your life."

"It really presents a problem for me. This is a photo session, and when I put one of those things on I look like I've gained thirty pounds. My advisors and image makers don't like that look. They say it makes me look like a bloated politician on the take. Of course, if I wear it on the outside I would look like an army commando in Syria. So I'll just take my chances, and of course rely on you boys to take care of me," Lewis said, flashing his charismatic smile.

"What a price for looking good," Chuck said with a sigh. "But I wish you wouldn't take such chances on my watch."

"I've been warned. All right, let's get it over with," Lewis said, stepping in the back of the shiny black helicopter.

Then he said something to make Ernie's day. "Ernie, I know you were excited about getting to take the controls when you checked out the area the other day, and that you enjoyed the chance to fly. Why don't you sit in the front with Chuck and take a lesson in flying? That'll give me more room to work on a speech that I have to give on TV this weekend. Okay?"

Ernie broke into a huge smile.

"If it's okay with the passenger, it is okay with me," Chuck said.

Ernie got into the pilot's seat on the right again. The controls were complete duplicates, right and left, and so it made no difference to safety as far as Chuck was concerned.

Lewis took his place in the roomy back. He opened up his briefcase and began setting up a makeshift table on one side of him to work on during the trip.

"Everyone buckled up?" Chuck looked at Lewis in the back seat.

Lewis complied with the request, moved to the center seat, put the seat belt on, and spread his paper notes on either side of him.

"Mr. Lewis, if you need to talk to me, just put on this headset," Chuck said, pointing to a headset hanging from a hook on the ceiling. "The mic will automatically engage when you speak."

Seeing Lewis and Ernie were both harnessed in properly, Chuck started the take-off procedures with the whine of the turbine. When the temperature was up to the minimum, he engaged the two thirty-three-foot-diameter rotor blades and the sleek black helicopter began to rock about slowly as the big rotors began to turn. The slow rocking turned into a faster movement and, eventually, into a vibration as the rpm picked up and the rotor speed came up to near liftoff rpm.

"Can you hear me, Ernie?" Chuck asked through the intercom.

"Loud and clear," Ernie said into the voice-activated mic attached to the headset and sticking out in front of his mouth.

Chuck increased the power and the pitch of the blades and lifted the helicopter off the rooftop of the campaign headquarters very smoothly. After taking it up twenty feet, he rotated the nose down and the helicopter began to move forward. Soon they were eight hundred feet up and moving at a hundred twenty miles per hour.

Now well up in the air where it was safe to show a novice how to fly, Chuck began his instruction to Ernie over the headset. "Take the collective and the stick and fly us." Chuck relaxed his hands on the controls slowly when Ernie took them. "Do you have the feel of it yet?"

Ernie, very good at handling most types of equipment, found it easy to keep the helicopter going in a straight line and at a fairly consistent altitude. "This is cool," he said, but he kept his eyes ahead and on the gauges, instead of turning to look at Chuck and losing or gaining altitude in the process—a sign to Chuck that Ernie could become a good pilot. He let Ernie fly from that point on, but kept his hands ready nearby, an eye on the gauges, and used the radio to notify Southern California Coast Approach of the course they were following so the helicopter could be kept on their radar screens.

"Keep the needle here," Chuck said, tapping the gyro compass, "and we'll be on course. This one here—" He pointed to an instrument near it. "—shows us where we are. It's the global positioning satellite receiver. We will be there in an hour, cruising at one hundred thirty miles per hour."

Ernie nodded. "Anything else I need to do?"

"You just fly us, and I'll handle the radio to report our entering the various air spaces and speak to flight forwarding.

And relax a little. You're hanging on a little too tight. I won't let you do anything wrong. We have expensive cargo, and I can't afford a mistake."

"Okay," Ernie was holding the controls so tightly that he was practically bending them. He relaxed his muscles and tried to comply, as the sleek, black helicopter made its way south toward north San Diego County.

CHAPTER 58

Focusing the cross hairs on one head and then another with the adjustable four-to-twenty-four-power scope set on twenty-four magnification, Innocenti toyed with the idea of shooting the various taller people standing about in the crowd to pass the time until his target came. Only an inch of the barrel stuck out of one of the openings in the camouflage netting covering him and his rifle. The netting, although it covered the rest of the rifle and the scope, was so close to the lens of the scope that it was completely out of the depth of field of focus, such that the netting could not be seen in the field of view and did not interfere at all with what Innocenti could see through the scope. And, the netting over the scope reduced substantially the risk of a reflection off the scope front lens that one of the FBI or police might notice.

From the hill where the event was held it was absolutely impossible to see Innocenti under his camouflage netting where he lay like the perfect chameleon.

Waiting for Lewis and Ernie's arrival, he became bored and began to toy with the idea that he might very well try to hit his prey in the head. He held the scope on several heads to see if he might just do it that way. But five hundred yards was a long way to hit a head. Better to be realistic and just go for the torso. Besides, he would have to take the shots and get the hell out of there or get caught. The idea of narrowing in for a second shot in case of a miss to the head would greatly increase his chances of being seen and reduce his odds of escaping. Nope, torso shots they would be.

The shuttle van went up and down the narrow, steep road, taking guests up to the water tank near the top. The crowd walked about, looking at the view, and mingling with each other, waiting for the gubernatorial candidate.

Doty looked about for anything suspicious and then looked through the binoculars at the surrounding hillsides. There was nothing suspicious.

Innocenti—with additional time on his hands, looking through the rifle scope on the highest power—watched the people at the hilltop five hundred yards away. He let his mind wonder. *There is the FBI man, with binoculars. He has the little wire to his ear, for his radio. It has to be a fed, since he has a suit and not a California State Police uniform. He's the man. It will take quite some time for anyone to get to me. The canyon between us is fairly deep, the terrain rough, and there are lots of huge rocks. I should have ample time to get to the bottom to the road and get away before anyone will be able to catch up to me from the hill where they are near the water tank. I can get off the shots I need and scramble nearly straight down the hill behind rocks and brush, out of sight of the FBI and state police running toward me. Yes, I will make the hit. Both Ernie and Lewis will die today.*

Doty's cell beeped and vibrated, working now that he was on top of the high hill.

"Doty here."

"Dan, this is Bill. I tried you twice before, but got no answer."

"I'm up on top of the hill now, so that's probably why you could get through. Before I was down in the canyon. What's up?"

"I just got a call from Connecticut."

"And?" Doty was impatient as he wanted to get back to preparing for Lewis and Ernie's arrival.

"Nothing of much interest on Manelli, Bastini, or Indelicato—just an arrest on Indelicato years ago for drunk and disorderly at some wild party—no conviction. A few traffic tickets, and something with the building department with Manelli. But one of the four, Fiorello Innocenti, has a whole bunch of tickets for going very fast on motorcycles when he was younger. The tickets range from twenty miles over the speed limit to one that was for going one hundred and fifty-five in a fifty-five mile speed zone—that is a hundred miles per hour over the limit. He also has one for reckless driving, for going so fast as to be reckless. His license to drive was suspended twice between the ages of eighteen and twenty-five. Given the proximity to other states, there may be some tickets in surrounding states, but I haven't had a chance to check yet. Also, in Connecticut he has an arrest for a charge of discharging a firearm within the city limits, but it was dismissed—probably some plea bargain to pay court costs or something like that. Since this guy is some sort of hot-shot motorcycle rider, I called a road racing motorcycle magazine that had records of racers and found out that Innocenti was a listed road racer for at least two years in that same period of time. So I checked vehicle registration in Nevada. He has three motorcycles registered. One is a classic English road racer called a Norton Manx, an Italian Ducati, and the third a Suzuki Hayabusa—that is one of the fastest models ever made. This guy likes road-racing motorcycles. Since that's what the lady believes she saw from her kitchen window at your brother's murder—a road-racing motorcycle—I figured that was enough, and I stopped to call you."

Doty got excited. "A road-racing motorcyclist who likes weapons, connected to the hotel that my brother was looking into! That's the connection. No wonder, Ernie didn't recognize him from the mug shots—he isn't in the computer as he has no criminal record other than traffic, so we don't have his mug shot. He's the son-of-a-bitch who killed my brother!"

"You got it," Kanno said. "A new breed of mafia with clean records. No doubt they're in bed with some silent associates with records. And when I was in Las Vegas, I was told that the Equator had its own jet. I checked federal registration for planes and found out that the Equator Corporation has a Cessna Citation X registered to it with call letters N88888. I called the Las Vegas Airport tower. A jet with the same registration numbers filed a flight plan last night from Las Vegas to Palomar airport. I called the tower there and the jet is still at the parking ramp. That is less than twenty miles from you!"

"This is it! Today is the hit!" Doty exclaimed. "Call the control tower at Palomar again and tell them not to give that jet clearance to move. Send in the nearest local police and have them hold the jet where it is if they can."

❧❧

"This is fantastic!" Ernie said over the headset, while piloting the helicopter south. "Flying this turbine helicopter is like having sex with a movie star. Of course, I haven't done that, so I can't say for sure."

Chuck broke out laughing.

❧❧

Below the next hill over, on the curvy road at the base of the hill, where Innocenti was lying in wait, Capirchio sat behind the wheel of the van, waiting for his employer to come down the hill.

A uniformed state policemen drove along the lower road, came up beside the van, and stopped. The officer opened the passenger window "What are you doing in this area, sir?"

Capirchio gave his prepared answer. "I'm thinking of buying a lot in this area and building a house on it. I'm just looking around." Then he tried a diversion, "Is this a crime free area?"

"I don't work this area normally, so I don't know what the crime rate is. But, sir, but there is an event nearby, and I must ask you to move along. The area will be open in three hours. You can return then and look for your property."

"Can't I just stick around here a while? I just want to get out and look around some more. I have to meet my wife later and can't come back today."

"Please move along, sir. You'll have to come back later or another time."

Capirchio started his car, hoping that the officer might drive on. When he could see that the officer was not going to leave first, Capirchio slowly drove off.

The officer waited until the van was out of sight before he made a U-turn and went back to patrol the road nearer to the event.

Capirchio drove on reluctantly down the road, until he was out of sight of the policeman, and then pulled over. *Should I wait? If the same cop comes back, he will definitely check for registration and driver's license. If the cop runs the registration on the radio he could find out the van was stolen, and I'll be arrested. Innocenti will have no way ou—wait. I'll leave the motorcycle!*

That was the best solution. He turned around, drove to the place where he thought he was supposed to wait for Innocenti, rolled the motorcycle out of the back of the van on a two-by-twelve wood plank he used for a ramp, and put it near the edge of the road on the kickstand, leaving the key in the ignition and Innocenti's helmet on the handgrip. Innocenti would come racing down the hill soon, and now he had a way to escape.

Capirchio got back into the van, made a U-turn, and drove off toward Polomar airport.

The helicopter with Ernie, Chuck, and Lewis came within sight of the hilltop.

Doty saw the helicopter coming and commanded the officers present to stand around the helicopter on the west to form a barrier on that side, which he considered the only risk, and to be ready to escort Lewis over to the podium for his speech.

Chuck took over the controls for the landing.

Innocenti could see the helicopter coming in. Officers moved in, making a line to the west of the landing spot, which would block his shot as soon as the helicopter touched down. So, he'd have to get his shots off before it landed.

Chuck brought the helicopter to a hover over the landing spot, twenty feet above it, as he set up for landing.

The nose was pointing to the southwest, its right side toward the west where Innocenti was.

He looked through the scope until he found the two men in the front seat, but the movements of the helicopter, although slight, were enough to prevent him from getting a good fix on the face of either person. He could see someone in the back.

He happened to know a little about helicopters and recognized this one as a Robinson. He knew that, in the Robinson, the pilot always sat on the right instead of the left, as in most other aircraft.

That meant that either Ernie or Lewis would be sitting on the left. He would take out the person in the front first.

He fixed his scope as best he could on the person in the left front seat and squeezed off a round.

Ernie saw a puff of smoke off to the west. The smoke was always seen first in gunfire, as light was faster than sound and the noise of the gun, especially at a long distance. Ernie fixed his eyes on the puff that lingered in the calm air, which was in between two large bushes, five hundred yards to the west and slightly below the hill of the event where they were to land.

Then there was an explosion, and the acrylic bubble canopy completely shattered, followed by a huge "BOOM!" as the sound caught up with the bullet. The noise was muffled to Ernie because of the headsets, but it was very loud to the police and others on the hilltop, and because of the rolling hills, it reverberated with echoes, like a noise in the Swiss Alps.

It only took a moment for Ernie to get over the shock and put together what happened. He was, after all, there as a target decoy. The puff of smoke, the blown up bubble canopy, and then a look over at poor Chuck, who had been hit in the middle of the chest, which had largely exploded from the impact of the big .50 bullet. The bullet proof vest he wore was inadequate to ward off a special 750 grain, .50 caliber, pointed-nose bullet. Chuck was very dead, and parts of his insides were blown about the cabin. The acrylic bubble canopy was mostly gone, except for a few pieces where it fit into the metal frame.

Chuck had jerked back involuntarily on the controls when he was blasted. The helicopter was pointed nearly up and out of control. This was a hypercritical moment for Ernie, as the helicopter was a second or two from flipping upside down or tumbling down the hill in a fiery crash.

It was up to Ernie to take over. He took the controls and was able to stabilize it, somewhat, pointing the nose back down, and returning it to a nearly level position. He braced himself to attempt a landing, which he had never done and did not know how to do.

Innocenti's mistake as to which side the pilot was on ruined his plan. He was going to hit Ernie in the passenger seat, kill him, and then hit Lewis in the back seat. Now, he wasn't sure who he'd hit, as he couldn't focus with the helicopter bouncing all over the place, but he realized that he better do whatever he was going to do very fast and get out of there. He tried again to focus his rifle, but the movement of the helicopter was too great to allow him to get a fix on any occupant, since whoever was flying it now couldn't hover it properly. Innocenti had only a few moments to make whatever shot or shots he was going to take before the helicopter set down, as there would be a line of police in front of it that would block any further shot.

His decision was to simply begin shooting in hopes of wiping out whoever was in the helicopter. With the scope looking at the body of the helicopter, he shot three more rounds at it as fast as he could. Given the recoil of the .50, rapid fire was hardly like a regular semi-automatic, and each shot was nearly two seconds from the last, as he had to gather his senses after each recoil and get the target back in sight, since the .50 kicked like a Missouri mule.

Two of the shots hit the helicopter, but not in a vital spot, going through the aluminum skin around what was left of the canopy. It was not clear to Ernie where the helicopter was hit other than the bubble canopy, but one definitely went through the rear doors. It hit the monitor screen of Lewis's open laptop, which was sitting on his lap, exploding it and cutting his fingers with shrapnel. More acrylic from the exploding windows was thrown into his neck and face. Another bullet went through the front canopy again, missing anything important. Lewis was not hit, but Ernie didn't know it yet. He cut the power which made the helicopter drop hard and unsafely, and it bounced hard off the ground.

The hitman quit shooting when the helicopter hit the ground as the officers blocked any further shots. Doty had three other FBI agents and nine state police on top of the hill for the event, and he quickly commanded them to surround the helicopter on the west side to get Lewis out, hoping he was not hit. They quickly and bravely came in to grab Lewis and Ernie and bring them out.

Lewis undid his safety belt and the men brought him out fast and low, like the Secret Service saving the president. Chuck was so obviously dead with his chest blown away, that they didn't attempt to get him out at the moment, trying to save Lewis.

Doty had several police surround Lewis, scurrying him in a crouched position to safety behind a cluster of the huge rocks that stuck up out of the hilltop. Having set those police in motion, Doty turned and commanded the other officers to get Ernie out.

Unlike Lewis, Ernie did not unbuckle, but just sat there, five brave men forming a barrier between him and the shooter to the west. He took off his headset when he saw Doty yelling at him.

"Come on, Ernie, get out!"

Ernie pointed over to the west and shouted, "The shots came from over there!"

Doty spoke into his radio, the mic of which was fastened to his wrist. "I want six officers to get over to the west, guns drawn. Shoot anyone with a gun"

The available men started running over the rough terrain toward the west. Some were moving cautiously and appeared reluctant to charge into possible live fire.

Innocenti assumed he hit Ernie. Through his scope, in between the officers, he saw Lewis get out of the back seat, escorted quickly to safety surrounded by officers. He figured that he couldn't get another shot at Lewis. It was time to go. He left the camouflage netting and sandbag, slung the heavy rifle over his shoulder, and charged down the hill toward the road where Capirchio was supposed to be waiting with the van. He could not be seen by any of the officers yet, due to the cover of the rocks and brush.

Instead of bolting out of the helicopter as one would expect, Ernie sat there, assessing the situation.

"Come on, Ernie, get out of there," Doty yelled again, beckoning with his right arm.

Ernie looked again at the very dead Chuck next to him on his left. He knew the shot must be from the same hitman he'd seen under the *Hookup*. Images raced through his mind of the deaths of Dwight and Poladian. What a great guy Dwight was, the long descent toward the abyss at the bottom of the ocean saving Lewis, the wounds to his ribs from the air saw, the pain and the hospital, the ten-bore shotgun shooting at him and ruining his motorcycle, the man who came in the woods after him with the ten-bore. The hospitals. The injuries. And now, the wonderful Chuck, who had given him the chance of a lifetime to pilot a turbine helicopter. Blood was splattered all about. And this bad man was getting away again.

Is this helicopter safe to fly? Ernie looked around at the sides of the fuselage, but could see no oil smoke. The gauges all seemed to be in the green on the instrument panel. The motor was running, the blades spinning. As far as he could tell, nothing super important had been hit. Chuck was definitely dead, so no need to wait to get him out.

Let the man who did all this escape? Not going to happen! "Wish me luck!" he yelled out to Doty in the melee.

Grabbing the controls, he yanked the helicopter up into the air. Luckily, it went up with little movement to either side. The danger to the police surrounding the aircraft was immense—if he tipped it too much, the rotor blades would wipe them out like a lawn mower.

Doty watched in amazement at what was surely an incredibly unsafe event.

Up twenty feet, Ernie could see to the west where the puffs of smoke came from. He caught a glimpse of a man wearing camouflage, running downhill, tucking in behind rocks and high brush with a big rifle slung over his shoulder. He looked at his friend Doty standing on the ground nearby.

Doty looked on in horror, as he realized what this new FBI deputy was going to do in an FBI helicopter. He could only think of one noble thing to do. He raised his right arm and hand, with his thumb up, in a tribute to Ernie, who was not going to let the hitman get away just because he only had a damaged helicopter and a dead pilot to chase him with.

Ernie couldn't take his hands off the controls to acknowledge the tribute, as he didn't know how to do that without crashing, but he nodded to Doty, turned the helicopter to the west, and flew off toward where he'd seen the man with the rifle running down the hill.

Innocenti saw and heard the helicopter coming. He stopped, put the rifle up to his shoulder, and aimed at the helicopter. Looking through the scope, he couldn't get anything in focus, as he had the scope still set on twenty-four power, far too much magnification for a moving target, especially when he had nothing to rest the rifle on and was shooting offhand from his shoulder and breathing hard from running.

He took a wild shot at the moving black shape in his scope, even though he had nothing in focus when he pulled the trigger.

Ernie heard the bullet go right over him.

Innocenti, not likely to make the same mistake twice, quickly reset the scope down all the way to the lowest power, four, but decided he better run. He slung the rifle over his shoulder, leaving both hands free to assist him in using rocks and trees for balance on his way down the steep hillside. Moving as fast as he could, he bolted down toward where he thought Capirchio should be waiting.

Ernie chased him overhead. He still had his pistol, but there was no way to take it out, aim, and shoot it without risking a crash. He also had on a headset, but he had no idea what frequency he was on or if the radio was still working.

"There he is!" Ernie cried out into the microphone. No answer followed, and he figured that the frequency was on the last one that Chuck used miles to the north, and no doubt, out of range because of the distance and the mountains. He had no idea of what possible frequencies that he should try on the radio.

And the helicopter was such a handful, that there was little chance of taking a hand off the collective or the cyclic to fool around with the radio anyway.

To the rear, Doty's men were coming toward the spot where the sniper had been, making their way as fast as they could in the rough terrain, running, climbing, and leaping over rocks and brush, but they were far behind and would not likely catch up before the shooter got away.

Innocenti was nearly at a full run, coming down the steep, rough hill, toward the road at the bottom. He didn't turn to stop and set up another shot at the helicopter, as escape was now all important and there was no time. He knew that there would be men chasing him, and it would be a foot race to the get-a-way spot.

Innocenti approached the bottom of the big hill looking for the van. It was nowhere in sight! Winded and panting, he reached the spot that he thought he had come up from, but no van! Where was it? Innocenti scanned both directions on the road frantically, then angrily. He wondered where in hell Capirchio was when he needed him desperately.

He cast about for any other option. There was little time. The helicopter was not far above and behind, and men on foot were chasing as well. He looked up and down the road some farther distance, this time more carefully. There! He'd missed it initially as it was much smaller that the van and farther away than the spot where he was expecting the van to be. But there it was, his motorcycle!

Innocenti ran to his motorcycle parked near the side of the road, two hundred feet away as Ernie closed in with the helicopter.

The key was in the ignition, and his helmet hung on the handlebars. He decided to keep the rifle slung over his shoulder, put on the helmet—needed for vision in high speed driving, not for safety—and mounted the crotch rocket. He fired it up, clicked the gear lever down into first, and let the clutch go. The front wheel going up in the air in a wheelie, he accelerated at a blinding pace down the road, out of range of Doty's men arriving at the bottom of the hill armed only with pistols.

Ernie could see the hitman accelerating rapidly away on the sleek motorcycle. He gave chase and was pleased with himself that he had not yet crashed the helicopter. As long as he was moving forward, he seemed to be able to control it.

Doty and another FBI man came along the road in a car. The officers who were on foot finally reached the bottom of the hill. Doty could see the tail end of the helicopter some distance away, following the path of the road. He sped toward the west on the road that Ernie and the hitman were on.

A section of the road that the motorcycle was traveling on came to a group of trees on either side of the road, such that it hid the road from above. Ernie went over, and past the trees, waiting for him to exit, lowering the helicopter and turning it to face the opening. Suddenly there he was, waiting to kill Ernie, off the motorcycle, a hundred-fifty yards away! He had the rifle lying on the handlebars, and was on a knee in a prone position ready for another shot.

This was the first confirmation to Innocenti that he had not killed Ernie earlier as now he recognized him at the shorter distance through the scope.

Ernie yanked the helicopter up and hard right. In making that maneuver, the passenger side, with the dead Chuck in it strapped in with the seat belt harness, was then turned to face the path where the hitman was shooting.

The man shot another round. But because of Ernie's quick reaction, the incoming bullet went into the left seat area of the cockpit.

The bullet hit the already dead Chuck, going right into his head, with all the force of John Henry, the steel driving man, hitting a railroad spike with a twenty pound sledge. Chuck's head exploded like a melon, and brains splattered all over the inside of the cockpit.

Do not think of the body parts all over the place, and get to flying, Ernie told himself so as not to get sick and abandon the chase. He raised the helicopter to an altitude of three hundred feet above ground, above the tree section, so he could not be seen by the assassin.

Innocenti slung the rifle over his shoulder and got back on the motorcycle, fired it up, and took off again. He appeared visible once again to Ernie when he came out of the tree section covering the road, zooming away at a high rate of speed.

Ernie gave chase once again. No regular pilot would have continued flying the damaged helicopter farther, but Ernie was no normal pilot, in fact, no pilot at all. And, the absence of the canopy bubble did not curtail his resolve, as he was used to having air in his face from riding his motorcycle and was at home with the wind blowing in his face at over a hundred miles per hour. He tilted the nose down and it picked up speed.

Innocenti's Japanese crotch rocket was much faster than the helicopter in a straight line, but the road had curves and Ernie flew straight, cutting the curves and shortening the distance, managing to keep the motorcycle in sight. Innocenti leaned the motorcycle over on the curves, going very fast.

Ernie looked at the radio on the dash and wondered what frequency he might use to call for help, but he dared not take his hands off the controls to try to find someone on a frequency. The narrow canyon highway that they followed straightened out for a stretch, and Ernie continued to pace the hitman.

Innocenti became irritated at the helicopter still being behind him and wondered if he should stop for a shot. He had the rifle on his shoulder and would have to come to a complete stop to use it. No, better not. Speed was his asset, as long as he had a straight highway, and his daring bountiful.

He saw the freeway ahead. Once on the highway, the Palomar airport was not far away, and the Equator company jet was waiting. He got on the on-ramp, and accelerated at a blinding rate on the freeway, soon reaching the top speed of the motorcycle. Ernie saw him accelerating away and went up slightly to keep him in sight. It was also a good way to keep from crashing into an overpass coming up.

The helicopter was doing one hundred and thirty as the oncoming wind pounded against Ernie's face through the missing bubble windshield. Having gone up in altitude, he was able to see the highway come to an end, where it interchanged onto the north-south Interstate Highway 5. The hitman would have to go to the north or south. As Ernie watched, the motorcyclist took the south route and accelerated. Ernie was losing him again with assassin's ability to go faster than the helicopter. Ernie pulled the helicopter up a few hundred feet to increase his vantage point.

Ernie could see an off ramp ahead leading to an airport. He didn't know where he was as he had not been to San Diego County, except to get the skunks. The airport was not a huge one, but it appeared to have jet service, probably for wealthy homeowners in Orange or San Diego Counties. An expensive Gulfstream business jet was on approach to land from the east, and a twin turbo prop Beechcraft King Air was climbing just after takeoff to the west on the single east-west runway.

There he is! The hitman had taken the off-ramp and was heading toward the airport on the far side, although Ernie did not know if he was going to the airport or around it. He cut the distance again by turning ahead of the intersection. The Gulfstream business jet and Ernie were both heading for the airport at the same time, and one would have to yield to avoid a collision. Ernie didn't yield and kept moving along his course, nearing the airport, keeping the hitman in view on the far side of the airport traveling alongside it to the west.

Ernie approached the edge of the airport. Maybe someone at the airport would be on this frequency? He decided to try and pushed the radio button on the cyclic. "Would the airport I'm flying over please identify itself?"

The question came over the radio of the control tower. Palomar Airport was small, but it had a control tower and was home for a number of expensive private jets owed by the very wealthy living in Orange and San Diego Counties. Timothy Peabody, Senior Air traffic Controller at Palomar Airport, had been looking at the sky with his binoculars, his way of relaxing.

"What?" Letting his binoculars fall to his chest on their straps, he turned and looked at his associate Roger Barns. "Did you hear that? We should identify ourselves? Never in my thirty-three years as a controller have I heard anything like that! Who in the hell is that?"

He saw a blip on the console radar screen. He looked at the area with his binoculars and found the black Robinson helicopter.

"Roger, what in the world is that?" he shouted to his. "He's entering our airspace!"

Peabody turned his transmitter to the helicopter's frequency. "Unidentified black helicopter, this is the Palomar control tower. You are in violation of controlled airspace. Execute a one-eighty to the right immediately and leave the area! You are endangering the airport and traffic!"

Ernie was relieved to finally hear someone over his headset. This was the first he had heard from anyone since he left the event. *So, I'm at Palomar, wherever that is.* He radioed back. "I'm in pursuit of a motorcycle that is presently heading toward your airport. Make way for me as I'm not turning around!"

"Identify yourself and your aircraft and do as you are instructed at once," Peabody ordered angrily, his temper straining on its leash. "This is controlled airspace and you are in violation of federal regulations by entering without clearance."

"This is Ernie, and I'm in a damaged FBI helicopter. I don't have a pilot's license. Clear the sky of other airplanes and look for the motorcycle."

"Is there a licensed pilot on board?" the frustrated Peabody demanded, his voice full of angst.

"Yes, but his head is missing!"

In the tower, the two federal air traffic controllers gaped at each other in amazement. This was a seriously dangerous situation. A person who had no pilot's license was about to fly over their airport where other planes were landing and taking off, and the airport was no longer safe.

Peabody quickly issued instructions to the incoming aircraft that was ahead of Ernie and about to land. "Gulfstream Two Six Four Sierra Whiskey, clear the airport by continuing downwind until further notice. Traffic is a black helicopter at two o'clock. Do you have him in sight?"

The Gulfstream pilot pushed his throttles forward to spool up his turbines. "Two Six Four Sierra Whiskey continuing downwind. We have the helicopter in sight."

"Put the safety crew on alert," Peabody said to Barns,

Barns rang the emergency truck and put it on alert status.

The land line phone in the control tower rang. "Palomar control tower," he answered.

"This is FBI Special Agent Bill Kanno, Los Angeles office. I've been trying to get your number for some time, and just got it. Is there a Cessna Citation parked at your airport with call letters N88888?"

Startled, Barns picked up his binoculars and looked at the several jets on the parking ramp area until he found the jet. "There it is. Yes. It's here!"

"Do not let that plane leave," Kanno said. "Call the local police and have them send any cars in the area to prevent anyone from trying to leave in the jet, and tell them to contact me at this number." He then gave his number. "Is there a black Robinson helicopter in the area?"

"I'll say. Some lunatic who says he's Ernie is just flying over. He says he has no license and he's endangering the entire airport!"

"Give him help any way you can," Kanno said. "That's our man and our helicopter. Better give him lots of room. He doesn't have a pilot's license!"

"There are no police at this airport," Barnes told him. "The nearest police are the highway patrol who may take some time to arrive."

"Do what you can to get them there," Kanno said. "If you see a motorcyclist, warn anyone around to exercise extreme caution. The rider is armed and extremely dangerous."

Ernie ignored the order to make a one-eighty to the right and flew right over the airport at three hundred feet above the ground. Peabody and Barnes watched in utter amazement and horror. Peabody's blood pressure was at the limit.

Ernie could see the hitman slowing down to a stop at an entry gate that led right onto the tarmac. A white limousine, that had dropped a passenger off at a twin Beechcraft that had just taken off, was leaving the field and the gate opened for it. This gave the hitman the opportunity he needed and he went right in. *Where would he be going on an airfield?* Ernie wondered. *Must be to a plane. Maybe he plans to go to Mexico. What plane?*

Innocenti answered the question by heading right to the Citation parked on the short term parking ramp. Innocenti rode up near the jet, the rifle still over his shoulder, parked his motorcycle, and raced up the several stairs that folded down in the door, taking his rifle with him.

Inside the jet, the startled pilots, who had no warning that anyone was arriving, put down their magazines and got up to meet their employer.

"Get this thing in the air. *Now!*" Innocenti bellowed, closing the door behind him.

The pilots hurried to their seats to make ready for an expedited take off. The pilot in command turned on the avionics switch. "I'll fire up the engines, and you call ground control and get us clearance to the active runway," he said to the co-pilot.

The copilot dialed in Palomar ground control. "Citation N88888 on the ramp, requesting taxi to the active."

"The FBI agent said not to let it go," Barns said to Peabody. "Maybe you should stall him while I call the FBI."

Peabody grimaced and keyed his mic. "Citation 888," he said, using only the last three digits as controllers often did. "Contact ATIS."

This was Peabody's way of slowing him down. Before taxiing, pilots had to tell the tower that they had been briefed with the latest news from the Automatic Terminal Information Service. The continuous, recorded broadcast of weather, measured ceiling, winds at the airport, and similar information that was transmitted from each tower. By telling the pilot to contact ATIS, Peabody was telling him to obtain the latest broadcast, and that he must dial into that frequency and hear the recording before taxiing. The pilot could then give the call designation of the most recent information, which changed regularly, by announcing he had the current alphabet name of the latest information, such as Oscar or Hotel. This was a regular requirement and would possibly delay the takeoff for a few minutes.

"I'll do what I can to slow them on the taxiways and to the active runway," Peabody said to Barns. "But there isn't much

I can do if he wants to ignore me and proceeds without permission."

Ernie, now approaching the Citation in the helicopter, saw the hitman go in and close the door. Ernie lowered the helicopter and made a pass over the Citation, at only a hundred feet above it, and then began a wide turn to come around again for another pass as he thought about what to do.

I'm not going to let him get away. He felt the collective in his hand to see if there was a lock for it. *Yes!* He locked it in place, freeing up a hand, took the cyclic in his left, and took out his .45 pistol with his right hand. In the process, he nearly went out of control as he had not learned to fly it that way yet. He put the pistol in his lap, and put his hand back on the collective and stabilized it.

He locked the collective once again. Holding the cyclic in his left hand—the collective on lock, feet on both pedals—he lined up a pass over the Citation, beginning at the left wing tip, heading right across its wings, lowering the helicopter to just high enough to clear the fuselage on the pass.

Peabody looked on in utter horror.

As the low pass began, Ernie stuck the pistol out of the helicopter, which wasn't hard since there was no canopy left. As he passed over the wing, he fired rapidly, aiming his .45 at what he felt certain would be the fuel tanks along the center cord of the wing. He let off four rounds in rapid succession into the left wing, pulled up just a few feet above the fuselage, and put another four in the right wing.

After that pass, he lifted it up and began a slow, wide turn for another one, during which he loaded up a spare clip in his pistol and made ready for another run, this time from the other side. On the second pass, he fired four more shots into the right wing, then went over the fuselage, barely missing it, and fired four more into the left wing.

The holes were more or less evenly spaced along the wing, and hit the wing tanks, going right through the aluminum skin of the top of the wings and out the bottom skin as well.

"*Jesus!*" the captain yelled. He ducked as the helicopter flew very close to his jet. "We're under attack!"

Innocenti rushed up, leaning over to enter the cockpit, and stopped behind the captain's seat. "What was that? Someone's shooting at us?"

"Yes. Look out at the wings! There are holes all over them!"

Innocenti looked out the captain's window to see the bullet holes in the wing.

"Over here too!" the copilot said, looking out at the right wing.

Innocenti moved over to his window to look out. "Take off anyway," he commanded in desperation.

"I can't!" the captain exclaimed, pointing at the wing on his side with the holes in it. "And look in front of the wing!" Streams of fuel could be seen draining to the tarmac below, forming puddles. "The bullets went right through the skin. We can't take off. If I try to start the engines and move, the raw fuel will catch fire as soon as we taxi over it and when the exhaust hits it, we'll be blown up! Anyway, we couldn't get very far with the fuel draining out. I only had the wings filled since no one asked beforehand for an extended-range flight. The wings hold seven thousand pounds of fuel. There is another six thousand pounds capacity in the belly, but that's empty. It would take quite a while to fill up, and no one will fill us up now with the fuel pouring out. We're not airworthy. Forget flying this thing!"

A highway patrolman, called by the tower, arrived at the gate. The tower called the hanger where there was someone to open the gate, and the person there opened it for him.

Innocenti considered his options and made a decision. The motorcycle was still a method of escape. Between the registration on the motorcycle, and that on the plane, they would be able to find him. The best he could do would be to get lost in a crowd and then make his way to Mexico, where his partners would send him money and he could get away somewhere from there. If he could just get to a crowd somewhere on the motorcycle, he could do it. He was about to be caught, and desperate moves were in order. He went to the door and lowered it.

The highway patrolman was exiting his patrol car and walking over to the Citation, his gun drawn. Innocenti's motorcycle was right by the patrol car, and there was no way to get to it without taking out the patrolman.

Innocenti picked up the sniper rifle he had set down against a chair in the jet. He laid the rifle over the back of one of the seats near the entry door and aimed carefully at the highway patrolman. Due to the light reflecting off the skin of the fuselage, the patrolman couldn't see inside the jet and didn't know what was coming.

Innocenti fired, hitting him squarely in the chest. The patrolman had on a bullet proof vest, but the massive .50 caliber bullet went right through it, exploding his heart, and then out the back of him, easily piercing another layer of bullet proof vest on the back. Both he and the pilot Chuck had useless vests for that magnitude of weapon. The officer was blown backward from the impact, dead.

Innocenti decided to leave the long, heavy rifle behind, so as not to draw so much attention to himself on the motorcycle, should he make it to a crowd, and also so as not to slow him down for the getaway as he intended to ride fast and hard. He ran down the steps to his motorcycle, mounted it, and sped off.

Peabody sounded a warning horn. The airport fire truck came out and headed for the leaking Citation. Its pilots were scurrying off the plane, in case it caught fire. Several mechanics and others from the hanger nearby were scrambling about, now aware of an actual fire emergency, very likely to burst into flames.

The confusion made it easy for Innocenti to race to the automatic gate and leave the airport. He went in between the small area of the wooden gate and the post, which had just enough clearance for a motorcycle.

Ernie, now catching on to flying the helicopter somewhat, raised it up to get a better field of view. He could see the hitman racing along the side of the airport, heading for the freeway once again.

He went for him, again cutting the corners.

As Ernie followed the assassin toward the freeway, he

heard the tower address him over the headset sarcastically, "Are you leaving our airspace now, Ernie?"

"Yes. Can you alert people for me that I'm on whatever frequency this is?"

"I'll alert Southern California Coast Approach, and the FBI that has called for you," Peabody responded. "A highway patrolman has been shot, and a jet with thousands of pounds of fuel is pouring out that fuel onto the tarmac, not far from fuel storage and other jets inside the nearby hanger. This is all because of you, you lunatic!"

Ernie paid the tower no mind and chased after the hitman, who was now back on Interstate 5 and heading north at a furious pace. Ernie twisted the grip on the collective and went as fast as he could, with the wind pounding his face through the missing bubble windshield.

The two Citation pilots ran from the aircraft, distancing themselves from the fuel pouring out onto the tarmac, a genuine hazard. More officers were being sent in, as well as all available fire trucks from the surrounding fire departments, pursuant to a pre-arranged emergency fire plan when there might be a crash or other such fire risk at the airport.

"Where's the motorcyclist? And where is Ernie in our helicopter?" Doty asked Peabody over his cell phone as he raced toward the airport in an FBI car with three other agents. Two state police cars followed, their lights flashing.

"They're gone," Peabody answered.

"What do you mean gone?" Doty demanded.

"That unlicensed lunatic in the helicopter left toward the northbound freeway, following a motorcyclist," Peabody answered in a very excited state. "He flew into our airspace, with no license, and without permission. He then dipped down to just over the Citation jet and shot it full of holes in the wings! Then he did it again in another pass!

"Now I have jet fuel running all over the tarmac, a twenty-three-million-dollar jet sitting over the fuel, and that's very near the fueling station with several hundred thousand gallons of fuel in underground tanks, planes parked nearby, a jet hanger a hundred yards away with millions of dollars more of jets with fuel in them, and the whole thing is waiting to explode. The homes nearby are in the danger zone. A policeman has been shot, and I have a goddamn disaster on my hands!"

"Did you say north?" Doty asked, ignoring all the whining.

Peabody finally lost it. "Yes, I said fucking north! *Have you got shit in your ears?*"

cాపా

Taking advantage of the straight highway, Innocenti opened the throttle all the way in high gear, zooming around the light traffic until he reached one hundred ninety miles per hour. He had no fear of the motorcycle, or of much else, for that matter.

Ernie twisted his throttle until it would go no more, but he fell back, unable to keep up with the crotch rocket carrying the hitman. The Robinson refused to go past one hundred forty-five miles per hour, due to the drag from the broken windshield bubble, and was losing ground rapidly.

As Innocenti went screaming along, pushing the motorcycle to its limit, he wondered if he should get off the freeway as soon as he could. Surely the police would eventually put up road blocks. He went past an elderly couple in a SUV so fast that the driver was startled, drove the vehicle off the highway, and crashed into the ditch on side.

Doty was heading north on the freeway with the other agents in his car, but they were far behind. The Chevrolet federal car would only go one hundred thirty-five, and was not very stable at that speed. Doty had to slow at times, as he passed, or on the turns. There was simply no way he would ever catch the motorcycle.

Ernie lost sight of the hitman. Two more cars that he passed must have been so frightened that they pulled over and stopped on the side of the road, proving to Ernie that he was on the right track. Realizing that he needed a better vantage point, as the motorcycle was gaining ground so fast, he pulled the helicopter up a thousand feet. Still not in sight. Where had he gone?

Innocenti saw the road sign *Ortega Highway*. This was a popular place for motorcyclists to try out their skills as road racers, and there were lots of injuries and fatalities from failed attempts. The road wound over the mountains and down to Lake Elsinore. If he took Ortega Highway and got to the end where it ran into Lake Elsinore, he could ditch the motorcycle, mix in with the crowd there, and make his way to Mexico.

Decision made, Innocenti slowed as he turned and went up the off ramp to the Ortega Highway. He made the turn very fast and accelerated once again.

Now a thousand feet above the ground, Ernie could see the Ortega Highway heading off to the east of his northbound travel. Nearly two miles away down the winding road to the east, he caught a glimpse of a motorcyclist just before he went under the cover of some trees. That was his prey.

Innocenti had to slow considerably on the winding road, but his motorcycling skills had not left him, and he leaned the motorcycle over from side to side adroitly as he sped down the highway.

Ernie tilted the nose down and descended toward the Ortega Highway. He remembered the radio and pushed the mic button, in case anyone was listening. "This is Ernie. If anyone is listening, call the FBI for Doty and tell him the motorcycle is heading east on the Ortega Highway."

No one responded and he was alone in radio silence.

Innocenti raced through the mountain highway. Many of the better drivers of race cars were his age, but most top road racing motorcyclists were only in their twenties, as a lack of fear of injury or death got replaced with wisdom and a desire for longevity, and they lost their competitive edge. But Innocenti had no more fear of dying than a twenty-one-year-old thrill-seeking racer and kept up his familiarity with fast bikes by riding them often.

He leaned the motorcycle over from one side to the other, nearly horizontally, with the elegance of a ballerina, as he danced elegantly through the curves. Racing on the edge left not a nanometer of room for errors. He rode like the fabled motorcyclist Mike Hailwood. At the speeds he was riding, one mistake and he would crash the motorcycle and be killed—or worse, caught.

Ernie closed the distance by cutting off a half mile off the right angle of the intersecting highways, and by not having to twist and turn like the motorcyclist.

Looking at the gauges, Ernie realized that he was chasing the hitman without regard to the safety factors of the helicopter. The engine was revving past the green zone, well into the yellow, and touching the red. *Will this going past the red line explode the motor?* He thought about the enormous expense of ruining the helicopter, and then he looked over at Chuck with no head. His brains were in little pieces, hanging about what was left of the frame of the canopy. *Ruin it? Hell, I can't even land this thing. I'll crash it anyway, trying to land! What's the difference?*

Not altogether unlike a Kamikaze pilot, Ernie went faster than the Robinson helicopter was supposed to fly. He paced the hitman as he leaned from left to right on his motorcycle. Finally, the curves slowed his travel enough that Ernie caught up to him. He could not get close enough, or go slow enough, to try to use the pistol as he had shooting up the parked jet.

Two motorcyclists were cruising the Ortega Highway, riding side by side on large touring bikes, each with hard bags and a wife on the back. Innocenti could not pass on the left due to oncoming traffic, and so he pointed his motorcycle right in between them, traveling ninety miles per hour faster than they were going. His velocity and wind startled both of them so much that one went off the highway to the right, the other to the left, barely missing an oncoming car. Both crashed, one on either side of the road.

Ernie raised the helicopter up as he had before over the freeway to gain a viewing advantage from additional height, keeping a constant vigil. Looking ahead, he saw Lake Elsinore off to the south and down from the mountain road, with a mass of people, cars, and activities. If the assassin got to that crowd, Ernie would lose him. *Got to get him first!*

He could now get ahead of the motorcycle, due to the curves that it had to negotiate. Ernie headed south to where the road led. Ahead, before the city, was a clearing and a long slice of straight road. It was down from the mountain, on the flats, near the lake, leading to the milieu of people that use the lake for recreation. Ernie pointed the helicopter straight toward the clearing and, with the nose down, picked up speed. The speedometer went into the yellow danger zone, and then into the red as Ernie descended toward the clearing ending on the flats. The controls, and then the helicopter itself, began to shake as it was clearly going too fast. He was close to ending the flight in a way he had not intended, by breaking the helicopter to pieces.

Arriving at the clearing, well ahead of the rider, he tried to slow the helicopter by raising the nose, and twisting the throttle back. The helicopter went up again, and Ernie realized that he had a bunch of speed to lose and no idea how to do it. With all his excess speed, he overshot the clearing. He swung around into a wide turn with a high angle of lean, to lose the speed and to return to the clearing. The rotor blades were stressed to their maximum in the turn, and bent up too far for safety.

But by the end of the turn, Ernie had lost a good deal of the excess speed, and was at the far end of the clearing. Still too high, he had to lose five hundred feet. Holding the nose up and cutting the throttle, he got it to descend until he was facing the spot in the trees where he expected the motorcycle to exit. He was two hundred feet in the air. The motorcycle came out of the last turn before the clearing.

Innocenti saw Ernie and the helicopter, and rolled the throttle down, downshifted several times, and slowed to consider his options.

Facing the motorcycle, Ernie dangerously lowered the helicopter to fifty feet above ground, moving forward just enough to maintain control. He stopped over-controlling it, and relaxed on the controls, which helped keep it straight.

Innocenti weighed his options. *How about I just run straight ahead and make him move? If I make it to the crowd ahead at Lake Elsinore, I can ditch the motorcycle, mix in, and escape. There will be others coming for me soon, so there is no time to lose. If I go back, I'll be caught, for sure. If I get down to the Lake and crowd, I can go free. I gotta go for it.*

The decision made, Innocenti lowered his head and rolled the throttle to maximum, heading directly toward the helicopter.

Ernie lowered the nose of the helicopter more, doing his best to keep it flying level in that attitude and in line with the road. As he leaned the nose down, it picked up forward speed. It descended until the rotor blades were only ten feet above the concrete highway, dangerously close.

Innocenti upshifted the gears, zipping through eighty, one hundred, one hundred twenty, one hundred forty, and still accelerating on a machine capable of two hundred, all the while gaining speed as though the laws of physics did not apply.

Ernie, in the sleek, black, but much slower accelerating, damaged Robinson helicopter, stopped it from descending down when the rotor blades were getting close to the ground. He accelerated through, sixty, seventy, eighty, ninety and was still gaining speed. The rate of closure between the two machines was becoming staggeringly fast.

Innocenti had made his way through life by never giving in and by intimidating people into backing off. He was not about to change now and be caught at this most critical moment. He counted on his bravado and on the fact that officers of the law and pilots had families and would not jeopardize their lives just to make an arrest.

That might have been true with regular law enforcement officers and pilots, worried about their wives, children, and pensions. But Ernie had none of these. He did just the opposite and increased his speed by leaning the helicopter forward, tilting the rotors down even more. The thirty-three foot rotors went down to only four feet from the ground as the helicopter moved down the middle of the highway accelerating toward maximum speed—a dangerous attitude even for an expert pilot.

From the other direction, the motorcycle, with its aerodynamic fairing, sped directly down the middle of the road, also accelerating. It became a game of chicken.

I am not about to give in, no matter what. This is the man who destroyed my motorcycle. He killed that great guy Dwight Winger. He killed the pilot Chuck. He killed the highway patrolman. No backing down. No chance. No way. No compromise. This is it!

They continued to accelerate toward each other, the motorcycle reaching one hundred eighty and the helicopter one hundred thirty.

The tips of the rotor blades hit the assassin in the head, just above the tiny road-racing windscreen on the Japanese crotch rocket. The blades went right through him after exploding his head. His entire upper body then blew apart as well. In the tiniest fraction of a second after that, the two machines hit, the curved top of the fairing of the motorcycle grazing along the curved underside of the front of the helicopter. Although a grazing hit, the speed of each vehicle was so great that the force of the impact slammed the motorcycle down, compressing its forks until they bottomed out, which then propelled it sixty feet up into the air, tumbling end over end many times, flinging the hitman's remaining body parts many feet in all directions.

The sudden stop of the rotors on the helicopter, combined with the force of the motorcycle striking it underneath, caused it to bounce up in the air as well, and it tumbled end over end three times, finally coming to rest on the side of the road in the dirt, upside down, with helicopter parts falling from the sky for some time afterward.

CHAPTER 59

*W*here on earth is this place? What happened? Where am I? So much white! Heaven?

Ernie woke up disoriented. He was lying down and tried to sit up. In attempting it, he was hit with a sharp pain. Looking around, he saw a pleasant nurse in her twenties. He tried to focus and, after a short time, could see that she wore a name tag bearing the name *Roxanne*.

"I'm alive!" he exclaimed aloud, realizing he was back in hospital, the third time since he came to Los Angeles to work for an insurance company.

Moments later, the all-too-familiar-and-welcome face of Special Agent Doty came into the room, smiling. "Not to worry, I have spoken to the doctors, and, incredibly, you have no broken bones and haven't suffered any internal injuries. But you have sprains and the like. You've been out since yesterday with a concussion. How do you feel?"

"Like a giant redwood fell on me while I was having sex with a spotted owl."

Doty laughed heartily. "From eye-witness reports, you apparently chased the suspect down the highway to Palomar Airport, where you took out a Citation Jet that the bad guy was trying to escape in with the FBI pistol I gave you. Then you continued to chase him all the way to the Ortega Highway and along it to the end of the road near Lake Elsinore. You then attacked him head on while flying the helicopter next to the ground. When you crashed into him, your helicopter fortunately grazed off the top of his motorcycle, but enough that the impact threw it up into the air, and knocked you out, unless that happened when you crashed. Your shoulder harness and belt held you in as the helicopter did somersaults. From what I gather, your extreme low level, head-on confrontation was an incredible bit of flying. Naturally the news media has followed it and reports you as a flying ace.

Ernie lay back and tried to remember what had happened. He began to recall flying the helicopter but not the crash. Slowly he recalled the earlier events and the dead FBI pilot Chuck next to him.

Doty produced a printout of a Nevada State driver's license with a picture of Fiorello Innocenti. "Do you recognize him as the man under the boat who tried to kill you? The answer is yes," he said, giving him a bit of a prompt in case Ernie had any difficulty in the biased one-person photo lineup presented him.

"Yeah, I guess that's him. Of course, I didn't see him up close on the motorcycle."

"The suspect you just identified is Fiorello Innocenti from Las Vegas."

The doctor, who Nurse Roxanne summoned, came into the room wearing green cotton hospital scrubs. He was a youngster, trying to act the part of someone important.

The young doctor walked up to Ernie, put a light in his eyes, and told him to follow his finger from side to side. Ignoring him, Ernie looked around the doctor's head at Doty. "Did I get him?"

"That's an understatement. Apparently, the helicopter rotors hit him in the head and upper body, just before the helicopter grazed off the motorcycle fairing, and it literally exploded him. His body parts were all over the place, some landing several hundred yards away. We arrived shortly after the crash and had you taken here by medevac helicopter. You're in a San Diego County hospital. You know that we lost the pilot, and a highway patrolman was killed at the Palomar Airport.

"What's the story on the man I got?"

"Fiorello Innocenti is one of four in a management group that runs a major hotel and casino in Las Vegas, called the Equator, and a smaller one in Reno called the Jackpot. One of his arms, hand attached, was found this morning over a hundred yards away from the scene, apparently catapulted by the force of the crash. We haven't found the other hand yet. We're still putting together his body parts and have several agents out there looking for those and any other evidence. We sent the arm we found up to our Los Angeles lab to get the fingerprints off the hand. We also found a piece of his lower jaw, and we're working on dental records. He had no wallet or identification of any kind—a smooth operator. By the way, he has no criminal record other than traffic tickets. But the jet he was trying to escape in belongs to the Equator, and we have the pilots in custody now as material witnesses." Doty paused for a quick breath. "Say, you caused quite a ruckus at the Palomar Airport by shooting up that jet. Luckily, the firefighters were able to keep the fuel from igniting and—"

"You must stay in one or two days more for observation," the young doctor interrupted, "given the fact that your concussion was severe enough to knock you out for so long."

"This is the third time I have been hospitalized just because I went to work at an insurance company," Ernie said. "I want to get back home to the safety of logging."

Doty broke out in a good strong laugh. "You're quite the hero. I have several newspapers saved for you, which I'll give you later. I'll have the front page stuff mounted for you as a present."

"I'm on duty today," the doctor said, irritated that he was ignored. "If you need me, push the button."

He then left the room, which was appreciated by all.

"So you don't need me to testify, and I can go?" Ernie asked.

"Yes, you can. And don't worry about the hospital bills. I've arranged for the government to pay the bills, as you were under our protection. Not to mention the helicopter." He smiled and shook his head as he thought of what Ernie did.

"What a guy," Ernie said a bit sarcastically. "Sorry about the helicopter."

"Good thing we have more than one," Doty said, trying to comfort him. "I'll be glad to pay for your return trip to Washington State as well. When you're ready, I'll send a car for you here to bring you back to the FBI building before you go. Some folks there want to meet you. But no, we don't need you to testify about Innocenti, anymore."

"At least you don't have to try him in court for months and see him get some jail sentence from a milk-toast judge, instead of death," Ernie said. "I gave him his trial, the death sentence, and handled all of his appeals for you as well as the execution."

Doty laughed as he thought of how it would be if all crimes came to an end like the one with Ernie. "If the FBI gave out medals to civilians, you'd be decorated. But I'm reasonably certain that you'll get a letter from the FBI director himself because of what you did." He paused to shake Ernie's hand. "Well, I have to go. I want to go to work on collecting evidence to connect Innocenti's partners to this, as well as whatever else we can get on them. Call me when you're ready to check out and I'll send a car for you."

Ernie found himself alone, with boring hospital walls as scenery. The daytime TV shows were mostly junk. Bored, he decided to get out of bed. Sitting up, he got a rush of pain in his head and realized his back was sprained as well. Everything hurt.

Overcoming the pain and getting up slowly, Ernie hobbled to the bag that Doty had brought down to see what he had left of his few possessions. His new outfit from Lilly was not there, and must have been ruined or cut off in the emergency room. He still had his jeans, a shirt, and boots. He had started out his big journey with his trusty motorcycle, and now that was gone. Fishing in the bag, he found the flash stick that he had made at Zelzah's. Oh, yes, he remembered. That was information from Majestik, including the instructional material. Ernie would probably never use it now. But you never knew. How to view it? He pushed the button and nurse Roxanne came in.

"Is there a way that I can get a computer or laptop and view what is on this flash stick?"

"No, not here," Roxanne said with a smile. "But I have a

computer at home, which is not far. Once you check out, you could come over and use it if you want."

"What time do you get off?"

"In just a few minutes."

"Will you take me there? I'm checking out of this place. To hell with staying in here for observation and that kid doctor sticking his light in my eyes."

CHAPTER 60

T his is my place," Roxanne said as she drove in the driveway with Ernie in the passenger seat of her older Honda. The house was a smaller, older one, willow green with cream trim, set back in from the street in between large trees, and rather attractive. They drove alongside the trees dividing the property from the next and parked in the back, in front of a garage. She led him in through the back door, which was the entrance she always used. It led right into the kitchen where she would normally unload her groceries, but in this case, her patient.

"Do you live here alone?"

"Yes. I was married, but I divorced over a year ago and we sold our house. I bought this with my share of the proceeds. It's smaller, but I don't need so much."

"Why did you divorce?"

She seemed like such a charming, unassuming girl, he couldn't resist asking, although it might not have been the most diplomatic subject to bring up.

"We were getting bored with our sex lives, and so I was fooling around on the Internet a lot. Sometimes I would use the camera. A few times we tried swapping with other couples in a swing club, and that was fun. But we were getting bored with each other, and so, after a while, we decided to just split things up and each go our own way. We have no children, so it was just a simple division. We're still friends. Now I belong to a local swing club and go once a week to some member's home for a party."

Leaving that subject, she studied him with a clinical eye. "You should stay here at least a day, in case you have any problems from being knocked out. I have tomorrow off and you can spend it with me if you like."

"This is way better than the hospital."

"Excuse me while I go change. While I'm doing that, would you like a glass of wine? I have some white wine in the fridge. Why don't you get us some?"

And with that, she left for her bedroom. She had on her nurse's white top, a white skirt, white stockings, and white work shoes with rubber soles.

Ernie found the wine, poured two glasses, and waited for her at the kitchen table. Roxanne came out of her room a few minutes later but, to Ernie's surprise, she was wearing the same white nurse's skirt and top she had on before, except that she had on white, high heel shoes. She had on white stockings as before. He noticed the aroma of perfume.

She picked up her glass of the wine, took a sip, and stood beside him at the table.

"I thought you were going to change."

"I did." She raised her white nurse's skirt to her waist. She must have put on different white stockings, this time with white laced tops, attached to a white garter belt. She wore no underwear, and was cleanly shaved, smooth as a ripe melon in season.

With a warm smile, she asked, "You like?"

⌘

In the morning, after coffee, Roxanne showed him to her computer. "Let's get it fired up."

Ernie pulled up a chair to her computer table and, as he did, he noticed that there were curious lipstick marks on the computer mouse.

Roxanne opened up the flash stick that Ernie got from Zelzah's place.

The first thing that came up was a letter to Tom McGinn, staff attorney at Majestik. Scrolling down, a letter to Alan Waterman came up, showing twenty million dollars to defeat Lewis, hidden in a transfer to the Chockpaws.

Wow! Unknown to him, everything that he had up on the screen, including the memo to McGinn, and to Waterman, as well as the MM file were copied onto the flash stick that day.

Twenty million dollars in a laundered contribution to defeat Lewis! Ernie had seen it at Zelzah's, but had not digested it or realized its significance.

This was information that might push Lewis ahead of his opponent to win the election. He needs know this at once.

Ernie read on farther.

Another topic was entitled, *List of Flexible Accident Reconstruction Experts.* Below that was a list of six firms in Los Angeles with addresses and phone numbers. Also following the firm was a brief summary of what each one had done on several cases. He read one of the summaries.

> *Matthews case: A woman was rear-ended in her car at a stop light by one of our insureds. She sued our insured, and this reconstruction expert testified that the woman was actually backing up at the time. The jury bought it. The firm charged seven thousand dollars to concoct the story and come up with the engineering, but it paid off.*

Wow, Ernie thought. *This is an actual list of experts who will lie for money, and actual examples of successes.*

He scrolled down to the next topic, which was Paper Shredders.

> *Everyone should have a shredder nearby. The person doesn't feel so guilty about destroying evidence if he can do it without someone watching. Anything incriminating has to be shredded. The legal department and the adjustors' offices are to be checked for shredders, to make sure that there is a shredder for at least every three (3) persons. There is not to be any cost savings in this area, and to try to do so is a very false economy. It has come to my attention that some volatile evidence that should have been shredded and destroyed

was not, in some cases, shredded, due to the fact that the nearby shredders were occupied, and then the evidence was forgotten about and inadvertently not shredded.

Ernie recalled what he had seen at Majestik when he actually saw those pieces-of-shit in-house lawyers shredding evidence. *They actually called me in to get a file from me so they could shred evidence in it and then swear an oath to the person suing that all evidence had been turned over. Crooks!* Ernie started to get angry.

He scrolled though a litany of topics, ranging from payoffs to the insurance commissioner and favors to judges, to redrafting of the company's insurance policies to make the limitations and exclusions more difficult to find and understand.

He came to a summary of the methods that McAteer had taught at the indoctrination on his first day.

This is hot stuff! He glanced up at Roxanne. "I must get this whole thing to Lewis."

"Do you mean the candidate for governor?"

"Same guy."

"Honey, you have some pretty important friends. The FBI and now the governor candidate!"

Ernie brushed off the notion. He found the paper he had in his billfold for Lewis. It had a personal email for him as well.

"Can you send him the entire flash stick?"

"Yes, honey, let me set it up for you."

CHAPTER 61

Gubernatorial hopeful Lewis lay in his bed, having decided to take two days off after being discharged from the hospital after ear operations. He had set up a desk in the study in his house for his senior aide, Sam Brenner, to receive messages filtered through his campaign headquarters. His wife sat beside him in a chair, as he clicked through the various news channels on the TV with the remote control, looking for news about his campaign and party.

"I've got to get out of here," he said to his wife. "This is the second day now, and tomorrow I'm going to get up and get back on the campaign trail. I can't take this lying around much longer."

"Darling, you know what the doctors said. You should rest at least one more day. Let me go find you something useful to do."

Brenner walked down the hallway toward the bedroom, with a handful of pages, just as Mrs. Lewis came out. He gave them to her for further filtering, as she had insisted on doing that while her husband was recovering.

"I have an email here that is signed by Ernie, but it is not from a computer with that name, so I cannot be sure if it is genuine or not," Brenner told her. "It might be a prank."

"Do you have any reason to suspect that it is not genuine?" she asked.

"No. But you know him so much better than me, so I think you should decide what to do under the circumstances."

She took it and went back into the bedroom. "Darling, I have an email here from an Ernie. But it did not come from his computer, so Sam says he can't tell if it is genuine or not. But considering that it might actually be from the real Ernie, I thought you would want to check it out."

"Ernie doesn't have a computer," Lewis said. "So it might be from him, using someone else's. Who's the name of the email of sender?"

"It's obscene."

"Let me see," Lewis said, holding out his hand, welcoming any message from Ernie. He picked up his reading glasses and read the message.

To: Mr. Lewis

From: SlapMyButtAndCallMeASlut

I obtained the attached file from actual internal communications recently at Majestik Insurance when I worked there. These are from the computer of the executive secretary to company president Robert Bradford and are genuine. I don't want her to get in trouble, so just use the contents without disclosing the source.

Sorry about you getting roughed up, but I think the man who shot at us in the helicopter is more sorry.

Ernie

(Here is the phone number where I am staying for a few days.)

Lewis read the contents of the attachment for some time and then leaped out of bed. "Hah." He practically shouted his laughter and excitement. "This is dynamite! This will make the difference in the election. Get Sam!"

Brenner hurried into the room. "Come on in, Sam." Lewis showed him the phone number. "That's a San Diego County phone number. Get him on the phone at once. If Ernie verifies it, I want you to call for a press conference immediately. Let's have it at news time tonight. I knew there had to be something behind that huge donation to the Chockpaws. Now we know. The announcement of twenty million dollars spent to defeat me and coming from an insurance company in this manner, and illegally, will surely turn a number of people against the insurance industry that's supporting our opponent and boost us over the top! And the rest is so beautiful. It may take us a while just to sift through it to put it to work for us, but I especially like the part where Majestik sets out how to systematically cheat people, and I know the public will too!"

⌇⌇⌇

Later, lying in Roxanne's bed, exhausted from her Olympic-level sexual gymnastics, Ernie turned on the late news to see what was happening with Lewis. Having been called by him earlier, and verifying the origin of the information, Ernie decided to rest the night where he was, as he had quite a headache from the concussion and was still sore from being bounced around in the crash.

He stopped surfing on a news channel. Lewis was being interviewed. "Is it true that you have discovered just today that a major insurance company, Majestik, put up twenty million dollars, illegally not disclosing it, to a straw man, an Indian tribe, to funnel it secretly to your opponent to pay for ads to defeat you?"

"That is exactly what occurred."

"What does the Indian tribe get in exchange for this?" the interviewer asked.

"One hundred fifty million dollars in a favorable loan to build a new hotel and casino. That shows you the magnitude of the amount of slush money these insurance companies have to waste on trying to preserve their crooked ways of doing business."

"Mr. Lewis, our hot line phone sampling voters' polls shows that this news release has already moved you up over your opponent. Are you pleased?"

"I sure am. I have told my constituents the truth about insurance companies and their systematic bad faith and illegal practices, and I'm glad to see that this discovery is showing people the truth of what I have been saying and the benefits of my platform. Details of the crooked practices, as admitted by Majestik in this discovery, are being put together and will be discussed tomorrow in a live talk show."

"On another subject, Mr. Lewis, Ernie, the very same man who saved your life in the heroic feat with the incident at sea where someone tried to drown you was with you when another attempt was made on your life again in San Diego. Your pilot was shot and killed, then Ernie, although not qualified to fly a helicopter, took off in it and ran down the suspect that the FBI now says is believed to be the same man who tried to murder you at sea. The reports are that this Ernie was involved in an incredible act of bravery in chasing down the man that we have been informed was Fiorello Innocenti of Las Vegas. Would you tell us about that?"

"The FBI is investigating the event, and so I'm asked not to say very much about it. But, yes, that's true. That Ernie is a real hero, and although he may not have been licensed to fly, I might have to disagree with you as to whether or not he was qualified. Ernie flew the FBI helicopter like an expert. Not even a pilot, he took out a Citation Jet with a pistol, and managed to chase down the assassin on a motorcycle traveling at very high speeds in a head-on contest of bravery." Lewis glowed in the limelight of attention and good press.

In San Diego, in Roxanne's bed, Ernie turned off the TV. "Enough of all this bullshit. Who wants to get involved in politics?"

He rolled over to see if Roxanne was sleeping. She was lying on her back, naked, holding both of her legs up in the air and apart, a subtle suggestion.

CHAPTER 62

Taking advantage of Doty's offer, Ernie called him when he was ready to leave. Doty sent a hired car to San Diego to pick him up—a black Lincoln that chauffeur services used for such purposes.

Roxanne walked him out, looking at the shiny black Lincoln. "Wow, what a fancy ride."

Ernie kissed her. "I want to thank you for everything."

She smiled. "Honey, you can come back anytime."

❦

At the FBI building, Ernie got a warm welcome.

"How is the man the news is calling hero?" Doty asked.

"Still a little sore from being tossed around so much."

"Come on," Doty said and then escorted him to the computer room where he had been before. "We don't normally talk about investigations, but in your case I'll make an exception—but of course, you realize this is confidential."

Ernie nodded in silent assent.

Doty put up a picture of Innocenti on the computer screen. "We have a lot more on the man you took out, Fiorello Innocenti. He was part of a group of four that run a major hotel's casino for a widow, and also a smaller one in Reno. He was brought in to a management group that was formed by a Salvatore Manelli who worked at the hotel's casino in management when the owner/husband died. His wife now owns it. Given complete management control by the widow, he brought in his old friends from Waterbury, Connecticut, who were Bastini, Indelicato, and Innocenti. We suspect they were all involved somehow. Innocenti was known for his bravery. He was a motorcycle racer when younger, and apparently afraid of nothing. We think he was cut into the illicit profits for his bravery, as he did not have the investment money to buy into the group. We don't have enough proof yet for an indictment, but we believe this group was also bringing in drugs and laundering profits with casino cash receipts, and then paying it out by overpaying money for extended auto warranties in Cayman for new cars, mostly from car agencies that the Equator owns. We may not be able to get an indictment against the others for murder, but it looks good for the money laundering and racketeering. Depending on what we turn up, we might also hit them with a RICO charge for the money laundering, among other charges. Hats off to you, for acting the brave decoy and flushing out the bastards."

"Good," Ernie said. The details were not of much concern to him. "Well, I'm going back where I belong. Do you think you could give me a ride to the airport? I think cabs cost a bunch here, and I'd like to head home today if you don't need me anymore."

"It'll be my pleasure. But I'll be sorry to see you go. You sure you won't consider becoming an FBI agent? I could set it up to get you an interview to get into the academy and, with a recommendation from one of our top people, it would be a slam dunk for you to get in."

Ernie brought reality to the idea with, "Don't you need to have a four-year college degree to become an FBI agent?"

Doty's enthusiastic smile fell when he realized that not everyone, like him and his deceased brother, had the privilege of a college degree. Realizing the blunder, he said, "Sorry."

Ernie was no man of letters or diplomas, nor did he want to be one. He eased the tension that was created by his lack of schooling with, "If I went to college, I'd probably end up rubbing shoulders with owl lovers." He then smiled to take the pressure off the awkward moment. "Say, did you ever find the pistol you got me?"

"Yes, we did. It was a long way from the point of impact. I'm afraid it won't be the same again. And anyway, we have to keep it in evidence as part of the case we're building. But don't worry. I have something for you." Doty produced a lacquered, wooden, presentation box with the metal logo of Sig Sauer on the lid, and ceremoniously presented it to Ernie, using both hands and with a slight bow. "As you were promised that you could keep the Sig Sauer .45, I got you another. Here it is." He handed Ernie a leather pouch with extra clips and two hundred rounds of ammo. "Since it was not a regular weapons order by the FBI, everyone here chipped in and bought it for you. I gave a letter to the gun dealer that exempted it from the required ten-day waiting period."

Ernie opened the box and his eyes widened in surprise and delight. It was a special, engraved, presentation grade Sig Sauer .45. The grips were gorgeous rosewood. On the side was engraved, *Ernie, FBI Deputy*.

Pointing to the engraved part, Doty grinned. "You were deputized for a while, and so it's true."

Ernie beamed. "Wow! This is the coolest present ever! Wait'll the guys at the chainsaw store see this!"

Hearing he was leaving, several agents came forward to meet him. They wanted to say that they had met the FBI hero, and all took pictures of them standing together with him with their camera phones.

At the airport, Doty insisted on charging Ernie's ticket to the FBI. And he went out on a limb and made it a business class ticket. Out of respect, Doty followed Ernie all the way to the gate.

Waiting to get on a different airplane, adjacent to the gate that Ernie was waiting at, was a Japanese girl. She scurried up to him, and asked, "Aren't you the person I saw on TV that saved Lewis's life?"

"It really wasn't much," Ernie told her.

"Could I get your autograph and photo?"

Ernie signed the paper she presented and her girlfriend took a picture of the two of them together. He then quickly turned away, not wanting to be a celebrity.

There was a short time before boarding. Doty looked at Ernie admiringly. "I would like to reveal something to you.

When I entered Quantico, I had dreams that one day I would do something heroic like tracking down an infamous killer like John Dillinger and shooting him in a gun battle. But after time I realized that I'll never achieve celebrity status. I'll just help others in the Bureau by checking records, interviewing witnesses, investigating from a computer, and once in a while participating in a team arrest. I'm sure that the instructors at Quantico will now tell students of your story, how you demanded to be deputized and to be given a gun, getting into a million dollar helicopter that you did not know how to fly and could never safely land, chasing one of the worst bad guys with it, taking out a Citation jet with the bad guy in it at an airport by flying low over it twice with only your pistol and shooting up the jet, and then attacking the motorcyclist head-on in what may become known as the quintessential chicken contest. You are the stuff that legends are made of. I heard that one of the instructors at Quantico told your story to new recruits, and they were spellbound. Your heroics may become FBI folklore one day."

Ernie's awkwardness at the attention was interrupted by a loudspeaker announcing the boarding of his flight. Doty faced Ernie and held out his hand, shaking Ernie's in a strong clasp of friendship. "You are especially important to me, putting a fitting end to my brother's murderer. If there is anything I can do for you, anytime, give me a call."

Ernie walked to the gangway. He stopped and turned around to smile and wave goodbye to his FBI friend. It would be the last they would ever see each other.

CHAPTER 63

Flying in a jet was a first for Ernie, and he felt a little helpless in the roar and vibration of the takeoff. He thought of his ruined motorcycle and his broken down truck. At home he would have to get out the insurance papers and make a claim. He needed the money.

At the Seattle airport, Ernie walked down the ramp, and there appeared the warmest and most friendly sight. "Lilly!"

There she was, smiling, holding out her strong, loving arms to greet him. More time having passed in her mourning of her late husband, Ernie's absence, and hearing about him in the news drew her closer to him.

He was still a bit too sore from sprains to run to her, but she hurried to him. He put his arms around her, picking her up off the ground and spinning her around, with a big hello kiss.

Walking through the airport, she said, "You were in the news. I was so worried that you might have been hurt. Weren't you in the hospital?"

"Yeah, three times, but I wasn't really hurt. How did you know when I was coming so as to meet me? I was going to take a bus home from the airport without bothering you at work since I'm unemployed."

"An FBI agent named Doty phoned the meat market and asked to talk to Rich, knowing he was the owner. The FBI man asked if Rich would mind if I took off to come down to get you. Rich was so flabbergasted to actually be called by the FBI that he insisted I leave and come on down for you. Can you imagine? A real FBI agent calling the meat market in Sedro Woolley? It was a major event."

"Ah, yes, that's Doty. He has a way of finding out anything

about anybody. I might have guessed he would have arranged something. Say, I got to fly a turbine FBI helicopter. In fact, I totaled it."

As they walked to her older, paint-faded car outside in the familiar Washington drizzle, Ernie remembered. "Oh yes, I wanted to tell how well the new wool outfit you got for me worked in the big city. I fit right in."

He was still completely unaware that when he had walked about in the insurance office with his oil tanned logger boots and his tweed wool outfit that he had looked like an extraterrestrial alien to the Los Angeles locals, except Zelzah, who thought his outfit was so outrageously cool that his attire must have come from Rodeo Drive.

She sighed, holding his arm. "I'm so glad."

Arriving at her beat-up car in the parking lot, she handed Ernie the keys. He always drove the two of them, except on the occasions when Lilly became the designated driver after a party. *Designated* translated that she would drive when Ernie could no longer stand.

Off they drove, north toward Sedro Woolley, with the familiar rain insulating them from the rest of the world as it poured down against her older car that listed to one side a bit due to a worn-out spring.

"Oh. I'm sorry to say that the outfit you got me got ruined in a helicopter crash," he said.

"Oh, well, you won't need it up here, anyway," she said, trying to convey that she wouldn't be angry at him for destroying the present she'd spent so much money on. She leaned over to hold him as they drove. The sound of the pounding rain, and the presence of Lilly were safe and warm as he returned from the condensed evil of the world of insurance.

CHAPTER 64

One morning the following week, the rainy weather broke for a while and Ernie decided he had better cut the grass around his trailer house. He got his gas-powered mower to fire up and went to work. He was nearly done when Lilly came barreling up in her car, excited about something. She had to be at work that day, which was the other direction from where he lived, so something was definitely up. Ernie shut down the mower.

Lilly parked hurriedly in his drive and got out with a newspaper in her hand. The break in the weather let rays of sunshine beam through the scattered clouds and illuminated her entry like daytime spotlights.

"Ernie, have you heard?" she practically shouted out as she hurriedly approached, holding a newspaper in her hand.

"No, what?"

"Zachary Lewis won! Your friend is the governor of California."

"Oh, boy, that's fantastic! I hope he socks it to those crooked insurance companies." Having heard the news, he sighed. "Well, all that politics stuff isn't going to help me get a job. The insurance company fired me but I thought that I'd done a pretty good job. Now I have nothing again." He didn't want to wallow in the subject, and so he changed the topic. "I had better get this lawn mowed while there's a let up in the rain."

Lilly didn't have to be in to work for a while, so she took a seat on an outdoor chair near the trailer house, watching him mow. They went inside when he finished.

"Coffee? I still have some pretty fresh brew here."

"Sure."

"Lewis really deserves that victory," Ernie said, finally addressing the subject, sipping his cup of coffee and coming around to discuss politics, even though he had just said he did not want to.

"Do you think he might do something for you one day? Maybe he could help you find work since you saved his life and all. A governor is a very important person. Of course, he's in California, not here. What'd you think?"

He smiled, put his stong arms around her, and gave her a big hug. "I think you should take it easy with all these ideas before you give me a headache."

"Well, darling, you don't even have any way to get around, since your truck is broken down and they ruined your motorcycle. Are you going to fix the truck or get a new bike when you get the insurance money?"

"Well, I have to wait for the insurance money to come in before I do anything. There's still no work, since Billings was shut down because of the silly owl."

"Do you want to use my car again today? If you do, just take me in to work and then pick me up later as usual. I'll make dinner for you at my place tonight if you want. I can bring home some tri-tip."

"I guess so. I could use a few supplies and things, so I'll take you in."

CHAPTER 65

We're all going to miss our most loyal friend, Fiorello." Bastini opened the meeting, addressing the remaining group, now just three, himself, Indelicato, and Manelli.

"He was the best," Indelicato agreed. "He always did things himself, not trusting others to keep things from screwing up."

"The best," Manelli repeated. "We'll give him a great funeral. It'll be a spectacular event in Waterbury. But there's something we should do now that Lewis won. Let's use the movie and see if we can still pull off the loan for Chief No Cloud."

⌘

No charges had been yet been filed against Indelicato, Manelli, or Bastini, and there was nothing in the news about them. They were hoping to carry on business as usual.

An Italian man who worked at the Equator in Las Vegas came to Zelzah's desk at Majestik in California. He was in his early forties; wearing dark-gray pants, a white shirt, tie, and without a jacket; and holding a small manila envelope. "I have a special delivery for Robert Bradford. I have to hand it to him personally."

"A lot of people want Mr. Bradford's time. He does not take mail or deliveries personally. That's why he has me. You will have to leave it with me, or not at all."

"Would you please ask Mr. Bradford if he wishes to take delivery of a package from a Miss Evette Evil?" He had been instructed to use her name if needed, as there must be no reference to Innocenti or the Las Vegas group.

Zelzah changed her tone. Was it something he ordered? That did not make sense—he would have told her he was expecting it. Was someone blackmailing him? Well, in any event, accepting the envelope would cause no harm. She tried again. "All right, you may leave it with me, and I'll give it to Mr. Bradford."

The man shook his head. "I have to hand it to Mr. Bradford myself. No one else may have it."

Zelzah thought a moment. She figured that her boss would want it rather than not. "Wait here," she said and headed into his office.

Bradford looked up from his work. "Yes?"

"There is a messenger outside who says he has something for you from Evette Evil. He won't give it to me."

Bradford's heart raced, but he maintained his boardroom stone face, without any change of expression. "Show him in."

She opened the door to his office for the messenger and stayed outside, knowing it must be something confidential.

Inside, the man walked up to Bradford, who was sitting at his desk, enmeshed in papers. "Mr. Bradford, sir, I have something for you." He held it out.

"Just set it on my desk," Bradford told him.

The polite man set the plain, small envelope down on the desk and left. Bradford did not want to signal any curiosity, and so he waited until the delivery man closed the door behind him before reaching for the package. When the door closed, he grabbed it anxiously and tore it open. Out came a flash stick. He turned it around, looking for markings or some other sign of what it was about, but there were no clues.

Bradford touched the button that locked the door and put the flash stick into his computer. As it started up, he recognized that it was a hotel room typical of the hotel he frequented with the ultimate orgasm Evette Evil each week.

Oh, no. He watched the scene on the computer in shock, his eyes opened wide, his face feeling flushed, and his respiration that of an Olympian in competition. There was Evette

Evil, in her leather corset that went from under her breasts to only the top of her hips, leaving her bushy sex very exposed. Long, leather gloves, a leather choker around her neck, and tall leather boots completed the dominatrix attire. In her hand was a sinister, long, thin black whip. Clearly visible and identifiable was Robert Bradford. The action was about to begin.

He shut the video down suddenly, realizing the import of what had happened. Blackmail! That whore Evette! This could ruin him. The board of directors would fire him in a nanosecond if they found out. Any such disgrace in the conservative insurance industry would be the end of his career. How did she get the tape? She had to have known it was being made. He would have to wait for the demand to see who was doing it.

He pondered his excesses and tried to think clearly as to how to hold together his sterling career. The private line on his desk from Zelzah rang. "Mr. Bradford, it's Mr. Manelli."

"Did he say what he wanted?"

"No. Did you wish me to take a message?"

Bradford suddenly knew. "Put him through."

"Hello, Mr. Bradford. This is Salvatore Manelli. I was wondering if you have made a decision as to the loan to the Cockpaws."

Bradford tried to establish his bargaining position. "I promised the loan only if Lewis didn't win the election. He won."

"I thought you might reconsider making the loan, anyway, as it's a good deal, and no doubt good press for your company to lend to an underprivileged Indian tribe. And, nothing is worse than bad publicity, don't you agree?"

That son-of-a-bitch! A lot of people wanted Bradford's job, and there would be no way that the directors would keep him if there was any leak of his relationship with Evette, let alone if the video itself got out. His career was still before him. If this didn't get out, he could stay on for several more years and tuck away several more million each year. If he challenged them, he would lose that extra money and have to retire in disgrace. Not to mention his wife and children! No doubt, he would lose them as well. There could be no question as to what to do. Anyway, he would have a private suite at the new Indian reservation hotel and favors for free, if he made the loan—such as hookers at the hotel. The decision was not hard to make.

"I've decided to go ahead with the loan."

"I'm so glad to hear that. As soon as everything is finalized, you'll get the remaining copy of the tape." Manelli promised.

Bradford sighed. "Very well, the matter will be signed in a few days."

The call was ended.

Bradford leaned his elbows on his desk and buried his head in his hands, pondering the situation. There was no way in hell he was going to the police or FBI and disclose the nature of the blackmail. If he did, it would leak out somehow. *Just make the loan, and forget about it. The company has the capital to do it. It's not my personal money. And I can have the special suite at the Indian hotel.*

Then he thought of Evette and the tape. He had never seen himself before from a camera point of view. *That Evette is some number. Somehow those mafia people got to her. But, what a turn-on watching!* He felt a surge in his loins and started the video over. This was too much. He pushed the button to unlock his door and beeped for Zelzah.

Zelzah came in, notebook and pen in hand, as usual. "Yes, sir?"

"Please lock the door. And a Martini, please. Make it two.

Zelzah complied, fixed him a double martini in a shaker with vodka and a wee bit of vermouth, and then poured the first in a chilled glass.

Bradford downed it, all the while consumed with watching Evette from an angle in the hotel room providing a new perspective.

Zelzah poured him a second, took off her high heels, raised her skirt, and took off her stylish pantyhose. He gazed at her sex for even more stimulation, got up, and came to the front of his desk, where she helped him out of his clothes. Facing forward from the front of the desk in his usual manner, he could not see his desktop monitor, so he changed the routine, and faced the desk, leaning over on it with his backside to Zelzah, leaving him just as vulnerable, but from behind.

He turned the monitor towards him so he could see it, watching intently.

Zelzah did what she usually did, only from behind. He remained face down on the desk, looking at the video. By continuing to bend over the desk, he beckoned for more as he watched. She repeated the act a number of times as the excitement continued. But watching the video gave him an idea for novel stimulation from Zelzah. He stood and motioned Zelzah to lay her face down on his desk, facing the computer screen to one side so she could see it too. He then mounted her from the rear. The two of them then worked up to one of their most exciting experiences, realizing just how much they both liked to watch.

CHAPTER 66

Three days later, Ernie sat in his favorite chair in his trailer, watching and listening to the Washington rain, the door open for fresh air, the sound of the rain satisfying the senses. He had to get something going soon, but there was no work available in Sedro Woolley. This doing nothing was getting old fast. But no more out-of-state work this time, after all that craziness in Los Angeles. Maybe he could find a job down in Seattle? Vancouver? What would he work at?

As he wondered what other work he might do, the US Mail truck drove up. It pulled into the gravel driveway, instead of stopping out at the street at the mailbox as usual. Willie, the familiar black mailman, got out and walked up to the trailer. What sort of mail deserved all this attention? Ernie wondered.

He opened the door to let Willie in out of the rain. "What's up, buddy?"

"I got a special delivery for you. You have to sign for it."

"Oh, oh. Usually bad news comes in certified letters. Somebody died. Or maybe the state ordered me to move out of my trailer since a bunny hugger claimed to have been a spotted owl flying over it."

Willie laughed out loud. "You still have a sense of humor, even though you're out of work." He had his cushy federal government mail carrier's job and felt a little sorry for Ernie. He handed him an envelope that was more of a square shape and made of heavy, rich, cream-colored paper. Ernie signed the return receipt with Willie's ballpoint.

"Oh, I got another one for you by regular mail." Willie remembered. The second was of cheap, thin, white paper with

Ernie's insurance company's logo printed on the return portion. It had a plastic window for Ernie's printed name and address on the single page letter inside to show through the window to save money by not having to type on or print the envelope.

"Oh, boy, this must be the check for my motorcycle," Ernie said with a big smile, grateful that he did not have Majestik for his motorcycle insurance.

"See ya."

"Thanks, Willie."

Willie went out to the boxy mail truck and drove away. Ernie went to his table and sat, excited he was finally getting the money for his ruined motorcycle. With a knife he opened the insurance company envelope anxiously, expecting a check. A single page letter came out, without any check, listing the claim number and, date of loss.

> *Dear policyholder:*
>
> *Regarding your claim for the loss of your motorcycle, please note paragraph 13 of your policy which states:*
>
> *"Loss occurring to the named vehicle when being operated is only insured when the vehicle is being operated by a person holding a valid driver's license in accordance with the laws of the state where the vehicle is being operated."*
>
> *You have reported that the loss to your motorcycle occurred more than ten (10) days after you entered the State of California from Washington to work for Majestik Insurance Company, which employment required you to use you motor vehicle in the course and scope of your employment. At the time of the incident and loss you were holding a Washington State driver's license, and not a California State driver's license.*
>
> *California Vehicle Code 12500 requires that "a person must hold a valid driver's license to drive a motor vehicle in the State of California. The license must be issued by the State of California, unless the person is*

exempted for a reason specified in 12505. Under 12505 (c), a person may not operate a vehicle in the State of California in excess of ten (10) days if the person is being employed for compensation by another for the purpose of driving a motor vehicle on the highways without obtaining a California driver's license."

At the time of the incident and loss, you were employed at Majestik using and driving your motor vehicle (motorcycle); you were in the state more than ten (10) days, and you did not have a California driver's license. Therefore, you were not a legally licensed driver by California law, and there is no coverage under the policy.

We must therefore deny your claim for the loss of your motorcycle.

Your Insurance Company

He yelled aloud, "I don't have Majestik for insurance! Can they all be the same?"

If a spotted owl was nesting anywhere near, the volume of Ernie's bellow would have definitely been scared it right out of its nest.

Breathing heavily, he went to the drawer where he had paper and angrily took out a sheet. "You bastards! I am going to come see you…"

What am I doing? He crushed the letter into a ball and tossed it at the wastebasket. *I can't do that! The insurance company could get the police to file criminal charges against me. I'll end up in jail.*

He realized he was breathing heavily and wished he was in the same room with the insurance claims representative who wrote him that letter. It would be nice smack him around for a while.

He stood up and went to the door to breath in the cool, rainy air.

I paid insurance premiums, which the company gladly took. And now the company denies my claim for my motorcycle that I had insured with it before I was hired in California. I

*can see more clearly now what Governor Lewis has been try-
ing to do. He's at least trying to get a start at making those
crooked companies do what they should. Good thing he won!
But I guess that won't help me.*

So upset receiving the bad news, he had completely forgot
the other letter in the expensive envelope.

He picked it up from the table and turned it about, noting
the thick, expensive paper. Opening it, he saw that the inside
was lined with copper foil.

Out came a very thick, cream-colored invitation with dark
blue colored script.

Who's getting married?

Greetings
*You are cordially invited to attend the Inauguration Ball of
Governor Elect Zachary Lewis*

The ball was at a fancy hotel in Los Angeles and the time
and date were provided. A table assignment card was also enclosed:

Table Number One
Party of Two

*Table number One? Wouldn't that be the Governor's own
table?*

An RSVP card and return stamped envelope were included.
The date of the party was the Saturday after next. Inside was a
personal letter from Zachary Lewis as well.

Dear Ernie:

*Enclosed is your invitation to come to my inaugura-
tion ball. It's for two. It was the news of the insurance
money laundered through the Chockpaw Indians fun-
neled to my opponent that made the difference in what
was a very close election. I owe you not only my life,
but the outcome of the election. And the people of the
State of California owe you a debt since, because of*

you, and with my election, legislation will be introduced curbing much of the deceitful and dishonest practices of insurance companies. There are many people who want to meet you personally, and I will be introducing you after the dinner and before the dance begins. You really must come to the party. Bring your girlfriend if you have one, if not, a date. I have the two of you sitting right next to me at my table. If it were not for you, I would be pushing up daisies in a cemetery.

As you are my most honored guest, I have arranged special transportation for you. One of my largest financial contributors has his own company jet. I have asked him to have his pilots come and pick you and your girl up personally at the nearest airport and bring you down in a private ride. He has a full time stewardess on board and a nice bar.

You will be picked up at the airport in a limousine and brought to the hotel where the party is to be held. I have reserved the best suite in the hotel for you and you can stay as long as you wish. A car and driver will take you anywhere you want to go while in town, and my secretary will follow you and pay for your shopping. You will be taken back to Washington in the same manner, whenever you wish. All of your expenses in Los Angeles will be paid by me.

On another matter. If you are still out of work, I have a proposal for you. As Governor of California I have the privilege of appointing directors. There is one for The Department of Forests. The position is open, and I nominated you to fill the post. The job entails becoming acquainted with the California forests and advising me and the legislature how to best manage them, how much timber to cut, where to cut, what replacement trees to plant, how much of the existing forests are needed to actually preserve wildlife, cutting fire roads for fire prevention, and other issues. You will have a great deal of influence as to what happens with our forests. It will put the police who patrol the forests, called

Forestry Wardens, under your command as well. You can continue to live in Washington if you wish, and you can fly back and forth to the forests and to Sacramento on a reasonable schedule, such as working out of your home on Fridays and Mondays, with many Tuesdays through Thursdays in the forests, in the capitol of Sacramento, or wherever you might need to be. These directorships are of the highest offices in the state, and carry a great deal of influence in many circles.

To view the forests, you will have a helicopter and other aircraft at your disposal. As I know you like to fly, I will see to it that the pilot is also instructor rated and with instructions to get you working toward a license.

As you would often be out in the forests, you will need to stay at the nearest lodging, all of which will be paid for by the state, including all transportation expense. Away from home, you will receive a per diem allowance for meals as well.

The job has a full medical plan and a very nice retirement plan. Due to the importance of our forests and the need for proper management, the pay will be $350,000 per year. The job is only as long as I am governor, but if you are good at your job, the next governor will probably keep you. I am keeping several of the last governor's directors in other areas, for example. And if, and when, you do leave one day to work elsewhere, you will have many opportunities open to you as you will have made many connections in the job.

You accrue retirement benefits for every year you are there. I hope to be governor for two terms, which is eight years. You are also entitled to a vehicle of your choice that the state will provide, including all maintenance, gas, and expenses.

The state self-insures, so you do not need to pay for insurance for the vehicle.

If you accept, I will announce your acceptance at the inauguration party. There is no doubt that you are absolutely the best man for the job, as you know the for-

ests from actual experience and how to deal with them better than anyone else I could ever find. Please accept.
    Your friend forever,
Zachary Lewis
Governor Elect
State of California

Wow! Ernie could hardly believe what he was reading. *What crazy pay*! He read it again and again to be sure that he'd gotten it right. *Imagine! Me getting to decide what to do with forests rather than some owl lovers. But what about the notoriety? Introducing me probably on TV and all that? Maybe I should think it over.*

He put down the invitation and went back to the open door, looking out at the heavy rain, wondering what it would be like to make so much money and have so much power. *My own police force! Getting to decide how the forests should be run, instead of having people who don't understand them making the decisions! This is the crossroads of my life, and maybe the only crossroads that I will ever encounter.*

He went back to the drawer and got another piece of paper, taking his pen in his hand.

    Dear Governor Lewis:
    Congratulations!
    As for your offer to attend the party, I would love to come with my girlfriend Lilly. We will probably want to stay several days as she has never been to Los Angeles. She's a butcher, in case you need anything for the banquet.
    As for your job offer, I have a question before I give you my answer. You say in your letter that I could have a vehicle of my choice. Could that be a new motorcycle?

End

About the Author

Brent Ayscough or Ace, as he is known to friends, retired from the practice of law and lives in a house overlooking the sea in Southern California. He has always loved machines, from airplanes to motorcycles, structural design, and other interests. He has enjoyed the acquaintance of diverse and interesting people, and is widely traveled. Bits and pieces of characters he has known, places he has been, seasoned with the spice of his imagination, help him create unusual stories and characters. Extensive collaboration with experts and sources, hopefully, make his stories credible and interesting.